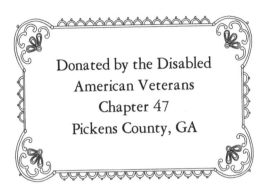

Donated by the Disabled
American Veterans
Chapter 47
Pickens County, GA

The
Chocolate
Kiss

The Chocolate Kiss

LAURA FLORAND

KENSINGTON PUBLISHING CORP.
www.kensingtonbooks.com

KENSINGTON BOOKS are published by

Kensington Publishing Corp.
119 West 40th Street
New York, NY 10018

ISBN-13: 978-0-7582-6941-6
ISBN-10: 0-7582-6941-2

First Kensington Trade Paperback Printing: January 2013

10 9 8 7 6 5 4 3 2 1

Printed in the United States of America

To Mia.
May your life be
full of magic.

Chapter 1

It was a good day for princesses. The rain drove them indoors, an amused little rain with long, cool fingers that heralded the winter to come and made people fear the drafts in their castles.

And Magalie Chaudron, stirring chocolate in the tea shop's blue kitchen, felt smug to be tucked into the heart and soul of all this warmth, not wandering the wet streets searching for a home.

Aunt Aja smiled at her in that quiet way of hers, her long black braid swaying hypnotically against the gold-brown silk of her *salwar kameez* tunic as she prepared a pot of tea. Aunt Geneviève had taken her giant umbrella and gone out for a stride, just to prove that rain couldn't confine her, no matter what it might do to anyone else. That was fortunate, because whenever Aunt Geneviève started feeling confined, the kitchen shrank to the size of a pin, and its other occupants weren't angelic enough to dance around each other atop it.

In the tiny *salon de thé* on the Île Saint-Louis, their first "princess" of the day, a businesswoman with straight, light brown hair, sat under the conical hats that filled three high, rickety wooden shelves wrapping around the entire room. Above the businesswoman's head sat a jester's cap, a stack of three shiny black and gold paper party crowns from New Year's 2000, and an Eiffel Tower–shaped hat that had shown up in a box in the mail one day with a note from a customer: *When I saw this, I could not resist sending it to you. Thank you for your beautiful haven. It brought me more pleasure than you can know.*

"Thanks," the brown-haired woman was saying to the business-suited man across from her when Magalie carried a tray out to Madame Fernand, whose poodle was, for a rarity, actually curled up on the elegant old woman's feet and licking up crumbs rather than trying to lunge at everyone else's table. Before going out, Geneviève had sprinkled crumbs generously under that table the moment she'd spotted Madame Fernand approaching the shop. The eighty-year-old grande dame had been bringing a dog everywhere she went for decades, starting back when she could still cling to physical proof of her days as a reigning beauty and train her dogs to behave. "This is perfect," the brown-haired woman said. She had a heavy American accent but was speaking in French. "Exactly what I needed."

"I thought you would like it," the man said with a smile. He was old enough to be her father, with a gold wedding ring so heavy and thick, Magalie was surprised he could stand to wear it. "It makes a nice break from meetings, doesn't it? Although I'm afraid they don't use your chocolate, Cade."

"No one in France uses our chocolate," Cade said ruefully. "That's the problem. But this . . ." She sighed and rubbed the back of her neck and then smiled. "If I ever run away to join the circus, this will be the circus I join."

Circus? This utterly stable center of the world? Magalie gave the woman called Cade a cool look as she served Madame Fernand. The wood-and-enamel tray held a generous portion of Aunt Aja's tea in a beautiful cast-iron teapot; a delicate, ancient, flowered cup with a tiny chip in the base; and a slice of rose chess pie, one of Magalie's contributions to the *salon de thé*'s recipes, the chess pie recipe inherited from her father's mother, the rose inspired one day by Madame Fernand's perfume.

"In a manner of speaking," the businesswoman-circus-dreamer said. While they nicknamed most of their female clients princesses, meaning women who indulged themselves with problems they didn't know how to fix, Magalie was kind of surprised at this one. The other woman *felt* strong. "Can you imagine? Making exquisite chocolate by hand instead of huge machines—all that mystery and magic? You would feel like a sorcerer. No wonder the owners call this shop The Witches' House. It must be wonderful to enchant people all the time."

The businessman across from her was giving her a blank look. The woman—Cade—realized it and straightened, smiling ruefully, and her dream sank right back down inside her, hidden under a professional, assertive calm.

Magalie gave her a disgusted look. What was the use of being assertive if you were asserting yourself over *yourself*? In the kitchen, she gave her pot of chocolate a firm glare, and—even though she knew she was being silly and that it couldn't really work magic on people, no matter what the aunts liked to pretend—she wished some gumption into the other woman, as she stirred the pot three times with the ladle: *May you realize your own freedom.*

Then she whisked up a separate cup for the businessman, because the last thing someone wearing that big a wedding band needed was to "realize his own freedom" while sitting across from a woman young enough to be his daughter.

"Give her this, too." Aunt Aja set a pot of tea on the tray as Magalie started to leave the kitchen again with it. The scent from this tea was spicier than Madame Fernand's rose and lavender, more adventurous. "Some nuts are harder to crack than others."

The brown-haired businesswoman's eyes took on a startled brightness as she breathed in the scents of the chocolate and tea slid before her. She reached out and touched the chocolate cup—hers was thick, handle-less, with a black-on-sienna African motif—tracing her finger along the rim.

The silver bell over the door chimed with such loveliness that Magalie gave it a startled glance. Maybe the rain had put it into a good mood. The two women who walked in with the chime had to be mother and daughter, the younger woman lithe, as if she was constantly in motion—dance, maybe? Her gold hair was caught up in a careless clip like that of a dancer between practices. Her mother was much stouter, her makeup too afraid of imperfection, her haircut the professionally maternal one of a woman who has long since decided to live only for her daughter.

"Oh, *look* at this, honey," she said, in American. "Isn't this the cutest place you ever saw?" Magalie was going to give *her* a cup of chocolate that taught her a sense of aesthetics. The place was not *cute*. "Can you believe how much of the world you're seeing?"

Her daughter flexed her hands, massaging between the tendons. "Mmm," she said. She looked tired. But her gaze traveled around the shop, curiosity and a kind of hunger waking slowly in her eyes. It was a look that Magalie, after working in this shop all through university and full-time for the three years since, had seen more times than she could count. "I wouldn't mind seeing more of it, Mom."

"Well, we *will*. My goodness, honey, you're touring New Zealand and Australia next month. With a stop in Honolulu! Should we take that engagement in Japan? It's good timing for the way back. Would you like that? We haven't been there since you were sixteen, have we?"

"I went with a group from school for a performance while I was at Julliard," her daughter reminded her.

"Oh, that's right. Your father had his operation, and I couldn't come."

The two women slid into seats at one of the tables in the tiny front room, tucked between the old upright piano and the window display: a dark-chocolate house in the middle of a menacing forest of enormous, rough-hewn, dark-chocolate trees, the house so covered with candied violets and candied mint leaves and candied oranges, it was almost impossible not to reach out to break off just a little bite. The daughter gazed at it but folded her hands, still rubbing her fingertips into her tendons.

If a few more princesses had spines, it would do them a world of good, Magalie thought with a huff of irritation, and back in the kitchen she shook her head at her chocolate as she stirred it: *May you love your life and seize it with both hands.*

Aunt Aja took that tray out, and just as she left the kitchen, the silver bell over the front door rang with a chime so sharp and true that it pierced Magalie straight through the heart. She clapped her hands over her ears to try to stop the sound, the ladle clattering across the counter, splattering chocolate.

But the tone kept vibrating inside her body, until she stamped her boots twice and slapped the counter to force it to stop.

A warm voice, not loud but so rich with life that it filled the entire shop, wrapped itself around Magalie and held her, making her strain with startled indignation against the urge to shiver in delight. "What a wonderful place," the golden voice alive with laughter was saying to Aunt Aja. "La Maison des Sorcières. The Witches' House. Do you ensorcell all your passersby, or do you enchant strictly children?"

Magalie tilted her body back just enough to peek past the edge of the little arched doorway that led into the kitchen. Through the second arch, the one that separated the tiny back room from the equally tiny front part of the shop, she got a glimpse of broad shoulders and tawny hair, a sense of size so great that a sudden dread seized her. If he should shrug his shoulders, the whole shop might burst off them, like staves bursting off a barrel.

But he was in perfect control of that size. Nothing around him was in any danger, not even the chocolate spindle hanging over the display case specifically to be such a danger and poke people in the forehead if they leaned too close.

Now *there* was someone who didn't need her help. She smiled at the ladle as she picked it up. What could she wish for a man so full of life and power? *May all your most wonderful dreams come true.*

The silver bell chimed again, dramatically. Aunt Geneviève came back in, taking a moment to shake her umbrella energetically at the street before it could bring in rain. Now two people of enormous character filled the shop, and for a second Magalie felt like a marshmallow that had just been sat on by an elephant.

"No, I'm sorry, nothing for me," the warm voice told the aunts. "I just had to peek in. Next time I'm here"—he laughed, and Magalie broke down at last and shivered extravagantly with pleasure—"I promise I'll stay and let you bewitch me."

The silver bell chimed again, glumly this time.

Magalie left the kitchen, hurrying to the archway into the front room. Through looming chocolate trees, she met vivid blue eyes looking back into the shop. While she looked straight into them, he likely could not see her, hidden as she was by the angle of the light. Raindrops fell on his head, and he shook himself like a lion shaking out its mane, saying something to the man in a business suit beside him. Then he strode on.

Aunt Geneviève raised her eyebrows, caftan sweeping out around her six-foot frame to dominate even more of the space as she turned to look after him with some interest.

Magalie retreated to the kitchen, her whole body relaxing in relief. She didn't know what had almost happened there, but thank God it hadn't. Absently, she picked up the cup of chocolate she'd been preparing for the lion of a man, cradling it in her hands as she drank from it.

Its warmth sank into her. "You know, I should have lent him an umbrella," she murmured vaguely. Some of the umbrellas princesses forgot to take with them when they left were very fine indeed.

"If you hand that man something, it had better be a gift, because if he likes it, he's not going to give it back," Aunt Geneviève said, propping her black umbrella against the kitchen's arch. Even folded, it came up to Magalie's shoulder. Geneviève was Magalie's blood relation in the aunts' couple—her mother's sister—but no one would be able to tell it by their sizes. "Anyway, it does big cats like him good to get wet from time to time," Geneviève muttered.

Chapter 2

Magalie was enchanting children with morsels of her dark-chocolate house two weeks later when the bearer of bad news burst in.

In this case, it was the toyseller from the quixotic shop four doors down. "Have you heard who's coming to the island?" Claire-Lucy gasped.

Magalie retained her calm, continuing to break off house pieces to pass around to the children. Even if Superman himself was stopping by to sign autographs, the island in the heart of Paris and Magalie's place in it would stay the same. And that was what mattered.

The aunts claimed a share of the credit for the chocolate house, but Magalie was the one who had designed September's display. It was pure dark chocolate, of course. They didn't really *do* milk chocolate at La Maison des Sorcières. But Magalie had fitted out the window frames with long strips of candied lime peel, and the roof was thatched with candied orange peel. Up the walls of it, she had twined such delicacies as flowering vines made from crystallized mint leaves and violet petals, both personally candied by Aunt Aja, a delicate, tricky business that involved the brushing of egg whites and sugar onto hundreds and hundreds of mint leaves and fragile violet petals with a tiny paint brush. Over and over. Only Aunt Aja could do it. Geneviève and Magalie soon started throwing things.

Feeding these works of deliciousness to impressionable young children was one of Magalie's favorite moments of each month. Aunt Aja had confessed that the first few times she and Geneviève had concocted elaborate window displays such as this one, they had been young and refused to destroy their work, leaving it to time itself to decay it with the pale brown bloom on the chocolate. At which point, it was no longer even remotely as delicious as it once could have been. The lesson, according to Aunt Aja, was one of recognizing transience. But Magalie hated transience, so she put it into other terms: one must always know when to yield magic into the hands of the children who wanted to eat it up.

So they made their displays fresh every few weeks, and from all over the Île Saint-Louis and the further hinterlands of Paris, children showed up on the first Wednesday of every month—Wednesday was the day children got off school early—dragging parents or nannies by the hand, to eat the witches' candy.

In front of September's witch house, lost in a forest of dark-chocolate tree trunks, a tiny black hen pecked in a little garden. The black hen had been formed in one of Aunt Geneviève's extensive collection of heavy, nineteenth-century molds, gleaned from a lifetime of dedicated flea-marketing. Deep among the chocolate tree trunks was also a chocolate rider on a white-chocolate horse, a prince approaching, perhaps to ride down the black hen and be cursed, perhaps to beg a boon. Magalie and her aunts never told the story; they only started their visitors dreaming.

She gave three-year-old Coco a violet-trimmed bit of vine that the child had begged for and studied their bearer of bad news. La Maison des Sorcères' eat-the-witches'-display-day was Claire-Lucy's biggest-business day of the month.

"You haven't heard who's going in where Olives was?" Claire-Lucy insisted. Her soft mouth was round with horror, her chestnut hair frizzing with its usual touchable fuzz all around her head. "It's Lyonnais!" She stared at the aunts and Magalie, waiting for them to shatter at the reverberation of the name.

Lyonnais.

Magalie's cozy tea-shop world was not crystalline or fragile, so it didn't exactly shatter on its own. It was more as if a great, Champagne-glossed boot came down and kicked it all open to merciless sunshine.

Magalie had been wrong. So wrong. Perhaps Superman could come through and leave her world untouched. But Lyonnais . . .

She looked at her aunts in horror. They looked back at her, eyebrows flexing in puzzlement as they saw her consternation.

"Lyonnais," she said, as if the name had reached out and tried to strangle her heart. She stared at Aunt Geneviève. Aunt Geneviève was strong and rough-voiced and practical in her way. She knew how to fix a constantly running toilet without calling a plumber. She was tough-minded. But she didn't seem to get it, her eyebrows rising as the intensity of Magalie's dismay seemed to build rather than diminish.

"Lyonnais!" Magalie said forcefully, looking at her Aunt Aja.

Aunt Aja was as soft-voiced and supple as a slender shaft of tempered steel. Her dimpled fingers could press the nastiest kink right out of a back. Wrong-mindedness had no quarter around her. Her gentle strength seemed to squeeze it out of existence, not by specifically seeking to crush it but by expanding until foolishness had no room left. Her head was on so straight, the worst malevolence couldn't twist it. But she looked at Magalie now with a steady concern that crinkled the red *bindi* in the middle of her forehead. Concerned not because Philippe Lyonnais was opening a new shop just down the street but because she didn't understand Magalie's reaction to it.

"Philippe Lyonnais!" Magalie said even more loudly, as if she could force comprehension. "The most famous pastry chef in the world! The one they call *le Prince des Pâtissiers!*" Was it ringing any bells at all?

Aunt Geneviève tapped her index finger against her chin, a light coming on. "That young man who has been stirring things up with his *macarons*?"

She spoke the word *macarons* lovingly, the way any Parisian would. Bearing no resemblance to the chewy, coconut-filled American macaroon, the heavenly sandwiches of air and lusciousness that were the Parisian *macaron* were the test of a pastry chef's quality. And, according to all reports, Philippe Lyonnais did them better than anyone else in the world.

"The one who stopped by here the other week?" Aunt Geneviève continued.

What?

"Weren't you around when he came in, Magalie?" she asked. "He seemed a bit rude to me, acting as if he didn't have time for us. And he certainly takes up a lot of room in a place," she added, not entirely with disapproval but not with any intention of yielding her own space, either. "Still, he's quite cute. If he can improve his manners, you might like him."

She gazed at her niece speculatively. Geneviève had originally been confused to learn that Magalie leaned toward the opposite sex in her preferences, since her vision of taking on her niece as apprentice hadn't included any male accoutrements, but she had long since resigned herself to it. Perhaps all the more readily because Magalie didn't accessorize herself with males very often.

"Mmm." Aunt Aja made a long sound that meant she foresaw trouble where Aunt Geneviève saw fun. "There was a lot of lion in him. And he *is* a prince," she warned Aunt Geneviève apologetically, hating to have to point it out.

"Oh." Geneviève looked disgruntled.

Magalie gave her a sardonic glance. In the whole history of the known world, there had been no mention of a romantic attachment between a prince and a witch. Lots of battles, yes, lots of arrogant royals reduced to toads, but not much love lost.

Which had suited Geneviève just fine for herself. But, given her niece's insistence on the male gender for her romantic attachments, it galled her that any member of that group—even a prince—might consider himself above Magalie.

"*Philippe Lyonnais,* the most famous pastry chef *in the world,* is opening another branch of Lyonnais right down the street from us." Magalie tried spelling it out in small words to see if that helped.

Geneviève started to frown. "You know, that is kind of nervy," she told Aja. "He could have more respect for our territory. *I* wouldn't go open a *salon de thé* right next to *him.*"

Why . . . yes, Magalie thought. That was a nice way of thinking of things. "But I don't think it took him nerve," realism forced her to admit aloud. "I don't think it took him any more nerve than walking on a bug he didn't see."

Aja smoothed her long burnt-sienna tunic over her *salwar* pants. Her eyebrows crinkled. "Why *didn't* he see us?"

Aunt Geneviève finally had the right focus, though. She stared at Magalie in gathering outrage. "You don't think it took him *nerve* to open a shop within *our* territory? You don't think it took him courage? You think he just did it without even noticing us?"

Magalie nodded. "I think he probably reviewed all the other shops on the island and his market base and decided there was no threat to him here."

Geneviève's mouth snapped closed, and within the bubble

of her complete silence, Magalie could almost see her aunt's head explode.

Aunt Aja traced the embroidery on her tunic soothingly. "I would not, of course, *threaten* anyone," she said. "I mean him no harm. However, it's perhaps better for a prince to learn young that looking before one steps is basic self-preservation."

Geneviève laughed in a way that put Boris Karloff to shame. "I won't 'threaten' him, either. He doesn't deserve the warning."

Magalie took a hard breath. Neither woman seemed to have noticed that the reason he'd treated them like a bug was because he *could*. He could steal their entire market base simply by opening up shop. He wouldn't have to *compete* with them. With five generations of pastry chefs behind him, he had been up against his own family heritage and every other pastry chef in Paris since he was born, competing with the *whole world,* and he had bested all of them. "I'll go talk to him."

It might as well be her. At least she had enough understanding of what was happening to be pissed off at the right thing.

Both her aunts frowned at her. "Why would you want to warn him? I hope you aren't going soft, Magalie," Geneviève said. "It's not because he's cute, is it? I can't see any good come from letting a man—especially a prince—take advantage of you just because he's cute."

"And no threats, either, Magalie," Aunt Aja said gently. "Remember karma: the fruit you harvest grows from the seeds you plant."

Aunt Geneviève snorted. "If anyone tries to boomerang a threat back at Magalie, I'm sure we can make him regret it." Aunt Geneviève believed in karma about like she believed in bullets: they might exist for other people, but they would most certainly bounce off her.

Aja gave her a reproachful look.

"*Enfin,* Magalie can make him regret it," Geneviève disavowed quickly. "I'll just . . . help."

Claire-Lucy clapped her soft hands together. "Can I watch?"

Chapter 3

Magalie was combing her hair in her white-on-white room high above the ground the next morning when a crow banged his head on her window. It shook itself on the sill, glared at her accusingly through the pane, and flew off to complain to a gargoyle on the next island over. As if she didn't already know what kind of day it was going to be without that. She'd have to face those gargoyles when she crossed the bridges into the rest of Paris, too.

She drew ethereal, streaming yards of gauzy white across her windows to avoid encountering any further crows and went to dress. The dawn she had been watching was never more than the faintest blush of yellow-pink on the horizon in Paris, anyway. It was one of the things about the city that made her wistful for her former home. In the South of France, morning coming up over a dew-strewn field of lavender could fill your heart with enough beauty to last through any kind of day at all. But Provence was her mother's place, and too scarred for Magalie. She had needed her own place and thus had come to this tiny island in the Seine.

She put on stylishly straight black pants that caressed her butt and hugged her thighs but showed a crisp, clean line around her ankles. She put on a teal flowing silk top because she knew the importance of a soft detail amid the black armor she was donning. She slid into her sleek, short black leather Perfecto jacket, which fit her torso and arms almost as closely as a knit top. She drew on ankle boots that had a subtle "rocker" suggestion in their pattern of black-on-black and their four-inch narrow but slightly chunky heels, a broader power base than her stilettos could provide.

She started to braid her hair to put it in a chignon but took one glance into the mirror and undid it. The look smacked of romanticism. Going into the city proper with a streak of romance showing was like going into battle with a gap in her armor right over her belly. She redid her hair without the braid, then deconstructed the chignon enough to make her look casually sophisticated instead of overly concerned with her appearance. She always enjoyed the irony of carefully pulling out wisps here or there to make her hair look careless—but in a perfect way.

On her way out, she stole one small chocolate witch from the shop to tide her over.

Down the cobblestones of the Île Saint-Louis, she walked with familiar confidence, no heels wobbling on the uneven pavement, ducking once or twice onto the narrow sidewalk to make room for the rare car to pass down the street—that of a wealthy islander on his way to work or a shop owner who lived off the island coming in. Thierry, the island's florist, was setting bouquets out in front of his door. He waved roses at her like a maiden might a silk handkerchief at a departing warrior and promised her his most beautiful bouquet on her return.

As she left the island, a violinist standing tall at the center of the bridge serenaded her, and she dropped some euros into the young man's hat for good luck. Both of the places she had come from had been so much smaller than Paris. Even after five years, part of her always felt, when she left the island, that she was making a sortie onto a battlefield where her weapons might not be entirely sufficient.

She passed the flying buttresses of the cathedral and crossed the great plaza in front of it, keeping well away from Notre-Dame's gargoyles. It was just the sort of morning when they might drop something on her head.

Pigeons skittered around her ankles as she walked but kept enough distance to show some respect. Her boots and her walk were still worth that much here, at least; no birds had the nerve to expect bread crumbs from her. On a low stone wall in the plaza, the pigeon woman sat with her arms extended, covered with the birds, while people in tennis shoes took pictures and dropped inappropriate forms of currency into her hat. Magalie nodded respectfully to her. The woman sat quietly in a place of enormous power and let birds collect on her arms through all the flashing of cameras. It never paid to be rude to someone like that.

Magalie held onto her uniqueness as long as she could as she crossed the Île de la Cité, the sister island, despite the increasing presence of cars and foot traffic. She exchanged a last firm look with the green king on his horse in the middle of the great stone bridge at the end of the island, then turned left and headed across more water into the city.

The ring of her boot heels started getting lost in the ring of other boot heels before she had even finished crossing the bridge. Trees rustling with late-autumn leaves extended along the river, forming the border between Paris and what she liked to think of as its heart, the islands in the middle of the Seine. She left the oldest bridge in the city, passing into the trees' dappled shadows, and then cut away from the river and its islands to the busy Boulevard Saint-Germain. She wanted to huddle into her jacket, but she didn't. She let it hang open, unzipped, as was proper fashion, and kept her chin up and her stride a long, powerful rhythm of heels against concrete.

Yet, despite her best efforts, the farther she got from the island, the more she felt diminished. Far from her power base, she became just another Parisian woman trying so hard to be the sleekest, the sharpest, to let her boot heels ring the crispest, but growing lost among the millions who did it as well or better, who had more money for higher fashion or longer legs, who had no idea she could make a *chocolat chaud* you would sell your soul for. Really. The aunts had a signed deed for a famous actor's soul behind the 1920s cash register among the chocolate molds, as a souvenir of a *sorcière's* power.

Around her, people moved briskly, harried out of bed by time and driven by it into work in the middle of a tense week, walking itself an aggression. Occasionally a tourist disturbed the flow, eager and bright-eyed and out early in the morning to soak up the city, with journals and cameras in tow. Unlike the tourists, Magalie did not stand out. Not in any way.

In her bathroom mirror, she had looked exquisite, perfect, exactly the effect she had wanted to produce. On the island, rose bouquets had saluted her in affection and respect. But here—here she was just another pair of boot heels ringing on the sidewalk.

By the time she got to Philippe Lyonnais's Saint-Germain shop, she was only a twenty-four-year-old woman with limited funds to indulge her taste for fashion, in a big, tense, polished, sexy city.

But he—his power was everywhere. His family name was on the Champs-Élysées, the rue Faubourg Saint-Honoré, here on Saint-Germain—all the power centers of this city. While she and her aunts kept enticing in secret from the heart of Paris, he stamped his supremacy down over the whole damn city and let people fawn over him. His coat of arms was the gilt lettering on his shop window. The exquisite nineteenth-century lines of his storefront reflected the glories of his family history. He came from a long line of rulers of Parisian tastebuds.

His shop door proclaimed that he didn't open until ten. She frowned at it—and was surprised when it slid open and let her into an empty shop. That was the kind of thing that happened when *Geneviève* frowned at things.

The interior was breathtaking. Panels of glossy wood and frescos were carved with the twining rosebuds that had been part of the Lyonnais décor since the first shop opened a century and a half ago. Lions' heads growled in the molding at each corner of the ceiling. Green marble pillars climbed above the gleaming glass display cases whose contents were more tempting than those of any king's treasure room and held more colors and richness than a chest of jewels. The tables and chairs seemed to come from a time when women wore sumptuous gowns of twenty yards of silk and men bowed over their hands.

Her skin itched. She wanted to turn around and leave. The presence of even one clerk might have helped, someone who could try to snub her and thus get her pride up. But the opulent perfection was empty.

Something congealed in her stomach, thick and treacly and sickening, as she realized her folly. Here, off her island, she was small and powerless. Glamorous, famous Philippe Lyonnais would look at her incredulously. He would dismiss her out of hand. Her territory was a small cave of a *salon de thé* on a small island. His rule extended over the whole city, and his influence stretched throughout the world.

She settled her shoulders firmly back and down and opened the door at the back of the salon. And she stepped into an alien world.

It was the first time she had ever been in a professional pastry kitchen or *laboratoire*. The quantity of metal struck her: the faces of cabinets and refrigerators under marble counters. Metal cooling racks. Great steel mixing machines. Shelves upon shelves, full of plastic boxes on top of boxes labeled with their contents. White-clad men and a few women bustled amid white tile walls and floors, bending intently over huge metal trays. One woman traced a circle stencil over and over onto a piece of parchment paper fitted into a huge metal sheet pan. Beside her, a man squeezed perfectly matching dollops of meringue out in row after row on similarly marked parchment paper. Another woman shifted *macaron* shells from a tray to a rack on a counter filled with racks.

Multiple colors filled that metal background: rich green *macaron* shells, peach ones, a garnet red. Someone squeezed ganache from a pastry bag into the upturned shells. A gangly teenager scooped out avocados with deft competence, piling the empty skins in a little tower.

Jokes and intense concentration seemed to intermingle, and someone passed with a great steaming pot, calling *"Chaud, chaud, chaud!"*

A big man with a wide lion's grin laughed suddenly, his mane flung back, his hands completely covered with some apricot-colored cream. A pastry bag had burst.

His laughter expanded into the whole room, his energy embracing everyone and everything in it. And that bell in her shop rang again, pure and clear, piercing her through the heart—which hurt like *hell*—and holding her there, impaled for somebody else's pleasure.

Philippe Lyonnais. She might not have placed him in their shop, but here in his, she recognized him right away.

Even if she had never seen his face in a hundred magazine articles and television interviews, she still would have recognized the ruler of this jungle.

She stared at him, feeling small and stubborn in her silk and leather. Defiant. *Dieu,* he had hundreds of *macarons* spread out here, every single one perfect. She had tried once to make *macarons,* spent hours in would-be perfectionism, and thrown the resulting flat, dry things into the trash. And she had no idea what would be done with those avocados. But she longed suddenly, intensely to try whatever it was they went into.

Her skills were rough-hewn, primitive. She could make

luscious hot chocolate. But surely everyone could, if they bothered. It wasn't hard. Pure Valrhona chocolate, milk, and cream, or sometimes water, a hint of spice . . . and that slow smile that grew in her while she stirred it . . . Not difficult at all.

It galled her to come, a humble petitioner, into such a prince's palace. She didn't have that pathetic role in her to play.

Was she to beg a boon from *him*? Big, vivid lord of all he surveyed. With his deep laugh like a lion's purr, filling the room with its vibrations. The hair on her arms rose to that vibration. That couldn't be good.

Again she wanted to zip her jacket, close the leather over the thin silk of her belted tunic, protect her vulnerable spots. But again, the gesture, the choice of self-defense over fashion, would have been an admission of her own vulnerability, and she raised her chin and refused it.

He saw her at that lift of her chin. Caught in mid-laughter, his blue eyes sparkled merrily as they met hers. His eyebrows went up, and he grabbed a towel to wipe off the apricot cream. His gaze ran over her once and then focused back on her face—and focused intently. *Alive.* She recognized the look. She had met males who thought to pursue her before. Quite a lot since she had moved to Paris, in fact. It didn't seem to mean much more than that she wasn't hideous and was of a nubile age.

He shifted, and anyone else who had even thought about asking her business faded away. They went back to their tasks, enticing her palate to follow them on a taste quest. Were those gold rounds to become caramel *macarons,* or mango, or . . . ?

"May I help you?" By asking the question, Philippe Lyonnais established his ownership of this world, his right to allow her to pass or to drive her out. Or to let her in and then close his forces around her, never letting her get away.

She had left her territory far behind. He didn't even realize it existed. He would ride his big white stallion right over her hedges and into her garden and never even notice that he had killed her favorite black hen.

Of course he would not help her. Fury at him, and at herself, washed through her, that she was here humiliating herself for nothing. Before *him.* The vivid life of him, filling this great, bustling space. The discipline and intensity that drew praise from all four corners of the world. She had thought the magazine shoots exaggerated his sex appeal, the way photo shoots did, with makeup and lighting and poses.

All those photos had been *nothing* in comparison to the real thing. Pale, posed, static images. Never once had a single photo caught him laughing.

She didn't feel like Magalie Chaudron, a witch of the Île Saint-Louis, who held the magic of chocolate brews in her hands. She felt like Cinderella at the ball, conscious that her fine dress was really ash-covered rags and intense make-believe, and wanting nothing so much as to slink out before the prince saw her.

She *hated* that feeling.

But she *was* Magalie Chaudron, whatever she felt like, so, instead, she spoke. Steady. Calm. A little cold, to punish him for that Cinderella effect. "Monsieur Lyonnais?"

He held out a hand. It took her off guard. She hadn't expected courtesy. Or contact. Especially when the contact sent little shimmers of warmth along her arm too fast for her own defenses to rally. The shimmers went racing all through her body, and her defenses went chasing lamely after, crying *stop, stop, stop* in vain.

"*Oui.*" His clasp was strong and gentle at once. What, did she seem that small in his world that he felt he had to be *gentle* with her?

She looked down at her own hand after his released it. Surely her hand had been enclosed so completely before.

Why had she never noticed it? She could still feel the calluses of his palm against her knuckles. The warmth seemed to linger, until her still-chilled left hand curled in jealousy.

He escorted her back to an office space minuscule in contrast to the spacious *laboratoire*. Books were piled everywhere, in towers on his desk, on shelves around it—great coffee-table books full of beautiful architectural photos and tiny paperbacks stamped with names like Prévert and Apollinaire. His laptop was pushed to one side, and across the center of the desk was spread what appeared to be a printed manuscript, a pen lying across it and little marks correcting details on the page. Scents from the *laboratoire* filled the space: strawberry, apricot, hot sugar, butter. Her stomach crawled with hunger, that chocolate witch she had eaten reduced to nothing.

He turned, staying on the same side of the desk as she was, making the room still smaller. Making her smaller. Even in her four-inch heels, she barely reached his shoulder.

His broad shoulders. He wasn't just tall. He was *big*. Wide shoulders and strong wrists and big square hands. His boxy chef's jacket hid the rest of him, and she tried to pretend its looseness concealed a potbelly. That was quite a strong, clean jaw for a man with a potbelly, though.

She suddenly wished he would unbutton his jacket. Just so she could know for sure what was under it. The space was so *small*, and he was focused on her so very intently.

She braced her booted heels and held her body proudly. "I'm Magalie Chaudron."

He smiled at her. The warmth of that smile turned his eyes azure and seemed to run over her body like a cat's tongue licking cream. *"Enchanté, Mademoiselle Chaudron."*

He said that as if he really was enchanted.

"From La Maison des Sorcières," she said.

It took him a second, but he did make the connection. "Ah!" Spontaneously, he thrust out his hand and shook hers again. Her right hand flexed involuntarily in delight. Her left hand curled sulkily against her thigh. "So we're going to be neighbors."

His eyes sparkled, quite alive at that thought, and subtly flicked over her body again, just once quickly, before coming quite correctly back to her face. But her whole body felt sensitized. A vague, burning curiosity seemed to linger most insistently in places like her nipples against the silk and, worse, the point of pressure between her sex and the seam of her pants. *What did he see when he looked at her?*

"I hope not," she said flatly, and his warm expression flickered.

"Pardon?"

She just could not get that boon-begging past her lips. Instead, she heard herself say, cool and clear, "I think you're making a mistake in trying to move onto the island."

He didn't change his stance, but something ran through his body, and the whole feel of his strength in that small space changed. The once-warm eyes flicked over her in an entirely different manner: assessing and dismissing an insignificant challenge.

It made her burn with rage.

"You do?" he said indifferently.

Indifference. Dismissal. Wrath crawled up inside her hands, making them itch to fist and pound against his belief in her insignificance. She dug her knuckles into her thighs.

"I don't think you realize how well known we are there. People come from all over the city—from all over the world—to our *salon de thé*. It's . . . special." How to make him realize how very special it was if he didn't see that, feel that, for himself?

"What a fascinating coincidence," he said coolly. His head was high, that beautiful, tawny lion's mane curling against his neck. Arrogance clipped his words and polished them, bringing out his privileged birth. "They do the same for me."

Magalie's knuckles dug harder into her thighs, as she tried to force herself to stay reasonable. "Exactly. That's why it might be better for all concerned if you sought different territory."

There. That sounded nicely neutral, didn't it? Neither warning him off nor begging him not to come. It was a tricky line to negotiate. She didn't want to err on the side of humility, that was for damn sure.

His eyebrows went up. He looked so very aristocratic— His Highness, lord of the jungle. "Are you telling me you don't think I could succeed down the street from you?"

She wished. "I think you will be competing for a well-established customer base."

The sharp edges of his teeth showed just a little. "I generally do."

As in, *once they taste me, no one else has a prayer.*

Her eyes narrowed, her anger no longer blunt fists but sharp points that knew exactly where they wanted to stab. "If you think you can move in there and try to put us out of business, I advise you to reconsider."

He inhaled with a hiss, as if she had reached out and grabbed him somewhere arousing. "Are you *threatening* me?" he asked with a little, curling, pleased smile. A smile that said, *Oh, good, the tiny mouse was rude. Now I get to eat it for a snack.*

"No," Magalie tried to lie. She had promised Aunt Aja she wouldn't threaten. But Aunt Geneviève's blood would out: "You don't deserve the warning."

His own eyes narrowed, his pupils dilated. He actually caught his lower lip with the edge of his teeth, as if he was tasting her there. "Oh, *really?*" The last word came out like a hungry little caress. *Tiny mouse, how kind of you to offer yourself to my bored palate.*

"My aunts have been there for almost forty years," she said, anger lashing. "We were there first."

He inclined his head. He had very beautiful, sharp, white

teeth. They looked as if they could cut through almost anything. "Then how thoughtful of you to come welcome me
to the neighborhood."

She snapped her own teeth together. It might take her
more than two bites to work her way through him, but she
could eat him up, too, if she set her mind to it. "You're not
welcome. If you insist on coming into *my* territory without
even a 'by your leave,' I'm going to make sure you regret it."

He took a step forward. His eyes glittered, sweeping up
and down her face and as far as her throat, which suddenly
felt overexposed. But she couldn't bring herself to lower her
chin. In the little office, she was well within grabbing distance of those big hands. Something in his eyes made that
very clear. "*Your* territory? Are you telling me I should *ask*
your permission to open a shop there?"

She took a half step toward him. She would have liked to
take a bigger stride, but, given the size of the office, that was
all she could do without running into him. "That would
have been better manners, certainly. But you would have
been denied."

He gave his head a hard shake. His gaze flashed back to her
throat and then up to her eyes. "You introduced yourself,
but maybe I should have done the same. I'm *Philippe Lyon-*
nais."

She sneered. She couldn't help it. The incredible arrogance in the way he said his name couldn't be taken passively.
"What, am I supposed to bow now?"

Their eyes locked. For a moment, there was nothing else
in the room but the war of locked gazes and the sense that if
ever either of them lost, it would be . . . delicious. Slowly,
carefully, he took a long, long breath and shook his shoulders, resetting his muscles. "Maybe we're getting off to a bad
start."

In the present context, that was so hilarious, half a laugh
surprised its way right through her sneer.

His gaze flickered over her face, and a hint of a wry, responding grin appeared on his lips. Abruptly, he cupped her elbow and led her out of the office. A gentleman escorting a lady to her carriage or a bouncer kicking out a drunk? she wondered dryly. His hand turned the supple leather armor of her Perfecto jacket into a wisp of nothingness between their bodies.

He stopped beside the long marble counter at which he had been working when she came in. The bag that had burst all over him lay there where he had abandoned it. Apparently his employees knew that he took care of his own messes and didn't expect someone else to do it for him. Near it lay the *macarons* he had been finishing.

He loosed her elbow long enough to scoop up one of the warm peach shells and sandwich it over the bottom shell, filled already with apricot ganache, tiny bits of apricot still visible in it. With a quick, casually deft hand, he sprinkled it with a dusting of pistachios chopped so impossibly fine as to seem like pixie dust.

"May I?" He offered it to her on a flat palm, a treasure to a princess, with a sudden, brilliant, confident grin. His eyes lit with pleasure in his offering, sure it would bring delight.

Who hadn't heard of Philippe Lyonnais's *macarons*? Food critics, food bloggers, magazines, television hosts . . . they all raved about him constantly. It would probably taste like she had been permitted to spend three bites of her life in heaven. Like the essence of apricot had come down and kissed a shy pistachio, and they had decided to hang out and cuddle.

If she bit into that in front of him, she would melt into a puddle at his feet.

And he wouldn't even notice. If he had a streak of the child in him, he might enjoy the splash around his shoes as he strode through it.

She looked from its promise of heaven to his warm, intense eyes.

Did he think he was *that* good? That all he had to do to make up for stealing three people's *lives* was to offer her one of his prize pastries?

"No, thank you," she said coldly. *Cold, cold, cold.* Drawing on all the force and warmth of her blue kitchen, far away on the island, holding its heat close and strong inside her, she gave him its opposite. His rejection from it.

She was looking straight into his eyes when she spoke. She saw the blink, saw his pupils contract to small points.

Why, she had found some way to have an effect on him.

He looked down at the pastry and back at her. "You don't . . . want it?" He sounded as if he was having to search out words in a new language that had no meaning.

He couldn't believe she had done it, could he?

Refused *that,* what he was holding in his hand. His life's work.

His face went stiff, her chill setting in, the dark blue eyes seeming to pale with the ice. He set the apricot-pistachio *macaron* very precisely down on the parchment paper from which it had come. His fingers rubbed slowly together, brushing away pistachio fragments.

If he had been anyone else, she would have felt guilty for bringing that look to his face.

She held his eyes and smiled. Then she turned her back on what was quite probably the most delicious thing she would ever encounter in her life and walked out.

And had the satisfaction of hearing her heels *click, click, click* into absolute silence as she did so.

Chapter 4

Philippe had been having a good day until he got cursed by a witch, and he stood there in shock, still unable to adjust.

He couldn't believe she had rejected one of his *macarons*. He had offered it to her fresh from his own hand. Not just his recipe, but *made personally by him*. And she had refused it.

His *Désir*. Apricot kissed by pistachio, with the secret little square of pistachio praline hidden inside, like a G-spot. Well, he didn't call it *le point G* in his marketing brochures, but whenever he created, he knew what he was doing: every pastry had to have its orgasm, its culmination of bliss that hit like a complete surprise. That made the eyes of those who bit into it shiver closed with delight.

The more expressive of his customers started making little moans of pleasure from the very first bite. He loved that.

He would have liked to take that intense, passionate anger of Magalie Chaudron's and make her moan with delight. It seemed the least he could do, given that his existence had so infuriated her in the first place.

She had walked in a challenge. Her leather armor unzipped, showing that silk and slimness underneath, daring him to get his hands on her vulnerable spots. Baiting him with it. Her chin up and her brown eyes so hot and cold all at once. As if she was trying to freeze into a weapon her burning desire to go for him.

So go for me, he remembered thinking, his chin up, his shoulders back. *Go for me, and see what happens.*

But she had only attacked with words. Words didn't give him an excuse to reach under that leather and grab her waist through that silk to, say, protect himself from assault.

You could grab a strange woman to protect yourself if she went for your throat. You could find out what that silk over muscle and ribs and softness felt like.

If he knocked those clicking boots off her, she wouldn't even come up to his shoulder.

Mmm. And he could pick her up and . . .

His mind ran through variation after variation on what he could do as he went back to work, dropping precise amounts of apricot ganache into the shells laid out on the tray. But as he worked, he gazed at the *macarons* for the first time in a long time with dissatisfaction. He had thought this recipe perfected.

But she had managed to refuse it.

"*Everything* in your power?" Aunt Geneviève said with delight. "You said that? *Everything in your power* to make him regret it?"

The three women were working on their new display, which promised to be impressive: the chicken-legged, windowless hut of Baba Yaga, the famous old witch crone from Slavic tales, complete with a palisade of glowing-eyed skulls—one dozen decapitated princes who had dared cross a witch. In the stories, one skull had usually fallen off a fence stake so that a wily prince could sneak in, but Magalie didn't plan on leaving any opening. Baba Yaga could just move over for the younger generation, a witch who knew how to protect herself properly.

She had been a little afraid the display might scare the children, but Aja, who had grown up on regular visits to the colorful and sometimes bizarre temples in India, had looked at Magalie blankly, while Geneviève had rubbed her hands gleefully and added still more frightening details. *"It's October,"* she'd said. *"They'll have been watching gory films from Hollywood. Might as well show them something really scary."*

Magalie thought back to her encounter with Philippe Lyonnais. "Something like that. I'm afraid I wasn't very conciliatory."

"I should hope not!" Geneviève said. Over the heat from the gel cap they had near them in the window space, she softened the tip of a chocolate post and attached a skull to it, its eyes gleaming with the bits of candied orange peel Aja had carefully placed. "Conciliatory! To someone who comes tramping into our territory without even asking permission?"

"I don't believe someone like him merits either conciliation or threats." Aunt Aja shook her head firmly. "Both are so bad for you."

"It's true, you gave him a pretty significant warning," Geneviève said, dissatisfied. "And you can't say that he deserved it. Unless it was how cute he was, after all? Did you fall for that?"

She considered her niece worriedly. Magalie knew that this whole susceptibility-to-princes thing concerned her aunt, because she had no real comprehension of such weakness but had seen it lead to the downfall of many a fine woman.

"Don't worry." Magalie's nostrils flared in disdain. "He's not my type."

"You have a type?" Geneviève checked excitedly, distracted. "Could you describe it for me? Tell me what to be on the lookout for?"

"Humble," Magalie said firmly.

Geneviève frowned in bafflement. And no wonder. Even

to Magalie, that sounded like a lie. Humble people were unsettling at best. All that lack of backbone. It was just creepy. Like talking to linguine.

"Were you planning to be on the lookout to catch one for her or to drive him away?" Aja asked dryly of her partner. Today, her golden tunic almost exactly matched the skulls' gleaming eyes.

"There's nothing wrong with being a filter," Geneviève told her spouse. "Especially a filter like me. I sieve tiny. It saves no end of trouble later."

Magalie waved at a young boy, one of their *habitués,* who had dragged his nanny to a stop and was now standing with his nose as close to pressed against the window as strictly enforced manners would allow, thrilled to catch this glimpse of the next display under construction. The nanny, a young Portuguese au pair, looked pretty thrilled, too. Oh, God, she was taking out her camera.

Magalie gave her a stern look, and the (barely) younger woman tucked the offending item back into her satchel guiltily. It was one thing to take pictures of the finished windows—that, they expected—but it was another to catch Magalie with her butt up in the air as she crouched trying to get three thick candied orange peels to look like a chicken foot.

"But did you say 'everything in your power' or did you say 'something like that'?" Geneviève asked.

Magalie sighed. "I think I just said I would make sure he regretted it."

Aja and Geneviève exchanged glances. "I liked 'everything in her power,'" Geneviève said wistfully. "It had such a ring to it. Like she finally realized she *had* power. But at least this way sounds more like a promise than a warning."

"Perhaps," Aja said. "I don't think we should be dealing in threats at all, but if you're going to, there's no point in inserting a *try* into it. You must admit that some people use the phrase 'everything in my power' to limit themselves. Then later they can say it wasn't in their power."

Geneviève looked offended. "This is my niece we're talking about."

Aja said nothing. Magalie suspected her of keeping thoughts to herself, as she often did. The two women, who thrived on their city and its *marchés aux puces* and other markets and quixotic stores, had long ago begun expressing hints of concern that Magalie didn't seem more at ease in the rest of Paris. They made her run all errands that took her off the island, and they were always quietly pleased—or, in Geneviève's case, sometimes loudly—when she went out clothes shopping. Between love of fashion and errands, Magalie got lured off the island at least two or three times a week. She could brave a lot for the clothes in this city.

But it was true that it always felt a little like leaving a peaceful, walled garden and heading out to war.

She went to work on her second chicken foot, her fingers sticky, and contemplated the growing number of skulls broodingly. "He seemed to think I was some peasant he could ride right over," she muttered, a dog with a bone.

Geneviève shook her head severely. "And he looked like such a fine young man, too. If you like that sort of thing. Peasant. Do you know, I don't think we should leave *any* post without a skull."

"There's always supposed to be a post missing a skull," Aja pointed out. "You have to leave one way in, if the prince is smart enough to find it. That's the story."

Geneviève sniffed. "Just because Baba Yaga got careless when she got old doesn't mean *we* have to."

It was October, Philippe reminded himself, looking at La Maison des Sorcières' window. He might be mistaken to take the display personally. A little wink and a nod toward the American Halloween could explain the chocolate skulls on chocolate stakes, the small bits of candied orange peel that made the skulls' glowing eyes, the orange-peel chicken legs peeking out from under the windowless, doorless chocolate log-cabin house the skull-posts protected.

This witch-house *salon de thé* had enchanted him the instant he saw it. It had been a major factor in his selection of this location. The Île Saint-Louis had been a natural choice, a luxurious island in the center of Paris, an enticing bridge away from one of the city's biggest tourist attractions, Notre-Dame. His shop was always in all the guidebooks as one of the top ten places to experience in Paris; as a polite gesture, he could make it easier for weekend tourists and not force them to choose between himself and Notre-Dame. That old cathedral had been through a lot, after all, what with revolutions and world wars, and he didn't want to make it feel any worse.

But this island was so blissfully peaceful. All the tension in his muscles relaxed whenever he stepped onto it, as if time had released him, and he had slipped into some idealized seventeenth-century world where everyone had money and time and the comforts of electricity. But, even with all those factors, he had researched other places before he bought the space here; the Luxembourg Gardens area had appealed. Then, walking this street, he had seen the witches' window.

And he had fallen in love with it. So different from the glamour he offered, but so enchanting. He had liked the thought of being just down the street from La Maison des Sorcières. Yes, his name alone was enough to give a street like this all the cachet it needed. But this quirky, bewitching place was like the bottom note of a perfume, that something you discovered later, that lent a richness to a neighborhood, that made it a place people came to linger. Where *he* wanted to linger.

It had never occurred to him that the "Sorcières" wouldn't

be thrilled at his arrival. Magalie Chaudon couldn't possibly understand the benefits his name would bring her.

Magalie Chaudron . . . silk and boots and leather, angled chin, and hot brown eyes, and all of it in a package he could pick up with almost no effort, which was good, because when he kissed her, he was going to have to lift her up to do it, and he wasn't going to stop for a long time.

But first, she had to regret that moment when she had flicked disdain all over his *macarons* and turned on her heel. He was going to make her crave him. First.

He searched the skull-posts and smiled a quick, feral smile of satisfaction. There, in the corner, where it was impossible to see from inside the shop and difficult to spot from the outside, one of the skulls had broken the chocolate seal between it and the post and rolled off by a corner of the log cabin.

His mother, the Jungian psychologist who had fallen in love with a real-life fairy tale in his father had loved to read him and his sister stories when they were little. So he knew what a man could do with a missing skull off Baba Yaga's barricade.

Find his way in.

A little silver bell chimed as he opened the door and stepped inside.

Odd things struck him as he moved into the empty shop. Odd things were meant to, he was pretty sure. He was a little surprised he didn't have to duck them flying at his head.

But no, he had slipped inside unannounced, and, for the moment, nothing and no one was bombarding him. He could take a second and look at things he had only been able to glimpse briefly before. The old pink scales on top of the tiny display case. The nature of the *tartes au chocolat* inside, a little rough and homey, as if they had come straight from someone's mother's kitchen. Not his mother's: their desserts had appeared almost magically from the Lyonnais professional kitchens, made by his father or one of their chefs. But someone's mythical mother, a mother who surely existed, the kind of mother who let her kids watch Disney movies without requiring a comparative analysis of them and *les frères Grimm* afterward.

A giant chocolate seahorse hung from the ceiling, twirling slowly as if to invite him to dance. An array of silver molds from another century filled the shelves behind the display case. An askew archway led from this small entrance area into a room beyond.

A voice called, "*Une minute!*" from somewhere back there.

He felt his chest tighten. Something happened to his breath, so that he had to concentrate to keep dragging it in. He almost recognized that voice. Except for its friendly welcome.

He walked back through the little second room and its astonishing array of conical hats, including old paper New Year's hats from 2000, a birthday princess hat, a medieval lady's hat, and, of course, some that were wide-brimmed and black. He glanced at it all, trying to take in what he was dealing with, but he couldn't hesitate. Something pressed him to reach that voice, and the owner of it, there through the last door.

He stopped just short of a little archway to a minuscule kitchen. Three coats, hung to the left of that doorway, puffed out enough to partly block his way in. Magalie Chaudron stood working at a counter of tiny blue tiles that would have driven him insane. How could she keep the grout between the tiles clean? What did she do when she wanted to roll out something—pull out a mat every single time? And how cool did those tiles even stay? How anyone could stand to work with anything but marble, he didn't know. Granite, *à la limite*. Small blue tiles?

She had two tart pans set out on it, and she was running a

spoon over the chocolate with which she must have just filled them. Imperfectly. He had to clamp down on the urge to grab a white towel and wipe it all around the edge of the tart pan to clean away the crumbs from her crust. He flinched a little when he saw some of those crumbs spill onto the chocolate surface itself. Which she didn't even make perfectly smooth. Her ganache had cooled too much before she poured it, and she left the path of her spoon visible on it. His palms itched so badly, he had to dig his fingers into them to keep from grabbing the spoon and taking her to task like a clumsy apprentice.

Behind her, close enough that in her place he would risk hitting it with his elbow every time he turned around, a pot of chocolate sat on a burner turned to its lowest heat. The scent of it reached out and curled around him. *Chocolat chaud.* When was the last time he had drunk *chocolat chaud*? Cold weather was settling in, leaves going brown, and the idea of curling up with a cup of it suddenly seemed so inviting.

She worked without even an apron, smiling a little. Her hair was coiffed again with that careless perfection he had seen the other day, another set of black boots adding ten centimeters to her height and helping her slim-fitting jeans do great things for her butt. A sweater in a blend of midnight blue and black dipped sexily toward one shoulder.

He took a long, deep breath of *chocolat chaud* as his gaze ran over that butt, then fixed on that glimpse of her collarbone. *And you wanted to take her to task like a clumsy apprentice? Keep your priorities straight, Philippe.*

She still hadn't seen him, concentrating on her chocolate. His chest was tight enough to make breathing an effort, and she hadn't even noticed he was there?

He stepped into the doorway. And just let his presence fill it. He dominated kitchens thirty times larger than this most waking moments of his day. She had to wear stilt heels to reach his shoulder. So he just stood in that archway and willed himself on her.

Her resistance surprised him, how gradually she came out of her chocolate. As he pushed his presence through the room, at first her smile deepened and grew more secretive. Her head rose, and a little shiver ran over her body, like that of someone cold who had stepped into warmth.

She looked slowly toward him, as if waking from a pleasant dream.

And jerked, her spoon smearing chocolate over the edge of the pan.

"Allow me." He couldn't help himself. The *tarte* was only one step from him. He grabbed a tissue out of a box as the only thing in her kitchen remotely approximating a professional's white towels, and he wiped the edge of her pan. One clean sweep, all the way around, getting rid of not only the smear but also those damn crumbs.

He might have yielded to the urge to grab the spoon and smooth that chocolate out properly, except that she looked as if she might hit him with it. He rubbed the dusting of greenish crumbs between his fingers and looked into her furious eyes.

All trace of her smile was gone. She was practically hexing him with her gaze alone. "What the hell do you think you're doing?"

His step to the *tarte* had brought their bodies together: his biceps to her shoulder, his hip to her ribs, his thigh to her hip. There was no space for her to give him in this tiny kitchen. He was pretty sure she wouldn't have backed up a step even if there was. It drove him mad with arousal, her inability to back up.

"Is that apricot?" On an unlit burner behind the *chocolat chaud* was an orange mixture that looked and smelled suspiciously like fresh-made apricot jam.

Apricots. The green crumbs of ground *pistachios*. She had made a *pistachio* crust. With an *apricot* filling. The exact flavors in the *Désir* she had refused a week ago.

Had she been thinking about it? A vindictive smile curled his mouth. Had she regretted what she had refused, until she tried to do something with those flavors herself?

If she had, she was outraged to have him discover it. "What. Do. You. Think. You. Are. Doing—in my kitchen? Get out!"

Excitement kicked through him. He shouldn't have interfered in her kitchen, that was inarguably true. The most basic etiquette. But now that he had, now that their bodies were touching and she was so mad, he felt an almost irresistible desire to crowd her some more and see what she would do. It unfurled in him, prickling inside him with claws, taunting him into action. "Why, *bonjour* to you, too, Mademoiselle Chaudron. You let a skull fall off one of your posts."

She frowned, glancing uneasily toward the display two rooms away, completely hidden from her by his shoulders, and that clawing thing inside him laughed and tried to push him forward. He liked the fact that his shoulders blocked her view. He liked the fact that his size overwhelmed this room. It was unsettling, how much self-discipline he had to call on to maintain some level of civilized behavior. Self-discipline was one of his greatest strengths, meaning that he wasn't used to having to think about it to get it to work.

She folded her arms, despite the fact that the movement bumped into him aggressively, and lifted her chin. "Did you come to apologize?"

He gaped at her. "Did *I* come to apologize? For what— how rude you are?"

She took a hard breath, and his eyes flickered over her chest, and then *he* had to take a hard breath. Maybe his self-discipline was getting out of shape. It felt thin and feeble before the pouncing-lion-thing growing stronger inside him.

"You open a shop right next door to us as if we aren't even here. You come into my kitchen and try to *take over*, as if you know how to do it better than I do."

He gave her *tarte* an incredulous look. He couldn't help it. He *did* know how to do it better than she did. There *was* something enticing about her *tarte*, true, like a childhood with a mythical mother he hadn't had, given that his mother had only set foot in kitchens to kiss his father. He wouldn't mind at all coming home from work and curling up comfortably to find himself offered a slice of such a *tarte*. It would make him feel . . . loved. But *his* chocolate *tartes* had a surface so smooth, you could see your face in it.

Her lips pressed together at that look, and a flush showed along her cheekbones, her eyes glittering. "You think I'm rude because I didn't curtsy to you when you forced your way in? Didn't thank Your Highness for riding your white stallion over everyone else's work and life?"

What? He didn't act like that. Did he act like that? Did she really see him that way? He folded his own arms. He had to be careful when he did that not to knock her in that proud chin, that was how much bigger he was. "I think you're rude," he said coldly, "because you are rude. Even if you have a problem with me, you could express it correctly. With some modicum of manners. At the very minimum, you could have accepted the peace-offering that I made you."

Her eyebrows shot up. Even though her arrogant chin just barely passed above his folded arms, she kept her boots braced and her body right in close, like a boxer refusing to yield. Blood roared through his veins, a genuine jungle roar, dying to be unleashed.

"That *macaron*?"

She said the word with so much disdain, his head nearly blew off. A Dubai sheikh had sent a private jet to pick up boxes of those *macarons*, so that his guests could have them at their freshest, just that morning. Multiple movie stars had them flown to Hollywood once a week. People bit into his *Désir* and then went online and blogged five drooling, raving pages about it. This weekend, he was making the desserts for a party for the President of France. And he wasn't even stressed over it. It was *commonplace.* He was *Philippe Lyonnais.*

He had told her that already, though.

"You have a big idea of yourself, don't you?" she said.

Well . . . yes.

"Come muscle in on someone else's territory, try to steal their customers, and offer a little bit of sugar to make up for it?"

"*Un petit peu de sucre?* One of *my*—" He caught himself, but unfortunately there was no rewind. He couldn't back up and erase the emphasis on the *my*. Her derisive look made everything inside him roil. "It was a nice thing for me to offer you. It was one of *my*—that is—" He broke off, then tried again. "I made that one with *my own ha*—"

Her lip was curling.

He dug his fingers into his biceps to keep from curling them into *her* biceps and lifting her straight off the floor. And to think he was known for his calm temperament in his kitchens. The non-volatile star chef. "You know," he breathed very quietly, feeling his voice going almost guttural, "you should have tried it. Just one bite of it might have been worth more than you think."

Her eyes flickered. *Yes.* She wondered at least a little about that, whether she had missed out on something incredible.

He thought about giving her another chance. The pressure in this room was enormous right now, the clash of two Titans in a space the size of an elevator. Hot burners to one side, no room for error, and the scent of chocolate, maddeningly powerful, overwhelming everything.

But if he could get her to bite down into one of his works of art, would everything dissolve away from her but his flavors on her tongue? Would all the muscles of her stiff neck relax in bliss? Would those molten brown eyes slide half-closed? Would she look up at him, when she had recovered from the first taste, with her lips parted, her eyes begging for more?

She smiled suddenly. He was so deep in his vision that it took him a second to realize she couldn't be smiling over any bite of him, because she hadn't tasted him yet. Uneasiness stirred. There was something very disturbing about that smile.

She turned away from him to the pot of hot chocolate. To turn away from him—that might be a yielding, right? It might show physical consciousness, at least, and a need to break free from it.

He looked at her bent head, the glossy black hair, the little smile on her face. She seemed utterly focused now on her chocolate. One perfectly manicured hand, nails some rosé Champagne color that matched the subtle gloss on her lips, stirred the pot with a wooden spoon.

It was strange how hungry the sight made him. Surely he got enough sugar just taste-testing his own work. And almost certainly his work was of higher quality, he thought arrogantly.

She lifted the spoon, unctuous chocolate clinging to it. Thick and pure, probably rich with cream and high-quality dark chocolate, the liquid slid slowly back off the spoon. The scent of it promised bliss. Chocolate and cream and . . . what was that spice? How odd that he couldn't recognize it. He could usually tell whether cinnamon came from Sri Lanka or Madagascar just by the smell.

"Enfin, bon," she said, "if you think I should apologize for *my* rudeness, maybe *I* should be the one to offer *you* something."

She stirred the pot exactly three more times and then dipped a ladle into it and poured the thick, rich liquid into a small, handle-less cup.

She held it up to him. With a little smile.

His heart beat hard, a warning drum. He looked from the cup to her. Why did he feel that if he drank the stuff, he would turn into a toad?

That was silly. Of course.

He started to lift his hand. Lifted it far enough that he could feel the warmth emanating off the bottom of the cup. *A little bit of sugar,* she had said, of his *Désir.* And, *That macaron?* with a sneer. And worse, far worse, that freezing, indifferent dismissal when he had offered it to her. *Non, merci.* Casually dismissing . . . everything. And turning away to walk out on it, the heels of her boots sounding as if they were walking right over him.

He dropped his hand away from that warmth. *"Non, merci,"* he said easily, as if the cup didn't tempt him in the slightest.

Had his face looked like that when she had refused him? As if he had been slapped? *Putain,* but he hoped not. He wasn't a baby.

He smiled at her.

Her eyes narrowed and spat sparks that burned his skin. He knew their bad start was getting even worse, and he *loved* it. To make his insult ice-crystal clear, he turned his back on her and walked out.

The little silver bell chimed as he went through the door. The back of his neck prickled, as if it had just been hit by a hex.

He glanced once at the display window with its skull posts. That was a good sign, wasn't it? If you could escape Baba Yaga's hut with your skin?

Why did he feel unsure he wanted to?

Chapter 5

Magalie was scowling at a skull hidden by a chicken foot when the aunts breezed in. It was one of her own posts that had lost its skull, too.

"That's probably a good sign," Geneviève said cheerfully. "That means we need another prince's skull for that post. And aren't we lucky? There's a prince insisting on barging right in."

Aja looked thoughtful. Magalie crinkled her nose, dissatisfied. She knew she wanted to do something to make Philippe Lyonnais sorry he had thought of her as a peasant, but somehow his skull on a post wasn't quite it. If she just cut his head straight off like that, he wouldn't have a chance to beg for mercy.

Neither Aja nor Geneviève seemed to realize that having him beg for mercy or having his skull on their post was a *fantasy*. That, in reality, the invasion of this "prince" might be the end of their world.

What if he took over their island? What if they lost all their *habitués*? What if all the tourists who might otherwise wander to their end of the street stopped instead at his store? *Lyonnais*. It was a name to stop traffic, all right.

What if their business was destroyed? What if Aunt Geneviève could no longer afford to pay the taxes on this building a lover had deeded to her so long ago, and they found themselves kicked off the island?

She felt physically sick every time she thought of it. And, with Philippe coming, she couldn't stop thinking of it.

Some suppressed part of her had always known she would be wrenched from this place. How could she belong in Paris? She wasn't even French. Born in America and packed up like a suitcase to be hauled back and forth between the lavender fields of Provence and Ithaca, New York, all her life.

A match made in heaven, her parents. The beekeeper who had fallen in love with the girl in the lavender fields. Only he was just starting an ambitious, tenure-track position in entomology at Cornell, and her mother's attachment to the family lavender fields was so profound, she almost couldn't live without them.

A love that could cross two worlds. And cross them, and cross them. Good God, had they crossed them. Stéphanie Chaudron's pregnancy far from her parents and her precious lavender fields had not gone well. She had flown home with her daughter when Magalie was only six months old. Her father had followed two months later, as soon as classes at Cornell let out, and spent the summer. Her mother had resolved to try again and had flown back to Ithaca in late August.

And so it went.

From American kindergarten until she passed her French bac, Magalie had only spent four complete, but not consecutive, years in one school.

And Magalie had handled it normally. Superbly, even. Her parents were so proud of her, they could burst, their bicultural child who could jump from one world to the next without even a stumble. She spoke two languages as if they were her own, which they almost were. She had a very strong sense of who she was, separate from all others. Because she was always separate from all others.

The first time she "went back" to an old school after a year's absence in another country, at age seven, she'd been so excited. She just knew that as soon as she was back with those old friends, everyone would be so happy, they would play, people would love her, and they would have so much fun.

But it didn't work out right. There was a fracture, a disjointing. As if she was a piece that had been pulled out of a puzzle, but the puzzle had a life of its own; it kept growing and changing, and she kept growing and changing, and when she tried to plop back into her old spot, well . . . it didn't work. She had to try again and again to fit. And as that kept happening, over and over, the attachments on either side fractured and weakened; because the people she left behind also knew she wouldn't necessarily be around the next time someone got dumped by a boyfriend or needed a friend to go to the movies with.

At eighteen, she sought out two people who hadn't moved in close to four decades: her aunts Geneviève and Aja.

She had always known them by their boxes of chocolate. They would arrive twice a year, birthday and Christmas, straight from Paris, always constant no matter whether Magalie was in Provence or in upstate New York. Stamped with a witch flying across the moon. The witch looked as if its original had been hand-drawn with a ballpoint pen by someone with a drawing style as angular and cryptic as her handwriting. *"Ma chère Stéphanie,"* each letter would begin, "we hope this letter finds you well and, if not, that this little package will help. We have had a quiet winter so far, only one Sleeping Beauty-type and two Cinderellas, although I wouldn't go so far as to say the rest of the customers had their heads on completely straight. But the theater season has been excellent. Did you see *Médée* when it played in Avignon? I must say, Huppert captured the role beautifully. How is Magalie doing? Don't forget you must send her to us once she passes her bac!"

And Magalie would stare at her mother's chocolates, dark and rich and shaped like flying carpets and witches and cow patties (the chocolate sprouting orange peel hay), and sneak one when she could, and dream of the day she would take a train or a plane to Paris, to go to work in a world filled with those chocolates. In a world that stayed the same, for forty years.

And then one day she did. She was in the U.S. for her senior year, so she got her diploma, headed straight over to pass her French bac, and enrolled in l'Université de Paris. She spent one last August and the start of the wine harvest with her mother in Provence and then packed her bags and took the train up from that south full of roses and lavender, cicadas and sunburnt stone and sunshine, and came to Paris. Where the stone was just as old but grimier, grayer, where nothing smelled of lavender or roses, and where the world grew so packed with possibilities, she almost couldn't move at first. She wanted fewer possibilities, not more.

She took a deep breath and began the long walk out of the train station, which was cold and enormous, her small bag rolling behind her. She had preferred to pack light and go shopping. In Paris.

Paris.

She was going to live in *Paris*. And work here and breathe here. Her emotions tangled in an overload of nerves and hope and potential. She kept taking deep breaths of the car exhaust and the smoke fumes. And walking. Walking down busy sidewalks, past beautiful shop windows and café tables crowded with people enjoying the wonderful weather.

She reached the great river, braceleted with bridges, bejeweled with re-purposed palaces.

Her aunts had written her specific directions: Follow the river and cross one island filled with tourists and pigeons gathering before God. Thread through them, shake her head at postcard vendors, protect her bag from pickpockets, and come to the little garden tucked like a secret behind the cathedral, hidden by the big tour buses that lined the street from end to end. There, a bridge arched up, spanning the river in one graceful leap. And at the peak of the arch, a young man stood at the rail of the bridge. His long gold hair was tied with a leather strap at the base of his neck. His white poet's shirt rippled from the movements of his arm. He played the violin, intensely and with passion, old, rich music she almost recognized escorting her across the bridge.

How the aunts had known to mention the violin player in the directions mailed to her a month before, she didn't know. But they had.

His hat lay upside down at his feet. She dropped a coin into it the way one might toss a coin into a well and looked up at him for a moment. He dipped his violin in acknowledgment of her and kept on playing.

She passed onto the quiet island, a place her aunts had lived for nearly forty years. They never moved. This was their place, and they stayed. They had an apartment for Magalie, six floors above the *salon de thé,* and the clear intention of making her their heir, to let her hold this place forever.

Forever had no ending. Not ever.

On the island, all the freshly discovered hustle and bustle of Paris seemed to fade away. Stone buildings centuries old rose around her, never taller than eight stories, including the slanted one, under slate roofs. The rare car passed discreetly, inching its way through the people who walked easily in the middle of the street, looking up at old carvings on the walls, into storefronts filled with strange specialties. Time lay over the island like a cloak: the idea that you always had time, that it had been here for a while and wasn't going anywhere soon.

It was her place. The one she wouldn't leave, so no one could grow over her spot and take it from her.

Until Philippe Lyonnais decided to take it from her, anyway. He brought time in.

The papers announced the date he planned to open the store: January 15, after the Christmas rush. The islanders rushed to La Maison des Sorcières in great waves of pity, filling the salon each afternoon with promises of loyalty, as if Magalie was stupid. People didn't keep spaces for people when things changed. She just hadn't known that *she* could set herself in concrete and refuse to budge, and still the world could change around her.

Magalie did everything she could to make those last three months the best, to fill the shop's coffers so that they could at least last another six months, no matter how many customers they lost. She poured so much of herself into her chocolate that her aunts started frowning at her. "How can you be losing weight making chocolate, Magalie? Is something wrong? My dear, you don't have to blast them with the scent of it in Timbuktu. Just a whisper released into the air. It will make it to Timbuktu. Don't you worry."

Of course, two women who had managed to stay in one place for nearly four decades would have a false sense of security.

Workers went in and out of the storefront halfway down the street, and the sawdust got cleared away, and the pure glamour of the place started to gleam into the quiet neighborhood. Even her most faithful friends on the island would stand pressed against its windows, eager to get a glimpse of the palace that would soon be revealed: the lions in the molding, the twining of rosebuds around the gleaming green marble columns. And the display cases—oh, the exquisite, curving display cases, so simple yet gorgeous in design. What elaborate concoctions would fill them and make them the most beautiful sight in the whole fairy-tale chamber?

His name went up. *Lyonnais.* A stamp of gold across the mist-green front, a claim of ownership of the street.

Occasionally they crossed paths, Philippe there to insist on what he wanted from his workers, checking on the progress in the store, looking cool and collected in jeans and cashmere sweaters and lambskin coats. A lion wearing a slaughtered lamb—how appropriate. She gave him an ice-cold look and refused to even cross the street to him when he nodded, walking crisply on before he could cross the street himself. Not that he showed any sign of doing that. He just turned his head and watched her, looking ever so slightly feral.

He sent them a box of his *macarons* for Christmas. A treasure box, opened as cautiously as one that might contain an asp, to reveal the jewel tones of ruby, onyx, amber, jade, emerald *macarons*. *Avec mes meilleurs voeux, Philippe,* it said, so very correctly. When he hadn't even tried to barge into their store where he wasn't wanted since October, Magalie turned away from it whip-fast and boxed up three of Geneviève's cow patties to send straight over to him, with no message. Then she and her aunts packed their bags and headed south to spend Christmas and New Year's with her parents and grandparents.

Chapter 6

"Are you expecting someone you haven't told us about?" Noémie asked, amused and searching at once. If there was any chance Philippe might begin bringing someone to the family Christmas parties, his sister wanted to be the first to start the gossip and speculation.

Philippe glanced down at the place settings and the extra wineglass he held. Noémie twitched the stem from his hand. "How many times do I have to remind you? There are seventeen of us, not eighteen."

Philippe, Noémie and her husband, his niece Océane, his fathers' two brothers and their families, and his and Noémie's godfather, a longstanding friend of the family whose wife had died of lung cancer several years back, were all in the home of Philippe and Noémie's parents, proud hosts to the event this year.

"Right," Philippe said, and he counted out eighteen of the silver knives a duchess had given his great-great-great-great grandfather after a particularly successful reception of a king.

Noémie took back the extra knife and gave him another glinting, searching look.

"Seventeen," she reminded him as he started counting out the multiple sizes of forks they would use.

"I can count to seventeen," four-year-old Océane announced proudly. "Do you need help, Tonton?"

Philippe laughed and ceded the counting. Noémie made too much out of a man trying to help set a formal table for a large crowd.

But as the family ate, stood and stretched their legs between courses, laughed, and tried to keep the children up until midnight for the presents, Philippe did keep feeling as if there was someone missing.

Maybe it was just the holidays highlighting his singleness. The couples around him were so happy, despite their frequent sparring. His parents surveyed the crowd, exchanging smug parental looks with each other. Nice to know he and Noémie made their parents proud, even if he often drove his father crazy.

His father was of an average height for a man. His Alsatian mother had passed on tall German genes to her children. His tall mother and average-sized father were of an exact height, in fact, something that pleased both of them enormously. His mother only once in a while put on high heels to show off. His father wolf-whistled when she did.

He wondered what they would think of the woman who needed ten-centimeter heels to not quite reach his shoulders. He grinned, imagining bringing that black-haired witch into his tall, tawny family. His whole left arm itched with a sudden and passionate desire to be able to pull her in against his side. Right then. Right there. To stand with her tucked up to him as he chatted with his family.

So that was who was missing. He laughed a little. He never could pick anything easy, could he? She had sent him chocolate *merde* by return courier in response to his Christmas gift the day before. He had sent her a true treasure box and gotten back dark chocolate made to look like oozing cow patties, with slivers of candied orange peel poking out like undigested hay. It had made him laugh until he had to bend over his desk and clutch its edge in a fit of desperate arousal. Which was very bad luck for him, because he didn't think the cow shit had been intended as a friendly message.

He hadn't dared eat the things. God knew what she had put into them. Belladonna, probably. But they still sat there on his desk at work, the most incredible temptation despite the plethora of his extraordinary Christmas desserts in the *laboratoire,* desserts that should have overwhelmed that whisper of hunger that snuck out from the cow patties and followed him around his kitchens.

"What's so funny?" his father asked him.

"Oh, just wondering if someone liked the *macarons* I sent for a Christmas present." Secretly, in his pocket, his hand curled into a fist as he tried to physically will her to eat them across however many miles. Was she even in Paris today? *Taste them. You'll never recover. Put one into your mouth, and you'll melt for me every time I look at you.*

"*Ça dépend,*" his father said. "Did you send her some of mine or those new concoctions you're always trying? Olive oil and banana. Who makes a *macaron* of *l'huile d'olive et banane?*"

Philippe grinned at his father, who was pretending not to eye their two desserts jealously, one made by Philippe, the other by his father. It was a source of both pride and rivalry to the older Lyonnais that Philippe was considered to be the best pâtissier in the world. His father had been considered one of the best before his son swept the field.

Half of Pierre Lyonnais was entirely proud, since he took credit for Philippe's training, but being in his own son's shadow made him grumpy sometimes nevertheless. Philippe raised his glass to him. "You taught me how to make the best chocolate *macarons* out there by the time I was fourteen, Papa," he said with a grin. "I got bored."

"*Rebelle,*" his father said, but with affection.

★ ★ ★

On Christmas Day, Magalie's parents kissed under mistletoe. They gave each other special presents they had been dreaming about for months during their separation. They hugged at odd moments. Her mother started talking about flying back to the States with her father for a few months, while the lavender was in its winter slumber.

"Look at my little *parisienne*," Stéphanie said of her daughter, eyeing her fashionable city clothes. "Magalie, I've always said it. You can make yourself at home *anywhere*."

Her father looked wistfully proud. Magalie got a lump in her chest at that look. Wherever her mother went during their daughter's childhood, Stéphanie had always taken Magalie with her. There had been no question of anything else. But the wrenching apart of Magalie's relationship with her father, over and over, was something that would probably never heal.

"You've always been so bright and strong," he said.

Geneviève and Aja gazed at her parents for a moment and exchanged a glance with each other. They didn't say anything, but a little later, Geneviève slipped her a chocolate witch, and Aja handed her a cup of tea. Maybe the two women really did know magic, or maybe the magic was in the gesture itself, but nibbling on the witch's broomstick and sipping the tea, Magalie did feel stronger.

She had brought the box of *macarons* with her, struggling against the temptation to serve them as a special treat at the end of the meal. But while her grandfather was uncorking the Sauternes to serve with the foie gras, she slipped out into the middle of their winter-dead lavender field. Its power was in abeyance, its hold on her mother loosened. Anyone would think her ambitious, determined, mild-mannered father was Hades, able to keep her mother in his world for only the four winter months of the year.

The plants' scent was a mauve, slumbering thing around her in the cold. Bundled in her coat, she opened the box to gaze into it. She had half thought she might sneak one, out here in the night, where no one would know, maybe not even him.

Instead, something wild and raging ran through her at their beauty, at the lavender fields, at her father's wistful look, and she threw the box to the ground, stomping and stomping on it, like a child in a temper tantrum, until it was nothing but muddy, obliterated card stock and gluey sugar.

It didn't make her feel nearly as strong as she'd thought it would.

The reverse, almost. It seemed to leave a fissure in her that she could not get to close.

Philippe was pouring a sweet Sauternes for the table, to accompany the foie gras, when he felt sharp-heeled boots shatter his heart and grind the crumbs into the ground.

His hand tightened around the bottle until the knuckles showed white. Noémie looked up from the family's momentary focus on the baby kicking in her belly. "Are you all right?"

"She didn't eat them," he said grimly.

That . . . witch.

Had she just stomped his *macarons* into the ground?

"Maybe try some classics next time?" his father suggested. "I hear women like chocolate."

But he threw his arm behind his son's back and gave his shoulders a squeeze. His father knew what it was like to pour his heart into his work.

Chapter 7

Magalie and her aunts returned to a freezing Paris to find an invitation to Philippe Lyonnais's opening.

The bright mood from the Christmas and New Year's festivities sloughed off Magalie like diseased skin. She just stood there, bleakness invading her. That bastard. He had to rub it in, didn't he? She had poured all of herself into her chocolate, but their doom was still approaching.

"Are you all right?" Geneviève asked repeatedly over the next week. "How can you act stressed making *chocolat chaud* and *tartes au chocolat*? It's not good for the chocolate. Maybe we're too busy. Do you want me to tell some of our neighbors to go away? They really don't need to sit in here every single day."

"I like that new combination of apricots with a pistachio crust," Aunt Aja mentioned.

"Don't you ever worry about the future at all?" Magalie asked, despite herself. She didn't want to worry them more by talking about the disaster fast approaching, but . . . how did they manage to be so oblivious?

Geneviève tilted her head. "I used to worry about your mother. Comes from being the older sister. But she turned out all right."

Aja exchanged a look with her.

"Almost all right," Geneviève amended. "In her own way."

"I worried before I left home," Aja said quietly, referring to her emigration to France. "I was about your age. But it turned out all right."

Worry about Lyonnais! Magalie wanted to shout at them. But if worrying did no good, why inflict it on them?

As the two older women went to the kitchen, Magalie pressed her forehead into the cold glass of their front door, angling to stare down the street at the name *Lyonnais*. If she could have brought herself to ask him for a favor, could she have saved her aunts? No. How? From the moment he had set his sights on this island, this street, from the moment he had bought the shop, their doom had been sealed.

She straightened from the door and reached into the window display to adjust a great chocolate fir tree that looked in danger of falling. Then she glanced up and nearly jumped out of her skin when she looked straight into Philippe Lyonnais's blue eyes. He was standing beside a tall woman with silky, gold-brown hair brushed straight and smooth to her shoulders, a woman with a distinct bulge in her belly.

Magalie felt as if she'd been kicked, right in her own womb. Was Philippe Lyonnais *married*? She had never seen mention of it in all the articles she had read on him, but, unlike the American press, French reporters wouldn't talk about his *vie privée*.

No, that was . . . Wait. She was seeing tawny hair and tawny hair, blue eyes and blue eyes, tall and tall. . . . That was a family resemblance, wasn't it? Why was she so relieved to find one? Because she might feel some pangs about crushing to his knees the father of a happy family?

Oh, yes, maybe that was it.

"It will be a shame if you crush them out of business," Philippe's sister said a little regretfully, as they left the display window of La Maison des Sorcières and headed on toward the end of the island. Philippe wanted desperately to turn around and go straight inside, grab Magalie Chaudron's shoulders, and squeeze that look of horror off her face, but his sister's presence stopped him.

Philippe gave her a betrayed glance. "What is it with everyone? Do I act like I go around crushing people?"

"Not on purpose," his sister said affectionately. The winter wind swept off the river, down the corridor provided by the street, and buffeted them. Noémie had been working on the last touches of his shop's interior design but complained that the baby was kicking her too hard and she needed to take a walk. "But no one is going to come here when you're a few doors away."

Philippe glanced back at the display window, not entirely sure of that. Sometimes *he* wanted to come here from half a block away. Just slip into a world that wasn't his but where he kept feeling he should have an entry. Even one he had to force open by jamming the toe of his boot in the door.

"You know you'll steal all their customers," his sister said. "You have to admit, it's a little bit of a shame. That place is like one of the seven wonders of Paris. The hidden one."

"And I'm the obvious one," Philippe said. His sister coughed oddly and bit her lip. He glanced at her, but she just set her hand on her pregnant belly, with her teeth solidly in her twitching lower lip, and said nothing. "So that works out perfectly for them, I would think. I draw people here, and more of them will discover this secret in passing."

"That's true," Noémie said thoughtfully. "That might work."

"I don't know why they can't be more grateful, then." He scowled, thinking of the evil little smile on Magalie's face as she'd offered him that cup of chocolate. One would think that, at the very least, he wouldn't have to worry about being poisoned by her. "You know I'll be bringing in people from all over Paris and a lot farther than that. Not everyone will have the patience to wait in line. They can have my overflow," he added generously. The witches didn't really deserve it, the way Magalie kept treating him, but he could hardly set up a barricade between his half of the street and theirs to stop it.

"You could be right about that." His sister could assess a business situation just as fast and as matter-of-factly as he could. That was what happened when you grew up with such decisions being made routinely over breakfast, breakfasts consisting of *pains au chocolat* and *croissants* regularly voted the best in Paris. "You really might be good for their business," Noémie admitted.

"Of course I'm right," Philippe said indignantly. Getting respect from one's own family was like trying to draw blood from a stone. His mother was the only one who could manage to produce some, and then mostly when his father wasn't around to feel jealous. "You never look at that scrapbook Maman collects on me, do you?"

"You mean the one Maman collects on *us*?" Noémie asked dryly. "On Lyonnais, and my design of the stores, and all that?"

Philippe tried to look suitably chastened. "The one about my fantastic interior designer, yes. And the brother who helps show off her designs by making world-famous pâtisseries to display in them. Anyway, you know and I know there will be lines down the block. You would think she—they—could appreciate that."

Ungrateful witch. He glanced back at the shop window, his shoulder blades prickling. "Do you ever get the feeling that someone could turn you into a toad?"

Or a beast. He felt much more like a beast when he got near Magalie Chaudron and her chocolate.

"Me? No. But in your case, we're not talking about a major transformation."

Chapter 8

The day the new Lyonnais shop opened, La Maison des Sorcières didn't have a single customer. Not even one loyal neighbor. Its emptiness was a huge hole in Magalie's middle, one she kept trying not to fall into. What if she and her aunts lost this place?

Her heart gave a little thump of relief and gratitude when she saw Madame Fernand step out of her building down the street and head their way, her poodle darting back and forth, right toward the wheels of a slowly passing moped, leash tugged ineffectually by a gloved hand. But Madame Fernand didn't even pull her fancy hat's broad brim down to hide her face in shame as she walked right past the tea shop and on toward Philippe's.

He was probably gloating over how completely he had taken over; there was no one in front of their shop, everyone in front of his. No, who was she kidding? You couldn't gloat over something you didn't notice at all.

Before his shop, a party-like crowd gathered, as if heralding the arrival of an emperor. *In new clothes,* Magalie thought maliciously, trying to imagine Philippe Lyonnais appearing before the hordes supremely oblivious to his nakedness.

"Are you all right?" Aunt Aja asked

Magalie blinked, coming back from a long way away, and realized that she had both forearms braced on the curve of the display case and her head lowered almost to rest on it, as if she was thinking of drowning herself in one of her own *tartes* just below.

"I . . . yes, I'm . . ." Whoever had come up with the idea of imagining one's enemies naked to rob them of their power should be shot. Guillotined. Burned at the stake. Something vile, anyway.

Aunt Aja handed her a cup of tea. Magalie took a long breath of it, the scent seeming to spice up her brain and clear out an unnoticed fog in the back of her eyes. She desperately wanted to know what was in it but knew better than to ask. If Aunt Aja gave you tea, you accepted it or refused it, but you didn't ask questions.

"I can't believe he sent us an invitation," Geneviève said grumpily, pulling the heavy card from where it was tucked by their 1920s cash register and tapping it on the display case. "It takes all the fun out of showing up unannounced and cursing him."

"He might be smart," Aja mentioned, as if it behooved her to point out the possibility.

Magalie turned away. She couldn't get that crushed box of Christmas *macarons* out of her mind. What magical array of flavors might he have sent her? What would the shell of one of his *macarons* have felt like under her fingers? How might it have yielded to her teeth? *Smart.* She brought up a hand and rubbed the back of her neck. Yes, Philippe Lyonnais was very smart.

Politic, even. He had probably sent the same box to a hundred different people that Christmas—reliable suppliers, major clients, third cousins.

She looked at her tea again. It took a lot of courage to toss out one of Aja's teas undrunk. It would be easier to drop a treasure chest back into the sea unopened. At least with the treasure chest, you wouldn't risk offending Aja. But it took just as much courage to drink it, blind. What if you didn't want to have the fog at the back of your eyes cleared, for example; what if you wanted to just remain stubbornly blind?

"It wouldn't have to be a curse," she said.

Aja smiled at her in quick, surprised approval.

"Oh, ho!" Geneviève said. "So you *did* think he was cute. Don't worry. After nearly forty years of working with all those would-be princesses who wander in here, I think I can land you a prince, if you're sure you want one."

Magalie narrowed her eyes at her aunt and tapped one booted toe. *If* she wanted such a "prince," which she did not, the reason she did not want him was *not* because she thought he was out of her reach. It might be because she thought *he* thought she was beneath his reach, which wasn't quite the same thing. She hadn't drunk the damn tea yet, so she didn't have to admit that if she didn't want to. And if she were, for example, to completely lose her mind and decide she did want a prince, she did *not* need her sixty-year-old aunt to land him for her.

"We might offer a gift," she said.

"Ooh." Geneviève pursed her lips and gave a silent whistle of approval.

Aja, on the other hand, stroked her tunic.

"You would agree that humility is a gift, wouldn't you, Aunt Aja?" Magalie asked her.

"I'm not the one who has to agree. You are. If you think humility is a gift—the kind you would like given to you—by all means."

Magalie hesitated.

Geneviève leaned past her, ostensibly to dust off the antique chocolate mold sitting near her on the display case, and whispered loudly into her ear: "Don't worry. I'm pretty sure that if anyone tried to give humility to you, it wouldn't take."

That was true, Magalie thought smugly. Still cradling Aja's cup of tea in one hand, she went back into the little blue-tiled kitchen. She took another deep breath of the tea and almost took a sip but then hesitated and set it on the counter. She looked at the pot of hot chocolate, currently going to waste for lack of customers.

"You will throw the rest out when you're done with it, won't you?" Geneviève called back. "We can't go randomly inflicting—I mean, gifting—humility on every passing stranger."

Magalie sometimes wondered if Geneviève genuinely thought Magalie could stir wishes and curses into chocolate. Or if she just liked to believe she believed it, which was not quite the same thing.

Magalie didn't *believe* it. That is, if someone asked her if she could do magic, she would scoff. But she didn't *disbelieve* it, either. She always made sure to stir in a wish, because whenever she dipped her spoon into the chocolate, it felt as if she could.

For Philippe, she stirred three times. Imagining all that confidence stripped from him. Imagining him looking *up*, not down, which meant, with his height, he would have to be kneeling at her feet. Her stirring slowed. Imagining his shirt half-ripped from his body, in tatters. Wanting something from *her*, coming to her in a petition she could carelessly crush.

Her ladle still, she looked down into the warm brown chocolate for a long moment as the vision tried to sneak inside and steal something from her. She took a breath and poured the chocolate into a side-handled *chocolatière* Geneviève and Aja had picked up just the other day at a *marché aux puces*. Rounded and carnival-colored, with broad stripes and squiggles, and polka dots up the handle, the pot looked like a Gypsy celebration for a prince. Not too much, she hoped, like something the prince's Fool might own.

Geneviève clapped her hands together at the sight of it. "Look!" she said gleefully to Aja. "We come bearing gifts."

"I'm going to give him some tea," Aja said firmly. She declined to say what was in it.

They were disappointed when Magalie just watched them get ready to leave. "You're not going to come?"

She shook her head. She didn't know why Geneviève and Aja could show up at Philippe Lyonnais's triumph like bad fairies swooping in to spoil the christening, while she was afraid she would be mistaken for a tribute-bearer to his court. But there it was.

She watched them head off, neither one wearing anything more against the cold than Geneviève's thin cotton caftan and Aja's cotton *kameez* and *salwar* pants, the gaily painted chocolate pot in Geneviève's hands, a cast-iron teapot in Aja's, making them vaguely suggestive of Three Queens of the Orient. With one Queen left behind sulking.

Oh, *bon sang*. It might be the season for the Magi, but he was *not* the Prince of the World. No matter what he thought himself.

The two aunts were talking as they got farther away, Geneviève in the low voice she mistakenly used whenever she didn't want to be overheard. When she lowered her voice for secrets, it went bass, acquiring a carrying power that Magalie's mother claimed had gotten her banned at a very early age from any discussions of Christmas presents. ". . . self-confidence," Genevieve said in that stage whisper. "Do you think she's ever going to learn some?"

Magalie's eyebrows flicked up, and she wondered who they were talking about. It couldn't possibly be her.

She pricked up her ears, but now Aja was answering, and Aja never said anything you didn't have to be close to her to hear.

Abruptly Magalie felt abandoned, alone with the scent of her chocolate. As if she needed to jump onto a camel and head after them, pursuing some bright star. The emptiness of their shop lodged a hard knot of anguish in her middle, and she couldn't understand how Geneviève and Aja didn't show the strain.

She grabbed Aja's tea, pressed the cup to her cheek, and almost drank it. Instead she set it down again and pulled on her wool coat. No sorties in thin cotton for her. She had no idea how Aja and Geneviève did it.

She turned their sign to LES SORCIÈRES REVIENNENT DANS CINQ MINUTES, picked up the tea again, and walked not toward Philippe Lyonnais's gloating success but toward the opposite end of the island, crossing the Boulevard Henri IV, named after the same green king who always saluted her. She passed through the small park, where two brave souls sat on the benches despite the cold, and descended the stairs to the quay and the tip of the island.

Their local *clochard*'s German shepherd wandered up, sniffing for food, and Magalie gave it a guilty look as she handed an old, battered pot full of chocolate to the dog's homeless owner. She always forgot to keep things on hand for non-chocolate-eating creatures. The street-dwelling *clochard*—who sometimes let Magalie call him Gérard and other times insisted he was one of the Notre-Dame gargoyles in disguise, but who always insisted that he was *not* homeless, he simply preferred to live life out in the open—took the pot with a noise of appreciation. Magalie wondered what the wish for happiness she'd stirred into it could possibly do to help someone in his situation, but then again, it surely couldn't hurt.

No one else was there, which used to make her uneasy, when Gérard, alias Gargoyle, had started hanging out there, but they had gotten used to each other over the years. Gérard frustrated Geneviève no end, however; she couldn't get his life straight no matter how hard she went after him, and, generally speaking, Geneviève was to other people's lives what a heavy, old-fashioned iron was to clothes.

The water flowed winter-brown and high from recent rains, splitting around the point of the island. Bare trees stretched away along the banks, offering little of the soft shelter from the city that they suggested in the summer. The bridges that braceleted the Seine thinned out a little past this point, and the arches of the Pont d'Austerlitz were small in the distance. She could see, farther on, the shining and impractical book-towers of the Bibliothèque Nationale.

Naked.

The word flashed back through her like a stab in the back. It had a lion's arrogant grin on it, and she pictured him surging up in his own nakedness, shoulders broad and powerful, and beyond that . . .

Beyond that, what? His jaw was lean. Oh, what a lean, powerful jaw that was. But the coats and chef jackets she had always seen him in left a lot to the imagination.

So why did her imagination provide a lean waist and a flex of abs and, above all, him glorying in it?

Well, of course, he would glory in his nakedness. That man gloried in everything about himself, didn't he?

Footsteps sounded on the quay, and Magalie braced instinctively, because even here, on her island, riffraff could occasionally wander in from the rest of Paris to annoy women standing alone. Then Gérard would urinate in very close proximity to the riffraff's feet, which was amazingly effective at driving them off, but awkward all around.

But her first glance spotted functional tennis shoes and a bulky jacket, and she relaxed. A tourist. She loved tourists. They usually meant no one any harm and were wrapped up in wonder. What was not to love?

Except . . . this one was carrying a box very clearly stamped *Lyonnais.* And more specifically, one also marked at each corner with the *PL* Philippe Lyonnais had added to the logo of *his* Lyonnais shop.

Magalie contemplated one trailing lace of those tennis shoes. One sudden fall, and those *macarons* would be crushed. And the German shepherd would be happy. She sighed and bent her head, slipping her gloved hand under her scarf to rub the back of her neck. She probably really did need to drink Aja's tea. It would be nice to stay the kind of person she could like. Wanting to trip a tourist, for God's sake.

The river curved two great, protecting arms around the island, shielding it from the hustle of the rest of the city. Holding her untouched tea in one hand, Magalie contemplated the banks across the water. From here, the critical, brisk, sharp-dressed people moving along them were just part of the view. The tourist set his box down on a bench and took some pictures.

Her feet aching in her boots, Magalie eyed again the white pillows that passed for shoes on the tourist's feet and, just for an errant second, imagined wearing them.

She caught the image back. She wasn't in Ithaca. People who belonged to this island in the heart of *this* city never wore running shoes.

But her gaze flicked up to the comfort of the tourist's outfit, not too unlike the comfort of the clothes she used to steal from her boyfriend back in high school, because she liked to bury herself in them and pretend she could never be dragged out. What would it feel like to put on those baggy sweatpants and the giant sweatshirt?

She gave herself a shake, like a dog flicking off water. No sense going that far.

But the idea teased at her. Tennis shoes. Running shoes. What would it feel like to go running through the city? She had gotten interested in track when she was fourteen. She'd done well that first year at her American high school but then missed all the spring meets when her mother just couldn't resist another spring in Provence, and the coach hadn't let her back on the team. She was too small, anyway, to have ever been a star athlete. But she had liked it, there for a while.

Occasionally she saw women running in Paris. Mostly

very slowly, very fashionably, chatting with a competitively fashionable friend the whole way. But what would it feel like to really run?

Floating through the city like some seagull, detached from it yet part of it. With no armor, no clicking of boots, no competition. Not giving a damn what others saw when they looked at her.

It was a very odd idea, and maybe it was because of that oddness that it kept hold of her as she headed back to the shop. It curled around the nape of her neck, as if with just a nod of permission it would massage all the tension away.

When she got back to the shop, a couple was standing in front of the display window, the man tall and lean, with over-long black hair and an intense, sensual, poetic face; the vaguely familiar-looking woman slim and considerably shorter, with light brown hair just past her shoulders, in that absolutely straight, silky look that was still fashionable. She was dressed in a way that proved sometimes money was just wasted on people. The woman's clothes spoke of the highest-end stores on Faubourg Saint-Honoré, but she wore them with a streamlined elegance that just barely escaped being *bon chic bon genre*. Magalie, with the same money, would have come out of those Faubourg Saint-Honoré shops with *flair*.

"You're right," the man was saying. "This is fantastic."

Magalie smiled.

"*Tu vois.*" The woman nudged her elbow gently into his side. "I told you you had to see this." Her accent was clearly American, but her French was accurate.

A quirk of a sensual mouth as the man glanced down at her, but all he said was, "I don't see why you made me go to Philippe's opening on the way. As if he wasn't full enough of himself without me stopping by."

"And here I thought it was *my* presence that would flatter him," the woman said dryly.

Magalie could see the man's eyebrows flick up incredulously at this idea—maybe that the woman's presence could
be flattering at all to Philippe, or maybe that anyone's presence could be more flattering than his own—but he politely
smoothed the expression away before the woman glanced up
at him. She gave him an ironic look, nevertheless. He smiled
at her. She immediately melted, smiling back.

Handsome, arrogant men who manipulated women with
a sexy smile were so . . . annoying. Right. That was the word
Magalie was looking for. Annoying. Nobody ever managed
to do that to her. And there was no reason at all that that
thought should make her *regretful*.

"Besides, he agreed to do our wedding. You know *you*
can't do it. The least we could do was come to his opening,
Sylvain."

"I might make one little thing for our wedding," Sylvain
said discreetly.

The woman narrowed her eyes. "Sylvain, if you spend the
forty-eight hours before our wedding trying to make sure
your 'one little thing' outshines whatever Philippe brings—"

Magalie drew in a startled breath, her heart speeding up
like that of a sixteen-year-old about to throw her panties to
a rock star onstage. This was—could this be *Sylvain Marquis*?
The best chocolatier in the world? Oh, God, and he was
standing there looking at their display.

Three dangerous-looking witches flew over a forest, on a
long journey, each with a gift behind her on her broomstick.
The small chocolate chests were slightly open, revealing
frankincense of gold-colored candied lemon peel in one,
myrrh made from bits of golden and brown raisins chopped
fine in another, and real gold leaf in the last. High up was a
great chocolate star with eight points, flecked with gold leaf.

They would have to take it down soon. The Fête des Rois
had been last week. But the season stretched through January. Magalie and her aunts, for example, were going to an-

other Feast of Kings that weekend, hosted by the friend who had gotten the *fève* in the *galette des rois,* or King Cake, at La Maison des Sorcières's Feast of Kings the week before. Some of the people in the line before Lyonnais were probably buying his *galettes,* paying a fortune to have a little bite of fame at their own Fête des Rois.

Magalie took a couple of careful breaths and tried to make herself sound adult and confident and not in the least starstruck. *"Pardon."* She nodded to Sylvain Marquis and his companion in a friendly, firm fashion as she moved past them to unlock the door.

"Bonjour," the woman said with a bright smile, and she held out her hand. Confused, Magalie put hers into it and found it shaken confidently. Not just another American, but an American businesswoman, Magalie decided instantly. "I don't know if you remember me, but I was in here once before, when I was in Paris for some business meetings a few months ago. I'm Cade Corey."

Magalie searched her face. They had quite a few princesses come by, and she clearly was one, but now that Magalie thought about it . . . way back in the fall . . . a wish for someone to understand her own freedom . . . "Ah!" She smiled. "Did it work?"

Cade Corey tilted her head inquiringly. "Did what work?"

"Ah . . . nothing. Were you wanting some—some chocolate?" She was offering chocolate to *Sylvain Marquis*? "Or tea, perhaps?" Her tea was a lot safer to drink than Aja's. Happy people generally did prefer to limit their risks of being shaken up. "Please come in."

Cade Corey's gaze flicked around the shop as she preceded Magalie inside, her face lighting with pleasure. Sylvain insisted on holding the door for both of them. Magalie turned at once to see his face as he came in after her, and she blushed a little when she saw his slow smile of enchantment. "This is wonderful."

She could feel herself turning bright red. *Sylvain Marquis.* "I'll just—please sit where you like. I'll just get out of my coat. May I take yours?"

When she came back from layering the coats on the hook on the courtyard door, Cade was examining the child's drawings on her menu with great delight, and Sylvain Marquis was standing as close to the display case as he could without pressing into it, studying the shelves full of antique silver molds climbing the wall behind it. He had an avaricious gleam in his eyes.

Cade Corey looked up from her menu. "I don't remember it being this quiet," she said frankly. "Is it the Lyonnais opening?" she asked, just as intrusively as if they were good friends and she had the right to know.

Magalie knit her brow, not quite sure what to do with the other woman. Overall, she liked her; she liked that clear, open confidence she gave off. But how were these things Cade Corey's business?

That Corey name was vaguely familiar, calling to mind awful chocolate bars to which she had occasionally been exposed during the parts of her childhood that were spent in America. What an ironic coincidence that someone with that name should apparently be engaged to marry Sylvain Marquis.

Cade frowned. "I like Philippe, but if he puts this place out of business, I will kill him."

Magalie clenched her stomach muscles, a second too late to protect herself from the blow. That was bluntness with a vengeance.

Sylvain turned his head from the chocolate molds, his eyebrows going ever so subtly up. "You like Philippe?"

Cade grinned. "Not as much as I like Dominique Richard," she told him.

Dominique Richard was the name of another top chocolatier in Paris. Sylvain Marquis turned completely away from the molds and narrowed his eyes at his fiancée. She looked rather smug about how annoying she was being.

Before she could tease Sylvain more or, worse, twist more knives in La Maison des Sorcières' wounds, the door opened and Geneviève blazed in, followed by a very quiet Aja. The cold air swirled around them and disappeared, eaten in one bite by the warmth in the shop.

"*Bonjour,*" Geneviève told their two clients with warm approval, while Aja smiled at them. "I'm so glad to see someone with taste."

"It went that well, did it?" Magalie said dryly, rather relieved. If Geneviève and Aja had ended up on best-buddy terms with Philippe Lyonnais, it would have been desperately annoying.

"First of all, we had to force our way in." Geneviève looked about as dangerous as a woman who was six feet tall and wielding chocolate could. "There were lines, and he seemed to think we should wait in them."

Sylvain Marquis grinned. "How impolitic of him."

Geneviève waved a dramatic hand. "I don't say it was him personally, but it's certainly his responsibility to better educate his lackeys."

Aja smoothed her tunic back into clean lines as if it had gotten ruffled. "Everyone on the island was there."

Magalie's stomach tightened. "Even Claire-Lucy? Thierry?" Who had saluted her with a rose bouquet when she went off to battle? All those people who had sat at their tables for months, swearing their support?

Aja inclined her head without saying anything.

"However, we did make our way back into his kitchens," Geneviève continued grandly, "without—need I clarify?— waiting in lines. There, I must say, he seemed rather intrigued to see us. However . . ." She fell silent. Her mouth got as tight as a mountainside just before lava blew its face off.

"He declined our gifts," Aja said, as evenly as if this was entirely his right and choice and no matter to her. She ran one finger over the length of her black braid, smoothing everything within reach.

Magalie's right fist clenched. "Your tea?" she forced herself to ask first, courteously, as if that was the most important thing to her.

"He set it aside on the back of the counter, thanked us kindly for thinking of him, and promised to bring the pot back another day." Aja made a little gesture of her hands: *On his head be it*. She fixed Magalie with steady black eyes. "If you're offered a gift, and you refuse it, then you've made your choice."

Magalie tried to look bright-eyed, as if she had drunk her own cup of Aja's tea instead of throwing it into the Seine. With her luck, the tea had been meant to make her dreamy.

"And my chocolate?" she got out. That she had made with her own hands and all her heart, pouring out her desire to see him begging on his knees.

"Refused outright," Geneviève said crisply. She held up the carnival pot. "He asked us to take it back to you."

Magalie gasped as if the chocolate pot contained icy water that Geneviève had just dashed into her face. Such an open rejection. And in front of Sylvain Marquis, too.

"It smells delicious," the most famous chocolatier in Paris said instantly, although the aroma leaking from the pot was now thin and cold, a ghost of its former self. "I would love to try some."

Magalie was going to wish every wonderful thing in the world for him and his fiancée, she decided firmly. What a beautiful man. "Not that one," she said hurriedly, grasping the cold pot from Aunt Geneviève. The idea of Sylvain Marquis begging on his knees in front of her was just . . . wrong. Not at all what she wanted. "I'll make some fresh. Aunt Geneviève, Aunt Aja, this is Sylvain Marquis." She tried to sneak the subtlest emphasis in there, because Aunt Geneviève would fail to respect the President. Which was one thing, but failing to respect *Sylvain Marquis* . . . well, there were limits. "And Cade Corey," she added, trying her best not to make that name sound like an afterthought.

Cade looked wryly amused.

"I remember you," Aunt Aja told her. "It seems to have worked."

Cade squinted just a little. "What worked?" she asked again, a shade more warily.

"Sylvain Marquis," Magalie heard Geneviève say musingly as she went back into the kitchen to empty the carnival pot of chocolate and start a fresh batch. "I think I've seen you on TV. You're quite handy with chocolate, aren't you? Did you come to ask for my secrets?"

Pouring milk and a little cream into a pot, Magalie groaned silently and raised her eyes to heaven.

"As a matter of fact . . ." Sylvain said, and Magalie dropped her spoon. Chairs scraped. "I want to talk to you about your window displays."

By the time Magalie finished the chocolate and came back out, Sylvain and Geneviève were at a small table together, deep into negotiations for Geneviève to help him design a particularly magical window theme, and Cade Corey was looking like someone swelling with smug satisfaction and trying hard not to let it show through her professional demeanor. Completely unoffended by Geneviève's attitude that he was a young *arriviste,* Sylvain was wheedling the older woman respectfully, acting for all the world as if she would be doing him an enormous favor.

Cade Corey watched him do this, the love and affection in her face so discreet yet intense that Magalie stood there with the tray of chocolate in her hand, its warmth and wishes for their wonderful life twining all around her, and felt desperately lonely.

The door opened with a forlorn little chime, and she looked up, smiling with delight to see one of their old faithful returning. Madame Fernand came in with a sigh. "Magalie, *ma petite chérie,* I don't suppose you would mind keeping track of Sissi long enough for me to try one little bite at that Philippe's? They won't let me in with a dog."

Chapter 9

Opening day was over. Philippe's family and employees had all finished toasting him and one another with Champagne. The place was clean and polished, and, as was fitting, he was the very last one there, to linger over the day and contemplate its success.

To linger over the smooth, cool marble and the gleaming glass display cases, the molding and the embossed walls, the palace of *pâtisseries*. The lines had stretched almost to the tip of the island. He had gone out himself many times to pass out little tidbits of this and that and greet people as they waited, and they had loved it, every second.

But his shoulders prickled with dissatisfaction, a tension right between the blades.

She hadn't come. She hadn't come to see the success, to see how many people would wait an hour in the cold just to taste the *macarons* she had refused. She hadn't come to see his triumph, to see the worth of what she had rejected.

He had had a plan, to escort her in—no lines for her—to bring her into the inner circle of family and employees in the kitchens, to treat her with every courtesy. To shame her with the very degree of his courtesy in the face of her rudeness, to make her change her mind about him.

But she hadn't come.

Her aunts had come. Alarmingly.

But other than a minor tussle as they broke in line and waltzed in, they hadn't done anything to spoil the day. At least, he hadn't accepted anything from them that would spoil the day.

He didn't drink tea, and he wasn't going to start with a beverage brought to him by someone who considered herself a *sorcière*.

And as for Magalie's chocolate . . . the scent had twined through all the smells with which his *laboratoire* was filled, taunting him. His chefs had raised their heads from their work and looked around, hungrily.

He had had to get the stuff out of there, because—because he would be damned if he would pay her the honor of drinking her *chocolat* when she was treating his own highest refinement of the art of *pâtisserie* as if it were worthless. Plus, he was pretty convinced she was trying to turn him into a toad.

What could he turn her into?

Pure desire?

He took one of the *Désir* macarons from the walk-in refrigerator and bit into it uneasily, as he had more times than he could count since that day she had rejected it.

No, still, it was perfection. The little grains of pistachio on his tongue, the delicate crunch of the outside shell, yielding instantly to the melting heaven of the inside of the *macaron,* and then the thicker, richer apricot ganache, and, last, as you came to the heart of it, that tiny crackling surprise of the hidden salted caramel heart.

Any change would make it less good. He couldn't let that doubt she had sown in him make him ruin one of his most popular works.

Maybe she needed something different.

He rested his hand on a marble counter in his *laboratoire,* letting the chill of it focus his mind.

Something even more special. Something that would make

those brown eyes stop snapping with anger and widen with stunned desire. Something that would make her mouth soften, helpless around it, unable to compress in disdain.

Something so special that only he, in all the world, was capable of creating it.

She had called him "Your Highness", in pure contempt.

He smiled suddenly, his hand closing tight and tense, so that his knuckles rubbed against the marble. Maybe he should offer her a crown.

Chapter 10

One single customer, and she was a woebegone blonde with an elegant, feathered cut who sat by herself broodingly at the table under the medieval princess hat and the dusty and rather evil-looking carved owl. And, routinely, she would toss that feathered cut sexily as if, even though the shop was empty of everyone but a woman clearly not impressed by that kind of thing, she had to keep in practice.

"What do you think?" the woman asked Magalie suddenly, still gazing at the menu and its cryptic handwriting as if it was the enigma of life.

Which, given that Aunt Geneviève had written it, it *was*, but still. If she was really smart, she would be looking at the children's drawings on the other side.

The woman feathered her hair again. "If we had a really good time, and, you know, *that* part was fantastic, really, the best I've ever had, and he hasn't called since? It's been a week."

Magalie stalked back into the kitchen before she could start sounding like Aunt Geneviève and glared at the chocolate, thinking, as she stirred it, *Quit selling yourself short, and if you want a damn man so much, at least find the right one for you. Go after the best.*

The woman drank half of it down without any hesitation, which was surprising, considering how thick it was and how thin she was. Anyone would think she would be afraid of chocolate. And then she abruptly dabbed her mouth with the thin tissue so effectively that she looked quite elegant doing it, her lipstick intact and the tissue barely smudged, bought three chocolate witches, and headed off down the street. Magalie went to the door and watched as the blonde turned straight into Philippe's *salon*.

She gasped with outrage. *That's not what I meant by going after the best* at all.

She stomped back into the empty shop, stood there with her fists clenched for a moment, and then finally forced herself to decide that the place could use a really good cleaning.

Magalie was up on tiptoe on the top shelf of a ladder, dusting witches' hats, when the silver bell rang for the third time.

"Une minute!" she called. The top hat in the stack wobbled under her duster, and she stretched higher, the uneven ladder bobbling. Something thumped on a table, and then two hands closed around her butt. The fingers curled around her hips, hard into the hollow of muscle and softness just past her pelvic bone, and the heels of the palms pressed deep into her bottom.

Magalie jerked her dusting arm wildly, the stack of hats went flying, and the hard hands plucked her right off the ladder.

She flew, out of her own control, and her feet hit the floor, making her furious. She did *not* like floundering in midair. Or anywhere.

Hats scattered all around them, one plopping down over her face. She pushed a broad black brim off her forehead and twisted to glare up at Philippe Lyonnais. His palms dragged against her with her movement, sending frissons of desire out from the contact, down toward her hips, up toward her breasts.

He glared right back at her. "Are you insane?" He filled the room again, his shoulders taking over and blocking

everything else from sight. The streamer from the fallen medieval princess hat clung unnoticed to his shoulder. "Can't
you even think to take off your high-heeled boots before
you climb up a ladder like that? And what were you doing
on the top rung? There is no way those shelves up there
would hold you if you had to grab them for balance."

Magalie put her hands on her hips. "If you know how to
dust better than I do, too, then by all means, feel free to show
me your technique." She handed him the duster. "It's such a
privilege to have so much superiority deign to invade my
life."

He gave her a long, cool look, then took the duster,
righted and climbed the ladder, and began dusting the top
shelf. He didn't have to stand on the top rung, and he didn't
have to stretch.

Magalie stood beneath him, her lips parted in disbelief,
staring up. His butt was just a few inches higher than her eye
level, so she could see the taut curve of it under the hem of
his leather coat. He propped one foot a rung higher than the
other on the ladder, pulling the material of his jeans tight
over the defined strength of a very fine set of *fesses* and
thighs.

He was dusting her shelves.

Without comment or question, despite the annoyed com-
pression at the edge of his mouth.

He was dusting. Philippe Lyonnais.

Why would he do that?

Certainly not because she had told him to. To show her
how much better at it he was than she was? No man's superiority complex went that far.

"Did you send that woman after me?" he asked abruptly.
She had the sudden impression of a man simmering over
more burners than one.

"What woman?" She scowled.

"The blonde who plastered herself all over me on my way

out of the kitchens! She was carrying one of your bags. What did you do to her?"

Magalie's teeth ground, until she thought she might go find that blonde and beat her over the head with a chocolate pot. Or, preferably, one of Aunt Aja's cast-iron teapots. No wonder Mademoiselle Featherbrain's life was so screwed up if she kept misinterpreting clear messages. "No. I barely knew her. I don't see why I would punish her that way."

He shot her the kind of glance that should have accompanied a stabbing dagger and finished the shelf, like a man who had speed-cleaned quite a lot in his life—which was probably true, given that he had grown up in professional kitchens. He extended an imperious hand.

She looked at it blankly. Did he expect her to put her hand in it? Her own hand flooded suddenly with warmth at the idea, tingling with a memory of those calluses. It was January. How could her hand feel so warm?

Did he have vertigo? Did he need a steadying hand down from the ladder? It was the lamest excuse she could possibly come up with to thrust her hungry hand into his, but she had actually started to when he gave his crisp command:

"Give me the hats, Magalie."

She gaped at him. Had he just given her an order? In her own territory? And used *tu*? She was *not* his intimate, nor anyone with whom he had the right to be on even remotely familiar terms.

"I beg your pardon," she said icily.

His left hand clenched around the edge of the shelf, and he turned his head and gave her a look as if he was about to leap right off the ladder on top of her.

On the other hand, maybe even she shouldn't push a man who had just wielded a feather duster at her snippiest suggestion. She handed him the hats. Brooding over the fact that she was cooperating with him. Was that showing weakness?

He restored them to their positions on the shelves: almost *exactly* to their former positions on the shelves, as if he knew to the centimeter what those were, except here and there he would change the angle very slightly, the drape of the princess streamer a little, so that when he was done, the shelf looked even better. More fanciful and dangerous and mysterious and romantic. He did it in two seconds, automatically, without even realizing he was doing it. Probably the same way he did the finishing touches on all those beautiful concoctions in his shop.

Magalie studied his work, then sent a sidelong look up at him as he dropped from the ladder to stand beside her. He was disturbingly amazing. Why couldn't she have been a princess?

Oh, no, how nauseating. She hadn't just thought that, had she? As if she wished she could be *good enough* for him? Princesses were so . . . so *helpless.* They always needed their lives straightened out by Geneviève's witches, or Magalie's chocolate, or Aja's tea.

And Magalie was better than enough. For anyone or anything.

"Don't climb up that ladder in those shoes again," he ordered her, aggressively. "Or in any of your other ten-centimeter heels. Do you *own* anything sensible?"

No. In her apartment upstairs, all by herself, she went around barefoot, or at this time of year in fuzzy socks, her toes curling happily. "Oh!" she said excitedly. "You're an expert on how I should dress, *too*! How lucky for me!"

Philippe looked just briefly as if he would like to beat his head against the wall.

Good. She gave him a sweet, mean smile.

Immediately his focus changed, the desire to inflict pain turning outward. Carnivorous. As if, instead of hurting himself, he wanted to eat her up.

She leaned toward him, her ten-centimeter heels pressed firmly into the floor. Her heart was beating so hard. "Did you *need help* in some way?"

His head went up. Blue eyes flicked to the topmost, beautifully dusted shelf. "You're welcome," he said deliberately.

She took an outraged breath. "I did not need your help."

She had no idea what went through his mind at that, but his gaze suddenly ran the whole length of her body, down and up, and then he shut his eyes hard. A burning shiver ran through her.

He turned his head away, his eyes still closed. She could see the taut line of his jaw. "I brought back the teapot."

She followed the angle of his jaw to the heavy iron pot that must have been what had thumped on the table just before he caught her. Deep in her tummy, a whisper stirred: *You know he thought you were going to fall. You know he thought he saved you.*

I don't care. She stamped on that whisper ruthlessly. *He thinks one of his pastries is worth my life.*

"Did you drink it?" she asked despite herself, the hostility in her tone giving way to real curiosity. Almost sympathy. He and she had one thing in common; they had both recently faced the dangerous challenge of Aja's tea.

He finally opened his eyes, the blue very dark as he looked at her again. Why did vulnerability pervade her whole body just at one dark look from him, as if she would beg him to do anything he wanted to her? "It was a thoughtful gift," he said noncommittally. "Please tell your aunt it was very much appreciated."

He couldn't have drunk it. Right? She searched his face. He couldn't have shown more courage or courtesy than she had. Right?

"I brought a small token in thanks," he added, and she saw near the pot on the table a frost-blue box with *Lyonnais* stamped across it.

She swallowed.

All her attention narrowed to that box. And to the large, elegant hand that moved into her vision and lifted the box up. Holding it toward her. There was a small fresh burn on one of his fingers, and something purple-red staining two of his cuticles.

She wet her lips.

She could feel his gaze beating down on her. He had certainly seen that flick of her tongue.

"It's just something I've been playing with," he said.

She cursed herself for the fact that she had to clear her throat. "I'll give it to her." *Just don't open the box.*

The large, sure hand moved and pulled back the lid.

Oh.

Inside, an exquisite *pâtisserie* the size of her palm was covered with the green dust of pistachios as if it had been dipped entirely in them. Strawberry halves formed a crown on top of it, upright back to back in the center, so that they looked not only like the jewels of a crown but like . . . bare, naked hearts. Tucked into the tip of the strawberry crown, a golden flower trailed long tendril-petals over the red, revealed hearts.

Her body prickled all over. She wanted to reach into that box, pick up the pastry, and bring it to her mouth. Feel the crumbs of the pistachio against her lips. The smoothness of the strawberries, their tartness. And under it—what did the coating of pistachios hide? Cream or cake, flaky or smooth, or layer upon layer of surprises?

She found herself reaching out for support against the temptation. Her hand closed around leather and taut arm muscle. She jerked it away.

And looked up.

Philippe had somehow managed to grow even closer, more dominant. His blue eyes blazed with hungry triumph. His will seemed to wrap around her and *force* her toward the pastry.

She took a harsh breath, fighting for oxygen. For reason. "If you . . . come bearing gifts . . . *for Aunt Aja,* the least I can do is . . . offer you some hot chocolate." There. That hadn't come out with too many ragged pauses, had it?

She held his eyes.

His lips compressed with frustration. "Perhaps—some other time." The rejected crown of a dessert stayed held up toward her. "I've had too much sugar already today. Professional hazard."

In other words, her chocolate wasn't good enough to take priority over his own desserts, but he thought *she* should fall all over herself to eat his. "Well." It took everything she had in her to shrug and turn away. "I'm sure Aunt Aja will appreciate it."

His arms tensed, and for a second she thought she was going to find the crown force-fed to her, but the door blew open, revealing Aja and Geneviève. Cold air swirled with chocolate-scented air, like a carousel spiral, teasing the nose with the alternation of crisp and melting.

Geneviève gave Philippe one look like Boadicea to the Romans, Aja gave him a cool Kali regard, and they both blew Magalie away from him and into the kitchen by pure force of personality.

"What is he doing in our place?" Geneviève asked in that low voice of hers that went so bass in its outrage, it probably carried through all the walls on the island and rubbed gently and finally into the uncomprehending ears of tourists on the tip of it. "The man who didn't notice us? Who dismissed us? Is he here to beg forgiveness?"

Magalie picked up her spoon and tamped it down hard into the bottom of the current pot of chocolate. Even through the chocolate, its wood rang against the steel and copper. A drop spattered onto her knuckle, burning. "Not noticeably."

"What are you stirring into it? Something that will *make* him beg forgiveness?" Geneviève suggested vengefully.

"Never use chocolate for vengeance, Gen," Aja said serenely, although she didn't look any more merciful for all that."You know what we've talked about."

"Knowing when to ask for forgiveness is a very important lesson," Geneviève said righteously, still in that voice that could be heard through seven walls. "In fact, it could save him no end of trouble. Or you could wish humility on him like you tried before. He might need several doses before it takes, though."

The kitchen suddenly grew stuffed beyond overflowing; there was not enough air. Magalie looked up at Philippe looming in the doorway. His gaze ran over her face, her shoulder, down the length of her arm, to her hand on the spoon and the pot of chocolate. His eyes were wary, hostile, enraptured all at once. *"Humility?"*

Magalie lifted her hand and gently sucked the hot drop of chocolate off her knuckle.

He took a breath and turned on his heel. She stared after him, outraged. But he didn't turn around and come back. The silver bell chimed.

He had *left*? He had dug his hands into her butt and looked at her chocolate and walked out? *Again?*

"He just waltzes in and out however he pleases, doesn't he?" Geneviève said. Magalie gave her a betrayed look. Was that just a thread of respect twining through her offended tone?

They all filed out of the kitchen and looked at the crown of a dessert left sitting in its open box on the table under the witches' hats.

"It's for you, Aunt Aja," Magalie said very quietly, after a moment. "He wanted to thank you for the tea."

"I doubt it," Aja said. "You only open a present for the person it's for."

Chapter 11

The entire tenor of the street had changed. It was simple. Philippe had brought a team of twenty chefs and assistants into this contained place, and they were all of them fit, most of them young, many of them single, and nearly all of them male. When they came in, extremely early in the morning, or emerged at their odd hours for lunch and breaks, or got off in the afternoon, they walked down the street with controlled, long, graceful strides, those detail-hungry eyes of theirs eating everything up, as first they hunted for food, learning the best places to calm those greedy metabolisms, and then they started hunting for everything else the street had to offer.

Some of them were very cute, too, and all of them made a woman wonder exactly how carefully they might explore new tastes and textures.

Magalie was pretty sure Claire-Lucy could have caught one of them just by standing on her doorstep in a noticeable way, but she grew shy and retreated into her toy store. Where she created a display of retro toy cars, the extra-special ones that a little boy some twenty years ago might have craved and maybe never gotten.

Aimée, the gallery owner across the way, took up her own painting again and started doing it in the predawn hours in front of the Lyonnais shop—"for the light on the pastries," she told all the passing chefs who asked. Philippe and another of his chefs stopped beside her, then Philippe laughed, and the next thing Magalie knew, Aimée was strolling into the shop with them, before it even opened.

Magalie didn't even want to talk about why she was up at that hour of the morning, looking from her window down the street.

Geneviève, Aja, and Magalie had lined either side of their window with giant chocolate thorns. They circled the entire display, from the bottom to the ceiling, making a menacing frame to the three-dimensional tableau of a witch and a princess in a tower that paired subtly with the one they were working on with Sylvain at his place.

Magalie stepped back to the other side of the street when it was done and frowned in sudden doubt. It just seemed as if a certain kind of man might see thorns and immediately draw a sword.

She frowned harder and went inside, antsy and irritable, and accidentally wished so much gumption onto the diamond-waving woman at a table worrying about a cheating spouse that the woman walked straight down to Philippe's and right in the door.

I meant your own gumption! Magalie shouted in her head. *Not his!* And she dumped the whole batch down the sink in pure rage.

Late that evening, Magalie wiggled her hand through layers of coats to the doorknob, opened the door a sliver, and slipped from the kitchen into another world.

The courtyard door was so small that only she, Aja, and children could go through it easily. Geneviève had to bend. Philippe Lyonnais would have to. Maybe that was one consequence of Magalie's diminutive height: she had never had to learn how to lower her head.

Freezing air hit her as she stepped into the small cobblestoned courtyard. An old fountain against the opposite wall stood unused, the small basin under the lion's mouth full of herbs. She had wanted to clean it out and set it in motion again. Geneviève had resisted. Aunt Aja had said she wasn't sure it could be done without spending a fortune on plumbing. Now Magalie's gaze snagged on the lion, its stylized head so similar to the one in the corners of the Lyonnais ceilings. As if it had been crouched in her courtyard all this time, waiting for her to wake it so it could pounce.

She kept her distance from it as she crossed the courtyard to a white door that led to a winding stair. Narrow and steep, it climbed and climbed, past the second floor that the aunts occasionally talked about remodeling but instead filled with flea-market finds, past the aunts' flat on the third floor, past the fourth, fifth, and sixth ones, which they rented out to the wealthy and sporadic, like the fourth floor's famous American actor who only appeared on random weekends between film shoots. It climbed to the seventh and top floor, Magalie's little apartment, a small but airy studio with windows from knee-height to the ceiling, a tiny kitchen area, and room for a bed, a reading corner with a comfortable chair, and a little space to move around between the two without bumping into things, which was more than could be said for a lot of Paris apartments. The building had been a gift to Geneviève when she was Magalie's age from a lover, the wife of a powerful politician. The very act had infused Geneviève's youth with romance and power. Magalie couldn't in a million years imagine someone giving away ownership of a part of the heart of Paris.

Magalie's free lodging in it was one of her greatest perks, for her salary from La Maison des Sorcères was certainly not enough to cover rent on such a place otherwise. She accented the apartment's airiness with white sheets and white translucent drapes that floated away from the blue shutters, so that she ascended every day from her dark, warm cave to an ivory tower.

In her closet, she kept a lavender sachet, made by her mother from her family's own fields. She had a local artist's rendering of lavender fields on her wall, spiky semi-Impressionist blurs of purple. But her photos she kept mostly in a large album on a shelf near her bed. Partly she did so because the small size of the apartment required utter simplicity to avoid clutter, partly because so many photos were of her amid groups of friends to whom she no longer belonged that she liked to keep them contained between the album's covers, where they couldn't accidentally make her sad.

The first thing she did was kick off her boots, slide them neatly away out of sight, and pull on fuzzy socks in pink stripes with a silly kitten on them. Her feet flexed in delicious relief. It was one of her favorite moments, the first step in those silly, fuzzy socks.

She pulled off all her careful clothes, swapped them for fleece pants in a subtle pink plaid and a loosely clingy cream-colored knit top, over which she layered a huge, thick terry bathrobe. She pulled the clasp out of her hair, and it fell around her shoulders, the roots sighing at the release.

She took a clementine from the bowl of them sitting on her tiny counter and began to eat it, the oil from the peel scenting the whole room, the flavor tart and clear after an afternoon spent with chocolate.

And then she stood there wondering if she should have made herself go out, should have called her Paris university friends or gone to the theater, should have done *something* with her evening other than wallow in solitary comfort.

She was an early riser, particularly in winter, but that might have been a consequence rather than a cause of her tendency to sink into her bed so early and pull her covers up all around her. She loved sinking into her bed on evenings like this, but apparently she shouldn't, because it worried her aunts, who thought she ought to be out dancing. It worried her a little bit, too, because what if they were right, and because sometimes a great loneliness welled up in her and threatened all the dams she built to hold it back.

You couldn't cure loneliness by wallowing in it, up above the world, on an island removed from everything. She knew that. But she had such a hard time with all the cures. They seemed rough and brusque and brutal, as if they abused her skin with a pot scrubber, things like trying to go out with men she barely knew, or dancing in Paris nightclubs, or hanging out with friends in bars over in that world past the banks of the river.

She had been something of a party creature in her high schools, still was one to dance all night at New Year's celebrations or weddings when she went back to Provence, but there was something harsher about dancing here, forcing herself into a mass of people, a stranger among strangers. Occasionally, one of her friends from the university, the longest continuous friendship she had ever had, could talk her into it. But it was much more tempting to curl up with a book under her thick white comforter.

Still, sometimes after she curled up, she regretted her lack of courage and felt bleakly lonely.

It was important to have a *really good* book.

Tonight she stood looking out the window, eating her clementine and then some yogurt for supper, and fought a flashing vision of a cozy, warm restaurant, someone smiling at her from across the table, pouring her wine, talking over all the choices on the menu.

The man she saw in the vision shattered under closer attention. You didn't go out to dinner with someone who considered you to be the main course.

She huddled her bathrobe more closely around her, trying to stand near the radiator under the window and keep a little back from the chilled glass at the same time. It was such a cold, clear night, she could see three stars, rare in Paris.

Magalie braced herself for one last second, then shed her heavy terry robe and slipped under the covers. The shock of their cold hit her, and she curled into herself, tugging them tightly around her to warm them fast with her body, shivering.

The loneliness that had snagged her while watching Cade Corey and Sylvain Marquis jumped out of nowhere and grabbed hold of her again. She wanted a warm body to share this bed with, to press against as they fought the first chilly touch of the soft sheets. A hot, muscled strength that grinned a lion's grin at her and pulled her in tightly, letting her soak up his heat.

She pulled the comforter over her head, trying to block out that vision of honey-colored hair and muscled shoulders.

But it kept sneaking back, in bits and pieces, even after she'd read all the way through her book and curled up to go to sleep. She would roll over and dream an arm curving over her side, a hand resting against her tummy. She would rub her head hard into her pillow to clear it and imagine warm breath against her hair and neck. She would dream a laugh, a sureness in his strength that wasn't afraid of her.

Maybe she needed to date more. The tea shop didn't seem to attract her type, though. At least, it did attract humble people, but so far she and they just hadn't clicked.

For no reason, a vision flashed through her mind of Philippe Lyonnais rending some poor humble man limb from limb and dropping the body parts off the river wall, grinning bloodily as they floated past the island. His territory defended.

The vision made her hot all over.

With anger. Hot with anger. She was not his territory.

Maybe she should try fantasizing about Sylvain Marquis. He was pretty sexy. Almost married to a princess, true, but then, men like him always married princesses. That didn't mean she couldn't fantasize a little in privacy, did it?

Every time she tried to get a good black-haired fantasy going, though, she found herself running her fingers over tawny hair on a forearm, or golden-brown hair curling over a muscled chest, or through a thick mane that . . .

Maybe she needed to count sheep.

A lot of them.

And no lion had better laugh and eat one while she was doing it.

Half a kilometer away, Philippe pressed his bare forearm against the window in his Marais apartment. He let the cold shock him, then seep into him. After a long moment of gazing toward the Île Saint-Louis, as if he could see through buildings, he lowered his head to rest it against his arm.

He needed to go to bed. He got up at four-thirty in the morning. And he had had an emotionally trying afternoon, what with yet another beautiful rich woman showing up in his shop with a sack from La Maison des Sorcières in one hand and throwing herself at him. He didn't know why Magalie was wishing these women on him—whether as a red herring to protect herself, or in the hope of ruining his life by making him fall for the wrong woman. Neither plan was going to work for her, but the fact that she was willing to try it made his head explode.

How could she even stand the thought? It drove him *wild*. He sure as hell wouldn't send any men *her* way.

He was going to get her for that. He was going to make her eat her heart out over every single woman she had thrown at him.

And he was going entirely crazy, of course, to think that Magalie could create love potions any more than she could create potions to turn him into a toad. It was just a damn cup of chocolate, for God's sake, and one that was *completely inferior to his creations*, too.

He needed to just give himself some credit. If a woman filled herself up on witch chocolate and still got lured in by his windows, it was a sign of how great his power was.

Powerful enough to triumph over one stubborn little witch, anyone would think.

Damn it.

Magalie had some trouble when the man at the sporting-goods store directed her away from the classiest pair of running shoes to the third-classiest. She gave him an incredulous look. Sure, the idea was that she didn't give a damn what she looked like, but there was no sense going crazy, either. *"Je vous promets,"* he said, "they're better for the way your foot turns in."

In the clothing section, she chose black knit pants and an elegant running top that clung in just the right places, to make it clear she wasn't running because she *needed* to. She didn't care what people who saw her thought about her, but it was important that it be clear to those people that her indifference was justified, too.

She didn't tell anyone. She slipped out like a secret the next morning, just before dawn, the city all asleep. She didn't want to look too weird. Like she didn't belong here.

The island was silent. The witch-hat of a church steeple cast its dark silhouette against the first hints of light.

She walked quickly to the end of the island, trying not to let herself pause in front of the Lyonnais window. But she couldn't help noticing the treasure chest: a genuine jeweled chest several centuries old. He had probably bribed some collector with one of his pastries to lend him the piece, she thought irritably. The chest was tilted onto its side, and from it spilled his *macarons,* like something a dragon might die for:

blood red filled with dark chocolate ganache, garnet flecked with genuine gold, one that was pure onyx, another a green so rich it could be emerald, another burnished amber.

She walked faster. The websites on running said she was supposed to warm up, and there was no point in anyone on the island seeing her doing something they would think ridiculous. At the peak of the bridge crossing over to Notre Dame, the sky in the east showed pink. No violinist to see her on her way. No one. Paris before dawn was more peaceful than a child, as peaceful as an intense, sophisticated society queen in her rare few moments of repose.

Magalie set out, running surprisingly easily. It felt so light. To be here, not dressed for battle, concentrating only on the dawn-gentled city and herself.

The websites had said to walk and run, walk and run, going five kilometers but not all running. The walking part was the hardest. When she slowed down, she missed the feel of her high heels clicking, felt vulnerable and awkward. She ran more than the plan said she should to start, along the water, through the city, because she preferred the feel of flying.

When she unlocked the door to the shop at two that day (the aunts refused to serve desserts to people who didn't eat a proper lunch first), she was braced for another sparse day of rare visits from old *habitués* that felt nerve-gratingly like pity, or the occasional woman longing for some magic in her life. Instead, she found a vaguely familiar man standing there. Lean, tall, high-energy, an angular, intellectual face. Young, her age at the most. And he smelled . . . he smelled of caramel and bananas. He smelled of Philippe Lyonnais, in fact.

She stared at him, realizing that his vague familiarity was because he was one of the young men who were loosed from the Lyonnais kitchens at odd hours, to hunt the streets. He had something green stuck under a fingernail, and another streak of the green on his cheek. Yes, he was a chef. One of the Lyonnais chefs.

He smiled at her, his eyes brightening flatteringly as he took her in. "Are you open yet? I keep noticing your displays every time I pass, and I can't resist anymore."

In the absence of the prince himself, there was something immensely satisfying about suborning one of his subjects. Magalie smiled and beckoned him in.

Chapter 12

It took Philippe two weeks to realize that one of the reasons Magalie's chocolate seemed to taunt him so pervasively, even in her absence, was that his employees were bringing its scent back into his kitchen on their clothes after every damn break they took. One of his chefs had just strolled back to work with a hot-chocolate mustache that now stained the white sleeve he had scrubbed guiltily across his face at Philippe's fulminating gaze.

And he still had not gotten her to step into his own shop once. It made him want to rend things.

Instead, he escalated. *Putain,* but he would make her regret that.

The magazines and blogs raved about Philippe's display windows: "irresistible," "the epitome of temptation," "an ecstasy of touch, taste, and sight," "heartbreak itself to walk by and not walk in," and "no one can pass untouched."

Except one.

She was driving him mad.

She hadn't tried one confection he had put into his windows. He hadn't even caught her lingering for one mere second to look at them. She hadn't acted tempted in the least.

She sent other women his way, for God's sake. He was pouring everything he had into those window displays. And

she acted as if her whole, entire being didn't bleed with longing. As if she could sleep at night.

He couldn't. He woke up dreaming of *chocolat chaud*.

Thick, luscious, dark chocolate. Stirred in a warm cave of
a kitchen by a slim hand that wore its perfect manicure like
armor, a shell she couldn't go out into the world without.
Rich hot chocolate stirred in a kitchen where the aroma was
a drug that overwhelmed all who entered. What was she stirring into it? What wishes or curses? *I'll drink it, I'll drink it.
Can't you take just one bite of something of mine, so I can taste
yours?* Soon he was going to be begging her on his knees to
deign to taste one of his *pâtisseries*. His. Philippe Lyonnais.

He strode out onto the street for a breath of fresh air and
not to stroll by that witch house yet again. It wasn't his fault
the nearest park was closer to her end of the street. And that
he needed to stretch his legs a lot.

He glanced down the street, despite his best efforts.

A tall, dark-haired man stood looking at the witches' display window and then opened the door with easy familiarity.

Philippe stiffened through every muscle of his body. Sylvain? What the hell was Sylvain Marquis doing down there?

Not that he gave a damn what Sylvain Marquis was doing,
of course. The man made good chocolate—Philippe would
give him that—but that hardly made him a worry to *Philippe
Lyonnais*. But just what did he think he was doing on this
street in the first place? This was Philippe's territory.

And going into . . . A great clawed paw reached inside
him and raked. Was she eating Sylvain's chocolate? Was she
feeding him hers?

He started down the street, a long, angry prowl.

When he stepped into the *salon de thé*, the silver bell rang
a crisp warning note. Magalie, Geneviève, and Sylvain were
all bent intimately over a small table, a stretch of paper before them, Sylvain's poet's-cut hair falling forward to brush

the hair wisping expertly from Magalie's chignon, the black strands of both blurring together.

Philippe drew a choppy breath, rage pounding up inside him like some enormous drum that made it hard to hear anything else.

He knew that Sylvain Marquis was busy naming all his new chocolates after a pretty billionaire who melted every time he smiled; Philippe had just agreed to do the *pièces montées* for their wedding. But how well did he know Sylvain's character, after all? He looked like a damn ladies' man, certainly.

And his hair was touching hers. And Aja was bringing out a tray of tea and chocolate. That *Sylvain* could drink. Nobody was trying to humble *him*. And Magalie's eyes were sparkling with pleasure. The rage pulsed until Philippe's ears buzzed with it, a bass that was too close, too loud.

"Sylvain," he said, crisp and cool, as if the very neutrality of his voice could bring himself back to reason.

Geneviève gave something over the door behind his head a stern look. "I might need to fix that bell. How did you manage to get in again?"

Sylvain glanced up and lifted a quick hand to clasp his. "Philippe. How is the new *salon* doing?"

"As could be expected," Philippe said, which was about as modestly as he could put "record-breakingly well," and he had no idea why all three women gave him a look as if he had just been impossibly conceited and needed to be taken down a peg. He almost didn't care about the attitude of the older two women, but the withering dismissal in Magalie's eyes made his blood burn.

Only Sylvain seemed to respect his phrasing. "Congratulations." He reached out and clasped his hand again. "You've worked hard for it."

Sylvain would know about working hard for success in their world of ultra gourmet cuisine. It was maddening to have the one person in the room Philippe most wanted to lift up and throw out of it be the only one to give him his due.

"And now that you've shared that with us," Geneviève said, "you're welcome to go away. Advised to, even."

"Maybe," Magalie said with a silky, malicious smile, "he can't stay away. Maybe he wants some chocolate."

He stared at her for a moment, his breathing too deep, the scent of her chocolate filling his lungs until it was almost but not quite a taste on his tongue. *Bordel,* what would it taste like?

His impulsive stride to harry Sylvain Marquis out of his territory had brought him here with nothing with which to tempt Magalie in exchange. He felt the disadvantage keenly. Sylvain had probably brought the witches a damn gift of his damn chocolates. Which she had probably eaten. *Putain de bordel de merde.*

He tried to make out what was on the roll of paper over which they had all been bent. Drawings. Something fantastical. He recognized the slashing, flamboyant lines of Sylvain's sketching, as he had worked on special projects with the chocolatier before. The two other styles were a whimsical curving line, almost like a fairytale laced with a cartoon, and an angular, cryptic hand that spoke of another generation. That last must be Geneviève. Meaning that whimsy twined with laughter was Magalie's?

He leaned one elbow back on their display case, as purchase against the longing that swelled through him and tried to take him over. He was never going to come near her without something tempting in hand again. Something tormentingly, excruciatingly tempting.

All three women fixed his elbow on their display case with a cold look.

He kept it there, though. The cold, flat hardness of the glass was good grounding.

He searched his mind for a solid, practical reason to have barged in. He needed to stop coming here just because he couldn't keep away. It made him look pathetic. "I happened to spot Sylvain and wanted to catch him. To get your opinion on one of the *pièces* for your wedding," he added to Sylvain.

All three women looked at him with, if possible, increased disfavor. He wondered what they had wanted his motivation for coming down here to be. To beg their forgiveness for his existence, maybe?

Well, at least he had slipped in the fact that Sylvain was about to get married. In case Sylvain hadn't gotten around to mentioning it to Magalie himself.

Sylvain, the black-haired bastard, looked at him with a slight, perplexed flex of supple eyebrows. "You want me to give an opinion on your work?" he clarified neutrally.

"It's *for your wedding*," Philippe said, goaded. Surely that made it seem plausible?

"Well." Sylvain grinned a little. His gaze flicked lightning fast between Philippe and Magalie. "I'm always happy to give you any advice I can."

Le salaud. "Why don't we talk about this outside?"

Where Sylvain's forearm, lying across the drawing, wasn't almost brushing Magalie's, each of them clutching a pencil in happy harmony.

"I just got here," Sylvain said, looking so amused Philippe might have to hurt him. "But I'll stop by when I leave."

Philippe tried again to make out the drawing without seeming to. Sylvain lifted his forearm so that the paper curled back over itself and over Magalie's arm in the process, hiding the sketch completely.

Philippe dug his elbow hard against the glass behind him and curled that hand into a fist. "This is my street, Sylvain," he said, goaded beyond caution.

All three women stared at him, and then he could actually

feel the flame hit the gunpowder, the tension in the room flash a white heat. Geneviève rose and went to the door. "I'm sorry, but we don't open for another hour. And then not to you."

His face flamed with frustrated fury at this palpable lie. He was never going to get anywhere with them. Magalie had come out hating him; every step he took was wrong. And all he wanted to do was grab her and drag her out with him so he could have this fight in private where it belonged.

He held her eyes for one long moment. And then, *putain de merde,* gave a sixty-year-old woman the respect of letting her throw him out of her own place and walked back out the door. With Sylvain grinning like life was just one delicious spectacle.

"Your street?" Sylvain checked dryly an hour later. The kitchen was closed for the day, but Philippe had stayed.

Philippe plunged his whisk into egg whites and whipped them hard, by hand. He had excellent equipment for whisking egg whites, but sometimes whipping them by hand relieved a great deal of frustration. "It is mine. I've claimed it."

Sylvain opened his mouth again, thought better of it, and closed it. After another moment, watching the egg whites mount under the speed of Philippe's whisking, he said, as if he already knew the answer, "I don't suppose you could try the humble approach?"

Philippe dusted superfine sugar in and whisked still harder. "No."

Sylvain shook his head, started to speak again, and again changed his mind. As the egg whites stiffened to peaks, he finally said, "You know why I asked you to do my wedding, don't you, Philippe?"

Philippe looked up at him, surprised. "Because I'm the best."

"Exactly." Sylvain didn't seem to find anything wrong

with the statement. Sometimes it was nice to talk to a man who knew the difference between arrogance and accurate self-assessment. "*Enfin,* with the sugar and egg whites and all that." Sylvain made a wave of his hand, clearly excluding all Philippe's chocolate from claims to superiority. "So you don't need my input on the *pièces montées.*"

"Of course, I don't," Philippe said, annoyed. Trust Sylvain to be obnoxious enough to make him admit the ruse. He drew the whisk out, the egg whites light as air, clinging to it nicely. "Have you drunk her chocolate?" he asked, despite himself.

"Yes." Sylvain gave him a small, malicious smile.

Philippe wished he had more to whisk, but any more and the whites would start breaking down. "And?" he asked the man considered to make the best chocolate in the world.

Sylvain's smile got, if anything, more gloating. "You should try it sometime," he said.

Philippe slammed the whisk back into the bowl, and fluffy egg white spattered all over him. Sylvain brushed a bit off one of his black eyebrows and raised it diabolically.

"I'm not trying her chocolate until she tries something of mine!" Philippe snarled. "Anything. I don't care if it's a grain of sugar off the tip of my finger. Something. Of. Mine."

Sylvain's eyebrows shot right up to the top of his head. "She's never eaten anything you've made?"

Putain de merde. How had he managed to let that slip to the man whose fiancée had been willing to face prison just to get more of his chocolates?

"Not ever? Why? Is she diabetic? No, that can't be right. I've seen her eat chocolate."

While Philippe had never gotten close enough to Magalie to see her eat a damn thing. He snarled again.

Sylvain gazed at him with incredulous pity for a long moment, until Philippe could barely refrain from upending the bowl of egg whites onto the man's head. *"Eh, bien, tu n'es pas dans la merde,"* he said at last conversationally.

Since when did Sylvain use *tu* with him? They both knew that *vous* was the basic rule of survival for a professional, sometimes-cooperative rivalry such as theirs. Was it impossible to maintain *vous* with someone currently as pathetic as Philippe was? "I realize that I am in deep shit, *merci,* Sylvain."

Sylvain eased a long step back, probably to be out of reach of an upside-down bowl of egg whites. He slipped his hands into his jacket pockets and stood there easily as Philippe started dusting ground almond over his egg whites, still pretending to himself that these *macarons* were going to turn out all right.

"Been thinking of that grain of sugar on your fingertip a long time, have you?" Sylvain smirked.

"Get the fuck out of here, Marquis."

Chapter 13

Magalie finished hanging the moon just before a beast rattled the doorknob, so she knew it was going to be one of *those* kind of days.

Her favorite.

It had been a week since Aunt Geneviève had kicked Philippe Lyonnais out of the shop in front of Sylvain Marquis, and she was beginning to think he had given up barging in. She had started catching herself stirring the oddest wishes into the chocolate of his sous-chefs, as if through them she could find the chink in his armor.

But when she had stopped, in the secret of the predawn, before his display windows that morning, heading out for her run, she had seen his newest creation in pride of place, sugar spun out like two crossed blades on the top of a pale vanilla *macaron,* across which tiny individual grains of raspberry scattered like blood.

The battle was still on. She had had a very good run that morning.

She was up to three out of five kilometers now. And even the walking parts were starting to feel less awkward, as if the freedom of running carried through in her long, open walking stride, minimizing any judgment from those she passed. She had spent five years feeling as if the island was her walled garden and that stepping beyond it was launching herself onto a battlefield. But the long, curving quays of Paris and the city's arched bridges, with the cold wind streaming over her—they were starting to feel like hers, too.

At five or six in the morning, she didn't get lost in the mass of people, reduced to nothing; there were hardly any other people about, and she felt too free and herself to care.

The doorknob rattled again. The beast was out without a hat, despite the hint of snow, his honey-colored hair curling against his neck in a rich mane. Some people had blue eyes you never even noticed, so that after years of friendship you still might not be sure of their eye color. But not his. They pinned her right through the glass window, picking her out unerringly among the dangerous thorns and the looming, primitive, snow-dusted, dark-chocolate firs. A chocolate witch picked jewel-like flowers made from crystallized violets and mint leaves in the shadow of the trees. Farther off loomed a chocolate tower, from the one high window of which draped a long braid carefully made from fine strips of candied lemon peel.

The beast outside the tea shop stood slightly lopsided, because a little girl with eyes as blue as his was clinging to his hand.

Typical of him. To use a little girl to get into a witch's house. He knew *he* was banned.

She climbed down off the stepladder, trying so hard not to show how sore her legs were from her last run that she barely remembered to duck the moon she'd just hung. It dangled, chocolate so dark its brown was almost black, just a few inches above her forehead. Taller people would run into it if they got too close to the display case below it, but this was the type of hazard her aunts liked to have in their *salon*.

She unlocked the door and held it open, and the visitors passed her in a whirl of cold air from the street. The cold air freed a space in the rich, thick scent of chocolate, and just for a second she smelled roses and sunshine. A lion that smelled of roses and sunshine? What was he working on now?

She sneered at him.

He smiled back sharply, showing his fangs.

"Is she a weapon or a shield?" she asked over the little girl's head.

"A lock pick," he said, and closed the door behind him, confirming his entry.

She contemplated swirling a love potion into his chocolate, to make him fall in love with some horribly inappropriate frog in the belief that she was a princess.

If she could ever get him to drink her chocolate.

"Are you a witch?" the little girl asked, hushed and eager, looking around.

Magalie studied her. Her hair was the same tawny shade as Philippe Lyonnais's and curled over her shoulders in rough, large locks. A lavender pageboy cap attempted to restrain it. "That's an indiscreet question."

Oh, mouthed the little girl, her eyes growing rounder and even more delighted. She looked around at the conical hats of all descriptions, so beautifully rearranged by the beast holding her hand. Besides the hats, the shelves and walls were crammed with images from the aunts' artist friends—from pen-and-ink to mosaic to woven and needing a good dry-cleaning—as well as with teapots and strange, whimsical souvenirs and a cuckoo clock that looked like a house covered with elaborate candies. As the little girl looked at it, a witch suddenly popped out of the clock's bonbon door and laughed evilly.

That clock was always five minutes slow.

"My uncle is a prince," the little girl said confidingly. She flourished a little hand, clearly quoting all those stupid TV shows on him: *"Le Prince des Pâtissiers!"*

Not confident that her own laugh would be wicked

enough to follow the cuckoo clock's, Magalie settled for a curl of her lip as she turned away—turned far enough for the girl not to see it, but not so far that her uncle wouldn't catch it.

He curled his lip right back at her. He looked as if he was about to rip her gazelle throat out when he did that. And then run his tongue lingeringly over her blood on his teeth. *In his dreams.* Because he was so fit and powerful and dwarfed her, even in her boots, she supposed some blind outside observer *might* see her as a gazelle to his lion. But he would be very much mistaken.

"Yes, he's made his royal status clear to us," Magalie said.

He gave a little shrug of one broad shoulder, in an it's-hardly-my-fault-you-noticed way.

"You knew!" the little girl said happily. "See, Tonton? I told you everyone could tell you were a prince."

Magalie tapped the toe of her boot. "Oh, yes, he makes it very obvious. The Beast was a prince, too, by the way."

"I believe he was *turned into* a Beast," Philippe Lyonnais said in his rough, rich, I'll-eat-you-when-I-choose voice. "After carelessly opening his door to a witch."

"If you're a witch, could you find a beautiful princess for him?" the little girl asked.

The beast-prince stopped the snarling smile long enough to send his niece a betrayed look.

Magalie tried her own throat-ripping smile. "If I find the perfect princess for him, trust me, I will send her his way."

The look that Philippe sent her this time was pissed off and almost human.

"Oh," the little girl said, looking very happy. "I *know* you'll find someone beautiful."

Philippe set his mouth.

"Don't worry," Magalie reassured the little girl. "We get princesses in here all the time." With their window full of a great dark-chocolate forest, and witches swooping through the snow-sugar-powdered chocolate firs, they attracted all manner of princesses in search of magic to deal with the world in which they found themselves.

So did Philippe, though. He put mouthwatering treasures confected of sugar and heaven in his windows. And princesses walked right out of her shop and into his. Philippe attracted princesses in search of a prince for the ball.

"Perhaps you're one yourself?" Magalie asked the little girl.

"I haven't decided yet. I think I want to be a fairy. Or maybe an elephant tamer."

Fair enough. Philippe could have loomed there until he turned into a statue before Magalie seated him, but for the budding fairy's sake, Magalie showed them to one of the tiny corner tables.

"Bonjour," Philippe said to her pointedly as he sat across from his niece, his voice a low, rich, tawny thing.

Oh, no, he had *not* just corrected her manners. In her own territory. Which he wouldn't have even gotten back inside if it hadn't been for his four-year-old lockpick there with her curly hair. Magalie tapped her fingers hard into the palm of her hand, held low by her thigh, entirely unable to bring herself to say *bonjour* back.

Instead, she handed each of them a menu, rich off-white with its cramped and esoteric list of teas on one side and children's drawings on the back. Sometimes, when things were slow, Magalie would study whichever drawing was uppermost, trying to interpret the child's visions. Other than the frequent appearance of witches, most of them were not that obvious.

The little girl studied the crayon drawings on her menu a long time. "I want some of the violets and mint," she whispered carefully, looking around in case she was telling a secret.

Magalie gave her an approving smile. She liked people

who thought outside the menu. "Certainly. Three petals, three leaves, and a chocolate witch. How does that sound?"

The little girl beamed.

"And for monsieur?" she asked with a little, challenging smile.

He held her eyes and smiled right back. "I'll have a Perrier."

Magalie bit hard on the inside of her lip in a reminder that there was a four-year-old child present. "I believe we're out."

His big hand lay flat over the cryptic, enticing list of items on the menu. Completely blocking it from consideration. "Evian, then."

She drew a breath.

"Or if you're out of that," he added urbanely, before she could speak, "just tapwater is fine. I'm not fussy."

He was a bastard was what he was.

"Can I draw a picture for you?" the little girl asked wistfully. "I'm a good drawer."

"Of course." Her aunts would be thrilled. "We would be honored."

"That's a nice new display Sylvain's got up in his windows." Philippe's smile was thin, murderous. "The one with the witch looking for where she buried her heart. And her heart turns out to be one of Sylvain's chocolates. Very sweet for Valentine's Day."

He didn't sound as if it was sweet. He sounded as if he wanted to spit the taste of it out of his mouth.

"Did you spend a lot of time crouched with him in the window working on it?" he continued. "Cade didn't object?"

Object to what? "I think it was her idea." Besides, Cade hadn't been present much; her sister had recently been hospitalized, and she was spending a lot of time there, joined by Sylvain in the evenings. Magalie had figured out who Cade

Corey was. The billionaire chocolate heiress and chocolate thief—the Web and print media had been abuzz with her over the past months, but Magalie had never paid attention before she met her. Cade's escapades in Paris had made for fascinating reading once she had searched for the articles, though. Quixotically enough, the heiress to one of the world's largest mass producers of candy bars seemed to have a thing about defending and supporting small artisan producers, and while it was annoying that she seemed to think La Maison des Sorcières needed a champion, at least Sylvain wasn't acting out of charity. He just liked the tea shop's style. He had openly credited their role in his window display and had a stack of their business cards by his cash registers. "Aunt Geneviève did most of it."

Philippe shifted restlessly in his chair, looking as if he wanted something to kick.

Magalie shrugged. "It's not the witch's real heart, anyway." That had been her contribution. Sure, Sylvain's customers could think it was and find it *si romantique,* but no witch worth her chocolate left her heart in some sorcerer's hand.

"It's in your own window, isn't it?" the little girl said suddenly. "Her heart. I saw it. It was hidden in the witch's basket."

A tiny sliver of a candied rose petal, just barely peeking out. What a very perceptive child. It was a pity she had to show off that perception in front of her uncle. Magalie forced herself to give the girl a self-confidence-boosting smile, as if Philippe Lyonnais hadn't just been handed a dangerous secret. "That's right. She's taking it back in under her protection, now that she's realized someone is after it."

She felt rather than saw Philippe's stillness, because she was *not* looking at him. Even if he was quite rudely letting his long legs extend into her pathway, so that she had to weave around them every time she moved.

The tiny silver bell over the door rang, and two women

came in, layered in coats and scarves, looking around with wondering eyes. "We were looking for the new Lyonnais shop," one said, "but this is so marvelous."

Philippe tapped his fingers once over the menu but said nothing.

Magalie smiled at them. "We're known for our *chocolat chaud,* if you want to try it." She seated the women neatly within Philippe's line of sight and took herself and her heart back into her lair.

In the tiny kitchen, Magalie brought out two old enamel trays from their mishmash collection. Her aunts had never bought a single thing new, unused, lacking history. First she set out Philippe's tray. She ran the water from the tap, adjusting the temperature until it was unpleasantly tepid, and filled a carafe for him with it. She set a thimble-size shot glass down beside it, one of a pair of old shot glasses picked up at a *marché des puces* long ago and which Aunt Geneviève said felt as if they had been drunk from in great *joie de vivre* for generations. For the little girl, she chose an exquisite china plate rimmed in golden curlicues and placed, carefully, three purple violet petals, three green mint leaves, and in their center, one dark-chocolate witch. Geneviève's witches looked like the real thing, not someone you would necessarily want to meet up with in the dark.

For the second tray, she brought out a little blue Art Déco pitcher. She stirred her pot of chocolate on the stove with her ladle three times before she dipped, the scent of it rising off the pot like an embrace. She always loved this moment, preparing to offer her *chocolat chaud,* pretending it would change someone's whole day, whole week, maybe whole year. *A pleasant dreaming day,* she thought for these women in her last three stirs. *And may they end the evening the happier for it.*

She scooped the chocolate up, so thick she could feel it yielding to the ladle, and poured it carefully into the pot, filling it to two fingers below its brim. She accompanied it with two blue, handle-less china cups, not from a matching set. Next to each, she set a little white tissue.

The aunts liked to set this little challenge to those who came here: to serve them impossibly thick, sinfully luscious chocolate and give them only the finest wisp of a Kleenex to keep their mouths clean. It was always fun to see who left the premises with their lips neat and who smudged with chocolate.

She brought Philippe's tray out first, sliding it onto the tiny table without comment, careful not to disturb the little girl's drawing. She was coloring enthusiastically on the cream sheet of paper Magalie had given her; she seemed to be drawing lots and lots of triangles. The hats, Magalie guessed.

She waited long enough for Philippe to get a taste of that tepid water before she brought out the second tray. The aroma from it wafted over everyone as she passed, and the size of the tiny shop made it impossible for that same aroma not to waft very thoroughly under Philippe Lyonnais's nose.

She set it on the tiny table between the two women and moved over behind the cash register. The two arched alcoves in the walls meant she was still as close to the tables as if she were in the same room and able to see all that went on while seeming to have much better things to do with her time.

Philippe eyed the tray of hot chocolate right there in his line of sight with long-lashed, dark eyes. Sleepy, predatory, one hand flexing like that of a great cat kneading a worry. His niece picked up one candied violet with great precision and ate it, her eyes crinkling in delight.

The two women poured and then sipped the chocolate with many exclamations between them. Philippe's eyes tracked their movements. *"Si, si bon,"* one of them breathed to another. *"C'est délicieux."*

"It's like heaven," said the other. "I'm so glad we stumbled onto this place."

"I wonder what Lyonnais has that could be *better*," the second woman said incredulously. "It makes me happy just to drink this."

Philippe lifted gold-tipped lashes to look straight at Magalie, through the fertility figures and masks and the tattered remains of fabric that some chocolate-lover had once brought Aunt Geneviève back from Papua, New Guinea. She gave him a malicious look back.

Just as long as he knew what he was refusing. She wanted him to suffer for it.

"You're welcome," he breathed for her ears alone as she passed again, so softly that she could barely hear and had to pay far too much attention to the way his mouth shaped the words. Precise and controlled in a way that made heat roil through her body. "For the clients."

She couldn't believe the gall of this man. He had waltzed into their perfectly blissful, sheltered heart of Paris and stolen all their customers, and now he thought she should be grateful for a stray or two who wandered in while searching for his shop? Well, all their customers were strays who wandered in. Their refusal to advertise the tea shop was part of their policy. But still. What did he think, that she was a dog to whom he had tossed a bone?

"Océane, now might be a good time to give Mademoiselle Chaudron her present."

Magalie stiffened.

The little girl dove into the backpack she had been carrying, while Magalie raged internally at the false pretenses under which the Beast had entered her shop. The backpack was a very innocent red, with butterflies stitched all over it and a flower that had lost one of its petals. But now it proved to be a Trojan Horse for the box Océane brought out of it: gold on pale pink this month, in honor of the fast-approaching Valentine's Day.

She set her mouth hard. *Chocolat*, she swore to herself.

Her mouth was watering over the scent of her own chocolate, not whatever delicacy Philippe had brought to tempt
her with.

"How . . . thoughtful." Unfortunately, it was almost certainly true that Phillipe had thought a very great deal about
every single grain that went into the thing, with her as its intended victim. She tried to take the box so she could tuck it
out of sight in the kitchen.

Too late for the two women, who were starting to glance
from it to Philippe, brows knit. They had seen photos of him
somewhere, sometime, out of the five million magazine articles and television shoots in which he had been featured.
They were starting vaguely to wonder if he might be . . . if
he might be . . .

"*Non, non,* you have to open it!" Océane said, clinging to
the other side of the box. Philippe, who certainly should be
the one minding the girl's manners, said nothing at all to this.
The faintest curve touched his mouth, entirely sadistic.

Magalie looked down at the little girl's excited face. "Very
well," she said. It wasn't Océane's fault her uncle was willing
to use a four-year-old to deliver bombs.

But she made no move to open it.

Océane couldn't wait. "*Regarde,*" she insisted. Like most
children her age, she hadn't mastered *vous,* making her standing with Magalie sound strangely intimate in contrast with
the cool *vous* reestablished between Magalie and the child's
uncle ever since the falling-hats episode. Océane fumbled
with the creamy pink lid.

A large hand closed over it, steadying the box before
something happened to its undoubtedly fragile contents. Magalie felt her heart beating in her throat. Why did he keep
doing this to her?

Well, she knew why he kept doing this to her. Because he
wanted to beat her at their game. Because he wanted the satisfaction of proving himself irresistible, after all.

He lifted the lid of the box like a lover might reveal a ring and waited. From the table in the other corner came a murmur of delight.

A rippling wall of thin white chocolate rose impossibly high inside the box, like a tower, around its protected center. How could he get his white chocolate to stand that high? Peering down into the narrow well of it, she saw a dome of delicate, creamy gold, made from what, she had no idea. Would never have any idea, unless she tasted it. Two curls of chocolate, one dark, one white, crossed over the gold, and it was hard to tell if they were crossed in combat or curled lovingly together. Almost hidden under them was a little glimpse of gold, tiny bits of candied . . . grapefruit, she thought, cradled in a little dip in the gold-white cream. As if the creamy insides held treasure.

Had he done this before or after he had seen the tower theme in their new display window? Was he reading her mind or responding to it that quickly?

And framing that creamy white-chocolate offering were those big, square hands, holding the box open, their calluses visible on the skin and their delicate skill there for all to see.

"It looks like a tower!" one of the women behind her exclaimed in delight. "How *beautiful!*"

And then the other woman whispered to her questioningly, *"C'est Philippe Lyonnais?"* She breathed the name the way she might if she thought she had glimpsed the Prince of England at the next table. *"Oh, qu'est-ce que c'est romantique!"*

Why, he had just stolen back the two customers, Magalie realized. Bringing that exquisite weapon into their shop, he had as good as piped his flute to every breathing person there and lured them down the street to his glossy windows.

"Do you like it? Do you like it?" The little girl's excited voice penetrated Magalie's fog.

Magalie dragged her eyes away from the offering to Oceane's face. "It's beautiful," she said with an effort.

It was so beautiful, it made her heart hurt, as it had no doubt been intended to do.

The silver bell rang, and three more customers drifted in, an older couple with their adult child, tracking down this shop that Sylvain Marquis claimed to love. Initially distracted by the shop itself, they, too, exclaimed as soon as their eyes touched the Lyonnais tower.

"Oh . . ." said the older woman on one long, drawn-out murmur. "Could we have *that*?"

"No, it's for the witch!" Océane exclaimed aloud, confidingly. "Only"—she caught herself and whispered—"I'm not supposed to call her that." And loudly and proudly again, she announced, "My uncle made it!"

"*Oh, c'est si, si romantique!*" one of the first two women whispered achingly from their table. "*Philippe Lyonnais,*" she shared in the same whisper to the new arrivals, unable to resist the power of being the deliverer of that news.

Philippe's eyes remained fixed on Magalie's face. His big hands never shifted from framing his poisoned gift, offering it to her. He looked ravenous, as if the box was a trap and he was primed to spring it onto her fingers as soon as she reached inside for that work of art.

Magalie reached out, very deliberately *not* inside, and took the box from him. Her hands grazed his, soft skin against warm calluses, as she closed the box. She felt more than saw Philippe's hard breath. He didn't make a sound. But when she glanced back up, his eyes glittered with fury.

"Thank you," she told the little girl.

"It's really from Tonton," Océane said. "He wouldn't even let me help."

"Are you, are you—*Philippe Lyonnais*?" one of the women said from the table behind Magalie. She pulled a folded card in heavy stock out of her purse, opening it to reveal the Lyonnais "winter collection" of *macarons,* every single damn flavor. Her voice was hushed, embarrassed. "Would you—

would you mind signing this? We were really coming to your shop," she added in a rush, as if to assure him they weren't betraying him with Magalie. "But we got distracted."

Apparently, they weren't too worried about betraying Magalie with him.

"*Oui, bien sûr,*" Philippe said with great control, managing to transform that fury into a warm, dishonestly self-deprecating smile for the two women.

Not able to bear watching him autograph his damn *macaron* list in *her* lair, as if he was king of it, Magalie swept the box into the tiny kitchen. Her palms burned from the contact. On the tiny blue tiles of the counter, so hard to keep clean but so loved by her aunts, the pink box sat completely alien. As if a damned fairy godmother had snuck in while her back was turned.

She contemplated her pot of chocolate, a muscle ticking in her jaw.

A current of air shifted, the door to the shop opening, and she could feel the giant presence of her Aunt Geneviève instantly. It filled the kitchen to bursting. There was a murmur of voices as Tante Geneviève squeezed past the jackets to get into the kitchen. Immediately, her turquoise caftan and long cape swept out to take up any space her body didn't. Capes were in fashion that year, which was convenient for Aunt Geneviève, since her last one had been getting threadbare.

"He had to use a child to get in, did he?" Geneviève murmured. Of course, their customers could probably see the murmur ripple in their cups in the next room.

If they had water. Damn it! Magalie cursed under her breath.

"The main problem with curses," Geneviève chided, "is that most of them will melt in the chocolate, so you never know what will happen with the bits and pieces that survive. And you would have to throw out the whole rest of the batch so as not to serve it to anyone else. Think of the waste."

"No, I forgot to put the water on their tray." They never

left anyone helpless before Magalie's chocolate without at least a glass of water. Her chocolate took rich to a whole new level.

Magalie filled a crystal carafe for the two women.

"Oh." Geneviève looked a little disappointed about the curse. "What's wrong with you, anyway?" she asked after Magalie. In the small space, conversations could continue in normal tones even when someone was two rooms away. "You're walking very funny."

"No, I'm not," Magalie said, indignant. She was putting a lot of attention into not walking funny. Her butt hurt from running. Her calves hurt. Her thighs hurt. Maybe she should have paid attention to what the running websites had said about how fast she should be increasing her distances.

"Yes, you are," Philippe said, peeling the paper back from a crayon for his niece.

Her insides stirred unsteadily at the fact that he had noticed. "You're an expert on the way I walk now?" she said snippily.

The oddest, ironic curl touched Philippe's mouth. "As a matter of fact . . ." he murmured, looking at the tip of the crayon.

A disturbing, destabilizing warmth grew in her. "Then watch carefully," she told him. "There's nothing funny about it."

Just before she turned away to prove it, his blue gaze rose suddenly from the crayon and caught her. For a second, she couldn't move. His gaze was so hard and intense, like being pinned by a spear. "Certainly," he breathed. "It's the first invitation I've gotten from you. I can guarantee I won't refuse it."

Now she *did* walk funnily when she strode away from him, conscious of those eyes on her butt like hands holding it, caressing every step she took. What was wrong with her to have said that? Never give a man carte blanche where staring at your butt was concerned.

Especially not a man like Philippe Lyonnais. Knowing he was watching her walk made her whole body seem to soften and beg to offer him a lot more invitations.

"Could I have your autograph, too?" another of the women, one of *their* clients, asked him in a breathy voice.

Magalie picked up her spoon and stirred her chocolate with vengeful satisfaction: *May whoever drinks this get what he deserves.* Which just *had* to include a comeuppance.

You couldn't call that a curse, could you? And she could even serve it to both uncle and niece at the same time. That little girl could only deserve wonderful things, right? She hoped she didn't get Océane sent to her room for not cleaning up her toys. And she hoped having that pot of chocolate under his nose cracked Philippe like one of his sugar sculptures.

When she brought the tray out, Philippe had just finished signing his *second* pamphlet with a dull blue crayon and was politely responding to the women's eager questions.

Magalie slipped firmly between the two tables and slid the tray right under Philippe's nose.

Philippe stared down into the pitcher. From her angle, above his head, the chocolate's warm darkness seemed infinite below the rim of the pot, as if one could wallow forever in its depths. He drew a long breath and then immediately, visibly regretted it. He actually brought a hand up before his mouth and nose, pseudo-casually, to defend his senses from the scent.

"Just a little thank-you for Océane's artwork." Magalie smiled. "It's on the house."

Philippe's other hand tightened around his tepid water.

"We're coming to your place tomorrow!" one of the women at the other table promised him.

"So where did it come from?" one of the threesome who had arrived last demanded of the two women and of Philippe. "That beautiful pastry? Do you have a shop near here? *Mon chéri,* what do you think? Maybe we should go there instead."

Magalie bent her head down, low, to Philippe, almost as if she was going to give *bises* on each of his cheeks in thanks. "I'm going to get you," she hissed into his ear.

Philippe's hand flicked up fast, as only someone with minute control of his hands could move, catching the one lock of hair that must have slipped from her chignon, stopping her lift of her head with a jerk that stung her scalp. He locked her there, far too close. "No," he breathed back, his teeth a snarl, his eyes molten blue. "I'm going to get you."

He dropped his hand and let her go.

Chapter 14

M agalie stood in her ivory tower in fluffy socks, thinking about her efforts to turn egg whites into feet. The term *feet* annoyed her. Who would look at the ruffled bottom of a glossy smooth *macaron* shell and call it a *foot*? And what kind of person did it take to keep pursuing the perfection of such feet when it *never, ever worked out right*?

Probably she should have gotten Philippe's book on the subject. The beautiful, glossy *Macarons* had taunted her, face out, on the bookshelf over at Gibert Jeune. And she wasn't getting very far with the only other book the store had had on the subject.

But she would be burned at the stake before she bought his book. Or before she went down into the better-equipped kitchen of the shop and let her aunts see her trying this.

She couldn't get the *macarons* to work for anything. She whipped them. She folded the cocoa into them, and she *tried* to be careful. It was tedious, folding cocoa and almonds in. She placed them in their little circles drawn on parchment paper. She baked them exactly how the recipe said. And they came out flat as crêpes, stuck through the paper to the pan so that they shattered as she tried to get them out, and the pieces tasted dry and grainy.

So the next morning, on her way back from aunt-invented errands, she stood scowling at Philippe's famously perfect *pieds* in his shop, the little ruffled feet of his *macaron* shells, the way those shells rose up from the foot into such a perfect, smooth surface, not a hint of grain. Instead of her dull, dry, pale brown, his chocolate ones looked rich and inviting.

And then there was the crown dessert he had offered her. And the tower. Luscious. Perfect. Taunting.

"You're welcome to come in," a rough-purr voice said from behind her.

She jumped and tried to disguise the startled move with a pivot on her high heel. Turning, she was already furious with him—for catching her out, for making treasures and putting them at the heart and center of his display windows *every damn day,* for startling her enough to give him the satisfaction of seeing it.

He was so close to her, he blocked off any escape but the door into his shop. That avenue, by the angle of his body, he left open. He was so close that, as she turned, the edge of her jacket must have touched him.

"Merci," she said flatly. *"Non."*

"It would be my pleasure." He was mocking her. She knew it. He thought himself some damn lion inviting a gazelle to dinner. Or a prince inviting in a bag lady, probably. *"Je t'invite."*

Her jaw jerked higher at the *tu*. How dare he? He held her eyes with that sharp, predatory smile, refusing to take it back at her frigid gaze. Which left her with . . . what? An overly intimate *tu* or continuing to use *vous* in the face of his *tu,* which his royal, arrogant bastard of a Highness would probably take as nothing less than his due.

"I wouldn't stoop," she said clearly, her nostrils flaring in disdain.

He looked past her shoulder, at the pure temptation sitting in his window. She had a sudden desperate fear that he could see the print from the tip of her nose on the glass, like a child's. She held her chin up and refused absolutely to glance back at that concoction herself to double-check. His gaze returned to her and lingered over that chin. "Suit yourself," he said, his voice smug and mocking but his blue eyes glittering with anger.

She wanted to stride away, but she couldn't get past him without either bumping against him, asking him to let her by, or stepping into his shop. Any of which she would be damned if she would do.

So she folded her arms and tilted her chin at him like a weapon. And he stood there looking down at her. Until awareness of why she wasn't moving began to penetrate his consciousness. He didn't shift back a step in belated courtesy. Oh, no. The blue eyes swept up and down the length of her body twice, darkening, and when they came back to her face were met with pure scorn. She had been in Paris for five years now. She had been on the receiving end of more clothes-stripping, aggressive gazes than she could count.

His eyes narrowed at her expression. The anger in them grew more intense, seething like the surface of a pot of chocolate just before it bubbled too hot and made an unsalvageable mess. He didn't look down her body again. And he didn't back up. He just stood there, blocking her, gazing into her face. His presence seemed to grow until it was pressing all around her, as if his will had become tangible and was trying to physically wring something out of her.

He wasn't touching her, and yet she could feel the press of him all over her skin. How did he do this to her? In his office at that first meeting, in her kitchen, every time he got close to her. How could he make her whole body burn? How could he make her feel both so strong, as if she could launch herself at him and fight with this man twice her size, and so strangely shaky, as if some secret, vital part of her might fail her during the fight?

He stood there as if he could hold her there forever. By

God, he had patience, this man who could stand and stir and stir and stir a simmering pot of sugar, facing the heat and the time until it was exactly perfect. This man who never, ever shortened a step or skipped it or took the easy way in his pastry making. Control. Patience. Intensity. Time. *Control.*

She put her hands on her hips and was surprised when her elbows didn't jab into him. He *felt* as if he was wrapped around her, as if she needed to fight him off with jutting elbows. "Do you think I'm a pot of caramel?"

The anger in his eyes flickered in surprise, and he laughed suddenly. It wasn't the big, ringing laugh that had greeted her the first time she had seen him, but it lit his whole face. A warm pleasure washed over her, stealing the strength from every joint in her body, while she scrambled to tell them they weren't supposed to behave that way. That laugh scared her more than anything else about him ever had. Its effect on her.

He grinned down at her, inviting her into his humor as if it was a warm embrace. "I was thinking of a meringue, but I'm glad you imagined caramel."

Meringue had to be whipped at high speed until every last grain of superfine sugar dissolved into the pure white and it was absolutely smooth and extraordinarily fluffy. It was part of why Magalie's failed; she got impatient. A pot of caramel was much hotter, it boiled and seethed, a molten gold that had to be kept under the most perfect control of the *caramellier* because it was so very easy to mishandle and let burn. Damn it. She felt herself getting closer to that burning point right then, at what she had just revealed.

His eyes were still laughing, still inviting her to come in out of this cold day and curl up in his warmth. The richness of their blue was incredible. The tawny hair seemed to pull in sunshine, promising that winter-cold fingertips might find it like treasure if they sank into its depths. "Do you think I'm a pot of chocolate?"

She shook her head, hard. No, oh, no. Chocolate was easy; it was rich and reassuring, and it always cooperated with her.

Disappointment flickered across his face. What had he been imagining?

Being melted and stirred?

Oh. Her whole body tried to rise toward him so that she desperately wished there was something behind her besides smooth glass, so that she could grab on and hold herself in place. "Chocolate does what I ask it to," she said crisply, and she turned to finally walk past him.

She kept her hands on her hips as she did it, elbows well out. Most men in nightclubs would give a little room to a woman keeping her elbows out, but Philippe just let hers connect with his ribs, let her arm fold back under the impact, her elbow slide across his midsection, her shoulder against his chest. He didn't even flinch at the impact. Probably his jacket had absorbed it all.

She shot him an annoyed glance, way up, from right in close to his body. He tilted his head down, his focus on her absolute. "You've never asked me to do anything, Magalie."

It was terrible, the power her name in his voice had over her. She understood now all those stories about giving away one's true name. But that claim was so outrageous that she stopped there and half-turned, the side of her arm still mid-rub against his chest. "I asked you not to come to my shop!"

"No, you didn't. You tried to threaten me away. You've never *asked* me for anything, Magalie. For all you know, I'd give it to you."

And *he* walked away from *her.* Into his shop with a long, confident stride, the king sweeping into his throne room.

She was still simmering—and trying furiously not to think of a master's hand stirring a boiling pot of caramel—when she returned from Gibert Jeune's with the fresh boxes of crayons and drawing paper Geneviève had sent her out for. How dare he try to get her to *ask* him for something? Never.

As if she could . . . petition him.

She had tried. She had tried to make herself ask when she first went to see him, to save her and her aunts' place. But to walk into that beautiful royal kingdom of his and be a beggar . . . she just couldn't.

She scowled briefly at the customer sitting at one of the tables in the back room and then realized it was Claire-Lucy. *"Ciao,"* she said tersely. If Claire-Lucy didn't remain loyal to Magalie, she didn't see why *she* had to keep a space for the toyseller. Claire-Lucy had been spending a lot of her afternoon teas down at Lyonnais. Probably huddling shyly in a corner, hoping one of the cute chefs would notice her, which was the kind of thing that drove Magalie completely insane.

Of course, it could be worse. Claire-Lucy could be going there because his desserts were so insanely delicious that once a woman tried them, she could never, ever say no to them again.

"Hi," Claire-Lucy said glumly. She was sipping some of Aunt Aja's tea, which was brave of her. If she wasn't careful, Aunt Aja might wish her gumption, and then she would be trying all kinds of things she didn't dare now. And that would teach her for being such a traitor.

"I like your vintage car display," Magalie said dryly.

"Nice thorns," Claire-Lucy retorted.

"I know." Magalie felt a little smug.

"What other toy do you think cute, busy men might like besides cars?"

Magalie shrugged. "You, probably."

Claire-Lucy flushed and tried to smooth the frizz out of her hair.

"Claire-Lucy, you aren't seriously enjoying the idea of being someone's toy, I hope."

Claire-Lucy sighed. "What are *you* doing for *la Saint-Valentin?*"

"Nothing," Magalie said triumphantly. Another year over, and her walls were still intact. Was she good or what?

"Me, neither," Claire-Lucy said, drooping.

"Well, good for you," Magalie said. "You can come over here like last year. It's a nice, supportive atmosphere for women who don't want to be toys."

Claire-Lucy gave her an indignant look. "You know, I *like* toys, Magalie."

"Well, then, I give up," Magalie lied, because she had never given up in her life. Instead, she went back into the kitchen and started warming chocolate.

Aunt Aja, quietly painting rose petals with egg white, smiled at her. "Geneviève is downstairs in the *cave,* looking through some of our old chocolate molds."

"I mean, it would be kind of nice to be some man's toy if I could be his pretty Barbie doll," Claire-Lucy said wistfully when Magalie stepped back into the archway. If Aunt Geneviève heard that, she was going to rise up through the floor like an outraged goddess from the depths of hell. "Instead of which, they always think of me as some kind of Raggedy Ann." She stroked her frizzing hair again.

First of all, Magalie thought, they made hair products for that kind of thing, and second of all, she was not entirely sure rescuing idiotic princesses was the right business for her and her aunts. It seemed as if at some point they might just start grabbing heads and conking them together.

She went back into the kitchen and gave her chocolate a stern look. *You could try finding a man who can see straight, who goes after what he wants, who knows how to appreciate a beautiful woman.*

Claire-Lucy finished her whole cup of that chocolate, draining the last drop, and sat there a moment thoughtfully.

Then, still sunk in thought, she paid and left, heading down the street.

As Magalie watched from the door, Claire-Lucy walked straight down the street, stopped in front of Lyonnais, ran her hand through her hair, straightened her shoulders, and walked in.

Magalie ground her forehead against the display case, then yanked a big chocolate thorn off and started eating it.

Maybe she had snuck him something after all, Philippe thought as he exchanged his fine leather jacket and cashmere sweater for an easily washable pastry jacket over a thin knit shirt. Maybe the drug was in the very air he'd breathed in that tea shop. Because he couldn't think of anything but her. Of pulling out that ever-perfect clasp and seeing how long her hair was. And what those dark, smooth—shoulder-length?—locks would look like when he messed them up. When he threaded his hands into them and held her head still on his bed while he kissed her.

While he took her, his brain flashed forward. And fractured into multiple fantasy paths at once, unable to decide between a vision in which she let him hold her still by her hair for his taking, and one in which she dragged her nails down his ribs to his butt, fighting him for control.

"I'll do the caramel," he told Olivier. "I'm in the mood for it this morning."

To Olivier's credit, he didn't show his relief. Philippe brought his sugar far hotter than anyone else before he deglazed it with the best butter in France and added in the cream, and Olivier had slipped up and burned it more times than he had messed up any other recipe. He was beginning to consider it his curse, which was unfortunate, as they were going to need a good *caramellier* for this shop, to free more of Philippe's time for creation and innovation.

Given that he had been making perfect caramel since he

was fourteen years old, it was probably a bad sign that *this* morning, Philippe brought his caramel too hot and burned it.

Right about the time the stink of scorched sugar was hitting his nostrils, and he was thinking about strangling Magalie with his bare hands, the *laboratoire's* door opened, and a young, somewhat plump woman with frizzy chestnut hair peeked in. "Hello," she said shyly, glancing around the room as if searching for someone.

She had a little sack stamped with a dark brown witch in one hand.

Claws pushed at his fingertips. Fangs grew. How could she, how *could* she, still be trying to save herself by sacrificing other women to him? "I'm sorry, we're working," he said flatly. "Hygiene laws. No one is allowed back here." He jerked his head at his intern to show the latest princess-victim of Magalie's out.

Grégory, closer to the door, moved in front of the intern and sent Philippe a reproachful glance.

What? How courteous was he supposed to be to Magalie's victims? Maybe they shouldn't drink her damn chocolate.

If *he* could resist it, he didn't see why everyone else had to be so weak-willed.

"I'm sorry," Grégory said kindly to the invader. "Did you need something?"

"I was just curious." She hesitated, casting a hopeful look up at him. "I own the toy shop down the street. I'm Claire-Lucy."

"Grégory Dumont," Grégory said warmly. "Don't mind Monsieur Lyonnais. So you've just come from La Maison des Sorcières? What do you think of their chocolate? Isn't it the best?" The door swung closed behind them as Grégory escorted her out.

Fortunately for him. Because, given that Lyonnais did serve *chocolat chaud* at its own tables, Philippe was that close to throwing something at him.

I am going to kill her, he thought.

But not before she looks at me with those brown eyes of hers and begs for more of me.

Not before she couldn't get the taste of him off her tongue.

Chapter 15

The city greeted Magalie with a hush, like a lover that didn't want to awaken. A lover who was, just for that moment before returning to consciousness, completely hers. The bare trees along the quays were etched black against the slowly fading sky, a thin wisp of gold clinging to the horizon beyond them. The lights that illuminated the Louvre in the night had switched off. The conical towers of the Conciergerie were black, like the trees against the sky. Just for a moment, everything was subtle, everything was gentle.

She could hear the dull thud of her feet on the paving stones, a gentler, softer sound than her aggressive daytime boots. The water was deep gray, the light as it grew allowing winter brown to seep back into its color. She ran between the border of bare trees and the wall above the river, along the upper quays.

Running like this, all her anger and armor against Philippe seemed unnecessary. When he crossed her mind, the vision of him made her smile. She saw his laugh as the ganache exploded over his hands.

Running, she didn't worry about La Maison des Sorcières, not after the first kilometer. Right now, it seemed as if they might be able to make ends meet on Philippe's employees alone. She kept wishing beautiful lives for them, on the theory that that was a nice, positive way to make them all desert His arrogant Highness and just spend their days drinking her chocolate, but so far, it didn't seem to be working.

She glimpsed the Gothic Tour Saint-Jacques down a side street to her left, cryptic and aloof but losing with the dawn that surreal sorcerer's magic it held under a dark sky or a full moon. The fountains of the Hôtel de Ville were stilled for the winter, the ice rink that lay now before it empty and chill, the utter loveliness of the Renaissance façade making one forget the drama and violence the city hall had witnessed over the centuries.

She turned her head to gaze at Notre-Dame across the water, against the pink and gold rim of clouds. Breathing hard, she barely noted the man in street clothes with a gym bag slung over one shoulder. As she came abreast of him, something teased through her absorption, and she turned her head toward him.

Just as she ran into the hard barrier of an arm thrust out. She bounced off it, and he didn't even try to catch her. *"Magalie?"* Philippe Lyonnais was staring at her with his lips parted, his gym bag drooping to the ground.

For a second, the quiet wonder of the morning stayed with her. She stared back at him.

The very last person she would have had discover her flushed from cold wind and internal heat, sweaty but chilled, her hair in a ponytail, her classy black and blue running clothes clinging damply in embarrassing places that showed exactly how much and where she sweat.

His hair was damp. There was a gym around here, wasn't there? He had been working out, too, but he had showered after and dressed in elegantly casual street clothes. And was heading now to make some diabolical concoction, which she would see in his windows as she came back onto the island.

She found her back to the wall that kept pedestrians from

falling into the Seine at moments like this. This time, he didn't shift his arm to the wall beside her to half lock her in.

Well, of course not. She was sweaty and nasty.

Philippe's expression was oddly . . . soft. Did the morning workout soften him, too, leave him clean and light? Focused? Because he was very focused, as he always was. On her. She ran a sleeve over her forehead, wiping away perspiration.

"You run," he said softly. He was studying her so intently. Still more softly, as if he was speaking to himself: "I never imagined you like this."

He seemed to blame himself, as if he had assumed he had imagined her every conceivable way. Which was rude. How could he ever presume to think he knew all her facets?

Unless he spent a lot of time imagining her . . .

Her breathing and heart rate didn't seem to be slowing down at all with her stop. There was no justice that he should see her like this. But, with the freedom of that dawn run still filling her lungs, it felt oddly . . . right.

She wished she had seen him twenty minutes earlier, sweaty and messy and pushing all his strength against weights.

Her breath caught. She had stopped running, but her heart rate actually began speeding up.

Or ten minutes earlier, his muscles still engorged from the exercise, stepping out of his shower . . .

She leaned over, clutching at her stomach with one hand and the wall with the other. Maybe she had overdone it on her run. She was starting to feel a little dizzy.

A hand closed around her shoulder. Shock stung her that anyone would want to touch her while she was so sweaty.

"Ça va?" he checked.

She tossed her ponytail off her neck, looking up at him incredulously. Not for him so much as for her. That gentled lion's voice, that concern, was doing something strange to her muscles. No, it was the run. It was the run leaving them weak.

Leaving them feeling so . . . soft. Malleable.

"*Non,*" she said, surprising herself with honesty. No, it wasn't going very well at all.

To her astonishment, she found herself being lifted, and then her bottom hit the cold stone of the wall, and hard hands held her firm there, making her sit but making sure she didn't faint and fall backward into the river.

She peered at him. Didn't he *want* her to fall backward into the river? Talk about a good laugh at the enemy's expense. She would probably only get hypothermia, not die.

He gazed straight back at her, from astonishingly close. Her position on the wall put their eyes at the same level. She could see the striations of the blue, the tawny streaked lashes, the crinkle lines around the corners.

She blinked first. Stirred or maybe even minutely swayed against the pressure of his hands at her hips. They flexed to hold her more firmly.

"*Ça va?*" he said again.

She stared at him mutely.

He tilted his head a little, that way he had when he'd seen her for the very first time.

And again, he just gazed at her. The cold was drying the sweat on her skin. But her heartbeat kept picking up and up and seemed to be almost sending strange hiccups through her blood. Behind him, a bare-branched tree rattled in the wind. He had set her between two green bookseller cases, partly sheltering her from the wind, but still that wind came off the water and whirled around them.

Her island was just on the other side of the water. A bridge away. He could see it, past her, her safety. She could only see him.

"Maybe you're too healthy to eat sugar," Philippe suggested, but softly, musingly, as if he was talking about theories for a fairy story. "Maybe that's it."

One hand left her hip and looped around her wrist, his callused thumb rubbing gently, searching for her pulse.

She knew when he found it, because his thumb stopped. His whole body gathered a great stillness, the one before a lion's spring. Why couldn't she get her heart rate down? She had stopped running. Maybe he would attribute—

He leaned in on her, almost without moving, his eyes holding hers.

"I prefer chocolate," she managed, still with that—that running-induced pant in her voice.

His thumb started to rub again, pushing up under the edge of her sleeve, tracing the fine veins and tendons while his index finger kept track of her pulse. "I can make you chocolate, Magalie. But I wouldn't presume."

"My own chocolate," she said with effort.

He smiled a little. "Of course."

"And Sylvain Marquis's," she added in pure defiance of her damn pulse.

His eyes sparked in annoyance, and his hand on her wrist tightened fractionally, but he only shook his head. His face drifted another centimeter closer, there in the shelter of the bookcases and the predawn. "That's because you haven't tried mine yet."

Her mouth watered, and it wasn't for chocolate. This was a really bad time for this conversation. She felt so . . . open. So unguarded.

It was well-known that running left you vulnerable to all kinds of infections for a few hours after. What had she been thinking, to breathe in his scent? Like a lethal illness, it seemed to be propagating inside her at an alarming rate.

And it didn't even have any sugar or vanilla or roses or lime on it. Right now his scent was just cleanness. A male body that had come only minutes before from a shower.

"Maybe," Philippe suggested softly, a hint of danger sneaking in, "you're afraid."

It was several minutes since she had stopped running, and her breasts still rose and fell just as hard. His finger never left her pulse. "I don't eat poison. But I don't live in terror of it. I know it can't get me unless I let it," she said defiantly.

His hands tightened on hip and wrist, and he pulled her body forward, as if on a surge of temptation to prove her wrong. He caught himself an inch from her mouth, his arms almost completely enclosing her, his chest expanding in a hard breath. His warning snarl heated her whole wind-chilled face. "Magalie. Do you *want* me to be a beast?"

Delicious fear burst through her like the *boom* the second before fireworks filled the sky with colors. If he were a beast, what would he *do*?

"You already are one," Magalie managed.

His hand spasmed up to grasp the back of her neck. "No, I'm not." He pulled her hard against his mouth.

The fireworks exploded. Searing through the air with a high, sizzling sound, and she found herself surging up with them. Her hands slid over his shoulders for purchase, and those shoulders felt so hard under the layers of leather and cashmere. The feeling of it was *more* even than she had thought, larger, denser, a press of sensation against her palms that drove them frantic.

She scrambled into him, dragging her hands over his back, one finding purchase in his damp hair, cold in the winter wind. Her head angled, her lips opened, as their kiss escalated immediately to an intense and intimate battle. Him starving, her starving, who would get to consume whom?

They kissed and kissed and kissed. Philippe held her hard against him, between him and the wall, her legs closing around him, her hips pressing into his lower abdomen, frustrated by clothes and the fact that the wall put her just a few inches too high for the pressure she wanted.

They kissed with tongues and teeth and, pulling back, lips that rubbed and enticed, and tongues that sought again. Her fitted running jacket and jersey seemed no barrier at all to his hands, but Magalie's ran frustrated over his leather, and one found the bottom of his sweater and slid up under it.

He took a fast breath, straight from her mouth, and flinched at the first press of her cold hand against his ribs. But then he just buried himself deeper in her, letting her cold hands run everywhere they willed.

Lights slid gently over them and past, an early-morning car on the boulevard beyond Philippe. Their intimate shelter was illusory, protected only by two green walls and dawn. And Philippe. His body blocked hers from view, wrapped around hers, his hand covering the back of her head, his mouth so hungry.

The muscles of his abs and back and chest under her hands felt hard and warm and resilient, still engorged from his morning workout.

He kissed her while the day broke, the passage from dusk to light a secret trace of pink, like the forgotten blush of a woman who had seen it all. He kissed her while more and more cars passed in the street. He kissed her until it penetrated that a couple of the honks might have been for them. He kissed her until the light drove them apart.

They stared at each other.

For a second, both were absolutely still. Philippe's face looked utterly naked. Meaning her own must look . . . Magalie pushed him so hard, she nearly shoved herself back into the river. He had to catch her to save her.

She felt a wild urge to hit him, kick him, do something to save herself. But she didn't even know entirely from what. Simultaneously, an urge drove her to turn her head, just a little, to rub the corner of her mouth, her cheek, softly against his lips. To see if, now that the first wildness had passed, he might press the most delicate of kisses just there by the lobe of her ear.

"I've got to—I've got to finish my run," she said. *What?* Oh, that sounded inane. Fumbling. *Imbécile.*

"Magalie." Her name was almost a whisper, it was so soft, so enticing.

She wriggled her body down to the sidewalk and away from him, plying her elbows to drive him back. "Cardiovascular and all that," she muttered.

"I don't think you need to worry about your heart rate slowing down, Magalie," he said, wielding that unforgivably pointed truth like a skewer to hold her in place.

She twisted away from it, trying to come up with a riposte. "I've got to finish my run." Pathetic.

"Magalie." Her name caught at her as she turned and took her first step. She glanced back. His muscles were all coiled, his body full of that menacing stillness just before the spring. "If you run, you damn well better feel like a zebra every step of the way."

Chapter 16

She was so pissed off at that sense of being a zebra by the time she got back to her apartment, she couldn't stop cursing herself for running. How else could she have gotten away? Walked? He would have kept pace. Caught a taxi? At six in the morning? And, anyway, any kind of running was running. She suspected he would have gloated at her zebra retreat no matter how she'd made it.

She was not a damned zebra to his lion. He was a toad to her witch. Or . . . a beast. A toad seemed a little . . . small and scaly. It might be she'd prefer to turn him into something she could sink her hands into.

Of course, the only choice to avoid the zebra role would have been not to retreat at all. But that might have left her . . . what? A zebra rug in front of his fireplace?

She was not a damn zebra.

She finished climbing the stairs, feeling her run-tired muscles all six flights. En route to a shower, she got stopped by the mirror and stood staring at herself.

Her hair had escaped her ponytail, whipped free by the wind. Her face was bare of makeup. She never wore a lot of makeup, anyway, but there was a world of difference between a skillful application of natural-looking improvements and seeing her eyes and mouth and cheeks completely bare, stripped further by the wind. Her face was flushed and sweaty.

She didn't understand.

He had kissed her when she looked like *that*?

She turned the water on hot and stepped under it, letting it pour over her endlessly like a substitute for the warmth she had fled.

She finally stepped out only because the heat of the water had faded to tepid and was moving to chilly, and the chill brought her some strength. But rubbing herself dry with her enormous white terry-cloth towel, she shivered again, her skin too sensitive, too hungry for texture and warmth and touch.

After five years of learning how to dress like a Parisian, she pulled out all the stops. Her armor that morning was invincible, designed to bring anyone to his knees while keeping her on her feet. Soft folds of silk fell around her shoulders: a shift one way could have that supple neckline spilling sideways to bare a shoulder, another and the extra cloth slid down between her breasts in a plunging neckline, another still and it drooped behind her, exposing the nape of her neck, a hint of her back. Below the neckline, it grew snugger, kissing the peaks of her breasts, her ribs and waist, and coming down over her hips to her upper thighs. A subtly patterned legging, with a motif up the sides that somehow suggested the old-fashioned line of stockings, disappeared under her top. Large green, fine filigree leaves dangled from her ears. She spent half an hour on her hair, the wisps escaping from her chignon just right.

Over the leggings she pulled on thigh-high boots. She had to make a special quick trip into the Marais to get them. She had been putting off buying them because they were so expensive, and now this year they were really already on their way out of style. But she wanted the leather climbing up her thighs. She wanted that toughness with its vivid, strong message beneath that silk.

When Philippe walked into La Maison des Sorcières, Magalie felt . . . like a zebra.

No. Not quite. A zebra didn't shiver with pleasure at the thought of being caught.

He didn't carry any box in his hands. The only temptation he brought was himself.

His gaze went once, hard, over her body, over the boots climbing to mid-thigh and the neckline currently drooping to a plunge at her breasts. That erotically controlled mouth of his tightened at the message in her armor, and his blue eyes blazed with a message of his own. *Zebra.*

No, I'm not, she blazed right back at him. *Go ahead and try to catch me. I've got teeth just as sharp as you.*

He abandoned her abruptly, like prey he could trap anytime, and zeroed in on the friendly, curly-haired man to whom she had been talking. "Christophe," he said coolly, clearly planning to rend the other man to pieces in order to leave a clear field for himself.

Christophe, who had just introduced himself to Magalie fifteen minutes earlier, gave Philippe an enthusiastic smile from his corner table and toasted him with a cup full of chocolate. When he brought the cup to his lips, a muscle in Philippe's jaw spasmed violently. "I should have known you would love this place, too. I'm lucky Cade mentioned it to me."

Philippe looked as if he wanted to yank that cup out of the man's hands and toss the author of the famous food blog Le Gourmand out into the street. Although it didn't even light on her, the look seemed to stroke Magalie's whole body, smoothing her in one long touch. So at least she was driving him mad, too, she thought. Oh, God, what he must remember of the way she had melted into him that morning. "I wanted to talk to Magalie."

Christophe looked delighted. *"Mais, bien sûr!"* He pretended to grow absorbed in texts, all while aiming his phone subtly. "Don't mind me!"

Philippe's mouth compressed.

"En fait, I was about to show Christophe how to make a couple of our recipes," Magalie said. "He wants to do some entries on us for his blog."

Philippe looked from her to Christophe and then beyond her to the tiny kitchen. A muscle ticked in his jaw. He shook his head once, slow and hard. "I don't think so."

Her chin went up. *"Pardon?"*

His gaze went to her throat and stayed there. Until it was all she could do not to cover it with her hand. The plunging neckline made her breasts feel, suddenly, very exposed. They tingled with the sensation.

Abruptly, something changed in his expression. A softening, and an intensifying. He turned so that his shoulder half blocked them from Christophe and shifted forward. Her elbows bumped the display case. She didn't think she had backed up—surely she hadn't backed up?—but this space left no room to maneuver. He ducked his head, ostensibly to avoid running into the tip of the moon, but the move brought his face very close to her upturned one. His body seemed to curve around her, enclose her without touching her. The chocolate crescent moon twirled slowly above his head.

"Magalie," he said softly and looked at her lips.

They flamed. Or felt as if they did, as if a flush condensed in them, making them too red, too soft, too full.

"Magalie." He touched one hand just grazingly to the wisps of hair allowed to escape from their clasp. The blogger who had broken the Chocolate Thief story was looking right at them. And holding a phone.

"You need a necklace," Philippe said.

"What?"

His gaze rested on the spot between her breasts to which the neckline plunged when it slipped its lowest, the look so vivid, she felt the imprint of a finger. "*Là*. Something green. And intriguing. Something that someone keeps wanting to see more of to figure out what it is."

Magalie took a deep breath that made his eyes, fixed already on her breasts, dilate rapidly. From somewhere, she managed to call up a smile as bright as a rapier. "Now you're going to tell me how to make men look at my breasts? What *would* I have done if you had never barged into my life?"

Philippe's jaw clenched, and for a second she thought he was going to bang his head against something. Since the nearest hard thing was her own head, things could get very ugly fast. What were those dinosaurs she had learned about in school, with the skulls made so thick just so they could batter each other with them? Her education had been spotty, back and forth as it was between school systems.

Philippe straightened so abruptly, he forgot about the moon, and it bonked him on the head and spun away wildly.

He reached up one hand and caught it, something it would have taken her a stepladder to do. Holding the moon still above their heads with one hand, he suddenly placed the other over her folded arms, right under her breasts, his hand big enough that it comfortably wrapped over both her forearms.

She was so surprised at the sudden, blatant claiming, even after this morning, that she just froze, her eyes widening enormously, fastened on his face.

He ran his hand deliberately from that point up one arm, a deep stroke that burned through the silk, tugged the neckline to the side so that it bared her shoulder for his palm, and finally cupped her chin, holding her still for him. His eyes locked with hers. "You *are* going to give in," he vowed.

She was going to give in? Was that how he had seen their kiss? "You're the one who can't resist a woman covered in sweat with her hair frizzing all around her face."

He had just started to turn toward Christophe, and he checked himself. All his focus came back to her, narrowed and dangerous. She smirked. Touched a nerve, had she?

He leaned in so close, his breath tickled her ear. "Do you think I spend all day being fanned by slavegirls and having grapes dropped into my mouth? You're welcome to come visit my *laboratoire* any time, Magalie. Trust me, I've seen sweat before."

"It's exactly what you look for in a woman, in fact," she sneered.

The jab failed to hit its mark. His mouth curved, a sensual lift of its corners that licked her whole body from toe to . . . somewhere around her breasts. The flame of it kept going, burning up her chest and over her face.

"I would be happy to make you sweat, certainly," he whispered to her.

And while her body was still clenching desperately around that idea, he stepped away. Easily. As if it was nothing.

"So, Christophe." Philippe sat in the chair across from the food blogger, easy and in command. Christophe covered his phone guiltily. "How badly do you want me to show you how to make my *Désir?*"

Christophe's eyes glowed with delighted greed. "You're thinking about it?"

"Stay out of that kitchen"—Philippe jerked his head toward the little room with its blue counters, and Magalie's blood went to instant boil— "and it's yours."

He got up and headed to the door, pausing just in front of her while Christophe scrambled for his things to follow.

"By the way, Magalie . . ." He cocked his head and gave her a little, smug smile that made her want to do something drastic. Then he leaned so close to her, her heart skipped a beat and started pounding like mad. "I make my caramel hotter than any other chef out there," he whispered. He held up thumb and forefinger a paper-thin width apart. "*This* close to burning. I thought you would want to know."

Chapter 17

Wen Philippe finally finished with Christophe, without strangling him even once, and got back to La Maison des Sorcières, Magalie had fled.

At least, he liked to think of it in terms of terrified flight, and that she had worried he was going to catch her tail every step of the way. Maybe he shouldn't have been so confrontational earlier, but she drove him insane, the way she'd put that armor straight back up, blades all out, after this morning on the quay. Just when he thought she was finally *yielding*.

Whatever it was she was doing, she wasn't there. Only Aja, who let him in with a benign look and offered him a cup of tea.

Oh, God. These women just would not give up on trying to turn him into a toad. He toyed with the cup and went to the kitchen door, to make sure Magalie wasn't hiding behind the coats. She was small enough. No. It was empty. But he slipped into the blue room to discreetly empty his tea into the sink and spotted . . .

Under those coats—how interesting. A little door, almost entirely hidden.

Philippe glanced back at Aja, but she was following the previous customer to the sidewalk, her back to the room, the two women speaking softly.

He pushed the door open, squeezing the coats against the wall. Outside, the cold air hit him with force, as if laughing at him for not taking one of those coats with him. But there was no wind. He stood in a small, cobblestoned courtyard. Ivy climbed up one wall, but otherwise the space was winter-bare. A lion face gazed at him from the opposite wall of the courtyard, the basin under it clogged with dirt and some brown dead plant.

He looked around but saw only one other door, in the wall to the right.

It opened into a stairway. Narrow and steep, its walls were plain white, giving no hint of what he might find up there.

He set his foot on the bottom stair, half-expecting Aja to come calling after him or Geneviève to come barreling down at him. Or Magalie. His body tightened with hunger. Magalie to confront him. Yes.

But there was no sound, except his own foot hitting the next step, and then the next. He picked up speed, mounting now quickly.

By the time he reached the seventh floor, his heart was pounding hard, and he didn't think he could blame the stairs. He took a long breath, staring at the door, his body tight all over. There was no peephole. She wouldn't know it was him.

How could she have no peephole in her door? That was crazy. This was Paris.

And the door hadn't even been pulled closed properly. He looked down at the knob, the latch not caught, ready to swing open at the first rap of his fist.

He knocked gently. The door nudged a little open, and he caught the knob to keep from barging in. No answer. "Magalie?"

Still no answer.

If she was taking a shower with her door unlocked and half-open, he was going to kill her. "Magalie?" he called, a little more loudly.

Silence. Maybe something was wrong. Had she tripped or hit her head as she came into the apartment? Had someone broken in—was that why the door was open?

He shoved it wide. "Magalie?"

No body on the floor. No signs of anyone, and the place was too small for her to be hiding. So she was all right. She just wasn't there.

Relieved of his fear, he could focus on the room, and the white on white hit him like a fairytale. Arousal ran through him like electricity. He had stepped into the sacrosanct heart of her.

White gauzy drapes streamed over the windows. White walls, not a glaring white but with some tint in it secretly to soften it; his sister would know—blue, maybe. On the wall, a splash of purple—lavender, he realized. A painting of a field of lavender. So that was Provence he had heard bouncing around in her accent, suppressed. There was something else, too, though. A tiny hint of the way Cade Corey talked, except so much more subtle that Magalie couldn't possibly be American. What was her story? Why did he still know almost nothing about her?

A white downy comforter covered the narrow bed, pulled over it a little carelessly. The bed was empty. A wry smile kicked his mouth at the thought of what Magalie would have done if she had been in it and woken to find him kneeling beside her, his kiss tingling on her lips. Waking the sleeping beauty in her tower.

She would love to see him on his knees, he had no doubt. But as for him seeing her vulnerable and kissing her while she was so—judging by that morning and her reaction to it, she would probably hit him.

For himself, he didn't fantasize about having her on her knees. But stripped of all her armor, defenseless in his hands . . . yes.

He crossed to the window, knowing quite well he should

go. But he had to see if she could make out his name on his shop from her windows. He pulled aside the filmy drapes. It was like being at the top of the world here. He could see the Seine, over to the left, past the tip of the island. And the towers of Notre-Dame to the right. And far away, a sliver view of the Tour Eiffel. His heart squeezed oddly at the thought of her standing there at night, watching it sparkle.

And there, yes, not as close or as dominating of her view as he would like, but she could see it: *Lyonnais.* If she liked, she could stand up here and watch for his arrival every day and cast hexes on him. Maybe that was why his shoulders always prickled when he walked into his shop.

He turned away and spotted telltale signs on a sheet pan soaking in her sink. She was trying to get off cooked-on egg white.

Macarons. His lips drew back in fierce delight. *Had* she been trying to challenge him at his own game? And if so, where were the results?

He glanced around for her trash. Now he was getting truly down and dirty, and after this he would have to leave before he started going through her underwear drawer.

Although . . . he had been wanting to know forever what her underwear looked like. Would she by any chance favor black lace, as some of her outfits suggested? Or would it be something airy and white like this room?

He glanced toward the drawers fitted under her bed. *Just check the trash, Philippe. That's bad enough.* He pulled open the door under her kitchen sink. The trash can slid right out, pulled by a chain on the door, and he smiled in feral victory.

There they were. Flat, dry, grainy, pitiful attempts to imitate him. Clearly not enough to satisfy her craving. Heat licked through him at the thought of her frustrated face as she scraped them off the sheet pan and dumped them into the trash. Had she been wearing her boots while she did it, or did she pad around her apartment barefoot? Did she paint her toes with that same perfect armor she wore on her fingernails, or did they get to be bare, here where no one could see? Had she gone to her window to glare down the street at the word *Lyonnais*? Had she imagined strangling him? And had she craved him, longing to sink her teeth into what he made? Or just skip to the source and sink her teeth straight into him?

He heard those heels of hers on the stairs before she got to the door, and he closed the trash away again. That could be his secret weapon, that he knew she was so hungry for him, she was trying to make her own feeble imitation.

As her footsteps got closer, he leaned casually in the window, for all the world as if he owned the place. He would be damned if he would be caught out like a furtive underwear-sniffer, and, anyway, the stance of ownership would drive her crazy.

She stopped abruptly in the doorway, staring at him in a first instant of—what was that? Stunned, hungry confusion? Or was he guilty of projection? And then, of course, outrage.

"What the hell do you think you're doing?"

She carried a couple of elegant bags from a Marais boutique in one hand. He imagined suddenly a scene in which she wasn't glaring at him for being there, a scene in which she modeled what she had bought and asked his opinion. He didn't even care if she was modeling a damn tennis shoe. It was the thought of her being happy and relaxed and eager to share. What a hopelessly arousing fantasy. Hopeless because it was as far away as the moon.

"Invading," he said.

The way she looked at him drove him insane. Her chin up, her throat exposed, until it was all he could do not to accept the challenge and lay his teeth against her skin. Feel the thrill of fear and delight run through her body just before she found out exactly what those teeth were going to do. She liked to look at him as if she despised him, but her eyes kept running up and down his body in a way that left him maddened with arousal. He doubted she even realized she was doing it, most of the time. Sometimes he saw her catch herself and try to stop it: the quick, involuntary flick of her gaze down his body and back up, the lashes that so briefly hid her eyes before the brown was forced back to battle his gaze. Or sometimes on the way back up, her gaze would get caught on his mouth and linger there, or run over his shoulders, or rest on his hand. It drove him *mad*.

She had control of that gaze right now. She was glaring at him.

Yes. Look at me. I'm very clearly not what you wanted. You didn't invite me. But I can make *you notice me.*

"The door was unlocked," he said. "And not even properly closed. You leave it that way a lot in the middle of the city?"

"It's our building," Magalie said impatiently. "Aunt Geneviève's. Who would come in?"

He raised his eyebrows and opened one hand, flicking his fingers just enough to make sure she looked up and down the body of one person who had gotten in. God, he loved it when she looked him up and down.

Rather than admit she was in the wrong, she just angled that chin at him more. "If it had been locked, I'm sure you would have just kicked down the door."

"Don't you have a deadbolt?" he asked incredulously. He glanced past her. *Bon sang,* she didn't. "Magalie. Are you crazy?"

"Aunt Geneviève owns the building."

He knew that. He had looked up the ownership of all the buildings on the island before he bought here. It was, doubtless, one of the things that allowed the women to operate a small shop in an outrageously expensive area. The property was worth multiple millions. The only question was how they managed to pay the property taxes. Not off a *salon de thé* with five tables, that was for damn sure.

"When the shop is closed, the door to the street is locked; the only people who can get inside are the aunts, me, and the tenants on the other floors."

Tenants. That explained the property taxes.

"You've never given any delivery person the code to get in through the courtyard entrance?" he asked dryly. They were a business. Half of Paris probably had the code to get in and leave shipments.

She frowned. "We know our suppliers very well."

Bien sûr, and every person who had ever worked as their delivery boy, too.

"Besides, my aunts would notice if anyone came through," she said with an insane degree of confidence.

He felt like strangling her. "Nobody stopped me."

She frowned at him as if that was further proof of his infamy.

"Get a damn deadbolt on your door, Magalie. And use it."

"I can't believe you!" she suddenly erupted, to his deep satisfaction. "I can't believe even you would have the nerve to break into my apartment and then stand there lecturing me! Get out!"

He folded his arms, so tempted to say *Make me,* he had to bite his tongue hard and think that through. He didn't really want to come across as a man who would muscle his way without permission into a woman's apartment and refuse to leave. She truly did manage to bring out the beast in him. And she hadn't even managed to slip him one of her potions yet.

"I've never heard of a prince getting kicked out of a tower this way. Not that I would presume to call myself a prince, but since you insist," he added in a tone designed to infuriate. "Usually he gets some kind of reward for his invasion." *A kiss, for example.* He refused to say the word out loud. Let her blame her own mind for leaping to the idea.

But Magalie gave him a scathing look that made him wonder if she was about to comment on the origins of those tales, when the invading prince was more likely to rape the sleeping princess than kiss her to wake her up. His head almost blew off. True, she called him a beast, and the prince label was an accusation of arrogance, not of gentlemanliness, and true, he had invaded her apartment. But if she even thought—if it even crossed her mind that he might—if even for a *second* she had the slightest fear that—

"I'm not a princess," she said dryly, proving her mind was off on a different track altogether.

"Yes, and, speaking of which, if you send another spoiled blonde my way, I'm going to feed her something that makes her fall in love with *you,* and see how you like it."

Magalie's arrogant expression flickered. Abruptly she seemed to notice the winter-evening dimness of the apartment and crossed to turn on the light by her bed. Her heels sounded wrong on the apartment floor, too aggressive for this space. He wondered if she usually took them off by the door. Had his presence required her to keep on her armor?

"I don't feed them anything to make them fall in love with you." She frowned deeply, seeming unsure where to put herself. Maybe usually she sat on the edge of her bed now, kicking off her shoes, curling up to examine her purchases . . . His blood surged long and slow and hot through his body at the image. "A poor, innocent princess? Why would I do something like that to her?"

"They don't look that innocent to me, but thank you for reminding me of moral considerations," he said politely. Really? She hadn't been sending those would-be seductresses his way? Something bitter was released in him, dissipating so fast, he had to struggle to keep his fighting form. "It's true, it would be quite reprehensible to make anyone fall in love with you."

Her eyes flashed. He almost laughed. This was fun. He felt aroused and infuriated and so alive, he held himself still only by his years of self-discipline. He knew how to pay precise, attentive care to the smallest of movements, how to wait as long as it took for something to be perfect.

She dropped her packages onto the bed, started to take off her jacket, and stopped herself. Oh, so she would usually shrug out of her jacket about now. And drop it carelessly across her bed or hang it up? No, hang it up. The room was so peacefully uncluttered. "If I wish anything on anyone, it's usually strength and courage and clear-seeing, which they never seem to have enough of. I have no idea why that would lead them to you." She looked as if she had bitten into something rotten in polite company and didn't know where to spit it out.

Strength and courage and clear-seeing. He felt himself draw a long, deep breath, like at the gym when he had just finished a punishing set of exercises well. Or at the Meilleur Ouvrier de France trials when the last, extravagant, impossible spin of sugar held. "Thank you," he said, "for the compliment." The extraordinary, beautiful compliment.

"It wasn't intended." She scowled.

"Yes, I gathered that." But maybe, when she stirred her chocolate and thought of strength and courage and clear-seeing, maybe some part of her thought of him. He reached out and caught her window frame, to give himself some purchase. His hand curled slowly harder and harder around it.

She had just undone him utterly with a few words and might, or might not, be willing to mold him back together again.

She folded her arms, and her foot made a little aborted gesture, as if she wanted to kick her bed. The lamp gave off a soft, warm light that seemed to embrace her tense body. Normally she would be relaxing in that bed, wouldn't she, soft and at peace? "How many spoiled blonde princesses are we talking about?"

"Since I've opened here?" Overprivileged young women who had walked into his shop and started throwing themselves at him as if he was going to catch them? "A few." And he hoped she could recall exactly how beautiful the women had been.

Her arms tightened under her breasts. He wondered if she could catch his gaze flickering over her body at movements like that, the same way he sometimes caught hers. Of course she did. And no doubt gloated. "So you've been having fun," she said dryly.

"*En fait,* Magalie, interestingly enough, I've been working nearly nonstop. Things will settle into a good routine eventually, and the new people I've brought in will learn their jobs enough for me to leave them to it, but for the moment, that's how this goes. And on the few occasions when I've stopped working, it hasn't been to provide an overindulged socialite with courage and strength she should be trying to find in herself."

It was to spend time with his family, because a man had to have priorities. To go to the gym, because it helped him keep his sanity. And . . . well, she was just going to have to figure out the third and dominating focus of his time and attention herself. He wasn't exactly being subtle.

"*I* don't have time to go shopping," he said, gesturing at her bags from the Marais. He regretted the words immediately. Was he playing for pity? That was *not* the reaction he wanted.

She gave his body an incredulous look, shoulders to feet and back again. And of course his body hummed deliciously in response. Pretty clearly, he didn't inspire her pity. So she liked the way he dressed, did she? "The jacket and shoes are from two years ago, Magalie. A fashionista like you can't tell? Plus, my sister likes to shop. And when it comes to clothes, I make quick decisions. I pass a window that has something I like, I buy it, and I keep going to my next appointment. It takes five minutes."

For some reason, that last seemed to annoy her. God knew why. Too arrogant? Too princely? Was she thinking he thought she was a sweater?

He sighed.

The silence stretched, and he wondered why she didn't tell him to get out again. Then a slow smile grew as he realized why. She couldn't, because if he just shrugged his shoulders in response, she couldn't take the embarrassment of not being able to enforce her own orders on her own ground. She couldn't throw him out, and she would probably die before calling the police or in any other way admitting she needed someone to help her against him. Her pride didn't allow her any way of getting rid of him unless he went of his own accord. She certainly wasn't going to *ask* him. And he didn't feel like volunteering to go. This pale room so high above the world, with the soft, luminous light falling all around her, filled him with a strange mix of peace and rightness and that vivid, hungry aliveness.

His own accord liked it right where he was. He grinned at her. That would teach her not to lock her door.

She tilted her head up at that grin and gave him a long, searching look. *Bon sang,* but she was going to kill him with that stretch of bare throat here in the vulnerable intimacy of her private tower. He wished . . . he wished she had invited him in.

She put her hands on her hips. "You know, this is exactly like you. To barge in where you aren't wanted and where you have no right to be, without even the courtesy of asking. Do you want me to show you my underwear drawer, too, or have you got a pair in your pocket already to take home with you?"

He laughed in pure respect for her technique. Drive him into a rage so that he stomped off. *Good luck*. It was *nice* up here. "Not yet, but I wouldn't turn down the offer."

She snapped her mouth shut, and her eyes fulminated.

He tilted his head. "According to Maman, the first time she read 'Rapunzel' to us, I was three, and when she told us about the prince coming back every day with another rag that Rapunzel could stitch together for her eventual escape, I said, 'Why didn't he just bring a rope the first trip?'"

She looked completely lost at this change of subject. What, was the reference not *obvious* to her?

"When I was about twelve years older, it occurred to me that maybe he didn't want to bring a rope. Maybe he was making Rapunzel earn her way to freedom one rag at a time with all kinds of sexual services. That one provided some great fantasies."

Her eyes widened a tad. He loved the brown of them. It made him want to get very close so he could see if her pupils had dilated. Her winter-pale skin flushed.

"But now I've had another idea. Maybe one rag at a time was all he could talk her into. Maybe she didn't *want* to escape. Maybe she liked it just fine in that tower with her witch guardian until some prince waltzed in and tried to drag her out of it."

Her brow knit. She was getting it at last. "I am not," Magalie said tightly, "a princess in a tower."

He only smiled a little and shrugged. "And you don't have to come out of it either, if you don't want to. I like it up here."

"Back to the sexual-fantasies theory?" she said sardonically, and then her foot twitched, as if she wanted to kick something else, possibly herself, for having brought the topic back up.

He grinned very slowly. He couldn't help the thorough look up and down her body as his insanely greedy brain tried to process fifty sexual fantasies at once. "I wouldn't object."

"You know what *I* remember thinking about that story?" Magalie said. The deepening of her flush made his body frantic with heat. "Just another over-entitled man forcing his way in where he wasn't wanted. And that the princess seemed oddly helpless for someone raised by a witch. I always felt like there must be parts to that story missing."

"Forcing his way in," Philippe repeated carefully. He looked once around the soft white of her apartment and down at himself.

"Yes. Someone exactly like you, for example."

"Over-entitled?" As if someone else had given his success to him? There was a reason he wasn't just another Lyonnais; he was *Philippe Lyonnais.* It had all come from his hands, his work, his sense of taste, his inspiration.

"Yes. You know, another selfish, self-absorbed, arrogant bastard."

His mouth set against the hurt of that. "Such flattery." Why did she so determinedly think the worst of him? He got on well with his family and showed respect, albeit sometimes mixed with exasperation, for his parents. He looked after his sister and babysat his niece one or two busy Wednesday afternoons a month, both to help Noémie and because he liked to. His circle of friends was small but very strong, and they could count on him when they needed him. He never beat out his rivals with underhanded tricks but with pure, superior quality. He took on interns to help them forge careers. Why did she always think so badly of him? How much damage had he done to her aunts' business, for God's sake? His staff was spending half their salary at La Maison des Sorcières.

"Christophe came to blog about *us.* He probably would have done two or three entries over time. A couple of recipes, a little piece on the shop. The most-read food blogger in Paris. And you couldn't *stand* it, could you? You had

to figure out a way to lure him off and get even more attention for yourself, even if it meant giving up one of your
prized secret recipes to do it."

He stood very still. He could feel it rise in him slowly, like
the tide, the rage, coming in wave after wave—hitting his
groin, reaching his heart, now his head. "You think I spent
the afternoon showing that damn, encroaching blogger how
to make my *Désir*—my *Désir*—because I wanted to *steal attention from you?*"

She folded her arms. It pushed her breasts up, as it always
did. It sent him a little mad, as it always did. "Clearly."

He turned his head sharply, staring out the window, because wrath was beating so hard in his head, he didn't dare
do anything else. Down below, two familiar forms exited the
shop, wrapped for once in capes against a night too cold even
for them. La Maison des Sorcières was closed for the night.
Dark, empty, full of pointed hats and chocolate lures and
danger.

"Where are your aunts going this evening?"

"A . . . friend's poetry reading," Magalie said jerkily, clearly
thrown by the question.

He turned his head back, still sharp. "What recipe were
you going to show Christophe? Your *chocolat chaud?*"

She hesitated, shrugged, and nodded.

"Your *tarte aux pistaches et aux abricots?* The one you in-
vented because you were dying for my *Désir macaron?*"

She narrowed her eyes. "I was *not* dying for it."

He held out an imperious hand. "Come show me."

Her jaw set. "Will you stop ordering me around in my
own apartment?"

"Magalie, if you will so very kindly come show me . . ."
The beast she woke in him uncoiled in starved delight and
roared. ". . . I will show you why I kept Christophe out of
your kitchen."

Chapter 18

Magalie didn't know exactly what Philippe was up to, but it didn't feel safe, which was probably why she was doing it.

Philippe Lyonnais, asking her to teach him her recipes? That was a triumph, wasn't it? He had finally cracked, and she had yet to taste one single thing he had tempted her with. So why did it feel as if she was placing herself in his power?

The stairs were dim as they descended, lit gently by low lights designed to give just enough illumination to see but not intrude under doorways and wake others. Philippe preceded her, his broad back very correctly between her and any fall down the stairs. But it meant she could not see his face. Just a glimpse of his profile when he turned at the landings, looking very primitive in the dimness.

The trip through the dark courtyard blasted her with coldness again. Nights like this were when she most wanted to be curled up in her bed in her apartment. Without invaders. But maybe with a warm, hard, welcome body curling around hers under the covers . . .

Philippe opened the door for her, and when she passed under his arm and looming body, all dark in the darkness, a thrill of something atavistic ran through her.

It was almost a relief when she turned on the kitchen light, a warm golden color that embraced them. But somehow her heartbeat only seemed to speed up, and she struggled to swallow. She could feel every movement he made through every inch of her skin.

Past the archway of the door into the rest of the shop, everything was dark. It seemed to make their space even smaller, a little intimate hollow of light into which darkness walled them. She could just make out the shapes of chocolate trees through the second archway, silhouetted large and black against the lights in the street.

Philippe very courteously moved behind her to help her off her coat.

It was, of course, what any prince with the barest modicum of self-respect would do. But why did it make her feel all silky and vulnerable, as if his hands had slid over her shoulders, when they hadn't, as if his breath had teased the nape of her neck, when it hadn't? It brought him close enough that she could smell him. He had been making caramel.

He hung her coat on the empty hook on the courtyard door and slipped off his own. The pressure in the little kitchen seemed to rise too high, as if too much air had been forced into a closed space. It didn't take much to fill this space. Magalie, small as she was, could command it all by herself. She and her aunts almost never shared the space, taking turns at making recipes rather than driving one another crazy.

To have Philippe in it, at the same time as she, over-filled it. And she was not even trying to battle him out of it but allowing him in. She would have to turn away from him, bend down, stretch up. To allow him to be that close to her without resistance.

"So," Philippe said, still in that courteous tone. "Which would you rather show me? Your famous *chocolat chaud* that drives men mad? Or the *tarte I*"—his voice silked out over the *I*—"inspired in you?"

"There's really not much to the hot chocolate," she said

uneasily. Drove men mad? Really? How mad did he feel? "It's a very simple recipe."

"Then why not show me both?" He opened a palm in the most chivalrous way imaginable. "I'm in no hurry."

She tried to work up anger at the fact that he assumed her time was equally at his disposal. But the attempt flitted away like an inconsequential distraction.

No hurry.

And when she turned to pull her pot out from the cabinet under the counter, her bottom brushed his thigh.

That thigh didn't move away to give her more room.

Her bottom and the back of her thighs seemed to flame, heat spreading from the point of contact and flushing through her sex.

Her hands faltered as she set the pot down, and it bounced and rang against the burner. There was a whirring sound from the clock in the next room, and a witch laughed evilly in the dark.

Philippe shifted, as if to get out of her way, but it put him just in the spot where her butt went the next time she bent down, to get the milk and cream from the under-counter refrigerator. A refrigerator that a kitchen expert like himself surely recognized behind its cabinet front.

She straightened too fast.

"Allow me," he said, as if the milk might be too heavy for her, and closed his hand around hers on the bottle. The calluses on his palms slid against her knuckles, warmth on one side of her hand, the chill of the bottle on the other, and then the warmth was gone, as he took the bottle and set it down.

"They're the best dairy," he confirmed, seeing the name on the bottle. "I use them, too."

This suggestion of complicity left her feeling oddly warm. Then wary, as if she had caught him sneaking up on her left flank. Since when did His Highness allow anything of hers to be equal to his? She started the burner and poured the milk and cream in, crazily self-conscious, so that she almost couldn't breathe.

The cinnamon scent rose from the cream as soon as it started to heat.

He tilted his head. "You've infused it already."

She nodded. She had made too much that morning for the bare handful of clients who had showed up, but she wasn't going to allow him to gloat by admitting that.

"With what?"

"Cinnamon, nutmeg, and vanilla."

He found all by himself the drawers where the spoons were, showing complete comfort in learning a new kitchen, and pulled out a small spoon. He dipped it into the cream and tasted it, his eyes intent. Seeking out whatever flavors she might not have told him about. He dropped the spoon into the sink without comment.

"The—the chocolate is right behind you." Her voice didn't sound quite right. And at that not-quite-right sound, he did a slow scan of her face that then drifted down her and back up, almost gently. As gently as if he had just brushed her bare skin with a feather the entire length of her body. She tried not to shiver, to ask him to brush her again.

There was the subtlest curve to his lower lip, held tightly down by his upper, an intense, triumphant satisfaction he was trying not to show. She realized suddenly that she could see the pulse beating in his throat.

"Where?" he asked, and if he hadn't turned, she might for a crazy second have told him where she wanted to be brushed with feathers. His thigh brushed against her again as he bent and hesitated before the two cabinets.

She tried to pull herself together. "Here," she said, automatically reaching under his bent body to the right cabinet.

"Ah." His fingers closed around the cabinet handle just a

fraction of a second after hers did, so that his hand in fact closed around hers. His arm brushed the length of hers. "I'll get it."

But when she tried to straighten, she found herself tangled somehow in him, her back running into his chest. "*Pardon*." He curled a free hand around her waist to steady her. "I must have—" He gave a slight laugh of apology as she shifted away from him just as he shifted in the same direction. She turned back—just as he turned back. Two more dance steps and twice the steadying hands on her hips before her body finally rubbed free of his. By that time she almost couldn't get her body to move away; like chocolate held too long, it seemed to want to cling to his skin. "It's a small kitchen."

It was, true, but for someone who was used to negotiating kitchens filled with dozens of chefs and assistants, all running around with things like boiling caramel, he seemed inordinately in the way. Maybe the prince of the kitchen had gotten used to everyone else yielding to him.

"Maybe I should call '*chaud, chaud, chaud!*' every time I move," she said dryly—the cry of "*hot, hot, hot!*" his chefs used as they negotiated one another's space and their pots of dangerous liquids.

That surprised the oddest crack of laughter from him, which he instantly muffled.

She had holes in her vocabulary concerning some of the cruder forms of French slang, but she remembered something suddenly from her last year in high school here. To call a woman *chaude* was to say that she was *sexually* in heat, and it was not at all the kind of thing a man would say to or of a woman he respected. She shot him a dark glance.

He held his hands up, palms outward. "*I* didn't say it." His mouth curved wickedly. "Although I wouldn't object."

Confused, she concentrated on something she could control, the giant black bag of *chocolat couverture,* flat, oval pieces of Valrhona chocolate that would melt perfectly into the milk and cream. She dipped her fingers into the bag, coming up with a handful that overflowed.

He slipped his hand under hers, fingers curling up to partly enclose it, before she could toss the chocolate into the cream. "Let me see?"

The rough feel of his palm against her skin was growing so erotically familiar, anyone would think she was Pavlov's dog and had been trained to associate it with satisfaction. Instead of tormenting, elusive temptation. A pleasure on the other side of a wall of pride.

She stared down at their hands, the chocolate in hers spilling out, a few ovals brushing his palm. She wanted to just stay there, her hand enclosed that way, until the chocolate melted in the warmth of their hands, or until—

She swallowed and upended the chocolate into his palm. But it was too late. Some of it still clung to hers, streaks melted against her skin.

She hadn't even put on an apron, and the box of tissues was on the far side of him. She brought her hand up and sucked the most obvious streak from the heel of her thumb.

When she looked up, Philippe hadn't moved, but his presence filled the kitchen like a physical force. A physical force that was lifting her up and pressing her back against a wall. His gaze was fixed on her mouth. Slowly he tilted his hand over the pot so that the dark ovals slid one by one, gently, into the milk and cream.

A drop of hot milk splattered up onto his thumb. On the inside of his palm, traces of chocolate clung to the heat of his skin. Her stomach clenched as she waited for him to bring it to his mouth, but he reached behind him for a tissue, gave it a rather exasperated look, and wiped his hand clean with it.

She reached toward the bag for a second handful.

He caught her wrist. "You should wash your hands."

It cut across her increasingly dazed senses. She frowned.

He dropped her wrist and cursed, low. She could swear he

was cursing himself. *"Pardon.* I'm used to professional kitchens."

Implying this was what? Her eyebrows drew closer together.

"And this isn't a professional kitchen, of course," he hurried to excuse himself. "But you do serve people."

He considered her so insignificant, so far beneath him, so unconsciously. While she . . . she was practically melting all over him. Like the damn chocolate that *he* had wiped off with a Kleenex. And given a disgusted look to.

She pressed her lips together, her eyes startling her by stinging as she turned to wash her hands. She took her time washing them, until that stinging was entirely under control. "Just exactly how would you describe this kitchen, if it's not 'professional'?"

There was a moment's silence. Then he moved in close behind her, his body brushing hers. His words stirred the hair on the top of her head: "Magical. Outside time. Outside anybody else's control. You probably turn health inspectors into toads."

She turned her head, tilted up to try to see his face, surprised and warmed all through. But he was too exactly behind her. To see his face, she had to turn around. She had to be willing to turn around, knowing that, as close as he was, her breasts would brush his chest, that they would be standing face-to-face, impossibly, intimately close.

She felt his breath stir over her temple and the top of her head, as he waited for her to do that.

If she did . . . if she did . . . Terror and hunger stirred in equal parts. *Did* he respect her, as the "magical" description implied? Or did he dismiss her value, as it had seemed with his comment on the unprofessional kitchen?

And if she knew for certain that he respected her, would she still be as terrified? Or even more so?

"I think my aunts handle the health inspectors," she said

vaguely. Not turning. Very much not turning. "I've never seen one."

A little laugh. "Maybe I should up our diplomatic negotiations. I wouldn't mind being under the umbrella of that protection."

When was he going to move? Never? Her back flexed involuntarily, as if he had just drawn his finger slowly down the length of her spine.

But he hadn't touched her. She twisted just enough to catch a glimpse of his face, her shoulder bumping his chest.

He lifted his gaze from the small of her back. His eyes were dilated, leaving only a narrow rim of blue. She could see the faint growth on his chin since that morning's shave, and the tiny scar that could be the result of anything from a kitchen accident to a boyhood escapade.

His head started to dip toward hers.

She twisted fast, as if to meet an attack, and just for a second they were chest to chest, and her breasts burned from the contact.

"*Le chocolat.*" She dipped sideways and felt his frustrated breath over the nape of her neck as he turned after her. It felt like the graze of a bullet.

But when he slipped back beside her, he didn't seem frustrated at all. She glanced up at him, puzzled and feeling . . . hunted.

What an exquisite and limitless amount of patience and persistence it must take, not to mention control of both himself and everything around him, to produce the desserts he did.

His hand slipped into the three-kilogram sack beside hers, brushing down her arm until he could bury it in the *chocolat couverture,* his fingers tangling a little with hers through the rounded, hard chocolate. "Let me," he said, as if his goal really was just to learn her recipe.

But that hadn't been his goal. Her mind fragmented under

the flex of his fingers as she tried to remember exactly what he had said just before they came down here.

He lifted out a handful of chocolate. "About this much?"

She couldn't tell. His hand was such a differently sized measuring cup than hers. She held her hand, palm up, and he poured the chocolate ovals into her palm. They slid over her skin, too much for her to hold. His other hand came up fast, just under hers, catching the overflow. And sandwiching hers, not quite touching, shielded by ovals of chocolate, between his.

She felt a kiss on her wrist above the chocolate, another on her temple. She looked up fast, but his face wasn't bent anywhere close enough for his lips to have actually touched her. Why did she keep imagining these touches? Was she so desperate for them, forcing wish-fulfillment into his glances? Or was that maybe what he was thinking, when his glance touched her wrist, touched her temple?

He smiled down at her, but there, lancing clearly through that smile, despite his best efforts, was the carnivorous edge of his teeth, the lion scenting triumph.

She dumped his big handful of chocolate into the milk and cream, equal to almost two of hers. This might be her darkest chocolate ever. The scents, in abeyance when they arrived, filled the kitchen now, overwhelming his caramel, making the world one breath of chocolate, wisped with cinnamon and nutmeg.

It took the chocolate only a few minutes to melt. She whisked it gently until the milk and cream turned a deep brown color.

"And that's it?" he said silkily, his body in too close to hers, dominating hers, like a spy trying to worm out her last secrets. "That's almost exactly what I do, Magalie. Except my chocolate comes from the finest plantation in the world and is sold to only a select few of us who have earned the right to buy it through our reputations. And I bring it to room temp correctly by itself and let the milk cool back down to match it the way you're supposed to and then whisk them together so that they're as smooth as silk. But all my chefs drink *your* chocolate. Are you sure you didn't leave anything out?"

He had just told her four different ways her chocolate-making wasn't up to *his* standards. And probably even she couldn't just dump the chocolate on his head. "Well. Usually there's a smile," she said.

"What?"

"When you stir it. There's a smile." She pressed her hand vaguely on her belly, that place from which the smile seemed to grow.

"A smile." He slid his hand over hers on the whisk, and warmth engulfed her before he took it away. "Like this?" He stirred the chocolate slowly, looking down at it, a little smile on that fine, sensual mouth that seemed to burn in her breasts and raise the hair on the nape of her neck.

"And . . . and the wishes," Magalie admitted.

His gaze rose from the chocolate and held hers. "What wishes would those be, Magalie? Wishes to humble a man? Wishes for him to fall in love with a woman who would torment him?"

"You didn't drink it," she protested quickly. How had he even realized she had tried that?

His body brushed hers so that she could feel the tiny change in pressure with every breath he took. "Maybe you're underestimating the power of the scent."

"Oh." She tried to pull back, but his arm shot around her and stopped her, protecting her from the burner. "So who do you think I've made you fall in love with?" she demanded hostilely.

He shot her a startled, confounded look, his eyebrows pulling together. "Someone . . . completely reprehensible," he said slowly, as if trying to digest something very strange.

His arm tightened around her, and he spun them suddenly, so that she was pushed back against the sink, out of danger of the burner.

Her body kicked with delight at being pressed between him and the sink again, but before she could make another choice—to melt or resist—he had released her and was turning back to the chocolate. And she stood there feeling deprived to have that choice taken away from her.

"A smile and wishes," he said softly, stirring the pot three times slowly with a very dangerous smile. He dipped a spoon into the mixture and blew on it gently, his lips so faintly pursed.

Her whole body seemed to dissolve in desire. She wrapped her hands around the edge of the sink. "Shall you try it, Magalie?" He proffered the warm but no longer burning spoon right to her lips, so that she had to fold them in to keep from tasting it involuntarily. "See if I've gotten it right?"

What would he wish on her? She wanted to open her lips around that spoon so badly that in pure terror, she put up a hand and knocked the spoon away, the chocolate spilling from it onto the counter by the sink and spattering on her sleeve.

"No?" He flicked off the burner and shifted back to stand very close to her, so that his thighs brushed her hips. The barest sway would bring his weight against her. "Have you figured out yet, Magalie, the real reason I wouldn't let Christophe spend any time at all in this kitchen with you?"

The reminder flicked through her, bringing her eyebrows together. "It's not your kitchen."

He took her hand.

She shivered all over. Embarrassed at how visible that reaction had been, she bowed her head, angling it away. She wished desperately that the war of pride between them was over, that they could just ball it up like a wad of paper and toss it away. If he wasn't who he was, she could melt against him now. But if he wasn't who he was, she wouldn't want to so badly.

He spread her fingers and closed them around his wrist. It took her a second to realize he had placed the tip of her thumb directly over his pulse.

Just where he had held her that morning, reading her every helpless reaction to him. Now he gave that knowledge to her. His pulse was racing out of control.

She rubbed her thumb, just grazingly, the same thing he had done to her.

He made a soft sound, and his body swayed into hers.

She looked up, pulled out of her own shame. That vulnerability—open, admitted, handed to her like a trust— undid her. She stretched up without even conscious volition, seeking the scent of caramel that must be hiding under all that chocolate, somewhere, there, in the hollow of his throat.

She, who loved chocolate so much, found herself burying her nose in the caramel scent like a warm and golden refuge.

He brought his free hand up, cradling her there, holding her face against him, his head arching back so that she could feel the muscles of his throat taut against her. The pulse under her fingers raced madly. The way he gave that to her, let her have that proof of his vulnerability . . . *that* crumpled the walls of pride between them like paper and dropped them at their feet.

She sank more deeply into him, boneless, relieved beyond bearing. How had she stood that hardness between them before? How had she kept fighting?

Her fingers climbed up his chest, flexing and exploring, digging into him, and it felt so *good*. As if he had been made for her to explore. As if his heat could take away every cold night that ever was.

He made a low sound that vibrated against her ear and buried his hand in her hair, trying to pull her head back as his own head bent. But she had the advantage of size. While he was all exposed to her, she could hide her face in him . . . and try to taste that caramel off his skin.

Both his hands tightened spasmodically on her at the flick of her tongue. He lifted her and whirled her, suddenly, her body pressed the length of his, to the one spot they could fit in that warmly lit kitchen and be completely out of sight of the street—against the courtyard door.

"Magalie." Her name was as rough along her skin as his hands, sliding up under the silk of her top. She shivered as they ran hot along her ribs.

He tasted warm and golden but not like caramel at all, something much more alive. He tried again to pull her head back, and again she resisted. She liked this spot. She liked being buried in him, wrapped in his heat and shadow, the feel of his muscles contracting under her touch, the way his body tightened all around her, his head bending over her, his arms wrapping around her.

He didn't use strength to force her head up. Instead, he pulled her kneading left hand from his chest and stretched it over her head against the door. Holding her prisoner, his hand wrapped around hers and his body pressing into her, he brought his mouth to her wrist.

And then he did things to her there that she hadn't even known the world contained.

Rough prickle of beard, silk of lips, graze of teeth, and the delicate tasting of his tongue . . .

Her muscles gave way.

"Let me," he murmured with prickle and silk against the sensitive skin. "Let me in."

Limp, she slid down the door until the only thing holding her up was his hand pinning hers to the wood, her body dragging on her arm. He could have supported her with the crush of his body, but he didn't. He pushed her sleeve up her forearm and tasted and prickled and petted her wrist until there was nothing left of her. No strength anywhere.

She was mindless, her fingers curling in and out of her palm. He caught them in his mouth, suckled them lightly. Those that were neglected curled against the prickle and hardness of his jaw, against the edge of his lips. He breathed into the center of her palm and scraped it tenderly and then gentled that scrape with his tongue.

No one ever in her life had done anything like this to her. Not ever. Taken one part of her body and rendered her mindless. Or rendered her precious? He made love to her wrist until they both knew exactly how helpless she was, her body dragging so heavily against the hand that held her that anyone would have thought she was past consciousness.

Then he pulled her up at last. Grabbing her hips and dragging her up on his thigh, dragging hard so that her sex rubbed against his leg. Her head fell back now, no muscles left to resist, and he took her mouth the same way he had taken her wrist—with prickle of beard, silk of lips, graze of teeth, the questing of his tongue.

The scents from their coats rose around her, hers, his, and the cold city scent the coats still carried from outside. The clasp at the back of her head hurt, pressed too hard against coats and door, and she pulled it out.

His mouth was open against hers, his tongue tangling with hers when she did it. She felt his gasp steal air from her as her hair spilled down.

His hands were occupied, on her torso: rubbing the silk over her skin, kneading it into her muscles and breasts and bone, slipping his hands under it, sliding everywhere. His hands taken, he pulled his mouth free from hers long enough for a gesture that entirely undid her: he pressed his face into her freed hair and stroked once the length of it to her shoulders, like an animal.

She buried her hands in the pelt of his hair, shivering.

He pushed her top up all the way to her shoulders and drew back enough to meet her eyes. A question.

She closed hers and lifted her arms above her head.

That gesture, waiting in the dark of her own eyelids for him to draw the silk over her head, was even more her undoing than his face stroking her hair or his mouth on her wrist. The moment of choice and the choice she had made—to agree to this, to all of this—left her hot and damp and fragile with arousal.

"Yes," he breathed, a growling purr. "Yes. I knew—" He broke off, his thumbs tracing the edge of her black lace bra, pressing gently into the soft skin, slipping under it, his palms cupping her nipples. They rubbed, and then rubbed harder as she arched.

"Knew what?" Still she had a trace of challenge left. How dare he *know*?

"Nothing." He gave a rough, strange laugh, as if there was so much tension in him, it squeezed the laugh almost to nothing. "I just dream really well."

She arched again helplessly, pressing her sex into his thigh as his hands grew greedier on her breasts. "Dreamed—me?"

"God, yes."

"Like this?" The coats burred against her bare back.

"It's one of the ways." He helped her with that ache in her sex, gripping her hips, dragging her hard up and down his thigh and then grinding her against his sex through his jeans.

Her thighs wrapped around his waist. Need pressed through her, frantic, relentless. Midnight-dark eyes, heavy-lidded, fixed on her face at that, and he ground her against his sex again, rotating this time, rocking her.

Her eyes widened desperately. She clutched at him, almost afraid.

"Yes," he said hoarsely. "Yes, yes, yes. Let me in." His hand found the side zip on her pants so fast that he must have located it sometime before and kept track of it just for this chance. He pressed his hand in through the tight fit of the panel over her pelvis, slipping his hand down to find the folds of her sex.

The silver doorbell chimed.

Philippe jerked his head up. Cold horror shot through her.

He tried. Cursing, yanking his hand away, wrenching at the coat behind her, he tried his best to get her at least covered.

But Geneviève and Aja blew straight back into the kitchen before he could even get the coat free of the hook.

Philippe was the only one who didn't freeze in petrified embarrassment. Cursing viciously, he kept his body between Magalie and them, slipping her paralyzed arms into the overlarge sleeves, zipping it up over her bare skin. One of her breasts was spilled lopsided out of her bra, the nipple rubbing against his jacket lining. Oh, God, oh, God . . . Philippe looked into her face and cursed again. "All right, go," he said, in furious resignation, easing back enough to pull the door open and push her through it, his body still her shield.

"What kind of poetry does your friend write, exactly?" he snapped at the aunts as the cold froze her bones and she fled. In all the times she had heard him angry, she had never heard him this angry. Wild with it. "Haiku?"

Chapter 19

Magalie would never, ever, in a million years forget the cringing horror of that moment. Caught half-naked in the kitchen by Geneviève and Aja with Philippe Lyonnais.

Oh, God.

She writhed with it, all night. She curled into it, in fetal humiliation, and then found her hand trying to take advantage of the position to slip between her thighs and relieve the desperate, hot, unsatisfied desire.

She threw herself back the other way, locking her hands in fists under her pillow, and saw Aunt Geneviève's face again.

Then she saw Philippe's, flushed and damp and purely furious.

Then she saw Aunt Aja's.

Then she wondered what the hell hers had looked like and flinched into a ball again. Since she had been half-naked at the time, what did her *face* matter?

She kept hoping the writhing would be interrupted by a knock on the door, the return of her intruder, so she could throw things at him or at least commiserate with someone. And then get rid of this hot desperation between her thighs. But he never came.

She thought about running away from home.

But she couldn't stand the idea of losing her place here. This was the truest place she had ever had.

She considered wearing a mask around her aunts for the rest of her life, and dark sunglasses with it.

Maybe not only around her aunts but whenever she had to walk by Philippe's shop.

Walk by Philippe's—

God, she was never going to be able to walk down that end of the street again. He had stolen half her island from her!

She tried to calm down and think of something else, and then flinched into her arms again, covers pulled entirely over her body, as she saw their faces.

That bastard Philippe. She would *kill* him.

He had done it on purpose. "I'll show you why I didn't want Christophe in your kitchen." He had *planned* it. In advance.

Maybe not planned to get caught by Geneviève and Aja, because a more appalled, furious expression than his when that silver bell chimed, she couldn't imagine. But planned to *seduce* her. As if she was some pathetic person who could be seduced by calculation.

Which, apparently, she was.

That bastard.

She had no doubt what that bastard had planned to do with his fingers just before they got caught. Oh, God, why couldn't that poetry reading have taken just five minutes longer?

She delayed as long as she could going downstairs the next morning, and thus ran right into Geneviève and Aja coming out of their apartment, having apparently delayed as long as *they* could. She jumped. They jumped. Everyone looked somewhere else.

"I'll just—I'll just go start the *tarte* crusts," Magalie said and ran down the stairs as fast as she could.

★   ★   ★

It didn't get better from there. Magalie dropped things. Spilled things. Aja and Geneviève cleared their throats at odd moments and gave each other embarrassed looks that she caught whenever she lifted her head.

She burned the crusts. She cut her finger just when she finished stirring a pot of chocolate and had to start all over because her blood dripped into it. And when one of Philippe's chefs, Grégory, showed up, she had just flipped a fresh *tarte* out of her hands and was scrubbing it off her shoes, trying not to cry. She glared at him. The employee of her enemy was not her friend. Plus, for all she knew, Philippe had been gloating to him.

No, now she was growing ridiculous. *More* ridiculous, if that was possible for someone who had gotten caught in flagrante delicto by her own aunts the night before. Even she knew that gloating over any aspect of his sexual affairs with his employees wasn't Philippe's style.

Grégory looked distressed by her glare and glanced for help at Claire-Lucy, who was sitting in her favorite corner, nursing a cup of chocolate. "I just, ah, was hoping for some *chocolat chaud*. Do you need help?"

"Probably," Claire-Lucy murmured. She was watching him very curiously, her mouth a little stained with chocolate.

Magalie was not letting another man into her kitchen at the same time as she, ever. If that damn bastard Philippe could get to her, she was clearly sugar that would melt at a drop of water. "I'm fine. Just give me a minute."

At least she hadn't worn any of her nice boots today. Of course, that was Philippe's fault, too. Cringing before even the slightest hint of sexiness in any combination of clothes she put on—had she marked herself as a slut?—she had eventually unearthed the only pair of flat shoes she had besides her running shoes—thick, fuzzy, warm snowboots, resistant to all kinds of ill-treatment. With those, she was wearing jeans and a heavy, dolman-sleeved, midnight-blue sweater that emphasized a small waist but otherwise did absolutely nothing to indicate sexual desperation in any way. She would have worn a sack, but the dolman sweater was the closest she could find in her entire wardrobe. She had twined her hair in one simple braid behind her head and left off makeup and was looking about as subdued as it was possible to look.

A decision that was already starting to wear on her.

"Are you feeling all right?" Grégory searched her face. "You look a little tire—different." His head tilted, as he digested the look. He didn't seem entirely turned off by it.

She went and got his chocolate. Sitting at the table, he gave her another crinkled, surprised look when she brought his tray to him. "I don't think I ever realized how small you are."

Maybe she should go back upstairs and change. There was only so much wallowing in humiliation she could take. This was getting old already.

"Monsieur Lyonnais sent something for you." Grégory looked wistful.

Magalie stiffened. And missed her heels in the worst way when she tried to brace herself aggressively. "I don't want it."

"Really?" Grégory brightened just a little. In her corner, Claire-Lucy ran a finger around the rim of her cup of chocolate, broodingly.

"Yes." Magalie folded her arms, just to make sure that whatever Grégory had brought couldn't be forced into her hand. "Why should he send me anything?"

To see if he had cracked her finally so he could gloat to himself that she had been the first to cave in? If Grégory opened some Lyonnais box on another tempting, luscious concoction, she would go completely mad.

Grégory looked puzzled. *"C'est la Saint-Valentin."*

She knew that, of course. That was the reason they had a witch hiding a rose-heart in her basket in their display case, to remind women not to hand their hearts out to any idiot who walked along just because of some stupid holiday. Aunt Aja made extra-strengthening teas today, and Geneviève made *tartes* that were pure chocolate darkness to nourish a woman's depths and fight off any silly feeling of emptiness.

Magalie stared at Grégory with a strange, blushing confusion. What did it mean that Philippe was sending her something—via an employee—on *la Saint-Valentin*? Unlike the confusing American version of Valentine's Day, *la Saint-Valentin* in France was pretty straightforward. No cards to be passed out to all your classmates, so no way you could be caught out cardless when you were five years old and your French mother didn't know and your American academic father was clueless. In France, *Saint-Valentin* gifts were for your spouse, your lover, or your very clearly declared intended lover, and that was about it.

She swallowed and folded her arms more tightly. "I'm not eating it, and I don't want to see it."

"It's not a pâtisserie." Grégory handed her a small sack that bore the logo of an innovative New Zealand-influenced jeweler in the Marais. Magalie had often lingered in front of her display windows. Beyond the island, the Marais was her favorite quarter.

The card inside it bore no message. Just one word, a firm, slashing signature: *Philippe.* The large square box opened to reveal a tiny green pendant, subtly intricate, so that you turned it and turned it to see a woman, held in a crescent, her slim form stretching up so that she strained to just reach the top tip of the crescent. A card from the jeweler also lay in the box, explaining the symbolism: the Polynesian goddess-heroine Hina and her moon. She glanced involuntarily at the moon above the display case, remembering Philippe rattling the door as she was hanging it. The chain stretching away from the Hina-moon pendant was pure, shimmery silver, so pale and shining it was probably platinum. And so spiderweb delicate, it looked as if the brush of a finger might break it.

"He's busy—that's why he asked me to bring it. He wanted to make sure you got it early. He said he would be by later."

He wanted to make sure she got something early—as if she should be *expecting* him to send her something on *la Saint-Valentin*? As if she could be hurt if he didn't? Magalie flushed crimson, staring at it.

She had to fight the urge to hug herself, cuddling something precious. If she had been alone, she would have.

"So you and he . . . ?" Grégory let his voice trail off, and there was that hint of wistfulness again. Magalie eyed him discreetly and realized something else Philippe had just done. By asking one of his chefs to carry this gift to her, he had very clearly marked her as his territory to that same chef.

It made her blood boil, but not in the nice, hot, rapid boil she was familiar with. It was more like bubbling chocolate, rich, tempting, something you ought to pull off the burner quickly before you ruined it—too slow, too delicious for a proper rage. Or maybe more like bubbling caramel, golden, hot—and, according to Philippe, something he'd mastered completely.

Not her. Her caramel was scorching.

"You should see what he's been working on today," Grégory admitted. He shook his head a little. Once again, his eyes met Claire-Lucy's, inviting her to share his ruefulness. "Or maybe, being you, you shouldn't."

Chapter 20

Philippe was afraid. He had seen Magalie's face the night before when her aunts found them, and he knew something could go very, very wrong here. She could cast him out farther than he had ever been, so that he didn't just need lockpicks and temptation and determination to get back in but a compass and very strong rowing arms to cross the vast, cold sea.

He was so afraid that on that busiest day of the year, when demand for his most perfect creations could not be satiated, when men got off work early and waited in line for an hour to find the one thing that would brighten a lady's heart . . . he delegated all of it. For the first time, in all the years of Valentine's Days, he had his own heart to worry about.

He focused until all the noise of the kitchen, and even the intern upending an entire tray of freshly finished *Couronnes,* crushing strawberries, pistachio, cream, and cake on the floor, didn't distract him. Someone told him later that it had happened.

At the half of a marble counter that he had taken for himself, he whipped aged egg whites. By hand. A little smile played over his mouth at the intensity of the whipping. God knew, he needed something on which to take out his frustrations after last night. That morning's brutal workout at the gym had not done it.

He dusted in sugar so fine that breathing on it raised a cloud around his hand, like the puff of a magic spell. He added coloring until the meringue was as brilliant red as heart's blood, knowing that when it cooked, it would pale to a perfect pink, and no one would ever know the intensity of the passion that had gone into it. He rubbed almond meal in his palm, ground so fine it felt silky and warm against his skin, processed it with equal parts confectioners' sugar, and folded it in.

While the meringue shells baked, he experimented with the ganache that would fill them. It was *la Saint-Valentin*. And she had indeed turned him into a beast. Maybe he should offer her a rose.

White chocolate and cream, rose syrup, and three drops of attar of roses. No, it needed something more. He prowled his shelves of ingredients, dry and fresh, in and out of his refrigerators. Occasionally he tasted something. He stopped before a case of rambutan, picked up from an Asian market in Belleville. The little red monster-fruit was prickly and hard on the exterior, but for the curious person who braved it, the skin could be split easily enough to reveal the silky, sweet interior, a clean, fresh flavor similar to lychees.

A little smile played around his mouth. If this was indeed the flavor that would match with the roses, how appropriate.

Splitting the skins on rambutan after prickly rambutan gave him immense satisfaction, especially as his fingers gained in deftness, and they fell to him more and more easily, the rubbery little thorns a pleasant defiance against his fingers. Especially as that defiance *yielded*. Rambutan, roses, cream, white chocolate . . . as the chocolate melted under the hot cream, as he blended the ingredients together into something unctuous and extraordinary, he thought of pale skin and pink secrets, of melting a person and making her body yield everything to his touch.

Let me in.

I will make *you notice me.*

Not the greatest anger or the greatest will in the world will keep your mouth locked tight against me.

Still it needed something. A heart. He thought of that rose heart hidden in the witch's dark-chocolate basket in Magalie's window. A secret in the middle, that last burst of bliss, her body helpless as he held it . . .

As the ganache cooled, he prowled the fillings they had made the day before, until a deep, intense red on one of the shelves of his cold-storage rooms caught his eye. Raspberry gelée. Normally intended to be tucked in tiny heart shapes into one of his dark chocolate *macarons,* for Valentine's Day, but he wouldn't offer Magalie chocolate. Her life was full of chocolate. The gelée was as intense in color, heart's-blood red, as the meringue had been before it baked to a soft, deceptively gentle pink. One small square, the exact size of his thumb on her pulse, on her breasts, on her mouth, on her . . .

He tucked it inside, nestled in the heart of the creamy pale ganache, hid it under the pink shell.

And stood back, uneasy. It looked so . . . naked. Vulnerable. The pink shells filled with pale cream. He couldn't do that to her. Maybe he couldn't do that to himself. What was inside this *macaron* deserved protection.

He bit into a raspberry from the flat shipped up fresh from his greenhouse grower in Spain. Sweet, tender, so fragile before his teeth, so perfect on his tongue. From those raspberries he made armor around the vulnerable edge of the ganache, nestled between the two shells, hiding it from the world.

He tasted one. Oh, yes, *perfect.* He glanced up. Despite the insane rush of Valentine's Day, half his kitchen had crept around him, eyeing the rose and raspberry *macarons* hungrily.

He held up a hand, and they launched back to their posts like trained tigers before a whip. But they looked over at his counter as they worked. He would be getting acid comments about sub-par *pâtisseries* in reviews the next day.

He stood looking at the finished product for a long moment.

Then abruptly he left the shop and walked down to the florist, standing in line behind all the other men waiting to buy roses. The florist, arranging and wrapping with ribbons and cellophane in a mad whirl, grinned at him happily when he finally got to the counter. "For Magalie?"

No, he hadn't been subtle, had he? How could Magalie not know?

"I loved the Valentine's post."

What?

"Le Gourmand," the florist explained.

He would have to find out what Christophe had done and murder him later. He couldn't spare the concentration now. His focus was entirely dominated by the creation waiting to be finished on his marble counter.

Back in his *laboratoire,* he pulled the petals carefully from one rosebud. He laid just one of those red petals, so perfect and silky and precise, on the top of the *macaron* shell, cocked his head a moment, and then pursed his lips and found some glucose syrup. Just one tiny bead of it, like dew, on the petal. And one raspberry, a hint of a crown. Or perhaps, he thought with a flicker of a smile, a hint of a nipple peaking to his touch.

He picked it up very carefully and laid it in a pink box stamped with his name.

Chapter 21

La Maison des Sorcières always felt quiet and secret after the glamour and rush of Lyonnais. Philippe usually felt a strange brush of peace when he stepped inside, as if he was peeking into a refuge that was denied him. But today it was oddly packed, and Geneviève and even Aja glowered at him, as if it was his fault. He knew right away, when his heartrate slowed down, that Magalie must not be in.

A woman in her forties was paying Aja for a small bag of crystallized violets and another of blue rose tea at the vintage cash register, while two more couples waited just inside the door. A woman sat by herself before a splendid tray of chocolate at the table between the upright piano and the display, writing in a journal. In the room beyond, an older couple dug antique silver forks into rough-hewn slices of chocolate *tarte* and smiled at each other serenely, no need on their Valentine's Day for Lyonnais glamour. But the three other tables were taken by couples who looked oddly similar to his own glossy clientele.

Despite the fact that the place didn't seem that peaceful today, all the tension left his shoulders.

And he stood there, rose-heart in hand, deflated, knowing that if Magalie were there, his shoulders would still be braced for a fight.

Geneviève drew him back into the kitchen, and she and Aja eyed him speculatively. Philippe felt a blush rising to his cheeks. And he hadn't even been the one half-naked last night. Maybe Magalie had jumped onto a passing barge and headed off into the unknown rather than face that look.

"What's this one supposed to do?" Geneviève asked, as he set the gift reluctantly on the blue counter. He had wanted to hand it to Magalie. He had wanted to see her face. "Break her heart?"

He sighed and rolled his shoulders. "I see where she got her trust in others."

Geneviève raised her eyebrows. "What she's got of it probably did come from us, yes. Very self-reliant, Magalie. I think she believes something of her will break if she ever lets herself need anyone. Besides us, I mean, but it took us a few years."

Was the woman actually giving him a hint? "And why is that, do you think?"

Geneviève snorted. "I don't think, I know. But you'll have to get to know her your own way. Or not, as the case may be."

"I did offer you some tea," Aja said peacefully, as if his difficult harvest completely failed to trouble her, since the seeds sown were his own.

"You have a tea for understanding Magalie?" Philippe asked incredulously. That seemed a little specialized, even for this place. Not to mention which, there were limits to all magic.

Aja gave him a serene look, clearly indicating that if he had wanted to know what her tea did, he should have drunk it.

"Where is she, anyway?"

Geneviève arched her eyebrows at Aja. "What was his name?"

Philippe's gut clenched.

"He said he had promised you not to set foot in our kitchens, so she agreed to go to his."

Rage rushed up in him like a volcanic explosion.

"I was surprised he talked her into it," Aja said with great approval. "Magalie is very attached to this place. He might be good for her, that Christophe."

Geneviève shook her head. "I don't know. Don't you think we should talk to her? This place is getting so crowded, I don't know if I can take any more. I should never have let those puppy eyes of hers and Sylvain's talk me into helping him with his window. And if she's going to get us written about in blogs next . . ."

"It reassures her," Aja said, like someone repeating an argument for the thirtieth time. "To know that she can attract customers despite *him.*" She gave Philippe a dismissive look.

"Yes, but we're the ones people come hunting in the depths of the forest! We're not the ones who put a castle on a hilltop and wave a flag to get attention. I don't *like* the kind of people who come just because they've seen a waving flag."

"It won't last," Aja said soothingly. "Let her get over this. It will die down eventually, or we'll close more hours and send them all his way." A slight flick of her hand, as if brushing crumbs off a dirty table for Philippe to scrounge.

"I hope it doesn't last! If this keeps up, we're going to have to dig up this shop and go hide it in a new place where no one knows where we are, and you know that would destroy Magalie. So we're stuck."

Philippe had a brief, terrifying vision of La Maison des Sorcières running off on chicken legs to an African jungle or something. He reached out and just barely stopped himself from grabbing Geneviève, who probably would have atrophied his arm with a look if he had. "*Don't* you move anywhere else."

Geneviève sniffed. "Well, keep more of your customers down your way. They're not my type."

Philippe ground his teeth, a gesture he didn't even know he had in him. "Magalie takes every person who comes to my shop and not yours as a personal insult."

Geneviève squinted at Aja. "When *I* was twenty-four, was I that confused and fragile?"

"I didn't know you when you were twenty-four," Aja said repressively. "But when you were twenty-six, the drop of a pin could knock you off center. She's doing fine. She's just small, still." She held up her fingers in a circle about the size of a walnut. "She has to crack through that shell, put down roots, and grow."

"Why would it be so traumatizing to Magalie to move this shop?" Philippe interrupted suddenly.

Both women ignored him. "I guess that's why we should let her keep on with this nonsense," Geneviève sighed to Aja. "Doing things like going to play in Christophe's kitchen are probably a sign of growth. Nobody said growing pains in others weren't annoying."

"Plus," Aja said sweetly, proving exactly how mean she could be to someone who had snubbed her tea, "it's very romantic to be going to make chocolate for a man on Valentine's Day, don't you think?"

Philippe had to turn around and walk out. He almost took his "heart" with him. It cost him. It cost him bitterly to leave it lying there outside his body, in witches' hands, while the witch it was for was away making her chocolate for that damn bastard Christophe.

Who would never, never, never set foot in any of Philippe's kitchens again.

Fury burned through him. As he went back to work, it ate at him until it seemed to spread out from him through his entire *laboratoire*. He worked in silence, his mouth a harsh

line, imagining two people in a kitchen somewhere across
Paris. He had Christophe's address somewhere. He had to
restrain himself from looking it up. Even he couldn't storm
in there in a jealous rage.

He kept his mouth a grim line, because if he opened it, he
didn't know what would come out. Even in his silence, the
force of his anger seemed to take over the kitchens, until
other people were snarling at one another. The desserts they
sent out, so deceptively beautiful, were probably going to
break up half the couples in the city. Or at least lead to some
passionate fights.

"What happened?" Grégory finally asked him, low. "Was
it the blog post?"

Philippe whipped his head to look at the younger chef.
And then he went into his office, shoved some books off his
laptop, and went to Le Gourmand's blog.

Chapter 22

Philippe Lyonnais aime . . . Christophe's blog post read for February 14, a takeoff of the *petits plaisirs* of *Amélie Poulain*. Under it was a picture of Magalie's chocolate, her own hand curved around the handle of the pot the way it should be curved around *him,* the liquid streaming thick and dark into a cup. Even with the Web's theft of some of its rich color, the photo was enough to make anyone starve.

He hadn't ever even drunk the damned stuff yet, Philippe thought in acute agony. Half of Paris was going to be flocking to La Maison des Sorcières, imagining themselves savoring what delighted *him,* and he would still not know what it tasted like. Or what it would do to him. What she wanted to do to him.

Putain de bordel de merde. What was she doing to Christophe right now? That man could wheedle himself into all kinds of territory where he didn't belong.

"On this *Saint-Valentin,* what does *le prince de pâtisserie* love? He loves rich, thick chocolate stirred by a *sorcière.*"

Another photo, this time a close-up of the tea shop's window display and the dark-chocolate witch with her little basket. One could just catch a glimpse, but probably not recognize, the tiny sliver of the rose-petal heart peeking out of the basket.

"He loves the magic brewed in this shop, La Maison des Sorcières."

An excellent photo of spilled crystallized violets made Philippe wonder suddenly if Aja would be willing to supply him some for a violet and chocolate *macaron*.

"Does he even love a witch?"

Philippe stood staring at the last photo. His own expression in it didn't surprise him in the least; he had known that about himself for some time. But Magalie . . .

"Philippe Lyonnais!" Christophe exclaimed happily. "You're the person who enchanted Philippe Lyonnais!"

Magalie stirred uneasily in his kitchen in the Ninth Arrondissement, a very nice kitchen, quite spacious for Paris, with a little island, even; but she really liked being in her own. The whole chocolate-making felt wrong here. Whom was she supposed to be luring?

Christophe was entirely likeable, attractive in a fun way with his curly hair and his enthusiasm, but she kept seeing Philippe's face every time she glanced down at the chocolate, and the thought of luring Christophe instead made her physically ill.

Christophe didn't seem to care so much about being lured, though. He seemed to be triumphing over the fact that he had lured *her*. But her worth to him seemed to come from Philippe, as if the world's best *pâtissier* had cast value on her just by looking at her. An idea that drove her insane.

"Do you know he was apprenticed part-time when he was fourteen? When he was nineteen, he took charge of the new Saint-Germain shop, and within the year he had a dessert featured in *Le Monde*? At nineteen! And he loves you! I haven't had this much fun since the Chocolate Thief story. *Thank* you for coming."

"I don't—I never said—Philippe Lyonnais—l-l-loved

me." Just trying to get the words out made her hyperventilate. *Philippe Lyonnais, love me? Love me?*

"I saw him myself. And I talked to his staff." Christophe made a kindly, dismissive gesture at her modesty. "Everyone knows he's obsessed. And *they* can't get enough of your hot chocolate. It's a beautiful story. And I get to be the first to tell it! Did you see my blog post for today?"

"No-o." Magalie's whole reason for working with Christophe had been to get a blog post from Paris's most famous food blogger about La Maison des Sorcières. She should have been delighted to learn he had already started writing about her. But given all this talk of Philippe's obsession with her, she was a little hesitant to see what he had actually posted.

"Look!" Christophe said enthusiastically, whipping out his laptop. "Don't you love this photo?"

Magalie looked at the title. *Philippe Lyonnais loves.* She blinked, feeling dizzy enough that her own pot of chocolate in the photo started to look like an abyss she could fall into.

He scrolled down.

And her body folded a little over the screen as if it had just reached out and punched her.

There was Philippe, leaning into her, the crescent moon over their heads, a bare inch between their lips. The hunger in their faces was so . . . naked. *She* looked as if she would die for him. Die to have him close that last inch of space and kiss her.

"I've already had 150 comments!" Christophe said gleefully. "There's another one right now: *Damn it, I hate her! I wish I could enchant him.* Don't take the hating thing seriously—you have to have a thick skin when you blog. And there have been thousands of hits. You'll have lines out the door tomorrow."

Yes, but at what price? She didn't *want* the whole world to see her naked. Good Lord, Philippe might be looking at that photo right now.

★ ★ ★

Magalie wanted a mask to wear on her way home. She told herself that, given the two million people who lived in Paris and the eleven million within its greater perimeter, thousands of hits on Christophe's blog did not make her notorious, but she felt overexposed. She wanted to put that deadbolt on her door that Philippe had talked about.

What had she been doing, trying to beat the lines at Lyonnais? She didn't *want* lines. She wanted to be private and secret and recognized only by those who sought out something rare.

She was glad to be back on her island, welcomed by its seventeenth-century calm. But when Thierry waved at her and asked if she had liked her roses, she blushed, her heart beating like some strange muscle that didn't know how to work anymore. Had Philippe sent her *flowers*?

She snuck glances at Philippe's windows as she walked past but could barely see them through the lines of men waiting to buy the perfect Valentine's gift. He was probably too busy even to gloat over the fact that he had such long lines and La Maison des Sorcières had none.

She touched a finger to her bare collarbone. She hadn't put on the necklace Philippe had given her. But she wished now that it lay there, in secret under her sweater, filigree chain and moon warmed by her skin.

There were no lines at all before La Maison des Sorcières, despite the blog post, and she felt exhausted. Maybe part of her didn't want to deal with Philippe-style lines down the block, but it hurt her that, even stripped naked for the world to see on a blog, she kept failing at the attempt to matter more than he did to people.

She discovered that the door to the shop was locked, and she focused on the sign written in Geneviève's cryptic, slanting script. *Morally opposed to Valentine's Day. Closed in protest.*

She sighed and let herself in, leaving the door unlocked

and taking down the sign. It considerably complicated her efforts to generate more business that her aunts continually sabotaged the attempts.

She showed Aja the sign in the kitchen, with a raised eyebrow.

"Oh, Gen just needed some space," Aja said easily. "I'm sure you can take it down now, if people have gone away."

Magalie sighed and threw it into the trash.

"So how did it go?" Aunt Aja asked. Dressed today in a warm brown *kameez* and *salwar* pants embroidered with golden yellow, she was humming while she boiled grapefruit peel three times. Three times, she said, was the key to clean all the bitterness out before she could turn it into sweet, intense candied fruit. *"Tu l'as aimé?"*

Did you like it? Magalie heard. She started to flush. "We didn't get that far," she muttered in embarrassment. Seriously, sometimes Geneviève seemed to have worn off too much on Aja, with the indiscreet questions.

Aja's mouth might have twitched. She poked at her grapefruit peel with a wooden spoon, watching the beads of air form under the surface but not quite rise to the boil. "After two hours in his kitchen, you don't know if you liked it or not?"

"It's *not* Philippe's kitchen. He can try to dominate it all he wants, but this kitchen stays *mine*. *Ours,* I mean."

Aja tucked her lips in, her eyes dancing. Bubbles began to rise to the surface of the grapefruit water.

"And it was hardly two hours," Magalie muttered. More was the pity. In two hours, they could have . . .

"I *meant* this afternoon," Aja said, with such excessive gentleness, it was clear she was trying not to laugh her head off. "Did you like *Christophe*? Really, Magalie. I *am* always a little curious about these male-female things, but I hope you don't think I would ask my own niece to describe her sex life to me."

Magalie choked. Damn French pronouns. They could be a little more precise. *Tu l'as aimé?* Anyone who was completely obsessed with an abortive sexual encounter could have made the same mistake.

"Unless there was some sex life with Christophe, too?" Aja suggested.

"No! *Tata!*"

Aja shrugged. "Well, that's what you choose when you keep your barriers up. Either you can have no one, or you can have lots of superficial someones. If you want to have something more than that, you have to make room for the person. And trust that person to make room for you."

Magalie hunched her shoulders, feeling sullen. Only Aja and Geneviève could make her hunch her shoulders. "It's not so easy. We're like ganache; when you make room in yourself, and then the other person is gone, your shape is all—funny." Her hands worked the air uneasily as she remembered the many times she'd ended up with that funny, unbalanced shape. Trying to get her chocolate ganache of a soul, long since cooled and hardened into what she had thought was its right shape, to lose the imprint of those missing others and return to a nice, smooth whole. Unfortunately, her soul seemed to be really lousy at melting again and stayed misshapen for a pathetically long time.

"Haven't we made room for you?" Aunt Aja said gently. "The way Geneviève and I make room for each other?"

"Of course you have!" Magalie said on a rush of love she didn't even know how to express, except by always being there, being the heir and apprentice they so wanted. Their needs and hers suited each other perfectly. If only she could keep this place safe.

"But it's true the spot could close, I guess, if any of us chose," Aja said wisely. "If you love someone, you have to make room for that person every single day."

Magalie shook her head involuntarily. She had often thought that Aja and Geneviève's relationship was like a fairytale, out of this world, those nearly forty years of constant, supportive life together. Aja's experience of couplehood didn't match what Magalie had seen of it elsewhere at all.

"Don't you think you are worth room in others' lives?" Aja went on.

"Of course!" Magalie's jaw went out stubbornly. For some reason, her own affirmation made her eyes prickle. She had been making room for herself, over and over, for so long, only to lose it again, it was like a bruise on her heart.

She couldn't stand prickling eyes.

"You're our heir, Magalie. In our wills, this shop and this building go to you. Didn't you know that?"

She had known it. And long been grateful for it. Her aunts had given her a permanent home. A place in the heart of Paris that would always be hers, if she didn't lose it. There were so many ways she could lose it, though. For instance, a small witches' shop could lose its economic viability.

"Do you think if you left, that room we've made in our lives for you would be gone?"

Well, of course. That was human nature. Magalie set her jaw, not willing to insult her aunt with the truth. Besides, she wasn't going to let the space for her here close over, because she was never going to leave it.

Aja studied her for a moment and sighed. "It's true that if friends can never count on you being there the next time they need you, the place they leave for you might be very small. That's self-defense. If you abandon people—even if it's not your fault—they will eventually get over you and find someone else. Good for them. But you're an adult now, and you can build things as deep and as long-lasting as you want to. I wish you wouldn't underestimate your ability to make people love you."

If her pride hadn't prevented her, Magalie would have wrapped her arms around herself protectively. "I think I'd almost rather talk about my sex life."

"Really, Magalie. I wouldn't want to invade your privacy." Aja dumped the water off the grapefruit peel, taking a layer of bitterness away, and half filled the pan again with cold water, still more bitterness to go. "Philippe left something for you, by the way."

She moved, and only then did Magalie see the pink box Aja had been blocking from view while she said what she needed to say.

Magalie's whole body kicked into overdrive, longing sweeping her. And fear. What would it be this time? What would she have to resist?

She took the box out into the little table in the entrance area and sat down to make sure she was stable. And very slowly opened it.

Oh, Magalie thought, as if she had been hit in the stomach. *Oh, oh, oh.* It was his most beautiful one yet. Exquisite shells of pale pink closed around some secret heart of ganache or buttercream, she couldn't tell. Couldn't tell because raspberries, pure deep red, circled whatever secret was inside, hiding it from view. One raspberry crowned it, beside one exquisite rose petal, beaded with a tiny drop that suggested dew but had to be glucose syrup. It was February, after all. The dark, perfect reds of the fruit and petal rested against paler pink, the surface of the *macaron* so glossy and smooth, not a grain of sugar left visible in the meringue that had made it.

Just for a moment, it was as if someone had brought an exquisite rose in the heart of winter into her dark, warm cave. She was having trouble breathing. It looked so utterly beautiful. She wanted so badly to sink her teeth into it. Slowly, carefully, with all due respect, letting her mouth linger over every instant of the pleasure: the delicate bite of the *macaron*

shells between her teeth, the tart-sweet juice of the raspberries spilling out, the unctuous cream inside . . .

It was a rose. It was a heart. It was a princess's crown, stud-
ded with red jewels. It was the treasure box that the third son
brought back from his quest to win the fair lady's heart.

It was a trap.

If she ate it, she might never be herself again.

And being herself was all she had.

If she ate it, he would win. He would know he had won.

He was flaunting his skill. He was gloating over her as he
so easily dismissed her *chocolat chaud*.

It looked so beautiful.

Maybe she could let him win.

Maybe she could let him make her into something else.

Was it really more important to her to stay Magalie than
to eat a bite of this?

She sat staring at it.

The silver doorbell chimed, and her head jerked up, but it
was only Madame Fernand, exquisitely dressed in clothes
that had gotten too big for her thinning body, with her
bouncy poodle pulling at the leash. Magalie ducked behind
the counter and bent down to pull out the package of tea Aja
had made for her.

It took her only a second to find it, but while she was
down there, she heard Madame Fernand make a soft exclamation.

She lunged up, hitting her head on the counter. Madame
Fernand was fighting with her poodle, its paws up on the
table. Magalie dove for the box, her body brushing past the
dog's as she caught it. She tripped over the chair legs, tangled
with the dog, and fell sideways, catching the rose-heart just
short of the floor. The raspberry fell off and rolled across the
wood.

The poodle scarfed it up and tried to snatch the pink *macaron* from Magalie's hands.

Magalie growled.

The poodle faltered.

"I'm so sorry!" Madame Fernand tugged ineffectually at the leash. "She was at it before I could stop her. I'm so sorry, *ma petite*. Was it from that young Lyonnais? He does make beautiful things, doesn't he?"

Magalie came to her feet, shaking. She couldn't believe the stupid poodle had eaten that raspberry. *Her* raspberry.

You've already touched it. Eat it now before something else gets it. Can we please just find out what it tastes like?

In private. She did not dare taste this gift in public view. She recovered the box and closed the *macaron* creation very carefully inside it, then set it on the top of the display case, out of reach of poodles. Madame Fernand kept excusing herself in her high, failing voice, as Magalie held the door open for her.

All at once, the dog jerked, sending the old woman careening. Magalie caught Madame Fernand as the dog yanked its leash free and darted down the street.

"Oh, dear!" Madame Fernand exclaimed. "I just don't know what I'm going to do with her."

Magalie righted the woman, making sure she was steady on her feet.

"Sissi!" Madame Fernand cried, in vain. Down at the end of the island, the poodle trotted across the street into the park.

"I'll get her," Magalie said.

Her boots weren't the best for running, but she found the dog at the tip of the island, down on the lower quay.

She stood still at the sight, her face flaming in outrage and humiliation. For the poodle had apparently run with a purpose. Gérard's rangy German shepherd was humping her enthusiastically, the poodle standing still for it, panting happily.

And all that from one raspberry.

Chapter 23

Magalie stalked through his kitchen, in pursuit. Philippe, caught off guard while correcting some apprentice's touch on a Taj Mahal of sweets, looked up, and his eyes flared. Bright, vivid. Hungry and supremely triumphant all at once.

He probably thought she was about to throw herself at him, wrap her legs around his hips, and kiss him for all to see.

"Those . . . those dogs." She could barely speak. "After the poodle ate that—that *perfidy* of yours, she—she . . . What do you think you're playing at? You obscene bastard."

"You gave my *Coeur* to a *dog*?" Philippe's voice built until the last word was a roar that knocked down a fantastical castle of spun sugar, *macarons,* and rose petals three counters away. His apprentice flinched, the ganache spurting out of his pastry bag in a jagged blob.

Philippe reached out and grabbed her, too hard, by the upper arm. He had never grabbed a woman like that, in pure fury, in his life, and when she nearly hauled off and hit him, her hand coming up, he shook his head, shook himself, and gentled his hold. She didn't hit him. Which he rather regretted. He didn't give a damn if she *beat* him at this point, as long as she took out *something* physical on him.

"Let's take this somewhere else," he growled between his teeth. He had a reputation for *not* exploding in his *laboratoire,* at least not with anything other than laughter. Or, fine, an occasional, "*Non, non, non, non,* non!" if an apprentice insisted on doing something carelessly *again*.

He swept her into his tiny office. She let him. She grinned savagely, as if he were inviting her to caged combat.

"What did you do while you were making it?" She turned on him as he shoved the door closed behind her, her shoulder rubbing under his arm. He took a hard breath and kept his arm right where it was, caging her. If she didn't mind him looming over her, caging her, he sure as hell didn't mind doing the looming. She was feral, dangerous. Any minute now, she would leap at him. Please. "Did you imagine me crumbling at your feet, begging, with every drop you put into it?"

His hand clenched against the door behind her. His voice went rough, as if she'd dragged it raw. "I *imagined*"—he brought his other arm up, both locked now on either side of her head—"superfine sugar spilling like dust over your bare shoulders. I made the shell of the *macaron* silk, such perfect, glossy silk, like the silk I rubbed over your skin last night."

The flame of a blush ran over her face.

"I imagined you turning just exactly that shade of rose." His eyes swept her face, and his pupils dilated further at what he saw. His voice got rougher still. "I didn't get the color dark enough."

Her hands flinched to cover her cheeks. She forced them down. She was probably battling that blush with everything in her. And failing.

"I imagined closing my teeth so gently around that raspberry, in the middle of that silky pinkness, that I didn't even break the surface of it."

Her nipples peaked; he could see them through her silk top. So she knew what he was talking about. And she liked it.

"I imagined touching it with my tongue. Still just texture. Still so careful that I didn't even have a taste of its tart, sweet juice. And then I imagined sucking it into my mouth . . ."

Magalie's head fell back against the door, her lips parted. Her anger seemed to be fleeing, melting. Like the flimsy excuse it had been in the first place. But *his* anger wasn't.

"The rose petal was because even I couldn't make from sugar something soft enough for your skin."

Her eyes were so dilated, so hungry. He hoped hunger for his touch ran over her everywhere, the way hunger for hers did him. He hoped she was *starving*.

"And what's inside it"—his face was so close, his lips were almost brushing hers when he spoke—"you'll never find out, because you fed it to a *putain de chien*."

He shoved himself away from her and walked out.

Chapter 24

Magalie sat in her room, high above the island, ensconced in creamy white. The radiator was on high, but she was cold. They were predicting snow.

Outside her window, the night sky was as dark as Paris got, the lights from the city flushing up on the underside of the snow clouds that tantalized it. Would it snow, or wouldn't it?

Magalie wrapped her bathrobe tighter around herself and curled her toes in her fluffy socks against the comforter and stared at the raspberry-bereft *macaron* sitting in her lap.

She brought the lid down over it to hide it and studied the name *Lyonnais* until it seemed branded somewhere inside her. As if he had laid claim to her soul.

She opened the box and gazed at the work of sensual art inside it again. The missing raspberry was like a blasphemy, an accusation of her cowardice. If she hadn't hesitated so long . . .

The drop of glucose still balanced perfectly on the rose petal, like a tear.

She curved her hands under it, the *macaron* shell glossy against her palms. *I made the shell silk . . . like the silk I rubbed over your skin.* She lifted it up to the level of her mouth.

It begged her to eat it. Just one bite.

She kept seeing Philippe's face. *You gave my heart to a dog?*

That was just a play on words, of course. He must have named this new creation *Coeur*, the way he named others *Désir* or *Envie*.

It looked so exquisitely beautiful, she couldn't understand how anyone could have made this for her.

She set it back into its box and got up suddenly, pulling clothes back on, an extra sweater, and snow boots instead of her usual heels because . . . well, it was cold, and they were predicting snow. And she felt . . . humbled. She bundled up in her heaviest coat, because it was a way of cuddling herself even as she ventured out, and went back outside into the evening.

The lights at Lyonnais were all out. Grégory was just locking the door.

Magalie stopped, burying her hands in her pockets. A plastic sack from a shoe store hung from one of her wrists.

Grégory turned away from the door and saw her. He paused, clearly surprised, then came toward her. "Philippe's gone home."

Oh. Magalie buried her hands deeper, fisting them so that she scrubbed her knuckles against the bottoms of her pockets. "Where—" Her voice was rough. She cleared it. "Where's that?"

The address he gave her was in the Marais. Not too far. She could walk it in under ten minutes. But over the bridge and across the water, off her island.

She rubbed her knuckles into her pockets again as Grégory said *bon soir*, his mouth twisting regretfully, as if he was saying *adieu*. The street was quiet. On the island, it grew quiet at night. In the Marais, there would be more noise. A lot more noise. It was Friday night, *la Saint-Valentin,* and couples would be filling the restaurants and bars and walking close together against the cold.

She stood still, there in the middle of her silent street for a while. The cold ate into her, and that teasing promise of snow.

She swallowed, lifted her chin, and set off.

Couples strolled, laughing and romantic, all around her as she stood in front of Philippe's seventeenth-century building, and for once no part of her felt as if she needed to brace herself a little, keep her chin up. For once, all these other people just made her feel . . . quiet. She thought they were charming, and she wished she was one of them, walking along with her hand tucked in someone else's. One particular someone else's.

She took a deep breath and pressed the button by apartment 3B and realized as a brusque *"Oui?"* came back through the intercom that she should have cleared her throat first. *"C'est"*—she paused and tried to swallow her hoarseness away. *"C'est Magalie."*

She heard a rough indrawn breath. And then a clicking sound as the door released beside her, and she pushed it open.

He met her at the first landing, running down the stairs in a T-shirt and jeans. Barefoot.

He stopped very still when he saw her. "Magalie."

She gazed back at him mutely.

A couple came out of the apartment on the same landing and nodded at Philippe politely and, by extension, her, although not without discreet glances at his bare feet. The couple was dressed for an evening out. She was reminded of how early it was for a city like Paris. Did she and Philippe *both* start getting ready for bed so early? Him, well, presumably because the work in most pâtisseries started around 4:30 in the morning. Her . . . because she liked to curl up in her own space.

Philippe hadn't even remembered to nod back at the couple. He had a way of focusing that shut out everything else, and right now he was focused on her. He held out a hand. "Come up."

It took her a second to realize that he wasn't going to lead the way up the stairs.

Of course, he wouldn't. Her mouth trembled between wryness and understanding. He was a prince. It was bone-deep in him to climb stairs behind the woman when she went up and before her when she went down. In case she fell.

His hand reached again, angled lower, starting to curl around the handles pulling at her wrist. She realized he was offering to carry her sack. She shook her head, climbing the stairs before him, conscious of his presence so close at her back.

From the door of his apartment, one could look straight across the wide-open living space and parquet floor to great windows through which came lights and colors and life on the streets a few floors below. Lamps glowed through curtains and blinds in the windows of the equally old building across the street. The open curtains on Philippe's own windows made her feel extraordinarily exposed. But no lights were on in the room to show her to those outside. The space was gently illuminated only by the lights in the street.

She crossed to the windows slowly, mostly so as not to look at him yet, conscious of the muted sound of her footsteps on the parquet, quieter still on the opulent carpet in the center of the room. *I come in peace,* her absence of heels seemed to say.

"Do you want me to draw the curtains?" Philippe asked just behind her shoulder. She did not start. Even though his bare feet had been perfectly soundless, she had felt him behind her every step of the way. The same way, no doubt, that a zebra felt a lion prowling behind it. That so pissed her off, the zebra image. "No one can see in unless we turn on the lights."

The activity in the streets below promised fun to anyone who ventured out. Just witnessing it made the evening seem exciting. She was not retired in her cozy room, where she had started feeling so lonely.

From his furniture came an impression of elegance and quality, a modern, clean look in muted colors. The thick carpet across which she had walked was a rich gray, for example. It surprised her, with the intense jewel tones and flamboyant structures he used in his work. Did he, too, seek something quieter when he retired into himself? Or was muted simplicity the best foil for his dramatic creations?

She turned to face him, and he stood a foot away, watching her. He did not move back to give her room. But he did not lean forward to make her feel enclosed, the way he had many times before. He waited. A pulse jumped in his throat.

"May I take your coat?" he asked, and her eyes flicked up to his. A second of silence beat between them. If she took off her coat, she was planning on staying. If he offered to take it, he was inviting her to.

"Yes," she said. And heard the breath he drew.

When he slid her coat off her arms, he did not touch her at all. She could feel him, behind her, not touching her. So graceful and practiced with that coat removal, with his elitist, Sixteenth-Arrondissement education.

She set the sack on his small dining table, in the kitchen area of the large living space, so cleverly divided by furniture from the "living room" area. She had seen an article a week before on his sister's interior design of his shops; she must have done this place, too, but it was very different. The clean, elegant juxtaposition of age and modernity was exquisite.

From the sack, she drew the Lyonnais box and set it, opened, on the center of the table, so that he could see the rose-heart *macaron*.

He said nothing. From behind her, she could feel the intensity of his focus. Waiting.

"The poodle only got the raspberry," she explained, and she had to clear her throat. "I fought her off for the rest."

Another beat of silence. "And may I ask what about that made you so furious? Other than the fact that it came from me, of course."

Her face flamed. She set her jaw, trying to force the explanation out. "It was—she only ate the *raspberry*, one raspberry—and then she, she let the . . . you know that German shepherd that wanders around the end of the quay?"

He made a half-strangled sound. Was that a half-strangled *laugh*? She gave him a burning look. "The, uh, the unneutered male German shepherd?" he asked. Oh, yes, he was definitely strangling a laugh. His voice trembled with his effort at neutrality.

She rapped her knuckles down hard on the table and said nothing. Her mouth set defiantly.

He burst out laughing, wrapping an arm around his middle and leaning forward to grab the back of a chair with the other. "I'm sorry, I can't help it," he apologized between gusts as she glowered at him. "I'm just—I'm seeing—oh, you must have been so *mad*." He said that with pure delight.

She glared at him, imagining him bursting into flames from her look alone. Oh, if only that were possible.

"And all that from just one of my raspberries?" he crowed.

She turned completely around, fists clenched hard. The bones of her fingers kept trying to warn her that it would hurt if she hit His Highness's jaw, but she could barely resist, nevertheless. "Do you think I am a bitch in heat?"

He stopped laughing, staring at her in shock. "*Bon Dieu,* Magalie. Of course not."

The shock was so sincere, the fury in her started to relax.

His lips pressed together. Laughter snuck up past them,

like steam escaping from under a pot lid. The lid abruptly abandoned its effort, and he burst out laughing again. *"Pardon, pardon,"* he apologized helplessly. "I just—I keep seeing—you must have been *livid."*

Well, he certainly enjoyed the thought of making her livid, didn't he?

She pulled the next item out of her sack and set it down with a thump.

Philippe stopped laughing as if she had flipped a switch. Next to his open box now sat a small Ziploc bag of *couverture* chocolate. Exactly as much as she would need to make a pot of *chocolat chaud.* In the same bag were zipped one cinnamon stick, nutmeg, and one vanilla bean. She pulled out a glass bottle of milk and set it on the table with a click.

The silence built between them until they could hear every laugh from every happy couple in the street below.

"Très bien," Philippe said. "A sip for a bite. Go ahead, Magalie. Do your worst."

Chapter 25

As she poured milk into a pot, and cream, Philippe took a small carton of raspberries out of his refrigerator, allowing Magalie a glimpse of fruit, yogurt, and not much else inside it. He bit into one of the raspberries, and her mouth watered at the thought of the sweet tartness on his tongue. Her breasts tingled as if he were closing his teeth around her. Satisfied with the flavor, he selected the largest, reddest raspberry in the flat and placed it exactly in the center of the *macaron*. It took him almost no time, as if he were a laser beam, so focused, so fast, and the result—once again stunning.

She had to tear her gaze away. She so desperately wanted to bite that *macaron* right out of his hands.

She dropped the cinnamon stick and vanilla bean into the liquid and added a quick grating of nutmeg, turning on the stove, and Philippe came to stand with one palm on the counter, watching her from less than arm's length away. He pressed the side of his head against the cabinet, his eyes slumberous and utterly focused at once. "I think this is the most erotic thing I've ever done."

She flushed and fumbled with the spoon. He just watched with lazy eyes that were not lazy at all.

"Or had done to me," he clarified.

She wanted to say something about taking things for granted, but when she met his eyes, she saw that he didn't

take this evening's outcome for granted at all. All of him—
every muscle, every nerve, every bit of intellect and
instinct—was concentrated on making sure that outcome
was what he wanted.

"It's as if I fastened my own wrists to a bed with silk
scarves while you looked me over," he breathed.

The flush spread to her breasts and filled them with so
much desire that it had to find an outlet downward through
her body, spearing through her, heating her.

"But the advantage is, I still have my hands free." His low
voice brushed her whole body up and down like fur.

She tried to concentrate on the stick of cinnamon, bobbing helplessly in the sea of white she was bringing to a sim-
mer. The scent warmed her face.

He shifted with the same easy, deliberate movement she
was using to stir the pot and came up behind her. One of his
hands rested on the counter to one side of her, his other
curled over the edge of the unused part of the stove. His
body did not actually touch hers but was held so close to it
with such a fine control that any shift on her part would
mean *she* touched *him*.

She could feel his heat running all through her body,
crossing that minute space. She shivered with it. It felt so
very much like coming in out of the cold. The shiver
brushed their clothes against each other.

"May I take your sweater?" he murmured, each word a
glide of warm air over the part in her hair. "These sleeves."
He fingered the open material draping from her wrist. "You
know you can't work in them properly."

She hesitated a long moment, head bent, his breath drifting over the back of her head, her exposed nape. Absorbing
the feel of him, just there but not touching. Absorbing the
moment. Then she released the wooden spoon and stretched
both arms at an angle behind her. Yielding him the sweater.

He could have pulled the cardigan over her head. He didn't. His arms circled around her enough to reach the buttons. Just enough. Still he did not tighten his hold into true contact. Very gently, the sweater tugging against her, he worked each button free—over her breasts, under her breasts, just over her navel so that her belly sucked in and the cinnamon-nutmeg-vanilla scents filled her lungs, down to the last one, just over the mound of curls hidden by her pants.

She swallowed the scents and bowed her head so far that the skin stretched taut over her nape.

He did not kiss her there.

The sweater glided down her arms with the gentlest of tugs, no hurry. He knew exactly how long it took to infuse cream so that a flavor permeated every part of it.

There was a soft sound, a puff of breath against her nape, when he saw what was under the cardigan. She shivered all over at that puff.

"Magalie. Silk?" He stopped tugging, the sweater pulled down to her forearms, her arms caught behind her back. One hand trailed delicately up her back over her top, the silk transparent to his touch. "You did it on purpose," he breathed roughly, but there was no accusation in his voice, only delicious, husky praise. "An impractical sweater for cooking. If I hadn't taken it off, would you have, Magalie? Complained it was getting in your way, and . . . and under it . . . you wanted to be able to feel my slightest touch?" He breathed on her nape. All the hairs on it rose to him.

His fingers skated up her back again—the slightest touch. Her spine arched helplessly.

He laughed suddenly, a rough, confounded sound. "Surely you weren't worried that it would only be slight?"

Not exactly. Her worries and desires were far too complex to say.

He pulled the sweater free of her arms and tossed it aside. His right hand closed hers around the spoon, as if he was giving her a lifeline. "Don't let my chocolate burn, Magalie."

Of course she would not let it b—

"How long do you let it infuse?"

"Fifteen minutes." Her voice was a thread of a whisper. Why did she let him steal all her authority?

He gave a small, exultant laugh. "You might want to set a timer." And his mouth pressed to her nape.

She made a small sound of such intense pleasure that his left hand closed around her left wrist and tightened there as if he had to squeeze something desperately or lose all control. *"Pardon,"* he said and released her before she could even protest the pain, closing both his hands instead around the oven door handle on either side of her.

While her spoon trembled its path through the infusion, sending cinnamon and vanilla rocking in a stormy white sea, he kissed his way down her spine. He never touched her with any other part of his body. Just pressed his mouth through the silk inch by inch, until he was kneeling behind her, his lips at the small of her back, just above the low waist of her pants.

She sagged over her infusion, making soft, helpless sounds. He laughed out loud, the triumph making her pride rear its head, the joy in it making her softer still and puzzled with wonder.

He surged up, his body brushing the length of hers in a burst of power as he came to his feet. "Is it ready yet?" He was grinning as if he couldn't contain his exultancy, but behind the warm fire in his eyes was still that intense, controlled focus.

"I—I don't think that was quite fifteen minutes," said Magalie, who had no idea. It had felt as if she had gone to heaven for all eternity while it lasted, but now that he had stopped, her whole back was begging for more.

His grin sharpened into something feral and hungry, but the blue eyes were rich with pleasure at what she had just asked for.

"Well, if there's one thing I know, it's that you must *never* stint on any preparatory step," he allowed and teased the spoon out of her hand with a long stroke of his index finger down the heel of her palm and under the curl of her fingers. Keeping her fingers peeled back, he lifted her wrist, wickedly exposed, and grazed his faintly rough jaw all along the exquisitely sensitive inside of her forearm from wrist to elbow.

And purred roughly with delight when she gasped.

"Your wrists handcuffed to the bedposts?" she managed dryly. She was so proud of that dry tone. It felt like holding onto a little bit of herself. *"Really?"*

Again he laughed, a soft, joyous sound, intimate and dangerous. "I don't seem vulnerable to you, Magalie? Submitted to your every desire?"

She twisted and for the first time gathered the strength of will to study his face, head-on, for a long moment. He just looked back. Her body was so much smaller, her position by far the more exposed and defenseless. And yet for that one long moment while he held her eyes, he did look vulnerable, almost as if he was tied naked to her bed, of his own volition, gazing at her as she prepared to undo him.

Arousal flooded her. Arousal that undid *her*. That had always been the problem. He undid her. And *her* was all she had.

She twisted back to the infusion fast, like a fencer might twist to avoid a killing thrust. She scooped the cinnamon stick and vanilla bean out of the milk with the spoon, dropping them onto a small plate on the counter. What had she thought she was doing, coming here? As she sat up there in her creamy tower gazing at his "heart," what burst of idiocy had said, *Yes, you can do this. You can give up yourself.*

Philippe brushed the faint prickle of his jaw over the nape of her neck.

Oh, God. She had never known that her perfect, pseudocareless chignons could leave her so vulnerable. She had never known that she could love it, that vulnerability. That she would be willing to just bow her body forward over the glass stove and beg him to do anything to her he wanted to.

The hot burner kept her straight. She scooped the ovals of chocolate with trembling hands and dropped them into the pot.

The milk spattered at her abruptness. With his jaw still at her nape, circling sleepy and sensual like a cat, sparkles from it running through her everywhere, his hands closed over hers, and he rubbed every burning drop of it away with his palms.

She had often felt those little burning drops while she made hot chocolate. She had never before had anyone there to smooth them away.

She linked her fingers through his and lifted one of his hands to her mouth. She kissed his knuckles, holding his hand cradled against her lips for a second. She couldn't help it.

Behind her, his body went very still. The cheek against the nape of her neck stopped moving.

When she brought her hand back down to stir the chocolate, he turned his head and kissed her nape, just the silk touch of his lips, no prickle at all. His palm slid slowly away from the back of her hand, a leisurely wandering path up her arm, over skin and then silk that whispered between his calluses and her skin, up to her shoulder.

She added a spoonful of bittersweet Valrhona cocoa, darkening her usual *chocolat* even further for him, and whisked the mixture into smoothness.

His thumb came up to trace the corner of her lips, which from his position behind her he could not see. The touch of his thumb made her want to nuzzle her face into his hand, to whimper and beg. "You're not smiling," he whispered.

No. What she felt was too intense to smile.

"I like the smile." His thumb teased at the corner of her mouth as if he could coax one to life. "It makes me feel in the most erotic danger."

A slow one grew, from some deep and powerful place in her belly. No smile before over her chocolate had ever felt like this one. Slowly she stirred the chocolate three final turns.

"What are you wishing for me, Magalie?"

To render him completely and utterly helpless with desire for her.

She shook her head, refusing to answer.

"You're going to make me drink it blind, aren't you?" His thumb traced over that dangerous smile, end to end and back, then stroked down, over her chin, down the length of her throat, to nestle in the hollow there.

"Do you have a chocolate pot?" she asked.

He did, sitting high up on the back of a top shelf of his cabinets, someone's idea of a Christmas present for a top pastry chef. He stretched up over her head for it, all the long strength of his body against her back, and brought it down for her.

She poured the chocolate into the pot, then slipped the *moulinet* in and rubbed the rounded end of the thick wooden stick between her two palms, hard and fast, frothing the chocolate to give it an exceptionally smooth richness.

A low, growling sound vibrated from his chest through her back as he watched the movement of her hands on the wood. Her hands slowed involuntarily, as she stared at the form of the wood and realized why. Her blush took over her body, and her hands faltered. She couldn't froth it properly. She was burning up.

She reached blindly for a cup, and he moved away from

her to stand just a couple of feet beside her, watching her as she poured his fate. For a moment, the silence was so absolute she could hear the liquid flowing from the pot, then the clink of the pot as she set it down.

The scent of chocolate now filled his apartment. As if she had made the place her own.

She swallowed and stared at the dark liquid in the white cup for a moment. All around them the apartment was dark, lit by nothing but the utility light over the stove and the illumination coming in from the street through the great expanse of windows.

She curved her hands around the cup, its heat against her palms, and offered it to him.

His breaths lifted his chest in long, deep movements. He raised his eyes from the chocolate to hers. Keeping his hands at his sides, he made a motion of submission with his chin. *"Vas-y,"* he murmured. "From your hands."

He was right. This was the most erotic thing she had ever done. Not that she had much for comparison. She suspected it might also be the most erotic thing she ever would do. What could match this?

She started to lift it to his lips, hesitated, then brought it to hers to blow on it a few times, making sure she would not burn him.

He made a sound, his hands tightening into fists at his sides. His blue eyes in the light looked almost black.

When she brought it back to his lips, he sat down suddenly at the little table near the window. His eyes as he tilted his head back to accept it clung to hers as if he was willingly drowning.

She watched the smooth, rich chocolate pass his lips, clinging to the sensual upper bow. He swallowed once. Twice. His eyes closed, and a long, slow sigh left his body, as if he was abandoning all fight.

He curved his hand around the cup, his fingers caressing its smooth heat and her fingers, and drank again. She stared at the chocolate clinging to his lips. What was going through his body? She had never been able to feel the power of her own chocolate.

Abruptly he pulled the cup out of her hands and set it on the table, then pulled her down on top of him. She tumbled into him, but because she tried to keep her feet planted firmly on the floor, her body stretched like a bow, her legs straight, her back arching so that her chest pressed against his. He spread his thighs so that her pelvis pressed against his, forced hard by the arch of her spine. "Magalie." How could her name on his lips sound like *ma chérie*?

His fingers skated up her spine through the silk again, arching her helplessly. He brought his mouth to her exposed throat. *Not a gazelle, not a gazelle, not a gazelle,* she reminded herself as he ripped not her throat but her heart out with a hungry little growl.

All her will dissolved under the feel of his mouth, his barest graze of teeth, the touch of his tongue, the burr of his jaw, against her skin. Maybe she could be a gazelle, just here, just for tonight. Maybe she could be completely weak. It was so dark, and he was so warm, and despite those great windows, no one could see.

"What did you wish on me, Magalie?" His voice was as dark as her chocolate, as if it had possessed him. He trailed his lips and rough jaw down toward her breastbone, arching her back over his arm. "Doom? Utter destruction? Complete helplessness at your hands?"

Was he going to show her how powerless she was, that what she wished on him in vain was what he could so easily do to her?

"I don't feel any different." He pressed her breasts apart with his chin, forcing a little space for himself in her cleavage. The prickles from his jaw ran all through her body, chasing after one another until they settled into her nipples and her sex, dancing and dancing there.

"It probably doesn't affect you," she said bitterly. Bitter as the chocolate she had used on him.

"Perhaps you wished something that was already true."

That he was completely helpless with desire for her?

She tried to pull her head back enough to get a good look at him, but the arch of her back didn't leave much room to maneuver. He made a pleased sound at the way the attempt thrust her breasts more prominently against his face. Then he lifted his head, and there was nothing for her mouth to do but meet his.

She sipped her chocolate off his lips. She opened her mouth over his and tasted it on his tongue. The chocolate that was supposed to render its drinker helpless with desire. He buried his hands in her hair, knocking the clasp free with the thrust of his fingers, and held her head as he took her in.

And by opening her mouth to take his, she let him in to take hers. His mouth moved over and in hers, slow and thorough, as if he was savoring something delicious. Something he wanted to roll around on his tongue, breathe in deeply, pull back to sip slowly . . .

He brought his hands to her ribs and lifted her suddenly, settling her across his lap. She kept kissing him through the move, and he kissed her back, as if he could kiss her forever.

But both his arms didn't hold her. One left her. Stretched across the table. And came back with his heart in his hand.

She wrenched her head away, burying her face in his neck. "Can't we just have sex?" she whispered. "That's what this is all about, isn't it?"

"No, it isn't." The hand still in her hair tightened, showing his anger. "Do you have to be so strong that you're stupid?"

She straightened a little away from him, eyeing that dessert with longing even while her mouth set mulishly. She had promised him the trade. She had come here with the intention of it. What was wrong with her to want to balk now?

"What do you think you have to lose, Magalie?"

She gave him an incredulous look. "Me." As if he didn't know.

"Vraiment." His palm rubbed a wandering path from her hip up her ribs to one tense shoulder blade, where it settled into soothing circles. "Not your pride. Not your anger. Not your strength. You." His tongue seemed to caress that last word, drawing it out the way one might draw out a slow, savoring spoonful of a luscious dessert.

If he was eating her in two bites, he was enjoying his meal. She wriggled resentfully.

"What do you think I have to lose, Magalie?"

She blinked. Frowned. "Nothing, probably. You said my chocolate didn't even have any effect on you."

He stared at her. The anger in him tensed the muscles in the thighs under her butt, pressed his palm against her shoulder blade, tightened the abs against which her arm was pressed. *"Bon sang. Quel imbécile."*

Was she really? In her witches' lair, surrounded by clients who couldn't quite get their lives together, she had always thought that she was the smartest person in the room. *Her* life was together. Nicely packed up and invincible. Until him.

"Here." He brought the *macaron* so close that the armor of raspberries protecting its insides brushed her mouth with their faint, silky, beaded texture, and the gloss of the *macaron* shells glided smoothly over her lips.

She opened her mouth and bit, snatching for it with her teeth like a starved animal snatching food out of the air. But as her teeth broke the fine crust of the *macaron* shells, her whole body slowed, the energy of the bite dissolved into a dream. The most secret, delicate crunch, the blissful, soft inside of the shell, and then, sinking down, the burst of raspberries, the luscious cream. Sex between two wings of heaven. Bliss and paradise, if the paradise was the kind that featured infinite debauchery.

An orgasm in one bite. As if hands ran all over her body. But more. It was the most beautiful thing she had ever tasted in her life. Made for *her.* It was so beautiful that tears stung her eyes, and she opened them to find Philippe's gaze consuming her face with a feral, starved triumph.

She stared back at him, from only inches away.

He rotated the *macaron* a half inch and proffered it to her lips again.

She couldn't describe what it did to her to take another bite under that savage victory. She almost couldn't *not,* her ability to resist more of that exquisite pleasure reduced nearly out of existence. And yet she could have. She was strong enough. She could have drawn from somewhere deep that resistance. She *chose* not to. It was as if she chose to strip herself naked at his snapped fingers and give all power over her body to him.

It was so erotic that she could barely breathe from it, from the desire to have him take her, then and there, laid across the chair.

He didn't. He fed her, holding her eyes. Grazing his palm over her throat as she swallowed him. Watching her shiver and her whole body clutch helplessly as she bit into that secret, intense, tart heart beneath the silk ganache.

He fed her every last bite. He stroked the rose petal over her lips and slipped it inside to lie on her tongue. He brushed the crumbs over her lips and made her lick them off his fingers.

He had tied his hands to a bed? His power over her was so absolute that it could not have been greater if she had put a slave collar around her naked throat and handed him the chain.

In fact, her erotic submission was so great that as soon as the thought came to her, she longed for it, to be stripped naked and used for his every desire.

He dipped the thumb she had just sucked clean into the cup of her still-warm chocolate and slowly, deliberately sucked it himself, still holding her eyes.

And then he slipped that thumb in through the tight fit of her still-zipped pants, finding her clitoris. With the first brush, she whimpered and writhed, clutching at him. Her eyes closed, but his didn't. She felt them on her, blazing dark. He pressed his thumb hard, and she came almost in the first second, shattering helplessly, curving her face into his arm and biting at his biceps.

And he *laughed*. He laughed in pure, utter triumph. A savage sound, a conquering sound as her body rocked and rocked to its rhythm.

Chapter 26

As the shocks to her body faded, Philippe began stripping her. The silk sliding over her hot, damp face grazed her plump, parted lips that did not want that teasing wisp of a touch, that begged to close around something hard and unyielding. To close around *him* and force him to the same helplessness. He left her bra on but scooped under its lace for her breasts, delicately pinching the nipples so that she cried out, and then pulling them free of the cups, so that they were pressed up but exposed.

He stripped off her pants, ruthlessly, lifting her up so that she stood with her legs apart before him as he did it, her breasts pouty before his mouth. He liked her black lace panties. He left them on. "God, I wish you had worn your boots," he breathed, squeezing his hand over her sex like he might squeeze the juice from a lime, and another ripple of aftershock went through her body, his hand coming away from her panties gleaming. "The ones that come up to here." He closed his hands around her thighs and pressed them farther apart, with that quick, savage lion's grin at what he saw.

But she had already come once, and she could feel the balance of power seesawing delicately. Because *he* hadn't had any relief. His arousal was desperate and desperately clear. It was possible that he had never in his life needed anything as badly as he right now needed her.

She was worse than exposed, but she didn't feel vulnerable.

She didn't feel helpless.

She felt stripped naked, yes. But *strong* in it. As if that was an absolutely beautiful, perfect way to be. She felt like Lady Godiva might have felt. As if she was a woman who could in fact walk naked through a crowd and never be touched by any look or word because her pride and her sense of self were unassailable.

She bent over him, with her thighs still braced apart the way he had spread them, with her breasts spilling toward his mouth, and ripped his T-shirt off over his head.

"Yes," he breathed, his body flexing with pleasure as the move stretched his arms over his head, so that muscles rippled the length of his torso. Broad shoulders, a tight waist, curls darker than his tawny hair across his chest. "Yes. God. Attack me."

But instead of letting her, he surged to his feet, grabbing her and flipping her around as if her body was as easily controllable as a doll's, curling her hands against the edge of the table.

A moment ago, his back had been to the window, the chair and his body hiding her. But now, she glanced sideways at the lights in the street, that great expanse of glass.

"They can't see us," he whispered, his penis pressing through his pants against her butt cheeks, as if to find its way to the thong that disappeared between them.

She was his doll, his puppet; he could do anything to her. She would let him. Over and over, every way he wanted, all night long.

"You had better hope so," she said, and she turned, pressing him back to the table instead. She curled *his* hands around its edge, and they tightened until the knuckles showed white.

She reached behind her, the movement thrusting her

breasts up, and took off her bra, tossing it away. She, too, wished for her boots, the thigh-high ones and nothing else, but thong panties and utter nakedness would have to do.

She pulled his jeans down over his hips and knelt with the movement. His slave, his very slave. And all the power was completely in her hands.

Com-plete-ly. Her hands closed over his penis, both at once, and squeezed hard. He made a harsh sound as if he had been shot, and his body jerked.

She opened her mouth and closed it over him in the same greedy rush with which she had first snatched at his *macaron*. And in the same way, the first silk-salt feel of him slowed her. She didn't want to rush this. Her tongue curled around him.

"Magalie. God. Please. Don't."

Don't? I'll do whatever I want to you, she thought. She would have told him so with words, but then she would have had to interrupt the more effective demonstration.

She took him in, sucking on him greedily, the way his body reacted making her own lower body weep again with hunger. His groaning growls surrounded her, vibrating down over her skin, her naked kneeling body, her bottom taut and bereft of his warmth against the cold air.

She couldn't take him all in. Her mouth was too small. But she flicked her tongue hungrily, curiously against his tip and stroked it around his head, the hardness and pulse of him, and brought both hands to grip the base of his shaft, the heel of her palms cupping his testicles.

"God, God, God," he groaned, and she loved it; she loved hearing him lose all his intellect, his control, just that long, growling plea for mercy.

She reduced him to nothing in less than a minute, his body shaking uncontrollably as he came.

And *she* threw back her head, naked at his feet with the taste of him on her tongue, and laughed.

Laughed in pure, glorious, giddy conquest.

★ ★ ★

"God." Philippe's big body seemed so utterly weak. Slowly, as the room felt colder, he managed to peel himself from the table. He picked her up. Confounding her. She thought she had made him weaker than she was. Too weak to pick her up as if she was nothing.

He carried her into his bathroom and turned the warm shower on them both, tucking his body against hers under the hot water, and then ignoring his own body thereafter. Pouring soap into his hand, he rubbed it, a warm, clean scent, all over her. Scraping her wet hair gently away from her face, he pulled her head back against his shoulder and let the water, at its gentlest pulse, stream over her face, her closed eyes. She had no strength left, although desire seemed to have grown again in a way that made her malleable.

The water and the soap and his body were such a blur of sensations, of slumberous longing, that it felt like a continuation of a dream when he turned her and lifted her astride him, sliding into her body. He tucked her face now into his shoulder, so that her hair fell around it, sheltering it from the spray, and the water streamed over the back of her head and down her spine as he took her, in easy, gentle thrusts, so that when she first began to come, she almost didn't realize she was doing so; the shocks just slipped up on her, seemed part of her, as if she was earthquake territory, and tremors were her constant.

Gentle and subtle though they were in their approach, they took control of her and would not leave her. Limp and clinging and wet, her arms wrapped around him, the water streaming over her, she came over and over, in long, soft vibrations, while he moved in her, slow, sliding thrusts.

His arms bulged on either side of her head when he shifted her back against the earth-tone tiles, but even at the end, his thrusts stayed slow, and long, and steady, and just very, very deep as his strength spurted up into her.

Her body trembled in those faint seismic tremors as he lowered her and drew her back against him again, scooping water and soap against the folds of her sex and washing her most intimately and thoroughly, as if he was exploring now at leisure something that fascinated him.

He wrapped her in a giant thick towel, for lack of a bathrobe, and picked her up like a child and carried her to his bed.

Lying in front of her, he laughed softly, wonderingly as he slowly peeled the towel away from her body. Unlike the living area, his bedroom was a cave, its window covered with heavy, pale drapes, the big bed a square, modern take on the canopied beds of centuries ago, so that the padded headboard rose high and formed a ceiling with the two square posts at the foot.

Philippe pushed their towels onto the floor and pulled the heavy comforter over them, wrapping an arm around her and pulling her back, a hot body against the cold.

"Magalie," he whispered just before she fell asleep, tracing a fingertip around her ear as if to draw her attention to an important secret. *"Je t'aime."*

The words glided over her with caressing, warm confidence, so that their speaker could have no idea that they speared her like a fish and left her gasping, out of the water.

Her eyes flared open, lashes catching against the hairs of his forearm under her head, and she stared into the white night of the comforter while his body grew heavy over hers, asleep.

Living between two languages, sometimes, with the rarer words, she thought a lot about what they meant. Her mother was the only other person who had said those same two syllables to her, *Je t'aime.* But her mother's accent had stretched it and bounced it, a gay little sound, not like Philippe's crisp, firm prince-of-Paris pronunciation.

While she was growing up, her mother had said it every day, often many times a day. *"Bonne nuit, ma minette, je t'aime,"* as she tucked her into the freshly changed sheets smelling of lavender at her grandparents' house, just arrived off the plane. *"Tu es ma petite chérie." "Oh, ma petite puce, je t'aime,"* on the plane from America to France, their father and Magalie's school friends left behind, as Magalie, cheerful and sweet and six years old, hugged her mother to stop her crying. *"Je t'aime, mon bébé. S'il n'y avait pas toi . . ."* If it wasn't for you . . . as she tucked Magalie into her bed in the States after flying back with their father to try again, the sheets smelling of Tide. *"Mais, Magalie, nous t'aimons,"* the desperate protest when Magalie had fought and won the right to go back to the U.S. by herself at sixteen.

In the vain attempt to create a home with a boyfriend who had said, "I love you" primarily because he thought that was what she wanted to hear in order to have sex.

No other person had ever used those exact words to her. Her aunts didn't say them. Her grandparents called her their *chérie,* their *petite puce,* and they clearly *did* love her, but they never directly said, *"Je t'aime."* Her father, like her boyfriend, used English, a steady, often regretful phrase, for wherever Magalie's mother went, Magalie had gone, too, which meant she had often been pulled from him. "I love you, sweetie."

Women sometimes said it about someone else, sitting at the tables in La Maison des Sorcières, a heartbroken, *"Mais, je l'aime."* And Magalie would roll her eyes and make them some chocolate that would put their heads back on straight.

What Philippe meant, she had no idea. But it made part of her curl warily away, into herself, because whatever he meant, it could only be a way to entice her own emotions out of her, to stretch them from her to him, where they would be ripped like over-tried tendons when . . . when . . . well, she didn't know when, because she wasn't planning on moving ever again. But some shift would occur, and with her emotions all out there, caught far away from her, instead of contained and strong within the island of herself, they would be torn to pieces when it did.

Chapter 27

In the morning, the apartment was empty, stretching away from her body, an alien, scary place, so that she jerked out of sleep in a moment of pure terror that she was a child again and waking on the other side of the world.

She pulled herself together, annoyed, and went into the bathroom to find toothpaste. First things first. And pulling herself together was always first. Her hair was a mess, having dried in uncombed tangles. She jumped under his shower again and dragged his comb ruthlessly through her hair while the water ran over it, so ruthlessly that tears sprang from her eyes, but she didn't stop.

A door closed somewhere. "Magalie?" Philippe called. "Magalie, you have to come see."

He found her under the shower before she could finish and actually . . . *blushed*. "I beg your pardon," he said, turning away, as if he had walked in on her naked.

Which he had, but still.

He, too, apparently got caught in the inconsistency, starting to turn back, hesitating, one foot moving toward and away from the door several times, as if his body didn't know where to pivot.

She turned off the shower and then couldn't find a towel, since they were all on the floor by his bed.

His head made up his mind what he wanted his body to

do, and he turned to look at her. He smiled, his eyes sparkling with pleasure, as his gaze ran over her dripping form, but his blush was very deep.

She shivered, goose bumps rising at the cold air and wet skin and the sense of exposure that she didn't know quite what to do with this morning after.

"Pardon," he said and ducked out of the bathroom to bring her back a big towel.

She wrapped it snugly around herself. Above the line of the fluffy white towel, every inch of her bare chest, shoulders, throat, and face must be a striking contrast of red, too. Maybe he could credit that to overly hot water.

His smile didn't grow wider, but it deepened, like good chocolate when the cacao was blended in, adding a richer element. Whatever he credited her redness to, he seemed to like what he saw.

"Viens voir." He claimed her hand and tugged. "You have to see this."

He led her to the bedroom window and pulled back the curtains with a flourish, like a magician's assistant. He was watching her face as she saw the great flakes falling, and the snow carpeting the narrow cobblestone sidewalks below. The coating on the street was still shallow enough that the pavement showed gray-black through it, but the old iron railing of his window had a good inch of snow clinging to it.

Paris in the snow. During the night, it had started snowing for them. She drew a breath at the magic of it.

"The baker didn't open," he said. "I gather the roads are icy. I hope you like yogurt. Or, if not, we can walk over to my kitchens, and"—he held her eyes with laughter and something else that sent a lick of excitement through her— "I'll make you anything you like."

He said that with great certainty that he could make anything she would like and make it better than any other time she might have had it.

"I mostly eat eggs and bacon," she said repressively.

"Like an American?" he said, taken aback, and she realized he didn't even know about that half of her. So, she thought, deeply reassured, she did seem to belong on that island in the heart of France.

"Tu es une plaie," he said, amused. *A pain.* "I can*not* do eggs and bacon." He said that the way a prince might say that he could *not* wax floors. "But I will be happy to make you the most exquisite *kouign-amann* you have ever tasted, instead."

A *kouign-amann* was an extremely difficult Breton concoction of butter, sugar, and dough layered through three elaborate days of turning, rolling, cooling, folding. It would blow her head off to try to make it. Philippe's miniature ones were world-famous, and he undoubtedly had some in the final stage of production in his walk-in refrigerators in his *laboratoire* at that very moment.

Which was presumably closed for snow, else he would be in it at this hour of the morning. He was going to have to throw out thousands of dollars of *pâtisseries* because of today's closing. And he hadn't even brought up one little, groaning complaint about it.

"You really can't do eggs and bacon?" she asked, intrigued.

He looked revolted. "Please."

"How can you not know how to cook an egg?"

"I didn't say I wasn't capable of it," he said with reluctance. As if he was afraid he might be put through the test of actually being asked to do it. "I'm sure I could do anything I set my mind to."

She had to grin at his blithe unawareness of his own arrogance.

He flicked a dismissive hand. "However, why I should set my mind to that, I don't know."

"To avoid diabetes," she suggested dryly. "You have to eat something besides sugar."

He threw an arm around her shoulders and hugged her

against his side, an impulse that completely undid her. "I love restaurants. Truly," he added, when she rolled her eyes. "I love them. I love having the best chefs in the world, or the secret unknown ones, cook for me. I love seeing what they come up with. I love looking at their menus, I love listening to their sommeliers advise on wines, I love plotting out the meal like an explorer's route through all the choices."

He made her hungry for something, standing in the warmth of his arm, watching the cold, glorious snow, listening to him describe his pleasure. She had explored new restaurants with family and friends; she enjoyed it. But he made it sound like a warm fire on a freezing day. Evenings with him in restaurants seemed to stretch out infinitely into her future, full of the senses and discovery.

When she looked away from the snow at him beside her, he was gazing at her with that something deeper than a smile in his eyes, as if he, too, had a vision, and she was sitting across the table from him in it.

"I don't," he admitted, "usually eat their desserts, but occasionally I am provoked to curiosity. So"—he squeezed her shoulders against him—"*kouign-amann ou yaourt?* If there's anywhere in the city open by this evening, I promise an excellent restaurant for dinner."

She swallowed, not sure what to do with all the warmth sliding over her. Her self-contained emotions kept wanting to stretch out and bathe in it. "I really live mostly on fruit and yogurt, and Tante Aja's *dal* and curries. And in the winter, Tante Geneviève loves to make great pots of soup."

He turned her around to face him, her still in his towel, the snow sliding over the window beside them, his eyes kindling with warmth and desire and something else, something that seemed to give meaning to those two syllables the night before. "*Bon Dieu.* I have a whole new world of flavors to give to you."

He said it like a man who could imagine no better gift.

She couldn't imagine a better one either.

What awed her was how clearly he desired to give that most precious of gifts to her.

He brought both her hands to his face and kissed the inside of each wrist, just at the base of the palm. "Come play with me in the snow, Magalie."

Paris in the snow was a gift. A rare gift for those who lived there, or those visitors who happened upon a miracle.

Magalie and Philippe, both early risers, made the first footprints in the snow on his street, only his short trip directly across to the closed *boulangerie* having come before. As they reached the end of the street, only one other pair of footprints headed off on the street perpendicular to his; who knew who had made them or where he was going or what he was dreaming? The stranger's footprints were blurring rapidly. The streetlamps glowed through the thick flakes.

Philippe had crushed her hair under one of his ski hats, an extravagant but warm knit with dangling colorful braids of yarn that he blamed on his sister and that made him smile every time he looked at her. Between her own sweater and coat, she wore one of his wool sweaters as an extra layer. It wasn't even touching her skin, nor visible to any observer, but it closed around her like some special, secret cocoon, an invisible superhero shield of warmth that was more than merely physical.

He wore a considerably more elegant gray knit hat pulled over his own hair. "Why do I get the one your sister picked up to make fun of you in a ski resort, while you get the one that came off Faubourg Saint-Honoré?" she demanded, disgruntled.

He tweaked one knit braid. "Because I'm bigger." His gloved hand curled under her chin and over her cheek, and he traced a snowflake off her eyebrow. "Do you remember how you always wanted snow on Christmas when you were a kid? This makes up for all the times it didn't come."

He bent and kissed snow off her lips, melting between them little sparkles of cold.

The streets under the thick snow clouds were still gray, the flakes falling slow and large, like small white feathers drifting down from the sky. Molting angels, Magalie thought whimsically, and she tried to catch one. It rested for only a second on her glove.

The streetlamps glowed magically through the flakes, as if their light was reaching the present through layers of time. Just for a moment, as they came into the Place des Vosges, all the lamps around the square were glowing in that muted, ancient way. Then they winked out, with the day arriving quietly under the blanket of snow.

Against the bars of the fence that surrounded the square, leaning bikes and parked mopeds were acquiring layers of white. The great, symmetrical buildings of brick and strips of stone framed it all, snow slowly muting their blue slate roofs, sliding over the steep pitch and grasping for purchase. Magalie and Philippe stood under an arch of the arcades, sheltered for a little while, as signs of life grew in the city around them, but the open park filling up with snow was too tempting, and they went back under the falling flakes.

Other people were starting to come out now, drawn to the thought of the Place des Vosges under snow: another couple on the other side of the garden, a mother and father with two small children who were jumping up and down, beside themselves. Snow gathered on the edges of the tiered fountains. It clung to the bare branches of the perfectly symmetrical marches of trees. Two teenagers burst in on the park from another side, one chasing the other with a snowball. An elderly man unleashed his small Jack Russell, which ran yapping and rolling in the snow with delight.

"This is beautiful," Magalie said softly. One of the most beautiful scenes of her life.

"I can't *believe* my luck," Philippe said, as if he was hugging it to him. "I could have been throwing pebbles at your tower window, trying to get you to come down and share this with me."

"I would have come out into the snow on my own," Magalie said, a little affronted. It was hard to tell if she would have wandered over the whole city in it, but she definitely would have explored the park at the end of the island, and the quays, and Notre-Dame. Probably would have gone as far as her green king on the Pont Neuf.

"I know, Magalie," he said very dryly. "It was coming out in it with me that was the trick. Let's build a snowman."

There wasn't enough snow yet for that, and Philippe was the first one who abandoned the effort to get his ball a decent size for a snowman base and instead threw it at her.

She shot her ball right back at him, laughing, and ran through the park, ducking behind stately rows of trees and fountains like great *pièces montées*. Magalie, paying more attention to what was chasing after her than where she was going, had to skid to a halt and swerve to avoid running straight into a stroller, its transparent plastic covering collecting snow, and she ended up on her butt.

Philippe loped up and hauled her to her feet, dusting off her butt with considerably more thoroughness than it could possibly need.

"Pardon," Magalie told the mother pushing the stroller. But the elegant woman only frowned at her with considerable disapproval and kept walking.

Magalie looked after the other woman's square but two-inch high heels and glanced down at her own flat snowboots uneasily. Damn it, had she copped out?

Philippe laughed at her, reading her mind. "You can make up for it when the snow melts. I've got plenty of ideas of things you can do in boots." He made a rueful, rough sound. "Far too many, I suspect."

Oh, really? She looked up at him, something hot running quick and hard through her under all the chill.

"*En fait,* we could work out some kind of exchange where you fulfill all my sexual desires and I supply you with all the boots you want."

That sounded quite enticing, actually. She cleared her throat and tried to look uninterested. "Would that include boots from Givenchy?"

"Magalie, you can't tell me you're willing to prostitute yourself for clothes but not for my *macarons*? That's messed up."

Her shoulders slumped. "I probably would be willing just for your *macarons,*" she admitted sadly. Now that she had tasted one, her mouth was watering already at the possibility of tasting him again. She had no fiber anymore. It wasn't so much moral fiber, because like her Aunt Geneviève, she thought this question of morals was made up primarily by Aunt Aja to annoy them, but just plain old backbone. "Although I wouldn't mind a bonus," she added wistfully. There had been this one pair of boots . . .

Philippe gave a crack of laughter, pulling her in for a hard kiss. "It's supposed to snow all day," he whispered into her frozen ear. "Why don't we go warm up for an hour or so before we come back out into the cold? I hear there's nothing better on a snowy day than a cup of hot chocolate."

When he led the way out of the square going in the opposite direction from his apartment, at first she thought he had been joking about the break to warm up and instead was heading toward the Seine to see the bridges in the snow.

They did walk down the Right Bank quays as far as the Pont Neuf and crossed over to watch the snow falling onto the statue of Henri IV on horseback that dominated its center—Magalie's green king. Snow veiled the monuments and bridges all the gray length of the river. Coming back through the Place du Parvis Notre-Dame, they saw other couples snowball fighting, and someone had left multiple snow angels scattered all over the plaza, as if a heavenly host was gathering around the great cathedral.

Behind the flying buttresses, they stood a moment on the arching bridge that connected Notre-Dame to the Île Saint-Louis, watching the drift of river and snow.

A couple passed on the other side of the bridge, cuddled close together under a red umbrella.

Philippe sighed. "I should have thought of an umbrella."

He watched the couple distance themselves, red bobbing over the dark coats so intimately pressed together, and looked down at her suddenly.

"You asked me the other night what woman I had fallen in love with." He was frowning, as if he was grappling with a serious structural issue with one of his *pièces montées*. "But there's something I don't understand, Magalie. How could you not know?"

She stared at him while snowflakes fell into her eyes, and she had to blink them into icy spiderwebs between her eyelashes.

Were they going to *talk* about this subject? It was one thing to whisper it when he was falling asleep after intense sex, but surely even he wasn't going to go around examining the subject in the light of day.

He didn't seem to have the slightest fear of it, though. At least, not here under this fairy-tale snow.

"I mean, Magalie—I'm busy. It happens, sometimes, that one of my desserts gets left on a plate. Not that *often*," he added, as if he could probably count the times as individual wounds in his body, "but maybe someone who is anorexic and likes to torture herself. Or someone who is pregnant, and suddenly her hormones revolt at the sight of what she has been craving. Or . . . or . . . maybe some businessman who is trying to survive a meeting but has the flu and his nose is all blocked up and destroying his tastebuds. I mean, it *happens.*"

Magalie curled her free hand around his forearm and gave it a consoling pat. Her mouth twitched, but truly it was pretty hard to imagine any other reason someone might leave a Philippe Lyonnais dessert unfinished.

"I don't go around pursuing those people personally with new and ever better works of art until they crack." A pause. "Well, not directly," he admitted. "I might make a new and better creation *for the whole world* anytime it happens, but I don't personally chase down the masochistic person who didn't eat the last one to try to win him over."

Magalie set her jaw mulishly. That verb *crack* did not sit well with her. It made her sound like a crème brulée, with nice, shiny burnt caramel on the top but all you had to do was get a spoon and tap it, and you would find the insides all soft and rich and vulnerable.

Or like a raw egg oozing out its middle. She scowled.

"Are you listening to what I'm telling you, or are you just getting mad?"

She looked up at him. Flakes of snow were layering his shoulders, and the hair curling from under his cap was damp from melted snow, making it look dark brown, hiding its gold. He was a beautiful man, strong, handsome, and very focused, and just standing still looking at him for too long made her feel like the snow, melting lovingly against him.

She frowned worriedly, pulling her lower lip in under her teeth. She was really not comfortable with the idea of being water.

Philippe heaved a quick, hard sigh at her silence and frowned. "I take it you're not in love with me."

Magalie gasped as if he had just shoved her over the side

of the bridge into the icy cold water. "I—I mean—I don't—I—" The feel of him, the taste of him, the laugh that swept out and embraced the world. Those feral, dangerous looks. One *pâtisserie* after another laid out before her like a dare. Her absolute inability to make him back up a step. The *taste* of him. His happiness right now. The way he had curved her face into his shoulder in the shower the night before, taking her against the wall. That curl of his hand over her, oh, God—as if she was precious.

"I . . ."

He didn't interrupt her. He didn't hurry. He didn't lose patience or seek to cut the moment short to protect himself. He just waited for her to stumble to a halt and stare up at him. A long way up at him. This damn slippery snow was really cramping her style.

With no more words, she could only stare. Wondering if he was going to turn around and walk away.

"*Intéressant,*" he said finally, a little flatly, when it was clear she had nothing else to say.

He took her hand again and led her onto her island. "Let's go warm up."

He stopped first at his dark and empty shop, which seemed a good place to linger to her. But he didn't shrug out of his coat, just stood for a moment with his hands in his pockets, gazing at the curving display case in the ornate palace.

"How about that one?" he said with a little jerk of his chin.

Magalie followed the gesture to the row of chocolate éclairs, glossy and perfect, voted the best in Paris three years running. Long, thick, blunt-ended, and . . . she gave him an indignant look, while a blush climbed up her face.

He looked innocent but with a little curl he kept trying to press out of the corners of his mouth. "It's chocolate," he offered, guilelessly.

Even a day old, they were probably exquisitely delicious. Just the right size for her mouth to close over it, her teeth to sink into the glossy dark-chocolate surface, finding the cool chocolate cream spurting into her mouth from inside . . .

She swallowed and folded her lips in over her teeth, pressing them together as hard as she could.

A blush was feathering his cheekbones, too. Whistling a little when he could manage the sound through his grin but moving stiffly enough to make her wonder exactly what was happening to his body under that coat of his, Philippe stripped off his gloves and pulled one of his pastry boxes from under the shelf behind the display case. "*Allez,* Magalie, what tempts you the most in here?"

Involuntarily, her eyes went to him. He was big and strong and controlled, his hair curling dark and snow-damp under his hat, his energy even in this quiet moment seeming to fill the whole elegant space. There was a drop of water clinging to his lashes, melted snow. He looked up at her silence, and the drop fell onto his cheek.

He grinned when he found her eyes on him, that quick, hot surge of triumph that both made her giddy with pleasure and made her want to stamp her foot and say she was not his conquest. "Why, thank you, Magalie."

She stuck out her chin.

His gaze went instantly to her throat. "May I say the compliment is entirely returned?"

She flushed slowly with pleasure, despite herself, feeling again a glimpse of that moment the night before when she had felt completely free and strong and proud in her nakedness, Lady Godiva. To be the most tempting thing in this room full of world-famous temptations . . . how could he possibly mean it? Was it true he felt that way about her?

He moved with sudden impatience, surprising her by the careless, quick way he selected half a dozen *macarons* and pastries and filled the box. He didn't do impatience, and most certainly not with his own works of art. *"Tiens. On y va."*

On the way out, he put his phone to his ear. "You guys able to move around in the vans?"

Magalie glanced at him in surprise.

"Go ahead and clean out the display cases when you get a chance to stop by," he said. "They might as well make someone happy. *Oui, bien sûr, à tout à l'heure. Restos du Coeur,*" he explained to Magalie with a shrug as he hung up.

The organization of soup kitchens and vans that fed the homeless and the hungry. "You seem pretty familiar with them."

"Well, they come by three times a week. There's not much I'll sell a day old." He shrugged again, stopping before the main courtyard entrance to her building. "I'm not the only person they'll get a windfall from today. Or a snowfall." His grin flashed.

She looked away from it, her heart squeezing too tightly again. He picked up her hand by the index finger and nudged its gloved tip against the code panel.

She realized suddenly that this had been his goal since at least the Place des Vosges. Not to go back to his apartment. He wanted to be in her place. As he stood close to her and therefore loomed over her in her stupid snowboots, his will tried to wrap around her body and force the code out of her fingers, his eyes hungry, eager.

She gave him a narrow look and, just to be completely annoying and keep up some boundaries badly in need of shoring, she curved her shoulder and left hand over the code panel, blocking what she entered from view.

"Nice, Magalie." Now there was an edge to his voice. Like her aunts, she was totally opposed to shame, but she felt it trouble her, nevertheless. The morning in the snow, his whisper in her ear, the heart of a dessert that had broken her own heart with its beauty, and she was hiding her entry code from him. Maybe particularly because of that rose-heart and its power. "Any delivery boy can have it, but not me?"

"I'm not worried about the delivery boys," she said and realized belatedly that that admission wasn't going to shore up boundaries at all.

He gave her a penetrating look, the line of his mouth relaxing. "Worried about me, are you?" he murmured as he followed her up the winding stairs. His voice came from about the level of her butt. It was probably just as well she was wearing a long, heavy coat.

"When the weather warms up, can you put on a short skirt and those lace leggings of yours and let me escort you home up these stairs?" he suggested, making her bottom tighten and the back of her thighs tingle. Did the man have one constant stream of fantasies going about her?

What an arousing thought.

She didn't answer him, but it occurred to her, oddly, that there was no reason they *wouldn't* be seeing each other in the springtime. It was mid-February. Warmer weather was only a couple of months away. And she wasn't planning on being moved out of this city by anyone, and he wasn't moving, so . . .

Her eyebrows knit in concentration, wondering if she could do this.

It was hard to trust in happiness, coming from another person, but . . . there was so much of it, around him. It squeezed her heart until she couldn't breathe.

He frowned at her doorknob, giving it a tug to make sure it was at least locked. "Magalie, *sérieux,* someone could break this lock with one hard kick."

She turned in the cave of space between his arm, his body, and the wood, suddenly enchanted by the feeling of it all. His size, his closeness, his presence at her door, the snow still melting on them, its scent losing its crispness. On the other side of the door was still her refuge, but at his approach, any loneliness or cold in it had already fled.

He brought both arms up to frame her head with his forearms against the door. "Let me in, Magalie?" It was the coaxing tone that made her realize how much he wanted this. How carefully he had been aiming toward it all morning, and maybe even longer than that.

She had a choice. It felt both sweet and therefore scary to rise up on tiptoe, kiss his snow-cold lips, and unlock the door.

Chapter 28

Philippe was in the witch's tower, and it was all he could do not to wave a damn sword in victory. He didn't want her to kick him out of it, though. She didn't have any visible thorns planted at its base to blind him, but it was a long fall, nevertheless.

He had taken over the tiny space between her little stove and the floor-to-ceiling window that opened inward from the iron railing of a pseudo-balcony front. His body blocked her miniature refrigerator and what there was of her counter space, but that was on purpose. He enjoyed shifting out of her way when she needed to access something and letting her movements brush him. Enjoyed it so much that his sword-waving was getting pretty obvious, now that his coat was off. He kept his stance open, not hiding it from her, wondering what she would do with the knowledge.

She had taken off her caked snowboots at the door, as he had his, but with a slanting glance at him, she had pulled on those thigh-high boots, turning him to molten lava instantly. Now she was stirring that chocolate of hers, and he might as well have been her cauldron, bubbling and melting at every turn of her spoon, thickening and rising and clinging to it, until with one stroke of her finger down the back of the wood, she would see exactly how desperate he was for her.

So he might as well tell her. She seemed to like that.

"You have no idea how hot this makes me." To be in her most inviolate space, with the snow sliding past her windows, and her stirring just for him the chocolate that was both the very symbol of cozy warmth and the epitome of pure temptation. And those damn boots. He was barefoot, a little sign of vulnerability and also of making himself at home, and she was in those boots she knew he lusted after. He loved it.

Her breasts rose and fell at his words. He smiled a little, looking out at her glimpse of the Eiffel Tower and his name down the street, blurred through the snow. Life was very, very good.

He had a lot of work ahead of him, but, God knew, he loved his work.

He slanted a glance down over her butt and thighs and the long leather of her boots and tried to keep his grin contained to something that wouldn't entirely tempt fate. Oh, yes, he had never shied from work.

"What are you wishing on me this time?" He was dreaming of running his fingertip from the top of her head down her spine and over that saucy butt to dip under the top of her boots and skirt around her thighs when he realized that he probably *could*. She might not throw the pot of simmering cream over his head, even.

So he did—from the part in her hair, down around the clasp that held her chignon, back to the line of her spine, down over the nape of her neck, down her back, over the small of her back, over one buttock, and then curling under the edge of leather, following it to her inner thigh.

Her spine flexed under his fingertip, her bottom tightened, and the fine hairs on the nape of her neck rose. Oh, yes, he thought with visceral satisfaction that surged arousal painfully through him. She wanted him. He had that.

He kept his finger tucked in her boot, there at her inner thigh, with malice aforethought, letting the trapped finger wiggle and flex from time to time, his other fingers drifting against that inner thigh, as if he might do something more purposeful with them. But never doing it.

It was so much fun to be cruel. Especially to someone who had just stabbed him, out there on the bridge in the snow.

"Are you wishing me to melt?" he suggested, letting his thumb drift so absently higher on her inner thigh and then tucking it down politely again as if catching an inadvertent stray. Her lips parted when he did it, and she had to pull the lower one in with her teeth. Her bent head tried to indicate a focus on her chocolate.

He never knew he was such a sadist. "Or trying to turn me into a beast?" He pretended his finger was uncomfortably twisted between her leather and legging and that he was trying to wriggle it free. His other fingers grazed randomly with his efforts over whatever was within reach. There was quite a lot of interesting territory that could be "accidentally," oh, so fleetingly in reach.

"Or maybe just to warm a man up on a cold day?"

She lifted eyes that were utterly dazed, her mouth open for him, her gaze clinging to his own lips.

He gave her inner thigh a little squeeze to thank her for his victory, and suddenly his hand found its way free, and he strolled over to her other window, the one he had to kneel on her narrow bed to look out of. His body pointed out to him that he was not just a sadist but a masochist, but he got a rush of hot joy out of abandoning her, nevertheless.

Look like he'd slapped her when he told her he loved her, would she?

Oh, yes, he was going to have a *lot* of fun this afternoon.

"Drink it and find out," she snapped at him. He allowed himself a very mean grin at the snow through her window. *Frustrée, Magalie?*

He rose from her bed, his knee marking the comforter with a stamp of possession that was a promise of things to come. She was going to let him into that bed. Oh, yes, she was. If he had his way, by the end of it, she would want to tie him up and never let him out.

You cruel bastard, quit torturing us with these images, his body begged.

He came back to sip some of the chocolate. She gave it to him hot, very hot, and he took his time playing with it, blowing on it, finally allowing himself one small sip. That sip shot straight through his body and grabbed a fistful of his heart.

He gave her his most vindictive smile. "I don't feel any different."

She thumped her own cup down onto the counter, making no attempt to drink it. He had never seen her drink her own chocolate. It was the kind of thing that could make a man really cautious about poison.

He leaned in and kissed her thoroughly, breaking apart the line her mouth had formed, turning it back into that soft and open and malleable thing and making sure she got a very good taste of her own chocolate off his tongue while he did it.

"Try some of mine, Magalie." He opened the pastry box he had filled at the shop.

"You didn't even make those for me." She sounded sulky, either about her chocolate or his tormenting of her, or maybe a combination. "They were from the display case."

"Magalie, everything I've made for the past four months has been for you."

The sulk softened out of her mouth. Her eyes rose and clung to his in the way they had multiple times last night and this morning, as if trying to find out the truth behind his façade. *What* façade? He had never in his dealings with her been remotely subtle.

She looked back at the box, and he knew before she even tried it that she was going to do something to steal her power back, just by the subtle, almost shy curve of her mouth. Slowly, she drew one perfectly manicured fingernail down the length of the choux of the chocolate éclair, just below the glossy chocolate glaze. His whole body seized at this effort to subjugate him.

She lifted the éclair from its paper wrapping, her fingers handling it so carefully, and brought it to her mouth. Her lips parted around it, and he had just a glimpse of white teeth before they closed over the chocolate. She let her lashes fall, her body sigh, a long, little sound of pleasure.

Arousal beat through him, a flood force that caught him up and tossed his body any way it wanted. He reached up and closed a hand through the handle of one of her cabinets, hanging on for dear life.

"Magalie," he said with thin, lethal warning. "I was going to do this to you anyway, but now you are really going to pay."

Chapter 29

Magalie was just starting to dream of taking control of the situation, her mouth closed around the lusciously suggestive pastry, when Philippe pulled it out of her hands, leaving the cream clinging to her lips and driving her to instant temper. What was wrong with him with his tormenting, broken promises, the touch pulled away, the taste pulled away? And hadn't he gotten her message with the éclair? Why couldn't he just be her victim? He had seemed to like it the night before.

He wrapped her hair around his hand and held her head back, studying that cream on her lips. She knew what he was waiting for her to do, and she tried to refuse him the gesture, but she couldn't, couldn't just leave that cream clinging to her lips forever. Involuntarily, eventually, her tongue slipped out and licked it off.

His teeth showed in fierce triumph. Eyes dilated blue-black. "Good girl," he said approvingly, and she gasped. She hadn't done it *at his command*.

But it nevertheless felt annoyingly and erotically like a reward for good behavior when he pulled her up off the floor and kissed her, lavishly, thoroughly, with no hurry to end. Pushing her back against the cold glass of her window, so that it seeped into her back and her butt while his heat consumed her breasts and belly and the thighs she lifted to wrap around him.

He kissed her . . . forever. Time seemed to blur, until there was nothing but their bodies and their mouths. Until she had always been locked away in this tower, not alone but with a man and his hardness and lips and teeth and tongue. Until she always would be there, the new Lady of Shalott, weaving bodies instead of threads, and a curse be on her if she stay. She wrapped her arms around him as tightly as she could.

He rode her pelvis over his arousal, adjusting her hips to his liking with every change in angle of his kiss. How could he be so deeply aroused and in so little hurry? He just kissed her and kissed her and kissed her, until all the rest of her life drifted away. And there was only his mouth. Only his body.

He tumbled them into her bed and made a rich, hissing sound as he hit it, one hand flexing into her pale covers, a great cat taking possession.

Rolling over her, he pushed his sweater off her, and then her own, and then her top underneath, laughing a little in triumph with each layer, like a person who just loved the box-within-a-box gift trick.

She was used to the first shiver of cold when she hit this bed in the winter, but he chased it all away, his body rubbing heat everywhere.

She protested when he moved to take off her boots. She had put on those boots on purpose. They were her mastery. They were what she would wear to take him over, to take charge, to make him helpless in *her* hands.

He cupped his hand over her sex, through the knit leggings. "Do you want me to rip these in two?" he asked conversationally.

The matter-of-fact menace made her sex bloom hot through the knit against his hand. Could he? The leggings were stretchy and strong and . . . He looked as if he could.

She gave him her leg, which felt like open submission and therefore made her unbearably hot and wet, and he worked the long leather boot down off her thigh over her toes to the ground. Then the next. Then her leggings. Her panties. When he had her completely naked, he smiled suddenly, a smile that made her whole body prickle with delicious vulnerability, and drew the boots back on, over her bare feet and bare legs, the leather gliding against her naked skin.

So, she thought, with a rush of victorious relief. He *did* like to leave the power in her hands. But when she tried to rise off the bed, to come astride him in her boots, he flipped her over as easily as if she was his teddybear and tucked her back against his chest.

His penis pressed hard against her bottom. His arm wrapped around her, holding her against his chest. One of her arms was pressed against his arm and the bed, captive. He curled his hand around her other bicep, a gentle, close hold.

His fingers slipped up and down her cleft, and it unfolded instantly for him. She couldn't have stopped her response. She had no control over it. He did.

And he was in no hurry. He explored her. Not as if he had any immediate goal to let her come. But with intimate curiosity, his fingers pressing apart her folds and tracing over them and inside them as if he could memorize their shape. Pinching them gently as if to learn their consistency, what she was made of.

As she tried to writhe, his easy hold tightened, pulling her back against his chest until his mucles imprinted themselves against her back and her breasts rubbed against the hair and muscles of his forearm. He contained her writhing. Effortlessly. She could barely move.

All her writhing had to transfer downward, to her hips, and even then he mastered it. He let her twist her buttocks against his sex with a laughing growl of approval, and when he decided he wanted to control that, too, he speared two fingers deep inside her. She whimpered and tried to curl over his arm, but he held her tightly back against him. All her inner muscles squeezed onto him, as if she could force him somehow to her nub, the lips of her sex clinging, as if maybe they could somehow writhe her clitoris to him.

But that was not physically possible. She could feel his hardness against her, how much he liked it. But he just kept exploring her at his own pace. No hurry. That man never rushed anything.

"I'm not one of your damn *patisseries,*" she told him.

He laughed.

That laugh drove her wild. She wanted to hate it. She wanted her body to shut down in revolt. And yet it just seemed to blossom further, the muscles of her sex trembling around his fingers, her hips writhing in a vain effort to get his hand where she wanted it.

His fingers, still in her, rotated a little, pressing outward against the walls of her sex, as if still testing what she was made of. She whimpered.

His thumb drifted toward the rear of her cleft.

Her body tried again to curl over his arm, and again he held it still without effort.

The heat washing through her was unbearable. "Philippe."

His thumb rewarded her with a fleeting hard press against her clitoris, there and gone so fast, her sex could only cling desperately to his fingers still inside her, her thighs trying to wrap around his arm. "Do you know that's the first time you've said my name? I like it."

"Please," she whispered. She could feel his hardness against her, his arousal. How could he do this to her? Did he not want her as much? She could make him. She could *make* him. But she couldn't take control while he held her like this.

His fingers spread a little inside her sex. The purr or growl inside his body reverberated through hers. "Yes, beg me," he whispered into her nape. "I like that. Say it again. Say it with my name."

"You bastard."

He pulled his fingers out. "No, that one I've heard before."

Her sex clung bereft to emptiness, and she tried to buck up to press herself against his palm. He pulled it away.

"I love you, Magalie. Have I mentioned that lately? And I want you to beg me."

The words *Je t'aime* washed over her, seeming to loosen something in her while making some other part more afraid. Combined with the open declaration that she should beg, it forced the most uncontrollable heat everywhere through her. "Why?" she protested furiously.

"I just do, Magalie," he said, so it wasn't clear if he was saying why he loved her or why he wanted her to beg. "I have for a long time. Since I met you, really."

"I *knew* you wanted me to beg you in that meeting."

"That, too," he agreed, and her body sparkled all over at the double admission. "You're begging me with your body already, Magalie." His palm rubbed lazily, heavily over her, deliberately just short of her clitoris. "You're so hot and so wet and so . . . open." His fingers flicked elusively over the innermost folds that were all exposed.

Her body jolted helplessly against his imprisoning arm.

"Can't you open yourself to me in other ways, too?"

She *did*. He was in her room right now with her.

"If you invite me in nicely," he breathed against her nape, "I promise you'll enjoy it."

"Philippe." She tried to arch and couldn't and made a little moaning curse under her breath.

"That's a start." His fingers glided in reward more deeply up and down the length of her sex. But he didn't touch that nub. He drew one little circle just around it but never touched it before his hand continued exploring.

Why was she so stubborn and closed and proud? She pressed her head back against his shoulder. "There might be some rewards in it for you, if you stop trying to play power games."

"You mean, if I give up and let you have all the power."

Given how powerless she felt, that was the height of irony.

"Besides, you're always complaining that I barge in where I'm not wanted," he murmured provocatively, the tips of his two fingers playing just inside her but not going deeper. "I'm trying to respect your territory."

"Philippe . . ." She put all the menace a naked, involuntarily clutching and writhing woman could into the word.

"*Allez,* Magalie." His chin was rough against her neck. "Say it," he breathed. "I'm begging you to say it. It excites the hell out of me when you say it."

He was begging her to beg him. That was—like the words *Je t'aime,* it freed something in her. She felt almost protected, held against him so tightly and so helpless. As if the strength of his arm was his promise: *Let go. I've got you.*

I'm as vulnerable as you. Which he couldn't possibly be, but—

"*S'il te plaît.*" She had never asked anyone for anything she desperately needed in French before. She felt, oddly, a spark of hope. It was like a new beginning. "*Philippe.*"

He bit into the nape of her neck like a cat and pressed his palm down hard, rotating her sex against her pubic bone. She jumped into him, convulsing against his hold, her body giving itself up so uncontrollably, everything in her dissolving and shattering while he held her together so tightly, that when she finally begin to sink limply against him again, tears were leaking out of her eyes.

His hand rode her down gently, caressing her through the aftershocks, keeping them going, and letting her subside slowly, slowly, until so much had drained from her that she was almost asleep.

Then he turned her over onto her back and licked the tears from her temples like an animal craving salt. He combed her hair back from her damp face and pressed it to the bed, holding her head still as he kissed her everywhere, all over her face, coming back to take her mouth again and again.

He wrapped both his arms under her and squeezed her up against his chest hard as he slid into her, as if he couldn't hold her tightly enough. Her body started to tremor again around him, tightening reflexively in what she thought at first were more aftershocks, and he made a low, hungry sound.

She ran her hands down his back, feeling the hardness of the muscles all in play, the arch of his spine. Finding tight buttocks and digging in, holding on for the ride as it got harder. She was close to coming again from the pleasure of that hard, steady ride, the use of her, the way he so clearly loved it, but she didn't think he realized it, his focus seeming to have drawn down, down, into his own body. She clenched again on him, and his body thrust deep, deep into hers, and he came, holding her tightly against him.

Afterward, when he eased off her and rolled them both to their sides, her body curled back against his in the position that had started this, she found his hand and slid it between her legs again. His muscles were all heavy against her, and she thought he was almost asleep, her second peaking like a secret. But his thumb curled up and cooperated, and he pressed a kiss against her shoulder when she finished.

He pulled the comforter over both of them, no cold left in her bed, nor in all the room. "It's not so bad being invaded, is it?" he murmured provocatively.

She smacked his forearm, but without force, and he nestled his head a little in the bed of her hair and laughed, drifting to sleep.

Chapter 30

When the contact at the Restos du Coeur called back to say they couldn't get a pick-up van through the streets, Philippe grimaced and pocketed his phone, gazing down through the snow at his shop. "Talk about a waste," he said. "And everything we had half-prepped for today is going to go, too. But"—he shrugged. *What can you do?*

Magalie came to stand beside him in her heavy bathrobe, tucked up against the warmth of his body, the cold of the window before them. "You should have a block party," she murmured.

"What is that?" he asked blankly.

"It's an American thing. It's kind of like a *fête villageoise,* but your village is your street. I mean, everyone on the Île is in their apartments all up and down here looking out at the snow. You should just invite them all over."

He gazed at her for just a second before a white grin split his face. "That would be incredible fun."

She grinned back, taken by her own idea and his enthusiasm for it. "It would, wouldn't it?"

"And I bet a lot of people are dying for a cup of your chocolate about now. You know, it's hot-chocolate weather."

She made a face. "Our place isn't big enough for that kind of crowd." Plus, she had been imagining herself at Philippe's side, having fun in this event, not down the street, feeling exiled.

Wait just a damn minute. When had being in her own place making *chocolat chaud* ever felt like exile?

"But, Magalie," he purred, "you know you are entirely welcome in my kitchens. *Je t'invite.*"

She prickled just a little, but the idea was irresistible. Grinning, they bundled up again, pounding on the aunts' door as they went downstairs, Magalie calling people she knew in different buildings to get them to start shaking out the neighbors: Thierry, Claire-Lucy, Aimée. Claire-Lucy was, in fact, at Madame Fernand's when the call reached her, having walked her dog for her to make sure the old lady did not slip and break her hip in the snow, and she promised to hold her arm all the way down the street.

Geneviève had applied her life-ironing abilities to getting Gérard to spend the cold night at his daughter's, but he was back outside already and regarding Geneviève with a particularly gargoylish glare. But he came, too, freshly showered at his daughter's insistence, and Philippe let not only him in but his German shepherd with him. "Because"—he grinned at Magalie—"I have kind of a fondness for that dog now."

Magalie clenched her fist but managed not to hit him. Sissi the poodle snubbed the German shepherd haughtily today, sticking to Madame Fernand at her little elegant table, over by a rosebud-entwined marble pillar.

Thierry brought all his leftover roses and passed one out to every single woman there, making some of them entirely happy. Claire-Lucy chatted happily with Aimée as each of them waved a red rose in one hand and a pastry in the other to punctuate their comments.

"It's too bad all that dough in the refrigerators still has to go to waste," Philippe said to Magalie. "I can't make all the kouign-amann single-handedly, though."

"We can do it!" Claire-Lucy exclaimed, overhearing. "Just tell us how."

Philippe exchanged a long, thoughtful look with one of the lion heads in the corners of his ceiling, presumably asking it for patience against the presumption that just anyone could make his pastries with a few simple instructions. Then he laughed suddenly, that rich laugh that had been one of the first sounds Magalie had ever heard from him, reaching out and grabbing everything around it into its vivid embrace. *"Allez. Pourquoi pas?"*

A laughing group spilled back into the kitchens, the fun and adventure of the snow party infecting everyone.

"You know a lot of women," he murmured to Magalie as he opened one of the walk-in refrigerator doors on shelves and shelves of dough. "The milk's in the next one, by the way. And the chocolate is in those cabinets. Are they all single?"

Her chin jerked up. "Why do you want to know?"

He just looked at her for a second. "You know, I might feel self-satisfied at the jealousy, if it wasn't so incredibly stupid." He pulled out his phone again, texting, then showed it to her. A group message to *Équipe Labo*, it read: *No, I'm not making anyone come in today, don't worry. But if you feel so inclined, there are one hell of a lot of single women who don't know how to cook trying to make* kouign-amann *in our kitchens right now.*

It was amazing, he said later, how passable the streets were with the right motivation. It was almost as if the city had a Métro or something.

Half an hour later, counters were lined with women and men leaning over them, some grinning, some intent. A group of children on stools were playing with dough on one floured counter. It must have gotten onto Twitter, because Christophe, Le Gourmand, had somehow slipped in, even though his apartment was way over in the Ninth, and he seemed entirely unaffected by the occasional exasperated glances from the store's owner. "Hi, Chantal," he said, stopping to stand near a woman Magalie remembered vaguely for her ability to toss her head and the fact that she had, like a lot of women who came to La Maison des Sorcières, a tendency to sell herself short.

Chantal looked up, stiffened, and looked awkward but oddly hopeful. Some old history there, huh? Christophe considered her for a careful, thoughtful moment. "Do you want me to help you?" he asked at last. "I'm not saying I'm up to Philippe's standards, but I did a long exploration of *kouign-amann* for my blog."

Chantal ran her fingers through her hair, which left it coated with flour. A little of the white stuff ended up on Christophe's cheek when she tossed her hair "Thank you," she said softly. "That would be nice."

Where had Chantal come from, anyway? She wasn't an island resident. There seemed to be quite a lot of people who had walked across Paris in the snow and found themselves here, and most of them asked for hot chocolate first thing.

"Wow," one murmured to another as they sipped from their cups, walking away from Magalie's pot of chocolate, a giant thing so big and heavy, Magalie felt as if she should be muttering *"Double, double, toil and trouble"* over it. "I think I'm glad that Sorcières place we read about was closed. I don't care what that blog said, their chocolate can't possibly be better than this."

Magalie ground her teeth together. Then she wrote a big sign and set it in front of the pot, saying, *Chocolate provided by La Maison des Sorcières.*

Philippe, helping Madame Fernand fold her *kouign-amann*, glanced across at her and laughed out loud.

Claire-Lucy looked up with flour on her nose and beamed at Magalie as Grégory put his arms on either side of her to show her how to fold. "This is fantastic," she told her. "I'll never forget this snowstorm in my entire life. What a fabulous idea Philippe had to do this."

Magalie, stirring her chocolate, bit her teeth together on an indignant protest. Philippe gave her a salt-in-the-wound grin.

A minute later, he helped Madame Fernand place her *kouign-amann* on a pan and came over to put his arm around Magalie's shoulders. "Let me have a cup?"

"You like to live dangerously, don't you?" Magalie muttered, filling it. But she could hardly try her first adventure in cursing chocolate when the pot was for such a big crowd.

"I should think that would be obvious by now." He lifted the cup to the gathering. "A chocolate toast," he said, and that easily, his golden voice took over the entire room and brought everyone's attention to him. Even Claire-Lucy's, and she had been busy getting Grégory to help her fasten a pastry jacket over her breasts. Philippe pulled Magalie snugly in front of and back against him. "To Magalie Chaudron, who had the idea for this party and so graciously agreed to make her hot chocolate in my kitchens for all of you."

Well, that was finally appropriate behavior on his part, Magalie thought. To give her credit where credit was due. It took her a second to realize the way everyone was looking at her: stunned, amused, pleased, indulgent, approving, incredulous, thoughtful in Aja's case, and outraged in Geneviève's. It was quite a range, really. And then they all looked above her to Philippe. She twisted her head back suddenly to try to catch his expression.

Smug. Unbearably smug.

Why, had he just staked his *ownership* of her out loud and clearly for the entire island? *Why, yes, I did win this battle, thank you, and she is* mine.

He waved his cup of hot chocolate generously, on cue, inviting his subjects to continue celebrating his victory.

She turned toward his chest so that no one else could see how tightly her teeth were gritting. "I might seriously kill you one day," she said between them.

"Believe me, I've realized that a few times in the past twenty-four hours." He took a sip of the chocolate. "But a man's got to die sometime, and it's hard to imagine a better way to go."

And while Magalie was sputtering over the meaning he had just put into her threat, flushing and wrestling desperately with the urge to dump the entire cauldron of chocolate over his head, he *tweaked her nose* where everyone could see and strolled off to make sure all *their* guests were enjoying the party.

In the end, when people were giddy from sugar shock, Aunt Aja orchestrated a stone-soup movement, and Philippe's kitchens filled with great pots of something bubbly and curry-influenced. Philippe and Magalie took bowls of it and tucked themselves up at his most intimate table, against one of the great glass windows, slightly sheltered from the room by a pillar.

The snow had tapered off, but the street outside was still lovely with it, despite or because of the footprints everywhere that showed the way their island of Parisians had played all day long. The streetlamps glowed beautifully against crystals of ice, rich gold warming the snow.

"Would you rather we sleep at my place or yours?" Philippe asked, and she curled her hands around the warm bowl with an involuntary burst of happiness at his assumption. Strange, how some of the ways he was arrogant hit her just right.

And, even more oddly, she wasn't even sure she cared about the answer. Attached though she was to her sense of place, either seemed just fine to her. "Your bed is bigger."

He smiled. "That has its pros and cons."

"But mine is closer to work. And less far to go in the snow."

"That has its pros and cons, too," he laughed. "I like walking with you in the snow. But I also like being tucked up warm with you in an apartment, watching it."

She smiled, feeling peaceful, as if she was resting on a great downy mattress of happiness and neither of these choices could really go wrong. "Let's see how late it is when the party breaks up."

He took a bite of his curry stone-soup concoction, eyebrows lifting a little in pleasure at the flavor. "Your aunt cooks like this a lot, you said?"

She smiled a little around an odd vision of him tucking himself up at their dinner table. It would certainly change the dynamic. In fact, she was not entirely sure his legs would fit under the aunts' table. Her head tilted as she considered the vision. She was deeply uncomfortable with changed dynamics inside her home, and yet it didn't feel wrong. More like the oddly enticing discomfort of the spice in Aunt Aja's curry.

Philippe took another bite, watching her. "Your Aunt Geneviève said you had trouble trusting others."

Magalie blinked. "I don't distrust others."

"*En fait,* she said you had learned what trust you do have from her and Aja, which I found disquieting, to say the least."

"It doesn't really come up," Magalie said, perplexed. "Trusting others. I mean, trust them with what?"

Philippe gazed at her with sardonic resignation. "Your feelings, for example."

"Why would I do that?"

He shrugged as if she had made his point, aggravating her, because she hadn't.

"My feelings are my own responsibility. I don't see what trust has to do with it. I can't go around handing them off to other people."

He toyed with his spoon. His mouth had an odd, wry curve. "I would try to take good care of them."

She gave a crack of laughter that made anger tighten his mouth. "You would not. You would try to take them over, do anything you wanted with them, if I handed them off to you."

Now he was seriously ticked. It ran through every tight line of his body. "What the hell makes you think that?"

"You just *would*. It's who you are. It's who people are, period, but you're worse than most."

"I am *not*."

Anger crackled so strongly in him, she could tell he could barely sit still. For once, she hadn't made him angry on purpose, so she tried to explain. "You're stronger than most."

"So are you, Magalie."

She sat back, thrown by how true that sounded. Her parents had always said the same thing about her. Her aunts had always shown it without saying it. She herself had always felt so impatiently competent and in control of herself compared to all the heart-torn princesses who wandered into their shop seeking consolation in a cup of chocolate. "But when I go out into the city, when I leave La Maison, I feel like I'm going to war."

Surely most people handled that more easily? Even princesses. Particularly princesses. Didn't her sense that she had to armor herself indicate her own weakness?

"Vraiment?" His anger faded as he reached across the table and curled just the tips of his fingers into hers. "That explains a lot." He studied her, as if he was trying to peer through a narrow gap in a fence to figure out what was behind it. "You still go, though," he said after a moment. "You go confront

arrogant princes"—he dipped his haughty head in sublime acceptance of his role as prince—"you brave shops for every delicious item of clothing you wear, you put your hair up in a ponytail and go running. Could I go running with you, Magalie?"

"No," she said instinctively, taken aback. His mouth set. The light in his eyes cooled, was shielded. "I like that time by myself." But even as she said it, a vision snuck in, of them running together quietly in the dawn, not speaking, in perfect peace and harmony. "Maybe sometimes . . ." she said slowly, softly, wonderingly. Was that something she could *share?*

He tilted her hand up so that her palm pressed against his and interlaced their fingers. His mouth softened. She liked the way his bigger hand spread hers just a little too much, a not entirely comfortable fit. She liked the way she was getting used to it, after a day of snow and lovemaking and that glowing warmth that had spilled everywhere from their neighborhood party.

It terrified her to realize suddenly that she was getting used to it. That was the one thing she most preferred not to do, with people. Get used to them.

It had taken her years to get used to her aunts, and despite Aja's claims of making room, she thought mostly she and her aunts did so well with each other because none of them did the jigsaw-puzzle thing. They just stayed the shape they were, and tough luck for other people running into their pointy, hard edges.

Nobody gave herself away.

Not even to a prince who smiled at her across a table and lifted her hand to kiss the inside of her wrist, just there.

It was astonishingly warm and comfortable to spend the night in his apartment, which was where they ended up, out of curiosity to see the rest of Paris in the snow one more time before they went to bed. Astonishing, because to hold onto one place had been so important to her for so long now.

But Philippe seemed delighted to have her, happiness expanding out from him until it filled the whole place like light, and he had to draw the curtains for once in case there was so much light and happiness inside, people could start seeing in. In the private cave of his room, he at first slept curled toward her, then eventually sprawled away from her on his stomach like a man not used to sharing his bed. She slept little, woken constantly by his movements in his sleep, but it wasn't until around three in the morning that she felt that little knot of cold and anguish in her again. That *What am I doing?* feeling.

She swallowed it as best she could. She had no patience with people who wallowed forever in their childhoods and sold short the rest of their lives. And it had never occurred to her before the past few days that she might be doing that.

She finally fell solidly asleep when he rolled back over and tucked himself into her breasts as a pillow, and then she slept late, but he didn't have the luxury. She felt him kiss her and woke to see his back as he left the bedroom and heard the outside door close behind him. She dragged herself home and went out for a slow and careful run through the icy patches of snow, which entirely failed to clear her head.

Magalie was working in the display window later that day, just before opening, when the timbre of a voice that came through the glass made her head lift and her heart perk up. In front of the shop windows, on a sidewalk salted for Madame Fernand's sake, Philippe was talking to Geneviève, who seemed to be acting quite pleasant. Magalie pricked her ears, but Geneviève wasn't trying to lower her voice, so no secrets carried through the glass. She leaned deep into the display window, ostensibly to scoop up a spoonful of crystallized roses. ". . . not enough self-confidence . . ." she thought she heard Geneviève say. *"C'est un vrai problème."*

Magalie drew back, frowning. Who *was* Geneviève talking about?

Philippe glanced at her through the glass and held her gaze for a moment without smiling. Her heart started to beat too fast, as his looks always made it do.

His eyes crinkled up just a little at the corners, a hint of a smile despite his serious expression, and he blew her a kiss.

She blinked and spilled rose petals everywhere, and he broke into a grin. He looked for a moment as if he was going to walk into the shop and kiss her for real, but instead he clasped Geneviève's hand, handing her a package, and Geneviève shook her head and kissed him on both cheeks.

Philippe rubbed one knuckle against one of those cheeks as he turned back toward his shop, looking rather pleased.

Geneviève handed the package to Magalie when she came into the shop, a soft, floppy package, the sticker on its wrapping paper belonging to a clever Marais designer. Geneviève stood over her, studying her and shaking her head. "It's like seeing your own child grow up to be a unicorn or something," she said. "It's hard to understand. But he's growing on me. I don't think I'll mind so much."

Flushing, Magalie concentrated on her package.

It was a scarf. Rich blue that matched *his* eyes, cashmere.

The card tucked inside had more than just his name on it, this time. It said, *If I have to work you out of this tower one rag at a time, we're definitely doing the sexual-fantasies version. Philippe.*

Magalie folded it quickly against her belly and looked up. Geneviève glanced away guiltily, trying so hard to look uninterested that for a second Magalie thought her aunt was going to start whistling. From the card against her belly, heat grew and stretched through her, pooling and concentrating in all kinds of areas she didn't want her aunt to know about.

"Don't you worry about Philippe Lyonnais at all?" Magalie asked and wished desperately that her tongue didn't curl around his name as if she were saying the king's.

"I tried to give him some tea," Aunt Aja said from behind them. She was sweeping the floor. That had once been assigned as Magalie's job, but Aunt Aja kept doing it no matter how many times Magalie went back over it. She said it was a very satisfying feeling, to sweep the floor clean of old messes. "If he refused to drink it, on his own head be it." Her black eyes held Magalie's.

Magalie tried to look as full of tea as possible. Aunt Aja had not offered her a cup of tea since that day a month ago when Magalie had secretly tossed her cup into the Seine. That *could* be because Aja thought that one cup was enough, but it could also be because Magalie was now labeled as an ingrate. But what if she had drunk it and it had made her too clear-headed to allow Philippe in, for example? That didn't bear thinking about.

"And I'm not that altruistic," Geneviève said. "If he had stopped, knocked politely, asked our leave, maybe. But he can't come in as if he owns this island and expect me to worry about him."

Magalie stared at both her aunts, for a moment completely confused. Finally, it clicked that they had misunderstood her. "I don't mean worry about him as if he were your child heading off down the wrong road! I mean, worry about what having him here is doing to La Maison des Sorcières."

The aunts gazed at her for a moment in deep concern. Clearly, though, for *her*. Then they exchanged a glance that made Magalie want to show them her report card from school and swear she was doing all right.

"Our customers!" she cried.

"Oh, those." Aja shrugged. "They'll go away eventually.

Besides, I really think the influx is more your fault than Philippe's. I told you you didn't have to make your chocolate call people all the way from Timbuktu."

"I meant not having *enough* customers!" Magalie fairly shouted in frustration.

"What, just because there weren't so many of them the first few weeks he was open?" Aja waved a hand. "We don't have to compete with fads."

A fad. Magalie grinned at a vision of Philippe setting his back teeth.

"Besides, we don't want too many people to know about us. The fun is being a secret."

"And *you* weren't here yesterday morning," Geneviève said severely. "People trying to rattle our doorknob off to get in on a *snow day,* because of that Christophe's blog about our chocolate. Rattling our doorknob. Is that polite?"

"The snow made them worse, I think. Something about hot chocolate and snow. It was very thoughtful of Philippe to host a party at his place to draw them off," Aunt Aja reminded her spouse. "At Magalie's suggestion, too. You see, they can both be taught."

Magalie had brightened. "That blog worked? You mean, we won't go out of business?"

Both the aunts stared at her for a long moment. They exchanged one of those glances that made her feel thirteen. "Maybe we should tell her," Aunt Aja suggested.

"I was *hoping* she would learn her own power," Geneviève protested.

"She's very young. You're rushing her. If she's still acting like this when she's in her forties, then we'll know there's a problem."

"By then it would be too late!" Geneviève sounded like a witch who had read one too many parenting books. "You can't change a person in her forties!"

Aunt Aja shook her head, dismissing parenting books as a

waste of paper. "Do you know how much we rent those other apartments for?" she asked her niece.

Magalie shook her head. "Several thousand?"

Geneviève gave Aja a disgruntled look and told her.

Magalie opened her mouth and closed it a few times like a gasping fish out of water. "That's twice as much a month as my annual salary." For one apartment. That explained a lot about why Aunt Aja and Aunt Geneviève only opened the shop from two to eight, five days a week, and closed for two months in the summer.

Geneviève gave her shoulder an affectionate pat. "Yes, you do help keep our overhead down."

"Can I have a raise?" Although, continuing the rental math, her own free studio apartment must be worth . . . also more than her annual salary. That was some gift Geneviève's old lover had given her, back when she was Magalie's age.

Geneviève gave her a severe look. "You would just spend it all on clothes."

Yes, well . . . "So?"

"You can't buy confidence in a clothing store, Magalie."

Magalie stared at her aunt blankly. "Are you kidding? This is Paris."

Geneviève gestured to her cotton caftan superbly. It might be a generational gap, but Magalie couldn't think of a polite way to express her reaction to the idea of wearing a cotton caftan.

"And what's this about confidence? I have plenty of confidence. People have been commenting on it all my life." In two languages. *Such a self-confident little girl,* her teachers used to write in their comments. *So centered. Si sûre d'elle.* To her teachers' credit, they had usually managed to make her sureness of herself sound like a compliment and not a danger to anyone else's authority.

Geneviève snorted. "As if they know anything about self-confidence."

Probably in comparison with Aunt Geneviève's, most people's knowledge of confidence could fit on the head of a pin.

"*I* know something about self-confidence," Magalie said, affronted.

This time it was Aunt Aja who patted her shoulder. "It's all right. You're still an apprentice. You've got plenty of time to learn."

"Go practice on that boy of yours," Geneviève added. "You don't meet many people who let you practice your self-confidence on them that way. The ones who do are either very weak or very strong." Her brown eyes glinted. "Which do you think he is?"

Chapter 31

At a wild guess, *not* weak.

Philippe created an immediate rhythm. Strong, confident, not asking for permission. Sometime in the early afternoon, usually within an hour of the tea shop's opening, he would stop by for ten or fifteen minutes. Then, later, when she and he both quit for the day, he would come back to take her out to a restaurant and take her home again, his or hers.

Geneviève was always glad to see him, as it gave her a chance to blame him for the flood of customers who were making her crabby. "First you move in here and attract everyone's attention this way, then your friend Sylvain begs me to help him with one of his windows and goes around letting people pick up our business cards, and then that Christophe has to blog about your crush on Magalie's chocolate. You're nothing but trouble."

"It will die down," Aunt Aja soothed. "Eventually. You know it will."

"I wish I could take all the blame," Philippe said, "but really I feel that most of your ability to attract customers is due to you three."

Geneviève narrowed her eyes at him as if she suspected impudence. Philippe just leaned back against the counter, his presence competing firmly with hers to dominate the overcrowded kitchen, until Magalie felt like the stuffed inside of a sandwich fighting valiantly to prove she was the best part.

"And you." Geneviève pointed a firm finger at her niece. "No more showing that Christophe our recipes in his kitchen."

Philippe beamed at her. "Tante Geneviève, I believe we shall deal very well together."

"*So* presumptuous," Aunt Geneviève said of him, resigned, and sailed out to deal with the customers who had just heard her complaining about them. She was trying her best to make sure her complaints were audible, but instead of driving people away, the complaints kept showing up on new food blogs as her "charming idiosyncracies." Now that Christophe had spoken, with no lesser authorities than Philippe Lyonnais and Sylvain Marquis to back him up, *all* the food bloggers were following in his wake. There had been some blog called A Taste of Elle that had used so many exclamation points about them, Magalie had double-checked the doses in Aunt Aja's tea. They didn't want to give anyone a heart attack.

Magalie hadn't yet told Tante Geneviève that her behavior was being labeled a "charming idiosyncracy," because, well . . . things could get ugly.

At her exit, Aunt Aja, too, picked up a tray and left the kitchen, making herself discreet.

"I'm pretty sure Christophe is dating someone new now," Magalie said. They had come by again the day before and sat there at one of the little tables for a long time, talking, Christophe and the woman named Chantal. She didn't toss her head nearly as much when she was around him, either, as if he reassured her somehow.

Philippe made a firm noise of approval at Christophe's dating someone else.

"Also, I think your chefs might be infiltrating the place. I've seen Grégory in Claire-Lucy's toy shop twice, and one of your guys—Olivier?—is definitely flirting with Aimée. Are they good guys?"

"I can't really claim to keep up with their dating habits, Magalie. You're the one who has been feeding my team hot chocolate for weeks. They're probably whatever you made out of them."

Magalie gave him an exasperated look. Now he was starting to sound like the aunts. As if he really *believed* her chocolate could change people, instead of pretending to believe it, the way she did.

Philippe smiled a little, shifting easily out of her way when she reached for something. He drank an espresso-size cup of her hot chocolate, watching her as he did it with warm eyes and desire slumbering in them, held in abeyance at that hour of the afternoon.

"What did you wish on me this time?" he murmured, sipping slowly, as if he wanted to savor the chocolate or the moment as long as possible.

That the afternoons like this, him stopping in her kitchen, and the evenings when he came back, could go on forever. She stared at the remaining chocolate in the pot, dissatisfied with her wishing, because wishes could only be for the inside of a person. You couldn't wish things from time. Besides, that one sounded like a wish she would have to wish on *herself,* and she wasn't sure her chocolate worked that way.

She wasn't even sure her chocolate worked. It was a nice game, but Philippe certainly seemed immune.

"I don't feel any different," he said. As he always did. "Unless—did you wish me happiness by any chance?"

Brightness spilled through her. He smiled and kissed her, so that she tasted the chocolate on his lips, and happiness unfurled inside her and tried to reach out and latch its roots into him.

She frowned, wondering if she could turn happiness into a container plant. She had been doing a really good job of it

before. Now the stuff was acting like mint, which her herbal-
ist mother had always warned her about when she'd taught
Magalie gardening in Provence. No matter what you did,
mint eventually escaped and sent its roots all over the place.

"Who's the lavender from?" Philippe asked suddenly.

She blinked. Had he somehow *scented* her thought?

"On the wall in your room. In your accent. On your underwear when you first put it on." A blush sparkled across
her cheeks at the memory of the times he had had his nose
anywhere near her underwear when she first put it on.
"Who did it come from?"

"My mother. You don't hear Provence as much with
Geneviève, because she came to Paris when she was eigh-
teen, but she and my mother grew up in lavender fields near
Chamaret."

He smiled a little, his gaze running over her as if he was
seeing a charming vision. "And you? Did you grow up in a
lavender field?"

"Sometimes," she said briskly, beginning to unload the
tiny dishwasher of its last set of thimble-size glasses and
handle-less cups. "Yes. All the summers."

His eyes sparkled. "I can see you as a little girl in a field of
purple. Can we take—" He caught his lower lip between his
teeth abruptly. His eyes flared, as if he had shocked himself.

What? Her head tilted, and she studied him, scenting after
something in his expression. What had he wondered? What
had made him so wary?

"Could we take a vacation there this summer?" he finished slowly, watching her very cautiously.

That wasn't what he had been about to say. Her eyebrows
flexed together uncertainly. Summer was only a few months
away, true. Not that much farther than the warming weather
he had mentioned the other day. Still, from winter to summer seemed like an eternity to count on anything. Even
though she had just wished for things to go on forever.

She took a deep breath. She wanted to say yes. She *wanted* to relax and count on the summer. But she felt physically sick when she tried to get it out. Her heartbeat raced, and her palms actually got clammy. "Um, yes," she said hurriedly, refusing to let her stupid old issues keep her down, but she had to turn around quickly and focus on her chocolate, breathing carefully, trying to calm her stomach. "We can," she said too loudly and too definitely.

There was a moment's silence behind her. Then his cup clicked on the counter. He wrapped an arm around her from behind and squeezed her back against him so tightly that her breath huffed out of her and her feet left the floor. "See you this evening."

He looped something silk-soft around her throat, tugging it just enough to make her feel leashed and a little breathless. "An advance," he murmured and was gone.

Released from his hold, the softness slipped down her arms over her fingers: a garnet-red scarf.

"So where is your father from?" he asked that evening in her apartment, come to pick her up for dinner, leaning against her little counter watching her consider clothing options. A layer of scarves draped from the hook on the back of her closet door. She was starting not to know where to fit them all.

"America," Magalie said in a tone that did not invite conversation.

Of course, Philippe ignored that closed door, as he did everything else that tried to keep him out. "You're American?" he said, astonished. "I never would have g—"

He was saying *I never would have guessed,* and she could feel the reassurance growing in her with the words, that confirmation that she did, indeed, belong here.

But he broke off, with that intrigued tilt of his head. "So that's what I heard, that little hint of Cade Corey."

Cade Corey very clearly did not belong in Paris. Her accent marked her unmistakably as foreign every time she spoke. She only belonged because Sylvain Marquis had accepted her. Magalie folded her arms, dikes in place, protecting her island. Her belonging depended only on herself.

"I'm both," she said, turning away. "American and French. Dual nationality." She walked over to her favorite window, the one from which she could just catch a glimpse of the Tour Eiffel when it sparkled.

"What does your father do?" asked His Highness, who thought all doors were there for him to walk through and missed the whole point about locks and keys and shutting him out.

"He's an apiculturalist."

"Bees." Philippe laughed. "Bees and lavender. *Bon sang,* I can *smell* them in you. Under all that chocolate." And then, abruptly, on another note entirely: "That *salaud* Sylvain. Is that where that new chocolate of his came from? The honey-lavender?"

She hadn't even known Sylvain had put out a new chocolate. Magalie turned and gave him an incredulous look. Intimacy was clearly not her thing. How he could imagine she was engaging in it with more than one person at once was beyond her. "I think the closest we've ever gotten was working on that window of his."

"That's close enough," Philippe said, pissed off. "He's got a very good sense of smell."

"He's also crazy about Cade Corey, you know."

Philippe made the sound of a man who hadn't been born in the last rainshower. "He's moved the date of the wedding. It was supposed to be in March, and now it's June."

"That's because Cade's sister is in the hospital. He told me about it while we were working on the window. She got hurt pretty badly in the Côte d'Ivoire, near some cacao cooperative. Trust me, no one is going to change Sylvain's mind about Cade."

Again that doubtful grunt. "Sylvain knows superior quality when he sees it."

Her heart gave a funny jump that seemed to spill warmth from it all through her. "Superior to a beautiful billionaire?"

"Clearly." Philippe sounded startled he had to point it out.

"I think he's latched onto her," Magalie said dryly. "I don't know how they're going to handle that question of place."

"That question of place?"

"Well, he obviously has to be here. He's the best chocolatier in the world."

Philippe shrugged. "He's not bad with bonbons."

Magalie bit back a grin. "And she's heir to a multinational corporation headquartered in the U.S. Here I always thought *my parents* had a tough choice between place and person."

He narrowed his eyes at her, that alert look, the one he had in restaurants when he was trying to identify an elusive taste. "Your parents? Bees and lavender didn't turn out to be the match made in heaven?"

"Oh, sure. But academic career at Cornell, lavender fields in Provence, back and forth and back and forth, trying to figure out a happiness that allowed them both to be who they wanted to be . . . There's no way Sylvain and Cade can do that; someone will have to give it all up."

"Cade," Philippe said, like someone in the know.

Magalie slumped in relief. "Oh, thank God. If Paris had lost Sylvain to Corey Chocolate, I might have had to kill her." But she wondered if it hurt Cade at all, to give up her place for Sylvain. Or whether she was just so convinced she owned the whole world, she didn't care what part of it she was in.

Philippe pressed his lips together. "Have you been eating his chocolates all this time you've been snubbing my desserts?"

"I like chocolate."

He folded his arms. "Magalie. I didn't want you to make me have to do this, because you're so sensitive about competition. But if you want chocolate, I can make you chocolate"—he leaned toward her a little, his teeth showing sharp—"that will melt your insides out."

She lifted her chin at him, feeling those insides melt just at the thought of him trying.

He, of course, went for her throat.

There might be more than one reason he kept buying her so many scarves.

Chapter 32

Two days later, Philippe brought Magalie one of his boxes. She opened it carefully, her heart racing in anticipation. It was simple. The simplest thing he had ever brought her. A *macaron* of chocolate, its shell glossy and perfect and freckled prettily with a dusting of darker cocoa that had been baked in. The *pieds,* the ruffled band around the base of each shell, were, of course, exquisite. She picked it up, mouth watering already, just from the texture against her fingers. The ganache inside the shell was a pale, creamy color, with maybe just a whisper of purple but maybe not.

She looked at him. He was excited, eager to see her reaction. But he didn't have that *go-ahead-and-strip-naked-now* look on his face that he did when he handed her some of his creations, either. So he wasn't convinced she would have an orgasm on her first bite. This was a softer look, intense.

She bit into it, and—his standards for orgasms must be extremely high, because she still felt a mild one. A rush of bliss at the whisper of a crunch and the yield in the chocolate *macaron,* then the crisp, scented, somehow familiar flavor of the ganache. She opened her eyes again, letting it melt on her tongue. God, he was so good. "Lavender?"

He nodded, his eyes alight with pleasure. But he leaned against her window, his arms crossed. Still waiting.

She took another bite. More lusciousness. How did he

manage to be so good? Lavender and chocolate. Her heritage and her present, her and her mother. Another bite, into the middle, and a thin cocoa shell hidden in the ganache yielded to her teeth, and its insides burst onto her tongue, a melting liquid honey caramel.

Oh. Her father was there, too. It was all of her. And it was delicious.

She looked at him, the bright, warm lion leaning against her cold window, so sure that she would love it. Had he spent two days on this? Dreaming up the best way to combine those three flavors in tribute to her?

Her eyes stung. She had to rub them quickly.

He came away from the window at once, scooping her up across his arms like a child, his eyes astonished. He laid her down on her bed and made slow, cuddling love to her, and they missed his dinner reservations.

"How much back and forth are we talking about?" he asked suddenly, later that night, as they headed out to get some falafel in his corner of Paris. There was still a softness between them, a gentleness that seemed to stretch from that earlier lovemaking into the evening. They were crossing the bridge over to l'Hôtel de Ville, Paris's other bridges stretching away from them over the dark water in bracelets of illumination, the façade of l'Hôtel glowing in the night. The ice rink had been removed. Spring was coming.

It was funny how, subtly, after five years of bastioning herself on her island, her sense of place was expanding. First the running, then the snow, then walking the streets with Philippe, focused on the two of them and indifferent to anyone else—sometimes she felt as if her soul was unfurling, like great wings that had been caught too long in a cocoon. Or maybe just as long as they'd needed to be to get ready?

"I don't know. Do you want me to try to count it up?"

"Yes."

Seriously, he just walked *through* doors, as if someone was supposed to be leaping to open them for him. How many times did she have to slam one in his nose for him to get the point that her doors were sacred? But she felt so soft. She didn't feel like struggling to hold this door closed. "I don't really remember from before I was four or so, but I know I was born in the U.S., and I think Maman tried the first year there, and then my dad pulled all kinds of strings to spend the next year in Provence. I remember kindergarten was in the U.S., and what would have been first grade, *l'école primaire,* was here. In Chamaret, not Paris. Dad came over for the holidays, spring break, and Cornell lets out in early May, so he spent that summer here. Then Maman steeled herself and tried to go back again but only made it through half the year. I guess it was pretty cold in Ithaca that year. I remember having fun in the snow and then all of a sudden being in the middle of the mistral instead. That was second grade. Then Dad got a fellowship for two years here. That worked out really well; everyone was happy. I misunderstood; I thought we were going to be able to stay."

Philippe's hand flexed on hers. But he didn't say anything.

"I was always misunderstanding things like that." She shook her head ruefully. "Then back and forth a bit more. Sometimes Maman and I would be here; sometimes she would dig in there again and try to stick it out. We were always in Provence for summers; they worked something out with my school when it was a U.S. one so that I could do May's schoolwork from a distance. A couple of times they talked about divorce and treated it as a trial separation, but they never did it. And when I was sixteen, he got a Fulbright-Hays for another two years here."

"He couldn't just get a permanent job at a university here?"

"He was at *Cornell.*"

"Yes." Apparently, he quite understood not asking a man

to sell himself short. "And she couldn't grow lavender there?"

"She tried." Magalie spread her hands. Or one hand. The other was held in his. "It wasn't the same at all."

"No," he said in a voice that spoke of a few summer vacations in Provence himself. "I can see how that would be."

They were silent for a few minutes, waiting at the light to cross from the quay to l'Hôtel de Ville.

"The Lyonnais family has been in Paris for over five generations," he said suddenly.

Well, whoop-di-do for you, she thought in American. "Shall I curtsy or just kiss your feet?"

His lips pressed tightly together, his fingers hardening on her knuckles. "You know, you wouldn't find me nearly as arrogant if you would quit inventing it in everything I say. I mean that we tend to stay in one place."

Her boot heels rang for two more steps.

"Forever," he added. "We *are* Paris."

Two more taps of her heels. Lyonnais was a part of Paris, that was true. For five generations, they had been marking the city with their *macarons* and desserts. They were as integral a part of it as the Eiffel Tower.

"I, for example, am never going to leave Paris, ever. I'm Philippe Lyonnais."

"And not arrogant at all about it."

He let out an annoyed breath. *"I'm just pointing it out."*

Yes, she was getting an inkling of what he was pointing out. She twisted her head just enough so that she could look up at him without him, maybe, noticing it. They walked that way for several paces before she realized that not only was he perfectly aware she was studying him, and keeping his gaze straight ahead to facilitate it, but that he was subtly guiding her around obstacles on the sidewalk to allow her to keep doing it without interruption.

Princes. She could see why they had driven traditional witches so wild.

"Now that I've opened that shop on l'Île Saint-Louis, there will always be a Lyonnais shop on l'Île Saint-Louis. Forever. Or as close to forever as *we'll* know. I'll pass it on to o—my children."

That still set her back teeth, his claiming of the island. It had been *her* street before. Hers and her aunts'.

"If they're interested in it," Philippe amended. "If they get some perverse, obstreperous blood from their mother's side that makes them want to thwart me all the time for no reason," he said broodingly, "and decide to become— become—*qui sait?*—engineers or something, then I'm sure there will be a niece or nephew who will continue the line."

As far as she was concerned, any child of Philippe's would have obstreperous blood. She caught her mind going off on the oddest, most delicious tangent and yanked it back in a desperate grasp, redirecting the subject before her mind could terrify her again that way. "Did you know my aunts don't really need the income from La Maison des Sorcières?"

He shrugged. She couldn't get over her knowledge of his body. Sometimes, when he shrugged like that under his coat, the thought of the way his naked shoulders looked as he did it, the easy flex of muscle, would run all through her. "I guessed. I researched the ownership of the buildings before I bought in the street, so I knew your Aunt Geneviève had owned that building for decades. You don't pay three salaries and the taxes on that kind of thing with five tiny tables and thirty business hours a week, ten months of the year. I always knew financial concerns weren't your real problem with me."

"And yet you managed to refrain from any cracks about *me* being a privileged princess?" While he carried a major business on his shoulders, his name and his skill its entire base, and never stopped moving.

He looked blank. "Everyone knows witches don't work regular hours. It's princes who have all the responsibility." His mouth curved a little at his assumption of the royal title. Probably waiting to see what reaction he could provoke. "Besides, you're the daughter of a lavender-grower and a professor. Don't kid yourself. You're a peasant."

"*You're* the son of a professor and a pastry chef!" she said indignantly. "Didn't boys used to be apprenticed as pastry chefs if they failed at school?" Although *his* family of pastry chefs had been making enough money to land them solidly among the Sixteenth Arrondissement set for generations. "Why aren't *you* a peasant?"

"Some people are born princes, and some people make themselves one," he said sublimely and shot her a grin, waiting for her next retort.

She rolled her eyes and refused to give him the satisfaction.

His next slanting glance warned her he was still digging for something. "So it must have been hell on boyfriends." She stiffened. His eyes narrowed, as if that stiffening was the ring of metal under his shovel. "That back and forth."

She shrugged. "I tried pretty hard once when I was sixteen. Well, fifteen when I first learned the move was coming; I had a birthday in there before we actually moved."

He stopped walking, there in the middle of the Place Hôtel de Ville, with the gleaming façade rising up behind him as if it were his royal palace. "Explain 'tried pretty hard'."

She shrugged again. What a stupid thing to make her eyes sting. Sometimes she wanted to shake herself. "I thought if I loved someone enough we could . . . stick. That it would make something permanent. That we would . . . belong together." Her hand slipped away from his arm. She hugged herself reflexively, a gesture that conveyed exactly what she had been trying to do. "I was a complete idiot. I didn't even want him to use condoms, so I could get pregnant."

"Good God," he said involuntarily.

"He was a little smarter." She made a face at the memory.

Philippe's eyebrows flicked up. "Not that great?" he asked sympathetically.

She wrinkled her nose. "It kind of hurt."

"The first time?"

"Just . . . sometimes." She shrugged. "I guess I take a while to warm up. To—" She shrugged again.

"To people?" he suggested, his mouth wry.

"That's not exactly what I meant."

"To places?"

"Were you even listening to what I was talking about?"

"To . . . things?" A grin slipped out. "Shall we say it takes you a while to warm up to . . . things?"

She pressed her lips together.

"So . . . it hurt sometimes. And you never told him to wait longer, change his style, or just get the fuck off you?" She blinked at the thread of anger in his voice. He studied her for a moment and then closed his hands around her shoulders, in deep approval. "You've grown since then."

Yes, she had. Hugely. Primarily, she didn't really need people anymore.

Except . . . there was this man right in front of her right this second, holding onto her . . .

She shrugged uncomfortably. His hands caressed over that movement through her coat as if he, too, could see her shoulders flexing naked. "I think it was more a question of forcing things."

"That's what it sounded like to me, too."

"I mean—me trying to force a relationship to work out for the wrong reasons. As if I could fall in love and create a firm *place*. And a relationship that could *last*. That couldn't be—" She made a little jagged motion of her hand, trying to express that fracture that occurred each time her parents went back and forth, the friends she had made whom she didn't see for a year, and then she was back, but the friendship was all different, interrupted. And just when she got a few threads picked up or a new friendship going, she was gone again. "And him, you know—I mean, he was sweet enough and sincere enough, but probably at heart he was just a seventeen-year-old wanting sex."

Philippe was silent for a moment. When he started walking again, he laid his arm across her shoulders instead of holding her hand. And when he spoke, it was with wry humor, shifting the load of the subject gently off her. "I wonder if my first girlfriend makes that face when she remembers having sex."

"That's pretty hard to imagine," Magalie said involuntarily. Deep down, in secret, the mention of former girlfriends made a knot of anguish squeeze inside her. Why were they former? What had caused the impermanence? He hadn't said anything about being in love with her after that first day of snow, and when it snowed in Paris, *anything* could be true. It would just melt later.

Unaware of that doubt, he grinned, and his arm squeezed her slowly tighter. "*Ma chérie,* I know you try to humble me, but you're not as good at it as you might think."

Chapter 33

He made her a dessert with armor plates of chocolate mounted around it, like the hide of an armadillo or a dragon. Just at the top, those plates had been deconstructed, so that instead of closing the dessert completely in a carapace, the last few plates climbed upward in what would have been for any other pâtissier an impossible spiral, leaving the soft inside revealed and vulnerable. He called it *Le Ventre du Dragon,* the Belly of the Dragon, and a few of the critics got the Tolkien reference, still others lauded the tribute to the Chinese New Year, and everyone talked about how it made them drool.

Magalie narrowed her eyes at it, understanding its primary message completely, but she ate it. It did melt her insides out.

Philippe knew because she pretended to exaggerate its effect, attacking him with a laughing growl, pushing him back onto her bed. But when she had him there and aroused just from the push of her hands and his willing fall back onto her comforter, when she was sitting astride him and had ripped his shirt over his head, her laughter died. Her gaze turned very sober. And she stroked her hands all over his chest and shoulders, gently, as if she was touching some precious find. It took all his breath away, turning his body too taut and hard and hungry to leave him air.

When she pushed him back and came down on top of

him, she looked like an erotic conqueror, which suited Philippe just fine. But the longer she touched him, the weaker she got. Her bones turned to water under his hands, until she couldn't hold herself straight off him and was lying on his chest, her lips pressing kisses everywhere. He could see how that would bother someone like Magalie, how malleable she grew while all his muscles engorged, as if he was stealing her strength.

He didn't think he stole it. Yes, he felt stronger, incredibly strong. But he gave her back all the power he drew from her. Only, he didn't know how to make her see that, except by what he was already doing.

He had to take over the rhythm with his hands hard on her hips, her body grown too pliant and yielding to maintain anything like the hard drive his own demanded. "Harder," she whispered into his throat. "I l—"

His whole body jerked, his hands pulling her down on him spasmodically. But she broke off, pressing the words back into her mouth with the kisses she rained down on his throat, on the joint of his shoulder.

Damn it, he *knew* that was what she had almost said. It couldn't be anything else. *I like it,* broken off, didn't sound like *I love you.*

With his hands on her body, with his mouth, with a taunting rhythm, he tried to get her to *say* it, to break down and say it. But she never even started to again.

"You just have no patience," Aunt Aja told him one day. *Him.* A man who could work on perfecting grains of sugar for a new pastry *all day.* "You have to do things so dramatically. You haven't let her have time to start counting on you. It only takes a few years."

"They say with really little babies, they cry whenever the mother leaves the room because they don't understand that she still exists then. It's something like that, I think," said Geneviève, who had never had a child of her own but could speak with supreme confidence about it, anyway. "Well, except the reverse. Magalie used to think things kept existing when she left the room and had to learn that most of them didn't."

They were walking back across the twin bridges behind Notre-Dame from Océane's birthday party, the first Sunday in March, when Philippe started probing again. The man was relentless.

Magalie had given Océane a collection of hats: a witch hat, a princess crown, a fairy garland, a firefighter's helmet, and a beekeeper's hat. Just making sure she kept the girl's options open. The firefighter helmet, she admitted, had been a little random, but she hadn't had much advance notice of the party. It had been a cute party. At least, everyone else there had seemed to find it cute, particularly her own role in it, tucked up against Philippe's side, being shown off like she was his Meilleur Ouvrier de France medal.

She knew vaguely that she was supposed to be annoyed by that, the whole tucked-up-under-his-arm-like-a-trophy thing, but she kept having trouble pulling it off. After all, the man had firsthand knowledge of the Meilleur Ouvrier de France competition, the Olympic training and intensity of it and what it took to win, so if he showed her off as if she was that valuable, it was hard not to be flattered.

"So I take it the attempt to create a home by getting pregnant at fifteen didn't work out?" Philippe asked. Winter was loosening its grip, and the day was prematurely springlike, so that he wore the leather jacket she had seen on him so much in the fall, unzipped, and under it a blue cashmere sweater showed through. She had bought the sweater for him the other day and thrust it at him in a way that defied him to make anything out of it.

Of course, he had ignored that signal and made about as much out of it as possible, ending by putting it on her naked body and making love to her in it. He had said he didn't like shopping and she did, and he wanted to get her trained to associate shopping for him with a great deal of pleasure.

Which meant he was going to get the most annoyingly smug grin on his face when she bought him another one, but what else was she supposed to do when he kept wearing this one every day? Honestly. Anyone would think it was the only sweater he owned.

"I did not get pregnant," Magalie said, annoyed. No thanks to her. Thank *God* she was so much stronger now.

"I assume he didn't turn out to be your home, either."

She sighed. This was such an embarrassing story. Why had she ever let him drag any part of it out of her? "Well, I did pitch such a fit those first three months back in Provence that my parents agreed to let me fly back to the U.S. for Christmas and stay at a friend's house. They were even considering making arrangements for me to live there, with that friend, and go to school there the rest of the year."

His eyebrows flexed together. "That's a lot of independence to provide a sixteen-year-old girl who doesn't know enough to use birth control."

She shrugged. "I was always very self-reliant." And if she *had* gotten pregnant at sixteen, she would have done just fine with it, thank you very much.

"Not much choice to be anything else?"

"What?"

"Nothing." He was clearly sitting hard on some opinions.

"Anyway," she said, speaking quickly, so she could dump this whole story into the trash where it belonged and get it over with. "He already had a new girlfriend, so all my fits turned out to be for a stupid reason, and I flew back after the break. Unfortunately, I had gotten the return ticket for the last possible day of the French vacation period and had to stick it out at the friend's house until then, but . . . lessons learned and all that."

Philippe was silent for a long moment. At last, he shook his head wonderingly.

"What?" she said defensively.

"Teenagers are idiots. I *think* I would have had the sense to wait a couple of months for you, even at that age, but God knows. The whole pregnancy thing probably scared him. And you were clearly much better off. I hope the next guy was a better lover."

Magalie's lips parted. Then shut. On a slow, slow smile.

Philippe let go of her hand. "Well," he said, rough and pissed off. "Apparently so. That's a much better expression on your face."

She looked up at his hard-set jaw and scowling blue eyes. Her own eyes snagged on his.

Philippe caught her chin. "Don't you *dare* look at me like that while you think of *him*."

She coughed. He was getting very much the wrong idea, but at the same time, the truth just couldn't be a good thing to let him know about her.

He pivoted, grabbed her hand brusquely, and started walking again, his footsteps hard on the stone slabs.

She cleared her throat, angled her chin off toward the flying buttresses of the cathedral, and tried to sound airy. "I don't mean to go to your head, Philippe, but you *are* a slightly better lover than a teenage boy."

Philippe tripped. His foot caught on the edge of a stone, and he stumbled forward, his hand wrenching free of hers. He caught himself against the metal rail of the bridge, all the locks lovers and tourists had attached to it clanging, and twisted, still holding onto it for support, to stare back at her. "Did you just say—" He caught himself and shook his head so hard, it shook his whole body, like a lion coming out of the water. "I must have misunderstood."

She folded her arms under her breasts and gave him a very stern, superior look. "I'm really very fastidious." She was, too. She had not wanted any sweating, stupid, grunting man in her space trying to take parts of her. She liked who she was.

And she hadn't wanted to trust one to make a space for her that would last. To value her the way she longed to be valued.

Philippe released the metal railing and walked back to her. His chest rose and fell visibly in the blue cashmere, and he shook his head again, very slowly this time.

"Wait. You've lived in Paris five years, working in the public eye, looking like you do so that a man can hardly keep himself from grabbing you and eating you up on the spot. You spent three of those years also as a university student, around hordes of men in their early twenties who must have been asking to borrow your class notes every damn chance they got. And you've *never* let any of those desperate men through your defenses?"

"I don't *like* desperate men."

"Oops," Philippe said, so dryly she knew she was missing something.

She waved a hand. "I mean . . . needy. Weak. I don't like weak men." Had he just said she made him desperate?

"Those are some walls you've got, Magalie."

She frowned at him. "Why not? I like who I am."

"I like who you are, too, Magalie. We're in public, so let's not go into the details of how much. I'm not asking you to change."

"Just to give part of myself away."

"All of yourself. But to me."

Clearly the fact that it was to *him* was supposed to make all the difference.

Which, oddly, it did.

"And you get to keep yourself at the same time. That's the way it works, I think. Kind of like flipping a Tarte Tatin. Or jumping a gorge. If you try to be careful or hold anything back, you end up with one hell of a mess."

"You would think that," she said repressively. But it struck a chord, vibrating inside her, knocking things loose. Lady Godiva. She'd bet Lady Godiva did *not* try to cover herself with her hair once she decided to ride naked through that town. She was too sure of who she was.

He shrugged. "I'm not strapped into a safety harness over here myself, Magalie. But it feels to *me* as if jumping that gorge to you makes me ten times bigger."

Ten times bigger than he *already was?* Good Lord. She looked up at him, the strong chin profiled against the back-drop of the river and Notre-Dame. The trees in the little park behind the cathedral were just starting to hint at buds of green. The wind off the water tousled his mane. That blue sweater she had picked out for him really did do wonderful things for his eyes.

He tucked her hand into the crook of his elbow, posses-sively, and started walking again. His mouth began to curve smugly, the curve growing and growing, so pleased with himself, she was surprised every other man who walked past him didn't try to knock him off the bridge, just to wipe that smile off his face.

"So . . . only me?" he said, trying and failing to get his grin under control. "I'm the only one you've let through? The rest of them just bounced off those walls of yours?"

"You don't bounce off much, Philippe."

"No, I don't," he agreed. The next little grin was impos-sible. "I like to penetrate."

She hit his arm, though not nearly as hard as she would have liked. "Will you shut up?"

"Did you ever play cowboys and Indians when you were little and always insist on being the Indian chief so you could do the wild, gloating, victory war dance?"

She had been an only child with no cousins, but she didn't interrupt.

"If we weren't standing right across from Notre-Dame, in the most civilized city in the world, I think I would be doing one right now."

"It's terrible being a sixth-generation Parisian, isn't it? The constraints of princehood. If you start gloating over me, I'm going to push you right off this bridge."

"You?" He gave a *pffing,* dismissive wave of his hand that nearly brought her head down in a bull charge. He was right by the rail. If she hit him hard with all her weight when he was least expecting it . . . "I'm not gloating over *you.* How many men do you think bounced off those walls of yours? Hundreds? Probably *thousands.*"

"Philippe, you're flattering, but I really don't remember ever having thousands of men trying to flirt with me."

"You never even *noticed.*" He threw back his head with such a fierce, triumphant look, she thought he was going to let loose that Indian war whoop right on the spot. "You never even noticed *them.*"

She gave a heavy sigh. She should never, ever have allowed him to get started on this subject. "You know, if I had ever imagined you in my future, I would have had a few more flings just to take your arrogance down a couple of notches."

He gave her a quick, hard look. "Bitchy, Magalie. But as I think I told you the first time we met, I'm not afraid of competition."

Yes, as he had pointed out, he wasn't the only pastry chef in Paris, but once people tasted him, the others didn't matter.

His grin came back. "I would still spoil you for any other man."

"Are you going to pretend wounded innocence again when I tell you how arrogant you are?"

"It's sad, but Sylvain Marquis is the only person I know who doesn't confuse honest self-evaluation with arrogance. Go ahead. Make me humble. Tell me why me." He pressed his lips together. A laugh bubbled through the corners of them. "Is it because of how I . . . penetrate?" He snickered.

He was really very full of himself right now, wasn't he? "I'm going to have to kill you."

He stopped walking and stopped laughing all at once, standing under a lamppost just at the start of the second bridge, the one between Notre-Dame and their—*her*—island. Even in the still-chilly weather, people lingered here, gazing at the cathedral. A tourist wrote in her journal with finger-gloves over her hands, and a group of buskers played jazz. She missed the latest young man with a violin. Violinists tended to head south for the winter, and a new one would pop up sometime in the spring. "*Sérieusement*. Why me?"

Seriously? Seriously, the honest answer was going to make him impossible to live with.

Live with. Was that becoming an option?

"I don't know if you remember, but when I first saw you, you were laughing."

"I remember. You cut across it like a whip." He touched a hand to his chest, as if he could still feel the sting on his skin. Was that where the sight of her had struck him? Right in the chest?

"I wanted that laugh."

He liked that. She could see the pleasure in the rise of his chest, in the way the corners of his mouth softened, in the way the blue of his eyes warmed. But he didn't know quite how to interpret her word *want,* his eyebrows flickering over it.

She closed one fist low over her abdomen, illustratively. "I lusted after you."

He made a sound as if he had just taken a soccer ball right in the midsection. Wrapping her up in his arms, he turned her back against the lamppost and kissed her, long and thoroughly, the flying buttresses soaring behind him, and no one on this bridge of dreams did more than even glance at them. The jazz band started playing a love song.

He raised his head at last. The wind that had been blowing his hair off his face now blew it toward her, little tendrils not long enough to reach her cheeks. "So if I had picked you up and put you back against my office door and eaten you up, the way I wanted to do, you would have *liked* it. And probably kneed me, hit me over the head with my laptop, knocked me unconscious, and never let me get anywhere near you again."

She remembered the heat in that room. "It's really very hard to say."

"Now you're just being mean, Magalie. I have fantasies about that meeting *all the time.*"

"It's hard to imagine me using something as impersonal as a laptop on you. Most of what I wanted to do required my bare hands."

He rested his forehead on hers. "Some of the fantasies I've had about that meeting are *so bad.* I think if I ever admitted them aloud, every female I know would disown me."

"Well." Magalie slipped her hands under his coat around his waist. "Nobody ever said Givenchy boots came cheap."

He wrapped his arms around her, squeezing her in hard, hard, so that she was enfolded in him and the panels of his coat, shutting out the cool March wind entirely.

When he finally pulled back, he was studying her, his eyes narrowed. "But you still don't want to admit you love me?"

She stiffened, a shocked recoil back behind her shield, her pupils contracting. His mouth went grim, and he straightened away from her. They walked on without speaking, the détente of a moment before broken.

Chapter 34

"I love you, *minette*," Stéphanie Chaudron said, and Magalie huddled into herself in the vast, noisy hall. She had forgotten how cold the Gare de Lyon could be. Cold enough to render the optimistic palm tree over there in front of the nearest TGV kiosk ludicrous. Full of people leaving, so briskly and firmly, as if that was just the way life was supposed to be. Masses of people who brushed past Magalie without a second thought, scuffing the toes of her boots with their suitcases.

She hated train stations.

"Me, too, Maman. You didn't stay long in Ithaca this time." Her mother was on her way back to Provence after a brief visit with her father in the U.S. Barely over two months.

"Oh, *ma puce,* the winter there. And I didn't even have you to snuggle up with." Her dark-haired, brown-eyed mother smiled down at her, a sweet smile reminiscent of those clinging cuddles between mother and daughter when all the rest of the world was well lost.

Magalie nodded. She kept trying to straighten her shoulders and open her arms to hug her mother good-bye, but the next thing she knew, she would be rubbing her hands up and down over her tight leather sleeves again, trying to warm herself. "How did Dad feel?"

"Oh, *pucette,* you know how hard it is on him. At least I

always had you." Her mother touched her cheek and gave her a soft smile. "You always made everything all right. You could handle anything."

Magalie couldn't understand why her heart kept trying to choke her, why her eyes kept wanting to sting. She *could* handle anything, certainly this, her parents' eternal Hades-Persephone relationship. She didn't know why she kept seeing her father's face, his hand lifted in a wave to her until she couldn't see it anymore.

Unless it was because someone had been forcing her heart open. Sudden terror seized her at how vulnerable it now felt.

"Don't you want to stay in Paris for a few days? You don't have to get straight on a train from the airport."

Her mother laughed. "You're my little Parisienne. I never could handle this city. But come down south with me. I'm sure the aunts could spare you."

"No, they couldn't," Magalie said quickly, so hard her mother's eyes widened in surprise. "They couldn't," she insisted.

Her mother laughed again, affectionately. "*Pucette,* I'm quite sure they could find some young woman to serve customers for a few weeks. I'll talk to Geneviève myself, if you want. She doesn't need you nearly as much as she pretends to."

Magalie stared at her mother. "Yes, she does." Her voice almost squeaked.

Her mother patted her cheek again. "I know sometimes people make a big deal out of good-byes and try to stop you from leaving, but you know they always get over it once you're gone. That's what it means to have a full life. You keep living it."

Magalie's breathing was so short, it was infuriating her. This couldn't be happening, this raw openness to things her mother had always said. This was *not* something she let get to her anymore. She did have a place now. She had made it, and she had never left it, so she got to keep it. No musical-chairs games for her. She knew how those worked. "They do, too, need me."

But for what? To serve customers in a shop they didn't even need to keep open, except for their own amusement?

"Pucette." Her mother tugged at a lock of her hair, look-ing wistful. "You could at least ask her and see what she says. I bet she would tell you to go without a second's thought."

The breath after that one physically hurt. Magalie bit on her lower lip until it made sense that her nose should sting. "I think that's your train, Maman. I'm glad I could catch you on your way through."

"Oh, *ma petite chérie.*" Her mother flung her arms around her and hugged her tightly. "If only you would come with me so we could see each other more. I'm sure everyone here could do much better without you than I can. I love you, you know. My little lavender girl, who would always make me smile, when I was missing your papa." She started to grab her suitcase handle, then flung her arms back around Maga-lie one last time. "Don't mind those two; they have each other, and they'll get over it if you decide to move back south with me," she whispered into her ear. "Don't let them trick you into thinking they need you."

And with a last quick kiss, she hopped up onto the train. And waved at Magalie out the window as the train slid away from the platform.

Magalie almost ran back to her apartment, the four-inch heels of her boots clashing with her need, forcing her to a brisk walk, to keep her chin up against all the opposing pedestrians who bumped past her as if she was nothing.

Philippe never had to dodge anyone on any sidewalk. People parted around his size and sureness. Slowly, she began to realize that the only reason the masses of Paris had seemed to respect her a bit more, recently, was that she was usually attached to him. It wasn't that *she* was growing bigger or more deserving of a place at all.

Reaching her building was such a relief. She ran up the stairs to change her suitcase-scuffed shoes, running a little late to open the shop, but that kind of thing had never mattered *because they didn't really need the shop and they didn't need her help,* a little voice whispered to her.

She shut it up with a firm shove of her key in the lock. It jammed halfway. She frowned, wriggled it out, and tried again.

It wouldn't fit.

The first shock, washing through her like a wave of sickness, made her reach out and grasp onto the doorknob.

She looked down at it. The doorknob was new, and there was clearly a deadbolt above it that had never been there before.

Her heart raced as if in a nightmare. Had something happened? Had the aunts decided to kick her out?

No. *Get a grip,* she told herself. *A firm grip. Don't be stupid.* Her aunts wouldn't do that. Maybe Geneviève and Aja had decided to update all the locks in the building and had not thought to mention it to her.

Frustrated, feeling hunted, wanting to at least peek into her room and make sure it was still there, she ran down the stairs to her aunts' apartment. They didn't answer her buzzing.

She ran all the way to the bottom and across the courtyard into the shop, gasping with relief when the door opened under her hand and she could get in.

"*Bonjour,* Magalie." Her Aunt Aja smiled at her.

"Did you—" Magalie took a hard breath, forcing it to even out. "I didn't realize you were changing the locks."

Aja's eyebrows lifted. "What locks?"

The wave of panic crashed back. "The lock on my door has been changed."

Aja's eyebrows flexed together. "Are you sure? Geneviève didn't order anything like that."

"Where is Tata?"

"She didn't say, but you know how she is. I'm sure she'll be back soon enough."

Magalie took rough breaths, feeling as she did at the end of a too-long sprint, as if she was trying to get her lungs to cool down. Insight and rage filled her in the exact same instant. She turned and headed down the street.

In his *laboratoire,* Philippe was bent over something on one of his counters, his fingers hovering just above it. He glanced up when she came in, and his whole face lit. "Magalie! Just one second. Here." He rubbed his hand over a blank space of marble near him, without really looking at it. "Sit by me."

Magalie stopped across the counter from him. Anger was beating in her like a drum. He didn't even seem to feel it, focused again on what he was doing.

"Philippe. I can't get in my door."

He looked up from the infinitely precise placement of a crystal of *fleur de sel.* "*Enfin!* I thought I was going to have to find someone else. Every time one of my contractors falls in love, they fall to pieces. It's ridiculous. *I'm* still getting my work done."

Her heart gave a little hiccup at that, but she repressed it firmly with anger.

"You hired someone to change the locks on *my* door?" Not only did he expect everyone's doors to open for him, he thought he had the right to take those doors over and lock them against the original owners.

"Just put in a deadbolt and a peephole. Didn't he do that?" She put her fists on her hips. She might have to murder him. "*My* door. You hired someone to change the locks on *my* door."

He shrugged and went back to the *fleur de sel.* "You're welcome."

Magalie dipped her hands into a nearby box of *rates,* the *macaron* shells that had been discarded for imperfections during the course of the day, and came up with a few weapons. "Did he give you a copy of the key?" she demanded between her teeth.

"Of course not!" Philippe said, so offended, it was clear he was priding himself on his virtue in not asking for a copy. "Although, if you wanted to offer it to me . . ." He let his voice trail off, invitingly.

Unfortunately for him, right now all she wanted to do was hit him over the head with the *macaron* shells. "He didn't give me the key, either."

For a second, she didn't think this was going to penetrate his obsession with a couple of grains of salt. He trailed crystals one way, made a moue of dissatisfaction, brushed them off, then trailed them in the opposite direction, in a single spiraling line. "Wait," he said, in delayed reaction. "Then who does have the key?"

She hit him precisely in the forehead with a *macaron* shell. It bounced off, and with lightning-fast reflexes, his arm shot up and blocked it from his current creation, protecting the sea salt.

Everyone else in the kitchen stopped moving.

The intern looked horrified. The more experienced chefs, like Olivier and Grégory, looked at the nearest boxes of discards wistfully.

Philippe picked up the *macaron* shell that had bombarded him and weighed it in his hand reflectively. "Magalie, this is a *professional* kitchen."

Magalie threw the next one. She couldn't help it. It was his continued conviction that he needed to tell her what a professional kitchen was. He ducked to avoid being hit in the nose, and the shell sailed past the next counter and bopped Grégory in the chest.

Philippe's return fire hit her right in the chin. If it had been a snowball, it might have hurt, but given that it was one of Philippe's *macarons* and therefore lighter than air, it just bounced off her, leaving a few sticky crumbs.

Olivier cracked, scooped up a *macaron* discard, and hit Grégory in the side of the face. Grégory whipped his head around. Laughing his head off, Olivier tried to pretend it had come from Magalie.

"This is a terrible example," Philippe informed Magalie, forming a protective shield with his body over his current creation while she launched a volley at his back and tucked-in head.

The intern and lower-ranking or newer employees looked too terrified to participate, but Olivier was getting into position right by the ammunition, rapid-firing at Grégory, who was heading toward Olivier and the box of discard-weapons with a clear sense of purpose.

"*Bon, bon, bon, ça* suffit!" Philippe roared, and Magalie made a moue at that last word, impressed despite herself. He really could fill a kitchen with that roar when he wanted to, and stamp his great paw down on a mass of rebels carrying knives and hot caramel and precious creations. Everyone stilled. Olivier, ducking to avoid Grégory's return volley, looked regretful. Grégory threw one last one, hard enough to hit Olivier right in the cheek, and then pressed his hands down by his sides to make them behave, trying to look innocent. "If one single pâtisserie gets messed up, I am *not* going to be happy," Philippe warned the whole kitchen in a perfectly normal tone. He didn't need to raise his voice again, because, post-roar, the loudest sound was a bubble coming from a pot of caramel.

"Magalie." He turned back to her and lowered his voice

for her ears alone. Or he tried to. Since everyone in the entire kitchen was dead silent and eavesdropping, the attempt at discretion may or may not have been successful. "Come physically attack me in private, why don't you?"

He pretty much had to drag her into his office. Her heels were dug in that hard. "I want you to quit forcing your way into my life, and I want you to *leave my door alone*. It's *my* place. It's *mine*."

"That's the idea, Magalie. I just made it safer."

"I can't even get in!" Her voice rose. Even to herself, she was starting to sound a little hysterical. She hated that.

"Putain." Philippe picked up a cell phone off his desk, scrolled through the numbers, and made a call. By the way his jaw clenched, she could tell he was getting voicemail. "Franck, this is Philippe Lyonnais. I need you to get back to me right away. It's an emergency."

He shut his phone, frustrated. "This is really traumatizing you, isn't it?"

"No, it *isn't!*" she shouted at him. She did not get traumatized. She handled everything with aplomb. She wrapped her arms around her middle abruptly, trying to force herself to sound as if she was handling this with more aplomb. "You had no right to do this. It's my place. It's mine."

"Magalie, this was just a safety issue, and Franck—I didn't even know he was coming today. I've been after him for two weeks. He was supposed to tell you what he was doing, and at *no point* were you supposed to be locked out of your place. Here, take my keys, if you want, and go to my place until I can get hold of him. Or hang out here and eat *macarons* and walk home with me when I go. It's not the end of the world, Magalie."

"What do you know about the end of the world?" she asked him furiously. "M.Sixth-Generation Paris. Have you ever had your world end?"

He stared at her with utter absorption, as if a harsh light was glaring through all her shields, turning them into transparent, gauzy curtains to her soul. "No. I'm sorry, Magalie. I just did it because I knew you weren't ever going to do it, and it was driving me crazy. I would have fired Franck already for taking so long, but I was there most nights or else you were at my place, so it didn't seem quite as urgent. But anyone could slip up there during the day!"

Her jaw set. She tried her best to be calm and strong. "It's my place." Her voice was too low. She couldn't get the tone nice and level. "You don't have the right to steal it from me. Nobody does."

"I didn't *steal* i—" His phone vibrated. He pulled it out. "Yes, Franck. The key."

He listened for a second and cut the connection. "He says he gave two copies to your Aunt Geneviève, who put them under a pot in the kitchen, where she said they would be the first thing you saw."

She turned fast, before she could say anything else she would regret, and headed toward the door.

"Magalie." His voice caught her. He had the drawer to his desk pulled open and was holding out a key. "This is to my place. If ever you get shut out of your place again, for any reason, this is yours. You can have my place, too."

She shook her head, fisting her hands as if he would try to force it into them. "I don't want two places. I only want one."

"This one isn't in another country, Magalie. It's five minutes away, in the same city. Consider it a backup. Take the key."

She curled her fingers more tightly. "You can change the locks on that door just as easily as you did on mine," she said bitterly.

His head went back. His eyebrows flexed, and he gave her

that confounded look he had given her once before. When she had asked him who he was in love with. "Do you really think I would do that?"

She turned her head away. She just didn't know. "If you were mad, or an ex-girlfriend was stalking you, or—you can't ever really have enough worth that when you're gone, the spot you left won't close over."

Philippe looked at her disbelievingly. "Yes," he said. "I can."

That was probably true for him, for the man who had made his mark on the whole world. Her heart clenched, stubborn and hostile. If he could make a place so well, why couldn't *she*? "I meant on a more personal level."

He looked wary, studying her as if he both wanted and didn't want to know the answer. "Would the place that I've made for myself with you—let's call it a tiny toehold, to be realistic—close over that easily, Magalie?"

Again her heart clenched, but in a frantic way, flinching from hurt. Goosebumps rose, as if he had walked on her grave. "No," she said curtly, looking away. More fool she.

"Your parents haven't found it easy to let the spot the other made close over."

"It might have been better if they could. They've spent twenty-five years torn between who they are and who they want to be with."

"They've got an unfortunate dilemma. I'm sorry for them, but I think they must somehow thrive on it, or they wouldn't persist in it."

"You've never even met them!"

"That's true. Perhaps I'm overestimating their willpower based on their daughter's."

Her willpower? What willpower? She was putty for him. "Based on your own, you mean."

He hesitated, then gave a slight, rueful smile. "Perhaps. In any case, I don't see any conflict between who you are and who you want to be with, Magalie." His smile faded, his face turning very serious. "Or maybe you could explain to me the conflict *you* see."

There wasn't one. There was just this hard knot in the center of her chest, this thing that she did not dare free.

He gave a sharp sigh and shook his head. "Magalie. Do you know what I was really going to say, when I asked you about vacationing in the lavender fields? I was going to ask if we could take our family there, because I saw you, a little black-haired and brown-eyed girl, and I wondered if we would have a little girl who would look like you. That was a bit of a leap into the future, but those are the kinds of leaps my mind makes when I think about you."

She stood still. Like some molten chocolate dessert, the outside still hard but the inside melting into a gooey mess.

He walked across the little office to her, looked down at her stubborn fists for a moment, then slipped his hand in through her neckline and tucked the key into her bra. "I want you to have it. What the hell you want from me besides sex and barricades, I do not know."

She almost made it to the door. But he had forced her so wide open. He had forced a *need* on her. The gooey mess of her insides was terrifying her. He could insert himself into her life and reshape her in any way that suited him. And she kept seeing that little girl in a lavender field. A proud little girl. A strong little girl. A little girl only her mother truly needed. A little girl who just could not stand to let herself change, ever again, for people who would forget her.

The key felt so warm, tucked into her bra. It shouldn't have slipped in there so easily. It should have warned her, all cold and metal, of what it was trying to do.

She turned suddenly, like a whip. "No," she said, low and fierce. "No kids. No little girls in lavender fields." Her voice was so ugly, compressing the tears so tightly, they came out like a junked car. "Don't you tear me apart. You don't *fit* in my life, Philippe. Stay the hell out."

Chapter 35

She fumbled under the pot for the keys without looking at her Aunt Aja, she got the deadbolt open, and she slammed the door shut behind her and turned the lock until it wouldn't turn anymore. And then she crumpled down onto the floor, her arms wrapped around her head, and she sobbed.

I can't do this. I can't do this.. He'll take this hole out of me I'll never be able to fill.

She rocked herself on the hard floor, her sobs coming in a low keen because her chest hurt too much for real sound.

I can't be that little girl in the lavender field again. I can't. Trying to play. Trying to be okay.

I can barely be the person I am here. Pretending with her stupid chocolate, pretending people needed her, that she was someone another person's world would bend for. No one even needed the *shop*, let alone her little role in it. Everyone had flocked to Philippe's as soon as it opened without a second thought for her. Her aunts didn't even need the shop. It was just some toy for them; it didn't even matter if it earned money.

And chocolate. God, anyone could make hot chocolate. They could teach the first teenager off the street to make chocolate, if they even really needed an extra person. It wasn't as if she was Sylvain Marquis or Philippe himself, the people no one could emulate. Someone no one could do without.

Except her. She could do without anyone. *She could do without Philippe.* That was how she had made her life.

Or had she made her life so that she kept trying to suck passing strangers into her orbit with her stupid chocolate, because she didn't really have anyone?

She scrambled up suddenly, her hand closing over the new lock, a lock that could keep everyone out. How ironic. Philippe had made her door into something even he couldn't get through.

Unless she let him in.

She backed away from it to huddle on her bed, but she could see his shop from there if she lifted her head, and so she sank back onto the floor again.

I can't, I can't, I can't. He's just too big. What will be left of me, when he—we—move on?

There was a careful knock on the door. "Magalie?" Aunt Aja called.

"I just want to be alone, all right?" Magalie yelled. "Is that so terrible? I just want to be alone!"

And then she buried her face in her knees and sobbed again.

Outside, a murmur from Aunt Aja, and then Geneviève's voice that, like Philippe, penetrated anything. "Leave her alone. A woman should be left alone if she wants to be left alone."

Footsteps on the stairs, and then they were gone.

And Magalie sobbed. And raged. She had no idea she had so much *rage* in her, she who had always handled everything. Rage for the little girl staring over her mother's shoulder in panic to see her daddy get so far away. Rage for the eight-year-old, hovering tentatively on the edge of a group of people who had once been her friends but who now barely remembered her. Rage for the fifteen-year-old and the clumsy, painful use she had allowed of her body just so she might have a chance at a place. Ready to give up her entire youth so that, like her mother, she would have one person who always was with her, one person who always needed her . . . until that child in her turn grew up and walked away and never needed anyone again.

Tried not to need anyone again.

Failed. Utterly. Miserably.

That was Philippe's fault, too, that rage. She had been doing just fine until his jaw had tightened so hard with anger when she told him about that fifteen-year-old, until his thirty-year-old's perspective on her painful first affair had made her realize that she, too, had an older perspective on it these days and writhed in horror and compassion and . . . rage. When she hadn't even *thought* about it, in years. Well, not really. She had been doing *just fine.* And that bad first affair had kept her out of all kinds of trouble ever since, when a man would hit on her, and a memory would flash, and she would wrinkle her nose and banish him from the beautiful integrity of the life she had constructed for herself, the life that finally did not reshape itself for anyone.

She buried her face and cried again, at the thought of her perfect, beautiful life in this perfect, beautiful, one-person-size apartment, on this perfect little island. Only when feathers stuck to her wet face and hands did she realize that she was clutching her pillow to her, and that she had battered it beyond recognition.

Which made her cry *again,* because . . . it was a strong, sturdy, expensive pillow, and she wondered what other strengths she might have just battered beyond recognition. She wondered what else she might have just broken.

She wiped her face slowly, which rubbed bits of down into her eyelashes, so that she finally had to step into the shower to get all the feathers off.

When she got out, she came face-to-face with herself in the mirror and stopped, studying the stranger who was trying to force her way into her life.

She drew a deep breath, lifted her chin, and settled her shoulders back, trying for Philippe's arrogance. *I'm Philippe Lyonnais,* she mouthed in that tone, as if all the world should bow.

No, wrong words. *I'm Magalie Chaudron.* There. No, that sounded ludicrous. No one was going to bow to her. Even Philippe, who had done one heck of a lot of things to her at this point, had yet to kneel at her feet.

She frowned at herself. And then her shoulders slowly shifted back and down again, and her chin came up. A natural gesture, this time. Settling back into herself. She didn't need Philippe's arrogance; she had her own. She didn't need to make the same mark on the world that he did. Or even to make the same mark on him that he did on her. She needed to make her own mark.

No. She said that as if she hadn't yet made one. But she had made her mark on him. The man was clearly crazy about her. *I mean, come on, Magalie. Even* you *can see that.*

The thought filled her the way she had always imagined her chocolate filling other people, warmth from the inside, swelling up until it heated all of her.

You can see it, if you want to see it. If you take off those cowardice glasses.

The same way she could see just how the aunts smiled at her, or tried to nudge her onto the roads they thought would do her good, the way they always made enough dinner for her, too, and checked on her when she disappeared into her room. The same way she could see that their old customers had drifted back to them so soon. Philippe had jostled this street when he had forced his way into it, but although routines had widened to include him, people still found themselves nestling into La Maison des Sorcières, needing her. Liking her.

There was nothing wrong with the way she was right now. She just needed to be herself, that was all. The person she had always wanted to be. The person she had been since she packed her bags and moved here to Paris with her aunts and decided her place was here.

Well, there was nothing wrong with the way she was, except one thing.

She needed to be herself. But that didn't mean she needed to be tiny.

Clenching the key she'd used to gain access to the apartment, Magalie tiptoed triumphantly and with a great deal of trepidation across Philippe's big living area, gently illuminated by lights outside. She paused near the couch long enough to strip down to her very sexy underwear, because she understood the value of being dressed just right for the occasion—and this occasion might require she make up for a few things. Like telling him to stay the hell out of her life. She tried for the first time to imagine what that would have felt like if *he* had said it to *her,* and she almost got physically sick. It was like being battered in the midsection.

So yes, she might have to make up for some things. She took a deep breath and slipped into the gorgeous cave of his bedroom, right up to his bed, and then stopped. The covers were flat. Which made her heart, already beating too fast with a sense of its own daring, pound into overdrive. Because if he wasn't in his bed, there was a very big predator loose somewhere in the dark, and she had just invaded his territory. Nearly naked.

Then she heard the shower. Damn. She looked at the sash in her hand with a great deal of regret. She was never going to manage to tie him up to make sure he listened to her if he was awake.

She slipped in through the bathroom door. Oh, now, what a beautiful view *that* was. Philippe stood naked, all that long, powerful body gleaming with water, one arm braced high against the shower stall, his weight slumped onto it, the shower beating down on his curved back and head.

He looked . . . tired. He looked as if he had been standing under that shower for a long time.

He looked almost . . . defeated.

Magalie's heart began to beat even faster, hurting her. She didn't want him to admit defeat. It didn't suit him. And there was only one subject on which he could be ready to admit defeat right now.

She took a deep breath and narrowed her eyes, trying to *will* herself into him, trying to make him feel her. Philippe did this kind of thing all the time. Just let his presence *fill* the room, and—

His head came up and turned.

She held up her key. "Surprise."

Defeat vanished from his posture in an instant. Replaced by . . . anger. Hard and tight.

He shut off the shower and jerked a towel off the heated rack, burying his face in it as the first thing he dried. Apparently it was a lot more important to him to cover his face than the rest of his naked body, gleaming big and hard, the water curling over him in all kinds of places a woman would want to touch.

She reached out, to follow a drop curling over the tight abs.

He caught her hand and pulled it away from him. The towel lowered, and blue eyes locked with hers. "You know what, Magalie? For once, I'm really not in the mood."

That hurt. Her chest tightened with anxiety, and her fingers clutched the key. "You said I . . . you said you wouldn't take this away."

"Yes, well, I didn't promise to never get mad in my whole, entire life. I'll sleep on the fucking couch."

He strode out, still drying himself with hard jerks of the towel.

Magalie followed him into the living room, oddly melted by the combination of big, angry body and what he had just said. *His whole, entire life.* "I just snuck into your apartment without your permission, but I get the bed?"

That seemed to make him even madder. His fist tightened on the towel, and he turned on her suddenly. "It's not without my permission, Magalie, or haven't you noticed that you're holding a key? What, do you think I pass those out to every woman I cross in the street? But right this second, I do not want *you* in *my* space." She flinched—all through her. "So go get into my bed and leave me alone."

Something warm flickered after the flinch, caressing the wound. She tilted her head. "You don't want me in your space, so go get into your bed?"

"Damn it, Magalie." Philippe clenched the towel and then threw it hard to the floor, turning his back to her. Which left him standing there completely naked and utterly gorgeous. The city lights falling through his broad windows turned his whole muscled body silver-gold. "I'm sorry," she said low.

His head came up a little at that, but then bent again, under too much hurt or too much anger, all those muscles too taut. "I don't want to talk right now, Magalie."

She stood there feeling helpless, exiled. Horrible. Staring at his back. There was the lean, tight lower torso and buttocks of a man who was always on his feet, always in motion, carrying, bending, crouching, always in a tight control that called on all his core muscles constantly. But then there were the larger muscles, particularly noticeable in his shoulders and arms.

"Why do you go to the gym?" she asked suddenly, hoping just to keep him talking.

For a second, she thought he wouldn't answer, but princely manners prevailed. His voice was short, though, cold. "I spend all day in intense concentration. The mindless exertion makes for a good . . . stabilizer." One shoulder shrugged, rippling those muscles. He added in a slightly more open voice, "It just feels really good."

It had never occurred to her what a buildup of tension there must be in his muscles over a day. "You know, you really might like it if I walked all over you," she murmured, touching a hand to the taut muscles of his upper back. She imagined laying him out flat on his stomach at the end of a long day, curling her toes into his naked back, massaging him with her weight.

He said nothing. She guessed he would love it but wasn't going to admit it under the current circumstances.

She drew her thumbnail down his spine, from his nape all the way to the curve of his butt, just one grazing trace. He flinched, started to arch, and then forced himself to stand stiffly, not allowing himself to flex into the touch. But those large arm muscles tensed, drawing her gaze down the length of them to the tight fists by his naked thighs.

"No," he said flatly.

She went on tiptoe and tried to kiss the nape of his neck, the way he did to her. With him standing so straight and un-bending, she had to grab his shoulders and pull herself up. She might need to work on her arm strength, she thought wryly, if she was going to play gymnastics with him. She held herself up there until her arms started to tremble, running her mouth and teeth and cheek over his nape, the way he did to her. She didn't think she could get quite the same results. Her cheek was too soft. She couldn't reproduce the completely shattering effect of the scrape of his jaw.

It seemed to do something, though, because his head bowed to it, his shoulders pulling at her hands with each heavy breath.

She sank down finally, her arms sliding down toward his waist, her breasts and belly dragging against his back. Such smooth, smooth skin there, compared to the curling hairs across his chest.

"Your back feels like silk," she whispered. It was like being let into a secret of him, or of masculinity: calluses on his hands from whisks and weights, hair on his chest and arms and legs and jaw, but his back was as smooth as a baby's.

All the muscles in that back were taut. Little shivers ran over his skin.

"You take more than you give, don't you?" he said bitterly.

That hurt. Did he think she was still playing power games, trying to prove she could overcome him with desire? "I think it's like making love when you're a virgin," she said ruefully. "You're . . . bigger than I'm quite ready for."

His stomach muscles contracted under her arms. One of his hands came up and curled around hers.

She pressed her lips against his back and let him feel her smile. "In more ways than one," she added mischievously.

He dropped his hand back to his side. *Ouch.* Apparently, no joking allowed.

"You said it before. It takes me a while to warm up to . . . things," she said.

She rested her cheek against those taut back muscles, slipping her hands lower around his waist, where she could reach all the way around. "This is perfect," she murmured. "Being right here."

He didn't answer, very stubborn in his wounded feelings, but his head turned. She couldn't see it, just felt the muscles shift under her cheek. Well, after a lifetime of making a place for herself, over and over, surely she could reaffirm her own space here. Make him turn to her and welcome her back into it.

"Isn't it funny that it would be so perfect? I thought you were coming into my life to tear it all to pieces. Destroy my tower like a spoiled kid knocking down someone else's blocks, just because you needed a few for your castle."

"Where this idea that I'm spoiled comes from—"

She stroked her hand down to his sex and curled her hand around him to shut him up. He knocked her hand away. Still stubborn, then.

"And that's kind of what you did, you know," she said. "You're very self—single-minded. You go after what you want, and tough luck for anyone else."

He tried to shrug her off and move away. Her arms tightened on him so that his first step pulled her with him. He stopped. His breaths ran deep through his abdomen, pressing against her arms.

She slipped around him, letting her arms slide, still clasped, until she was leaning now against his chest, his arousal pressing into her belly. "This is perfect, too," she said wonderingly.

She knew his head was bent to her because of the breath on her hair.

"So here I am, torn apart. I really didn't want to be torn apart. I liked who I was."

"You liked your tower," he murmured, his voice almost an apology. "Do you really think I broke it? I just wanted to make room for me inside."

She nodded slowly, unsurely, her cheek sliding against the hairs on his chest. "Well, I could probably repair it. But . . . I like it here."

"In the Marais? In Paris? Off your island?"

She tilted her head back until her eyes could meet his, her face still snuggled against his chest. "Here. Right here."

The meaning flared through him, softening him like chocolate against skin. His arms slid around her. "Right here?" She loved the way his voice vibrated in his chest and tickled her ear.

"I'm really quite strong. I can defend my tower."

A puff of breath against her hair. "No kidding."

"I can fight you off."

"Now that, I wouldn't be so sure of."

"But I think you might deserve me."

His arms tightened around her. "Why I am the one who always gets called arrogant in this couple . . ." he complained to the empty room, but without much heat.

Couple. Her arms flexed around him. "Sometimes I even think you might still be there when you walk out of the room. That you might not be . . . made of sugar."

He picked up one of her hands and began to draw it over his muscles, so hard and defined and resilient, stroking her palm over his chest, his biceps. "Now, what gave you a clue about that?"

She gave a little laugh against his chest, her head tilting down so that her gaze could slide secretly, under the fall of her hair, down his body. He was so aroused. If they could make peace, he would slide into her and . . . "You're what melts sugar," she said wryly. "A blowtorch."

"No. I'm what controls the blowtorch. You're just confused because I'm so hot."

Her mind did that little flip it sometimes did between the French and English uses of a word. *Hot for you,* he meant. *Deeply sexually excited.*

He gave her that little grin of his. "If only you were a little more like sugar yourself, I could do anything I wanted to you."

Her body, hot, crystalline, spun out under his hands, formed however he wanted it . . . "You do make me feel like sugar sometimes."

His penis leaped against her belly at that. His hands slid down to curve around her hips and bottom. He pulled her against him snugly. "Being here is my plan, Magalie. Did you think I told you I loved you as a way to get you out of your tower, and damn the consequences?"

She hesitated. Not really, but . . . "People do."

"That's probably why I took you to meet my family, too.

My four-year-old niece. My pregnant sister. My parents. People like that."

She stroked his abdomen. It contracted under her touch. "I don't say I love you, not for any reason whatsoever. I used to, when I was a kid, with Maman and Dad, to make them feel better. But I stopped when I was a teenager."

His fingers tensed against her buttocks, pressing into muscles sore from yesterday's run. "Is that a warning?"

"In a way." She stepped back from him, so that she could look straight into his face. "I do love you. It's hard for me to say. I'm still trying to figure out how to be myself and give me away, too. I do love you, though. You break my heart." Broke its shell wide open.

It was hard. But it felt like casting off an old, outdated carapace, something that had been pinching her far too small. She felt *huge*. She realized suddenly how he could dominate a room with his presence. He wasn't holding any of himself in. He controlled his emotions, but they were all out there, fully extended.

It was hard. But—she liked it. That sense of stretching herself out. It wasn't quite the same as latching onto him desperately, after all. Not done like this. It was as if the very center of her got even stronger. He had said it himself: it made him feel ten times bigger.

It was hard. But the look on his face, the way his hands went out to her, made it all worth it.

Chapter 36

There were five scarves in the box. Which—she counted back, blushing deeply with each mental tally mark. Right. Five. And all this time, she had thought the scarves were rewards for *his* orgasms.

"He doesn't have any other ideas for gifts?" Aunt Geneviève asked. "Do you look cold to him or something?"

Aunt Aja stroked a discreet, shushing hand down Geneviève's forearm. "I think this present was meant to be opened in private."

Great. Now her aunts were imagining her being tied up naked and spread-eagled with scarves up there several floors above them. Now *she* was getting a mental image of herself tied up, and . . . oh, for God's sake. Magalie bundled up all the scarves quickly and hurried into the courtyard to take them up to her room.

"Stop sending me scarves, you pervert," she told Philippe that afternoon in the blue kitchen.

He caressed the hot cup subtly and brought it to his mouth, gold-tipped dark lashes drifting downward a little as he drank the rich chocolate. "What do you want me to send you instead? A ring?"

Her eyes flew to his. His lips were curled, his eyes teasing, but under the humor, all that focus was there. And he just waited. Waited to see what she would do with the question.

She looked down at her hand, her thumb curling over the base of her ring finger as if testing its emptiness. She looked back up at him.

One of his eyebrows had arched. His focus had grown more intent, the kitchen smaller, all his muscles gathering for a spring.

She cleared her throat. She was supposed to be saying something repressive right now. She looked back at her bare ring finger again.

Philippe was starting to smile. Not in humor but in pure, glowing happiness. The lion's muscles were all bunched now. A breath, and he would leap.

She stared at him, wanting to save him the jump, wanting to walk right up to him and press herself against him.

Well, why didn't she? Hadn't she already found out that if she stopped letting him make all the moves, she felt much more in control?

It only took her two steps.

"This is nice," she whispered against his chest. "You feel really good. What have you been making today? You smell like lime zest."

The chocolate cup clicked on the counter. His arms folded around her. "I will never leave Paris," he mentioned. "I love it on the Île Saint-Louis. I come from a very happy family where people seem to have normally annoying relationships that last forever. I only ever pulled my sister's hair once when we were little, and it was because she knocked over this beautiful, three-tiered *pièce montée* I was making for our father's birthday. Fine, and I did kidnap her Barbie when we were playing cowboys and Indians and tie it up to an anthill, but anyone would think she would have gotten over that by now."

She tilted her head back and kissed him, feeling his response run through his whole body. What had been wrong with her, to let him do all the driving in their relationship so far? Things seemed to seesaw in her as she drew the kiss out, finding at last a sense of center that had him in it.

His fingers sank into her hair. "Every afternoon, I could come have a tiny cup of chocolate. Or you could come see me," he coaxed, "and sit on one of my counters, and let me feed little things to you while I work."

She kneaded her fingers into his chest muscles happily. This was a very nice place to be.

"And we could—well, I don't know if I could ever afford a family-size apartment on the Île Saint-Louis, but you know, it might be that your sense of place is too small. Maybe this whole city is your place. Paris."

Hmm. She hesitated. She really, really liked her apartment high above the island. Although le Marais was nice. But . . . She hesitated, the need to never move again clutching at her one more time.

"You're thinking about it, right?" Philippe said into her hair.

She nodded against his chest.

"That's all right, then." He lifted her hands from his chest and kissed the inside of each wrist, the way he liked to do. Then he slipped away just as her Aunt Aja came in from the courtyard.

At the door, he paused and glanced back. "What did you wish on me this time?"

To love her forever. She drew her eyebrows together, concentrating on him very hard. As if she could develop magic vision that would show her the chocolate running through his veins, taking over his body, making him hers.

He smiled. The smile seemed to grow in his whole body, pressing out from it for lack of space, filling the kitchen. "I don't feel any different."

Chapter 37

Magalie was crossing the Pont Saint-Louis between the cathedral and her island when a young woman who looked like a student grinned at her. That in itself was unusual. People didn't grin at one another in Paris.

Magalie hesitated, because the other woman was either crazy or they knew each other. Oh, or maybe she was simply hoping to soften any tight hold Magalie had on her wallet, because the other girl proceeded to open a violin case and leap onto a stand she had lodged against the metal railing, at the high point of the bridge's arch.

Her blond hair was caught in a ponytail, her jeans worn at the knees, and she held that violin as if it was part of her body, as if, without it, she would lose her balance and topple into the Seine.

Magalie took a step toward her. "Do I know you?" she murmured.

The girl laughed out loud. "You make good chocolate," she said and brought her bow down on the violin.

It was like being pierced with a thousand points of light. Heaven touched earth. It was the most beautiful sound Magalie had ever heard in her life.

Everyone on the bridge stopped. The waiters in the café at the far end of it froze and turned toward her. People stood from their tables to get a better look.

The other young woman was grinning, brilliant with joy. Her music washed over everyone, some great ode to freedom.

Magalie stared up at her, her jaw dropped, goosebumps chasing all over her skin. *May you love your life and seize it with both hands.* It came back to her. Wished long ago, on a young woman who had rubbed the tendons between her fingers while her mother delighted in how much of the world they saw between her performances.

Performances that had been in New Zealand, Hawaii, Japan, and here in Paris. She knew perfectly well—anybody with an ear who heard that violin knew perfectly well—her mother hadn't been talking about street performances.

And now the girl looked suffused with joy and freedom and profound, delighted mischief to be busking here.

Good God, maybe Magalie needed to be more careful with her chocolate.

She stood there until the "Ode to Joy" ended, her hands tucked in her back pockets. She had started at first to rub her arms, against the goosebumps there, but that had felt too closed to the world, when this radiant music was washing over her.

As soon as that bow paused and the young woman flexed her shoulders and lowered the violin for a second, her hat filled up. Magalie reached for her wallet.

The girl laughed and jumped down. "I don't really need it, but I suppose it would be better not to access my accounts if I can help it," she murmured to Magalie. "I *told* my mother's people to leave me alone, but I bet they'll put investigators on me. Still, in your case, I would rather be paid in chocolate." She winked at Magalie. Without the joy in music-making suffusing her face, her mouth was wide, her nose a little too pointed in proportion, her cheekbones strong, giving her face a not-quite-pretty look, too much of everything.

Magalie opened and closed her mouth. And opened it again. "Did my chocolate do this?" she whispered.

The girl—she was really only a year or two younger than Magalie at the most, but she bloomed with life and youth like a daffodil that had at last lifted its head out of the snow— laughed again. "No, I did this," she said.

Oh. Magalie felt a mix of both relief and disappointment. She tossed a coin into the hat, and some more prosaic bills on top of it—although she suspected the other woman had a lot more money than she did, in those accounts of hers—and started to head on over the bridge.

"Although that chocolate of yours is really good," the violinist said. "I still remember my first sip of it. It makes you just want to seize your life with both hands, to love every drop of it."

Magalie stopped and looked back at her over her shoulder.

The other woman wiped her face, took a long drink of water, stripped down to a white camisole, and leaped back up onto her post to play again.

Philippe had an entire marble counter to himself, and from the other counters his hardworking chefs and various assistants, interns, and apprentices kept rising up on tiptoe to peer at what he was doing or passing just a little too slowly with that *"chaud, chaud, chaud!"* pot she or he had to carry through the *laboratoire*.

There was an attempt to create a ring out of choux, filled with cream. There was a chocolate and lavender *macaron* whose center had been cut out, but he didn't like it, because where was he supposed to put the honey? There was a gorgeous, ring-shaped Paris-Brest, its whipped cream flavored with rose, and the powdered sugar on the top scattered with rose petals, and a pack of raspberries sitting next to it because he couldn't make up his mind whether scattering those around the rim was a good idea or not. There was a dark, dense chocolate creation he was currently easing free of its ring-shaped mold. He had flour in his hair and a streak of chocolate across his cheek.

And, of course, no one had the presence of mind to lock his sister out, so she came waddling in on him. And stopped. "Philippe, *what* are you—"

He gave her a harassed look. "I can't decide which one to give her."

"Oh, my God!!" Noémie's voice rose to a shriek he hadn't heard since their cowboy-and-Indian days. She grabbed her belly as if the baby had just given her a double-kick. "Are you—is this—*ooh-la-la!* Is it the girl you brought to Océane's party? Does Maman know? *Ooh-la-la-la-la-la-la*—where's my camera?"

She whipped out her phone and took a whole series of pictures of her brother looking growly and rather desperate, ring-shaped pastries strewn all around him.

"Don't you need to go have a baby or something?" he grumbled.

"Don't be a bastard, Philippe. She's not due for another two months. You always look fatter on the second one. Ha. As you'll find out!" his sister chortled in giddy triumph. "Is it that girl, Magalie? When are you going to tell her? If Maman knows and hasn't told me—"

Olivier, passing, whispered something into her ear, which was a shame, because it was really hard to find talent like his, and now Philippe was going to have to fire him.

Noémie clamped both hands over her mouth and then back over her belly. "I knew it! I knew it! I knew it! Maman's been printing up all the blog posts for her scrapbook."

Olivier, looking past her toward the door, made a sudden movement that sloshed crème anglaise from his pot over both him and Noémie's belly. Fortunately the crème was no longer hot, but while Olivier was busy cursing and apologizing, Philippe froze, caught by Magalie walking in.

"Bonjour," she said, looking surprisingly shy, for her. She probably didn't know how to make a peaceful entrance into his *laboratoire.* She was so used to storming it.

She walked toward him, and Olivier was too busy dabbing Noémie's belly for either of them to be useful and body-block her, and the intern over near the door lacked the sense of authority.

Philippe straightened slowly, his hands leaving prints in the powdered sugar on the counter. With nothing left to wear but his pride, he might as well drape that around him as best he could.

He watched her as she took in the counter. For the best pâtissier in the world, it made a pathetic spectacle.

"I'm still working on it," he ground out. Whatever he came up with would have been *perfect* when he was done.

She stood still, staring at it. Until she blinked. Then blinked again. Then brought her hand up to her mouth and blinked several times in rapid succession. "All of this is for me?"

Putain, she was crying. With Noémie and Olivier blocking his route to her, he didn't have much choice but to reach out and pick her up by her shoulders, hauling her across the counter, dragging her sleek black pants in the sugar.

She buried her face in his pastry jacket, which—this was *Magalie.* Crying into his chest in public.

Beyond her, his sister gave him two thumbs energetically up. Then she pumped one fist into the opposite palm and raised it in victory. Olivier had to dodge back to avoid an elbow. The chef was grinning and trying to look discreetly away, but his head kept turning back to them.

Magalie stood on tiptoe. "I really do love you, you know," she whispered into his ear.

"Don't say anything yet," he interrupted hastily, putting his hand over her mouth. "This isn't ready. I can do a lot better than this."

She lifted up a pale brown box with a witch stamped on it and opened it. Inside was a chocolate witch with an orange-peel broomstick. Caught on the broomstick was a man's wedding band.

Philippe fell back and hit the counter behind him. He scrambled for a grip on it, trying to get the damn counter to stop swaying and become solid marble again like it was supposed to.

The ring was a wide, strong band that looked like two tones of silver but was probably white gold—what did he know about actual metal rings? He had been focusing on saying it the way he did best, with pastries. She had placed her real ring there while molding the witch so that chocolate had hardened over part of it, so that he would have to eat the chocolate off it, even suck the last remnants of it clean, to get the ring.

Brown eyes gazed up at him. "I actually think I might trust you, with me."

Oh, good God, *he* was going to cry. In front of his own kitchen.

Dimly, he was aware of cheers and hoots and clapping. And a flash. His sister and her damn camera.

"More or less," Magalie said. "I'm still going to keep an eye on you."

He started to laugh a little. Happiness was burbling up in him like a spring, and it had to go somewhere. He was damn well not crying in front of his chefs. "Magalie, I can't conceive how anyone could not leave you a space."

"And we live in my apartment until I get sick of sharing such a small space with such an arrogant man and am ready to move."

One side of his mouth kicked up. "That might not take very long, Magalie."

"It will be at *my* pace," she told him severely.

He took one of her hands from the box and kissed the inside of her wrist. Then kissed the other wrist, nudging the box a little with his chin to find the most vulnerable spot on her skin. His sister's camera flashed again.

"So does that mean yes?" Magalie asked carefully.

He looked up from her wrists into her wide, watching eyes. "Was there a question?"

From the sidelines, his sister gave him a boo. Magalie narrowed those brown eyes.

"God, yes, Magalie," he said. "I told you once I would probably give you anything you asked me for. You don't even have to ask in words."

Chapter 38

Philippe was sitting cross-legged on the grass, with Océane using him as gymnastics equipment—climbing on his shoulders, clasping them with her legs, and tumbling backward off them into the grass, to climb back up and start again—while people milled everywhere. The wedding was huge; there had been no other way to do it, between their families, their friends, the professional contacts that were like friends, and pretty much the entire island, ever since that party.

He had been surprised, given his impression of Magalie as a solitary person, to realize exactly how many friends she did have, in her all-barriers-up way. Madame Fernand was there, and Claire-Lucy with Grégory. Aimée and Olivier had each come separately, but they seemed to be hitting it off pretty well. Sylvain had done some chocolate sculptures for Philippe's wedding in his turn, and Cade had come with him. Several people were talking to the busker who had played her violin for Magalie's entrance, urging her to consider auditioning for something professional. Philippe noticed that Cade, who had probably seen the busker perform in concert at some point just as he had, for two-hundred-euro tickets, was discreetly silent. The violinist, at least, had not come with a partner, something about which Geneviève had expressed strong relief. "Magalie was sublimating so much of her battle with you into that chocolate of hers, I was afraid we were going to get a reputation as matchmakers. And it's hard to get rid of something like that."

Christophe had managed to wiggle his way in, which Philippe had only realized when he was waiting at the altar, heart beating so hard he could barely stand, scanning the audience to try to give himself something steadying. And you couldn't really pause your own wedding to go strangle an old imagined rival, especially when he had some pretty blonde hanging on his arm, so he had had to let it go.

He was still bemused by how tall Magalie's mother was. Geneviève's size maybe should have given him a hint, but— he looked at Magalie again. No wonder she was obsessed with heels. Her mother was as tall as his own, albeit black-haired and brown-eyed like Magalie. Her aunt was nearly as tall as he was himself. Her father was tall, too, in a rangy way. "Was she adopted?" he asked Geneviève discreetly, puzzled. "You're the aunt with the biological connection, right? Not Aja?"

"Maman." Geneviève nodded to the little black-haired woman with the wrinkled face and the fiery brown eyes who was coming out of the house with a platter of something held high above her head, apparently in the belief that this put it above everyone's reach rather than right at their level. "Both her parents were Italian and moved here to get away from Fascism. She married an American soldier after she hid him from the Germans in a huge bed of dried lavender, where, the story is, I was conceived. My sister was always jealous of that story; she wanted to be the one conceived in lavender, she loved it so much. Our father was a big man, and my sister and I took after him. He died ten years ago. So, you see, it wasn't entirely unprecedented, romantically speaking, when my sister fell in love with Peter amid lavender fields. She never would have imagined he wouldn't stay."

"I like the story about your mother," Philippe said, wondering if Magalie would enjoy making love at midnight amid lavender fields or whether it would waken a score of childhood issues. He kind of liked the idea, himself. He was always up for exploring new scents and textures. Maybe not on a night when they were quite so likely to be discovered by the plethora of wedding guests, though.

"So Magalie is a throwback to her grandmother," Geneviève explained. "Although personally I always thought that her body as a child spent all its energy putting down roots, only to have them yanked out and broken over and over again. And then as she got a little older and realized the roots weren't going to work, her body poured all its energy into building her soul so strong and self-contained. Deep down, she never had enough energy to spare to make her body bigger."

Philippe looked at his wife, who had gone to help her grandmother and was now doing the exact same thing, imagining that she held the serving platter out of people's reach, except she was doing it in a low-cut, lace, Givenchy wedding dress with long, slinky, cream-colored, feathery things spilling out like lingerie all around her calves. Which were shown off not by Givenchy boots but by strappy, glittering Givenchy sandals, since it was June in Provence.

"Physically bigger," he added to be precise.

"Of course." Geneviève nodded. "We wouldn't have apprenticed a marshmallow. Although I think her soul's grown about twenty sizes since having to fight you." The big woman made a little circle with her two thumbs and index fingers, apparently indicative of Magalie's former soul, and then spread her arms out until she accidentally thumped Philippe in the chest. "You're good exercise."

His mouth curled. "Don't take this the wrong way, Tante Geneviève, but I really think I might like you."

Geneviève shrugged, indifferently. "You can like whomever you want. But this will reassure you, *jeune homme. I* am beginning to like *you*."

He grinned.

"Take your effect on her chocolate. Don't shake your head in despair over her or anything—remember she's even younger than you—but I honestly think she didn't really believe in her chocolate before. That she thought it was just a fun 'let's pretend' when she was standing over her pots with that smile on her face, wishing herself a place in people's lives."

"Is that what she was doing, wishing herself a place?"

"Of course, it was. Isn't that what you do, when you make your pastries? Not that she thought of it that way, of course. You could tell, with that straight back of hers and that refusal to need anybody. She just pretended she was wishing people happiness, freedom, their heads on straight, and that she didn't care at all if they valued her or needed her. But when you showed up, she had to skip that whole pretending step and pour herself into it."

He gave his new aunt a searching look, genuinely curious. "Tante Geneviève, do you actually believe you three can work magic on people? Like . . . turn men into beasts?"

Geneviève shrugged. "It depends on how much of a transformation it is. In your case . . ."

"I know, I know." His smile kicked all the way through him, as Magalie came across the grass toward him. "There wasn't that far to go."

"I wasn't going to say that at all," Geneviève said reprovingly, in that tone she used for his presumptions. "Weren't you listening to what I said about exercise? In *your* case, she had to stretch the full extent of her power."

He smiled, liking that, Magalie stretching to her full extent to get him where she wanted him.

Océane tumbled off him and ran toward the bride, stroking the feathery skirt.

"I notice that humility didn't take, though, did it?" Geneviève told him dryly.

He got to his knees at Magalie's feet as she stopped to look down at him. She looked absolutely beautiful in that dress. She looked so *happy*. That she had just married him. And she looked down at him as if—as if she trusted him with herself. As if not only his but her own most wonderful dreams had come true. "You would be surprised," he murmured.

Author's Note

All the characters in this book are fictional, but the Île Saint-Louis in Paris used to contain a tiny *salon de thé* called La Charlotte de l'Isle that was the most incredible, magical place and was the inspiration for La Maison des Sorcières. A place of the same name as the original Charlotte de l'Isle still exists, but over time its ownership has changed hands, and all the witch and other conical hats that lined its walls are now gone. But I think I, and maybe everyone who ever walked down the Île Saint-Louis while that little shop was there, owe a huge debt of gratitude to its original owner, Sylvie Langlet, for creating that magical place. Ever since I first stopped in front of its windows and looked at its chocolate witches and bowls of crystallized mint leaves, stories have brewed in my mind and, I imagine, in many, many visitors' minds. It is not everybody who can give so much magic to so many people.

As for other types of magic, pastry-lovers will recognize the inspiration behind Philippe's rose-heart *macaron*. The legendary Pierre Hermé's famous *Ispahan* has been marking pastry-making around the world since he created it, and I would like to thank him and all the other amazing French pâtissiers and chocolatiers for helping make Paris a world of wonder.

And I would like particularly to thank Laurent Jeannin,

head *chef pâtissier* at the Michelin-three-star restaurant of Le Bristol and *Le Chef*'s 2011 Pastry Chef of the Year, for his infinite enthusiasm, generosity, and patience with me, as he let me research the inner workings of one of the world's top pastry kitchens. And fed me an extravagance of amazing desserts.

It is truly a privilege to meet such exceptional people, as I write these stories.

A Witch's Chocolate
(Le Chocolat Chaud d'une Sorcière)

**A recipe shared by Magalie Chaudron
on the blogs *A Taste of Elle* and *Le Gourmand***

According to our guest, Magalie Chaudron, of that magical little shop on the Île Saint-Louis, La Maison des Sorcières, *chocolat chaud* should change with the weather and the person drinking it, and no recipe should ever be followed to the letter, because why do you want to imitate other people? That sounds oddly humble.

However, to get you started, Magalie has generously described her basic process for us, and we've added precise measurements to help out. She had never measured her ingredients before.

1. Smile. Just a soft curve of the lips.
2. In 2 cups (250 milliliters) whole milk,* infuse the following ingredients for 15 minutes, keeping the temperature below scalding so that steam rises very gently from the liquid but no skin forms (about 140–150°F):

---

*Up to ½ cup of cream can be substituted for the milk if you want a particularly rich and seductive texture.

1 cinnamon stick (½ teaspoon ground cinnamon)
1 vanilla bean, split (if you don't have a vanilla
   bean, it's probably best to leave out the
   vanilla altogether)
Dash nutmeg, freshly grated (less than ⅛ teaspoon); if it
   is not freshly grated, you might want a touch more

3. Remove the cinnamon stick and vanilla bean, and
any skin if you misjudged the temperature because
you were distracted by someone like Philippe. If you
prefer an even richer vanilla flavor, scrape the seeds
from inside the vanilla bean into the liquid.
4. Add 8 ounces (225 grams) high-quality dark
chocolate. How dark depends on whom you are
making it for, but Valrhona's 61 percent couverture
chocolate is a good place to start.★★
5. Let the chocolate sit in the milk for about 30
seconds, then whisk until smooth.
6. Keep over low heat. When you are ready to serve,
stir three times with a smile and a wish. If you wish
for dreams to come true, then be prepared for
upheaval. Dreams are like lions: gentle when sleepy.

P.S. This recipe drives Philippe insane. *His* recipe uses a hand-
selected blend of three chocolates and requires a careful low-
ering and raising to precise temperatures of both the milk and
chocolate (separately) before blending them together into
inimitable smoothness. Every time people prefer Magalie's
chocolate to his, he has to learn humility all over again.

★★From Ellie, of *A Taste of Elle,* for her American readers: This recipe
for *chocolat chaud* will still be much better than hot cocoa, even if you
use chocolate chips from the supermarket. But chocolate is the main
flavor, so go with the best quality you can. Also chocolate chips will
make for a grainier texture than a fine couverture chocolate, which is
made to melt smoothly.